D0389915

THE BOAT TO REDEMPTION

Also by Su Tong

Raise the Red Lantern (a novella collection)

My Life as Emperor

Rice

Mad Woman on the Bridge (a short-story collection)

THE BOAT TO
REDEMPTION

SU TONG

Translated from the Chinese by Howard Goldblatt

THE OVERLOOK PRESS
NEW YORK, NY

This edition first published in hardcover in the United States in 2011 by
The Overlook Press, Peter Mayer Publishers, Inc.

141 Wooster Street
New York, NY 10012
www.overlookpress.com

For bulk and special sales, please contact sales@overlookny.com

First published in China in 2009 by the People's Literature Publishing House

This translation first published in Great Britain in 2010 by Doubleday, an imprint of Transworld Publishers

Cataloging-in-Publication Data is available from the Library of Congress

Typeset in 11/151/4pt Berling by Kestrel Data, Exeter, Devon
Manufactured in the United States of America
ISBN 978-1-59020-672-0

PART ONE

Son

M OST PEOPLE live on dry land, in houses. But my father and I live on a barge. Nothing surprising about that, since we are boat people; the terra firma does not belong to us.

Everyone knows that the Sunnyside Fleet plies the waters of the Golden Sparrow River all year round, so life for Father and me hardly differs from that of fish: whether heading upriver or down, most of our time is spent on the water. It's been eleven years. I'm still young and strong, but my father, a rash and careless man, is sinking inexorably into the realm of the aged.

Ever since the autumn he has been exhibiting strange symptoms, some age-related, some not. The pupils of his eyes are shrinking and becoming increasingly cloudy – sort of fish-like. He hardly ever sleeps any more; from morning to night he observes life on the shore through fish eyes filled with dejection, occasionally managing to doze a bit in the early morning hours, as he fills the cabin with a faint fishy odour, the earthy smell of a carp, at times especially heavy – even worse, I think, than a dead fish on a line. Sighs of torment escape from his mouth one minute and transparent bubbles merrily appear the next. I've noticed spots on the backs of his hands and along his spine; a few are brown or dark red, but most glisten like silver, and it's these that are beginning to worry me. I can't help thinking that my father will soon grow scales on his body. He has lived an extraordinary life, and I'm afraid he's on the verge of turning into a fish.

Anyone who lives on the banks of the Golden Sparrow River is familiar with the martyr Deng Shaoxiang. Hers is a name that appeals to all, refined or common, a stirring musical note in the region's revolutionary history. My father's fate is tied up with the ghost of Deng Shaoxiang. For Ku Wenxuan, my father, was once Deng Shaoxiang's son. Please note that I said 'once'. I had no choice, I had to say it, however inconsequential a word it might seem to you. You see, it is the key to unlocking the story of my father's life.

The heroic deeds of underground Party member Deng Shaoxiang, of which there is both a long and a short version, are known to all local residents. The succinct version has been etched on a granite memorial stone and erected at the Milltown chess pavilion where she was killed. Each year, on tomb-sweeping day, children from throughout the region come to Milltown – on foot for those who live nearby and by boat or tractor for those coming long distances – and when they reach the pier they are greeted by road signs that point to a hexagonal chess pavilion to the southwest:

Tomb-sweeping, straight ahead three hundred yards

Straight ahead one hundred yards

Straight ahead thirty yards

In fact there's no need to bother with the signs, since on tomb-sweeping day a banner with a conspicuous slogan stretching across the top of the pavilion is visible from the pier:

SOLEMNLY COMMEMORATE THE HEROIC SPIRIT OF THE REVOLUTIONARY MARTYR DENG SHAOXIANG

The memorial stone, some two metres high and a metre wide, stands inside the pavilion, and while the homage is virtually identical to all commemorations of martyrs, children are expected to commit it to memory before returning home, so they can use it in school essays. But what visitors find most impressive is the bas relief on the back of the stone: it is the image of a woman with a basket on her back, awesome anger in her eyes as she gazes to the southeast; and if you look carefully, you can see a child's head poking up over the edge of the basket, a tiny round head. Look even closer and you can see a little tuft of hair.

Every place has its legends. Deng Shaoxiang's legend is a bewildering one. The most popular version has it that her father owned a coffin shop in the town of Phoenix, which earned her, his only child, the nickname Coffin Girl. Just how she strode on to the path of revolution is a bone of contention. Hometown people say she developed a loathing for evil people and evil deeds in childhood, and constantly sought ways to better herself. While other girls sought riches over poverty, she sought poverty over riches. She had uncommonly good looks, her family was well off, and yet she fell in love with an impoverished fruit-grower who sold Chinese bayberries at the school entrance. But when we sift the sands of gossip to find a kernel of truth, we see that this version reveals only selected facts about her life and is little more than propaganda: that is, she chose her path for love, for an ideal. A second version of events, once popular in and around her husband's birthplace of Nine Dragons Hill, tells a different story. Soon after eloping to Nine Dragons Hill with her peasant lover, so the story goes, she had a change of heart, unhappy with a life of tending fruit trees and enduring the taunts of the muddle-headed rustics around her. At first, she voiced her unhappiness only to her husband. But before long, her in-laws suffered from her tirades too, and the arguments grew so violent that one day she simply stamped her foot and marched off to join the revolution. Most people felt that this account had the air of marketplace gossip and made Deng Shaoxiang appear unsavoury. Had she joined the revolution simply because of unrealistic aspirations? Had she become a revolutionary out of pettiness? This version of events made the rounds for a while, like an evil wind, but it was relatively short-lived. A team of investigators was sent to stamp out the rumour. Three public-criticism sessions were called, at which one of Deng Shaoxiang's sisters-in-law plus the wife of a landlord and two ageing rich peasants were openly criticized. From then on, even among the poor peasants of Nine Dragons Hill, no one dared spread such talk.

People from both Deng Shaoxiang's hometown of Phoenix and her husband's hometown of Nine Dragons Hill found what she had done unimaginable. Who wouldn't? This frail young woman took on the perilous task of smuggling guns and ammunition to guerrilla fighters who, like her, moved stealthily up and down the banks of the Golden Sparrow River during a reign of terror. It was a role for which she was supremely gifted and well placed. The Phoenix coffin shop was an ideal operations base. News of a death in the area always travelled first to her father's shop, and whenever there was a need to bring weapons to the fighters, she would return to her parents' home, secrete the weapons and ammunition in a corpse-filled coffin, then dress in funeral garb and wail all the way to the cemetery. Once the coffin was in the ground, her mission was accomplished. The rest was up to the guerrillas. And so people said that Deng Shaoxiang relied upon three treasures to carry out her staggering task: a coffin, a corpse and a cemetery.

The mission that day was relatively easy: she was to travel

to the Milltown chess pavilion and deliver five pistols to an underground comrade known only as the Chess King. Disdaining the enemy, she chose not to find out if there'd been any recent deaths in the Milltown area, and neglected to learn the location of the Milltown cemetery. She merely confirmed the name of the contact and where he was supposed to be. For the first time, she chose a basket containing a child instead of a coffin to deliver the weapons. She could not have known that this departure from her three treasures would seal her doom: she would not return from Milltown.

After secreting the five pistols in the baby's swaddling clothes, Deng Shaoxiang hoisted the basket on to her back and boarded a coal barge for the trip to Milltown. At the pier she asked for directions to the chess pavilion.

'That is where men play Chinese chess,' a man said, pointing southwest to a six-sided pavilion. 'What business does a woman have there? Do you play?'

She patted the basket on her back. 'Me, play chess? No, the baby's father is watching the Chess King play, and I've come for him.'

Deng Shaoxiang stepped into the pavilion, where two men in long robes were in the middle of a game. One, a police commander in disguise, had a cultured look, exactly what she'd expected of the Chess King. The other, a fair-skinned, keen-eyed man wearing glasses, was peering around. Not knowing which of the two was her contact, she fixed her gaze on the chessboard and uttered the secret phrase: 'It's going to rain. Time to come home and bring in the corn.'

One of the men looked into the sky; the other coolly sized up Deng Shaoxiang, picked up a chess piece and placed it on his opponent's square. 'The corn is in already,' he said. 'Now it's time to take his general!'

Though the secret phrase had been answered correctly, Deng

Shaoxiang did not put down her basket. Seeing the chaotic setup on the board, she suspected that the men did not in fact know how to play. 'How will you do that?' she asked guardedly.

Momentarily stumped for a reply, the police commander glanced at the other man, forcing himself to remain calm, and said, 'Yes, how will you do that? Tell me.'

The second man gave Deng a sideways glance, his mind racing. 'Remove the chariot and jump on the steed,' he said. 'But the cannon, ah, what to do with that?' As he spoke, he let his gaze travel downwards, a salacious glint in his eyes. Then he burst out laughing. 'You are very clever, Coffin Girl, but do you know what the cannon is doing? It's aimed at you!'

Deng blanched and began edging her way out of the pavilion. 'All right,' she said, 'do what you want. I shouldn't have spoken. Who am I, a woman, to comment on how men play chess?'

But it was too late, for a gang of men sitting outside the tea shop across the way rushed over, as if attacking an enemy bastion. Deng stopped at the pavilion steps, seeing that she was surrounded, and stood still. 'Well, well,' she said. 'So many men to deal with a single woman. You should be ashamed of yourselves.' Her calm demeanour in the face of danger stunned them all. But her concern about her appearance nearly cost her her life on the spot. Seeing her reach into her bundle, the nervous policemen drew their weapons. But what she took out was a compact – she opened it, looked into the tiny mirror and began to powder her face. '*I'm* not worried,' she said. 'So why should you be? All I ask is for a few moments to powder my face before you kill me. Too bad I don't know how to use the weapons I've brought. If I did, I'd at least take one of you with me.'

Stung by the rebuke, a policeman ran up and snatched the compact out of her hand. So she reached back into her bundle and took out a comb. That too was taken from her. Then they took her basket. 'Hold on,' she said as she ran after it. 'You'll scare my baby!' Pushing her way past the policeman, she bent down to kiss the baby in the basket. 'All right,' she said. 'If you won't let me comb my hair, then I'm ready. You can shoot me now.'

With a sneer, the commander said, 'What do you take us for, a bunch of empty coffins, telling us what we can and can't do? First you smuggle guns, then you tell us to shoot you. Well, you're not getting off that easily.' He signalled to a man outside the pavilion, who ran up with a pole and banged it against an overhead beam, knocking down a cloud of dust and a rope. A noose dangled from the end. With hideous grins, the men clapped their hands.

Momentarily taken aback, Deng Shaoxiang gazed at the beam and at the rope swaying in the autumn breeze like a ghostly pendulum. Those who heard her last words would remember them all their lives. 'So instead of shooting me, you're going to hang me, is that it? Go ahead if that's what you want. All I ask is that you don't leave me with my tongue hanging out. That's hideous. You have a pole. Well, if my tongue hangs out, push it back in.'

After the martyr's death, the weapons hidden in the basket were removed. But what to do with the baby? Eventually someone – no one knows who – put the baby back into the basket, and someone else – also unknown – took it down to the river. Having heard that boat people were known for plucking children out of the river, he left the basket on the steps of the pier. But no boats came and there were no boat people to claim the child. What came was the water. The river rose that night and swept the mysterious basket from dry land.

Water carried Deng Shaoxiang's legacy downriver, floating from wave to wave. People on the bank who ran after the nearly-new basket spotted a clump of water grasses, like a tow rope, carrying the basket along in fits and starts, disappearing and reappearing, as if warning off anyone who might try to catch it. Ultimately the basket floated to a spot near the town of Horsebridge. Tired from its travels, it twirled once or twice before falling into the net of Feng Four, a fisherman. Driven by curiosity, Feng reached into the net and scooped it up. Inside he discovered an infant who looked strangely like an immortal, naked but for clumps of grass draped across his yellow skin, which was dotted with beads of water. When he picked the boy up he heard the sound of sloshing water. And there, at the bottom of the basket, hidden beneath some gourds, was a large red carp, which flipped into the air before slipping beneath the surface of the river.

My father was once that boy in the relief sculpture on the back of the memorial stone. The person who scooped the basket out of the Golden Sparrow River, the fisherman Feng Four, lived for many years after Liberation, and it was he who pointed out my father in the Horsebridge orphanage. What he recognized after the passage of time was not the face of the mystical child, but the birthmark on his backside. Seven orphan boys, all about the same age, were brought into the sunlight by attendants and told to expose their backsides for inspection. Filled with the importance of his task, Feng Four walked back and forth behind the boys. After eliminating four who bore no resemblance, he painstakingly examined the green birthmarks on the backsides of the remaining three little boys, his hand held high, twitching nervously; everyone present held their breath in anxious anticipation. Finally his hand landed on the bottom of the tiniest and scrawniest of the three. 'It's this one,' he said. 'The one with a fish-shaped birthmark. It's him, I know it is!'

Feng Four's hand had spanked the bottom of my father, and that loud smack settled the question. From then on, everyone knew that dirty little Wenxuan, the boy no one cared for, was in reality the son of the martyr Deng Shaoxiang.

For years people said that the boy found amidst clumps of water grass and a red carp was the son of the martyred Deng Shaoxiang.

But then everything changed. One year, a team of martyr-orphan investigators, shrouded in mystery, was sent by the district government to determine whether the orphan was in fact the martyr's son. Taking up residence in Milltown, they travelled to towns and villages up and down the banks of the Golden Sparrow River, sometimes openly, at other times in secret. The starting point of their investigation was the disgraceful personal history of Feng Four, whose word they had determined was not to be trusted.

Who was this Feng Four, anyway? In his youth he'd been a river pirate, but when he gave up the lifestyle – or as the Chinese proverb goes, washed his hands in a golden basin – he built a hut on the riverbank and settled down to the life of a fisherman. People who lived near the river agreed that he'd been a handsome young man who'd lived a dissolute life, choosing to become a pirate because of a woman. With a boat and a rifle, he'd pursued an amorous woman who peddled garlic from her boat. Later he went ashore because of yet another woman. He'd had his eye on a farmer's daughter who picked broad beans and gave herself to him in the field, but would not marry him. So he next turned his attention to a widowed seamstress in Horsebridge. She was happy to carry on a furtive affair, but not to live openly with him, and while she refused to marry him, she would not let him marry anyone else. In the end, he simply wove nets on the riverbank all day long, nets for catching both fish and women. A handsome, bold fellow who was favoured by the opposite sex, he caught more women than fish. One – it was never made clear who – passed on a venereal disease that not only forced him to keep his trousers buttoned from then on, but eventually ended his life.

It is wise to avoid examining these matters too closely. How could a man like Feng Four be qualified to recognize the orphaned son of the martyred Deng Shaoxiang? One of the members of the investigative team, a college student who knew his history, even suspected that Feng had done a swap, palming off his own bastard child as the legitimate offspring of Deng Shaoxiang. It was an audacious charge that took the other team members' breath away. Unwilling either to dismiss or endorse this theory, they wound up simply including it in the remarks column of their report as an item for consideration.

Everything centred on the birthmark. Drawing on the scientific study of heredity, the team rejected the fish-shaped-birthmark theory, announcing that the residents of the Golden Sparrow River region were all Mongoloids, who had birthmarks on their backsides. And if the birthmarks looked exactly like fish, that was mere coincidence, with no basis in science.

But the residents of Milltown hankered after things that had no basis in science. They went crazy that autumn looking for birthmarks on their bodies. At first the craze was limited to males around the age of forty, but it spread to children and then to old men, until nearly every male in Milltown was caught up in it. Walk past any public toilet, and this is what you might have seen: a man taking down his trousers or asking someone else to take his down so they could eagerly look for birthmarks on their backsides. And in public baths, it was rare for a person not to show off his birthmark, which frequently led to watery squabbles, not to mention the occasional fistfight. But despite the outrageous extremes of the birthmark craze, since people lacked eyes in the backs of their heads, they could not examine their own backsides. That, of course, was how the craze worked to some people's advantage, for there was always someone eager to analyse the prophetic symbols imprinted there. Several of the examined backsides revealed fish-shaped birthmarks. Some were like goldfish, others resembled carp, and some actually looked like pomfrets. But not all inspections ended happily. Some of the exposed flesh was dark as ebony, some white as ivory, but could boast no birthmark. Had it faded over the years or had it never been there in the first place? Imagine the consternation this caused these unfortunate individuals, who quickly covered up and would let no one else look. Left to taste the bitter fruit of failure alone and in silence, they suffered from a crippling sense of inferiority.

As for my family, the craze took a back seat as rising winds threatened to engulf our home. I ignored the gentle and persistent entreaties of my classmates at school and refused to be caught up in the entanglements out on the street, which all centred on one thing: they wanted me to drop my trousers. My backside was not for public viewing – end of discussion! I tightened my belt and heightened my vigilance, taking a brick along whenever I visited a public toilet, and keeping my hands in my pockets when I was out walking, eyes peeled and ears alert to all sounds. By forestalling sneak attacks, I managed to preserve the integrity of my backside, but was powerless to ward off the domestic storm that had been gathering for so long. It hit, in all its fury, on the twenty-seventh of September, when the visiting team announced the startling results of their investigation. Ku Wenxuan, they concluded, was not Deng Shaoxiang's son!

They said my father was *no longer* Deng Shaoxiang's son!

The events of that day are indelibly etched on my memory. The twenty-seventh of September – coincidentally the commemoration day for the martyr Deng Shaoxiang, the day when my father ought to have been wreathed in glory – turned out to be the day of his greatest shame. I recall that my mother emerged from her propaganda broadcast studio in a daze, looking like someone who had just escaped from hell. She wore a white scarf as a makeshift mask as she pedalled her bicycle precariously down the busy People's Avenue, weeping the whole time. People she passed noticed that the scarf was wet. Sending humans and animals scurrying out of her way, she careened into Workers and Peasants Avenue and stopped at a blacksmith's shop, where she borrowed a hammer and chisel. People said they saw her lips quiver under the scarf, though they could not tell if she was cursing or praying. 'Qiao Limin,' they said, 'what do you need those for? What's wrong?'

'It's nothing,' my mother replied. 'It's just my lungs, they're about to explode from anger!'

The twenty-seventh of September. I heard someone hacking away at our front gate, so I went out and saw that my mother had chiselled off the red plaque announcing that we were honoured as a martyr's family. She weighed the plaque in her hand for a moment before stuffing it into a cloth sack. Then, before any passers-by could open their mouths, she pushed her bicycle into the yard, closed the gate behind her and sat on the ground.

When my mother said her lungs were about to explode, it was no exaggeration. Her anger was so intense that her face had lost all its colour, and there were traces of tears on her cheeks. 'Go and get the first-aid kit,' she said. 'My lungs are bursting, I need to take something.'

But instead of leaving, I asked, 'Why did you take down the martyr's family plaque?'

She removed the scarf from her face and glared at the little table my father and I had set up in the yard the day before, on which a chess board and pieces rested. Another white-hot flash of anger filled her eyes. I stood watching as she walked over, picked up my father's chess set and flung it over the wall, as if she was dumping rubbish. 'So you like to play chess, do you? Well, from this day on, you're no longer a martyr's descendant. No, you're the son of a liar, and the grandson of Feng Four, a river pirate!'

Hearing the sound of shuffling feet outside the yard, I climbed the wall in time to see our neighbours scrabbling about on the ground, snatching up the chess pieces. Some got their hands on steeds, some on warriors; the blacksmith's son managed to get hold of a general, which he waved proudly in my direction. I had no idea why these people had gathered outside our yard, but now they were looking at me as if their eyes held secrets, happy secrets. A slightly demented guffaw burst from the mouth of one woman. Then she became serious. 'You!' she screeched. 'You gutless little boy, no wonder you wouldn't let anybody see your backside! A guilty conscience, that's what it was. Just whose grandson are you?' I ignored her, preferring to watch what was happening down there from my perch on the wall and to keep my eyes peeled for my father. I didn't see him; what I did see was a town in mutiny, now that the news had spread. I heard shouts of liberation and screams of joy from the heart of Milltown and beyond. Milltown was in uproar.

My father was not Deng Shaoxiang's son. That was not a rumour, not hearsay. He just wasn't. So who was the martyr's son? The investigative team would not say, and my mother certainly didn't know. Based on hope alone, most of the town's residents were caught up in the birthmark craze, running around making wild guesses, with no two people able to agree. *Who is Deng Shaoxiang's son? Whose birthmark looks most like a fish?* I heard several names being mentioned, including the idiot, Bianjin, whose birthmark came closest. I didn't believe that for a second. Nor did anyone else. An idiot like Bianjin could not possibly be a martyr's son. So who was it? No matter what anyone said, only the investigative team could provide the answer. And all they were prepared to say was that Ku Wenxuan was not the one. It was not my father.

There can be no doubt that the injustices I've suffered have their origin in those visited upon my father. Now that he was no longer Deng Shaoxiang's son, I was not her grandson. Not being Deng Shaoxiang's son meant that he was a nobody. And his being a nobody had a direct impact on my mother and on me. I too was now a nobody.

The next day I became a *kongpi*. And that became my nickname. Everything happened so fast that I was caught on the back foot. On the day after the news broke, before I had chance to amend my princely ways, I ran into Scabby Five and Scabby Seven on my way to school. They were standing in front of the pharmacy with their older sister, waiting for it to open; Seven's head was swathed in gauze stained by thick gunk that attracted hordes of flies, which encircled all three of them. I stopped. 'Scabby Seven,' I said as I gaped at the flies on his head, 'have you opened a toilet on your head? Is that why all those flies are landing on it?'

Their eyes were glued to me, especially Scabby Seven's, who was looking at the buttered bun I was holding. He swallowed hungrily, then turned to his sister. 'See!' he bawled. 'He's got a buttered bun. He gets one every day!'

With a little pout, his sister shooed the flies away from his head and said, 'What's so great about a buttered bun? Who cares if he's got one?'

'Who cares?' Seven complained. 'I've never tasted one. I ought to care about something I've never tasted, shouldn't I?'

His sister paused, glancing at the bun in my hand, and sighed. 'They cost seven fen,' she said. 'We can't afford that. I've never tasted one either, so let's just pretend we don't care.'

But Seven was having none of that. Stiffening his neck, he said, 'His father isn't Deng Shaoxiang's son and he's not her grandson. So how come he gets a buttered bun?'

His sister's eyes lit up. 'You're right, he's a nobody. Who said he can eat that for breakfast? He's mocking us.'

The siblings exchanged glances, and in that brief moment I had a premonition that something bad was about to happen. But not ready to trust my instincts, I stood there, unafraid. Then, as if at an agreed signal, they all rushed at me. Holding the bun over my head, I said, 'How dare you try to steal my food?' They ignored me. Seven jumped up and, like a crazed animal, grabbed my wrist. Then his sister prised my fingers apart, one at a time, until she could snatch the bun, now squeezed out of shape, from my grasp.

I was fifteen at the time. Scabby Five and Scabby Seven were both younger than me, and shorter. And their sister, well, she was just a girl. But by ganging up on me, they easily snatched the food out of my hand. For that I have only lack of preparation to blame, thanks to my princely habits, not ability or physique. Someone riding past on a bicycle turned to look at me and then at the brothers and sister. 'Stealing food,' they said. 'You should be ashamed of yourselves.'

They weren't. Scabby Seven's sister watched with a sense of pride as he took big bites. 'Slow down,' she said. 'Don't eat so fast, you'll choke on it.'

After a long moment I began thinking logically. This incident was tied up with my father. Since he was not the martyr's son, Scabby Seven was free to steal my bun, and bystanders could look on without lifting a hand. I understood what was going on here, but I refused to take it lying down. I pointed at Scabby Seven. 'How dare you eat my bun!' I shouted. 'Spit it out!'

He ignored me. 'What are you shouting about?' his sister said. 'I don't see your name on it. Buns are made of flour, and that comes from wheat, which is planted by peasants. Our mother's a peasant, so some of this belongs to her.' She dragged her younger brother over to the wall and used her body as a shield. 'Hurry up!' she demanded. 'Finish it. He won't be able to prove a thing once it's in your stomach.' Apparently she was getting worried, though she put on a brave front as she searched the faces of the people near the pharmacy. Then she looked at me again. 'What are you complaining about? You eat a bun every day, but my brother has to settle for thin gruel. That's not fair, it's not socialism! It gives socialism a bad name.'

She walked off, dragging Scabby Seven along with her and followed by Scabby Five. I took a few menacing steps towards them. 'Is this a rebellion?' I said. 'Well, go ahead and rebel. Eat up. Today the bun is my treat; tomorrow I'll bring you shit to eat!'

She raised her arm and gave me a threatening look. 'To rebel is right! Chairman Mao says so! Don't you dare come over here! If you do, you're thumbing your nose at Chairman Mao. Shit this, piss that. How about cleaning out that filthy mouth of yours? See those people? Are they coming to help you? The people's eyes are too bright for that. Your dad has fallen into disgrace, and you're nothing, a nobody, nothing but a *kongpi*!'

No doubt about it, that was a big loss of face. But I can't avoid the fact that, thanks to that girl, I had a new nickname. I was now Kongpi. I can still recall the glee on the faces of the crowd that had gathered at the sound of those two syllables. In wonderful appreciation of his sister's quick-witted sarcasm, Scabby Seven burst out laughing so hard he nearly choked. 'Kongpi! Kongpi! That's right, now he's a *kongpi*.' Their glee infected everyone within hearing. People around the pharmacy, early-morning passers-by on the street, and those standing beneath the family-planning billboard echoed their gleeful laughter, and within seconds I could hear those two syllables swirling triumphantly in the air all over Milltown.

Kongpi, Kongpi, Kongpi!

People may not know that *kongpi* is a Milltown slang term that dates back hundreds of years. It sounds vulgar and easy to understand, but in fact it has a profound meaning that incorporates both *kong*, or 'empty', and *pi*, or 'ass'. Placed together, the term is emptier than empty and stinkier than an ass.

River

IN THE winter of that year I said goodbye to life on the shore and followed my father on to a river barge. I didn't know then that it was to be a lifetime banishment. Boarding was easy, getting off impossible. I've now been on the barge for eleven years with no chance of ever going back.

People say that my father tied me to the barge, and there were times when I had to agree, since that provided me with the justification for a life of sheer tedium. But in the eyes of my father, this justification was a gleaming dagger forever aimed at his conscience. At times when I could not contain my displeasure with him, I used this dagger as a weapon to injure, to accuse, even to humiliate him. But most of the time I didn't have the heart for that, and while the procession of barges sailed downstream, I gazed over the side at the water and felt that I'd been bound to the river for eternity. Then I looked at the levees and houses and fields on the banks and felt that I was bound to them as well. I saw people I knew there, and others I didn't; I saw people on other barges, and couldn't help feeling that they were the ones who had bound me to the barge. But when we sailed at night, when the river darkened, when, in fact, the whole world darkened, I turned on the masthead lamp and watched as the hazy light cast my shadow on to the bow, a tiny, fragile, shapeless watermark of a shadow. The water flowed across the wide riverbed, while my life streamed on aboard the barge, and from the dark water emerged a revelation. I discovered the secret of my life: I was bound to the barge by my shadow.

Traces of the martyred Deng Shaoxiang criss-crossed the towns and villages on the banks of the Golden Sparrow River. The year I came to the fleet, my father's view of his bloodline was unwavering; he was convinced that the investigative team had viewed him with enmity and prejudice, and that their so-called conclusion was nothing more than murder by proxy, a crazed incident of persecution. The way he saw it, he was in the bosom of the martyr Deng Shaoxiang as he sailed the river with the other barges, and that invested him with an enormous, if illusory, sense of peace. Once, when we sailed past the town of Phoenix, he pointed out a row of wooden shacks – some tall, some squat. 'See there?' he said. 'The memorial hall, that one with the black roof tiles and white wall, that's where your grandmother hid the weapons.'

I gazed out at the town and at the building with the black roof tiles and white wall, which I'd never seen before. 'Memorial hall? So what!' I said. 'What about the coffin shop? Where's that?'

He erupted angrily. 'Stop that nonsense about a coffin shop. Don't listen to people who just want to smear your grandmother. She was no coffin girl. She relied upon coffins to smuggle weapons and ammunition to serve the needs of the revolution, that's all.' He pointed insistently at the ruins. 'It's there, behind that row of buildings. Don't tell me you can't see it!'

Well, I couldn't, and I said so. 'There's no memorial hall!'

That infuriated him. After swatting me across the face, he said, 'Your grandmother fought a battle for that place. Now do you see it? If not, you must be blind!'

My father moved his commemoration of Deng Shaoxiang to the river. Each year, at Qingming – the fifth day of the fifth lunar month – and on the twenty-seventh day of the ninth month, he unfolded a banner on our barge with the slogan:

THE MARTYRED DENG SHAOXIANG WILL LIVE FOR EVER IN OUR HEARTS.

Several months separated the two dates, and as I recall how the seasonal winds snapped at the red cloth on those holidays, I am visited by disparate and unreal visions: autumn winds billowing Father's banner cover our barge with a heavy pall, as if the martyr's ghost were weeping on the river's surface; she reaches out a moss-covered hand and grabs our anchor. 'Don't go,' she says. 'Don't go. Stop here!' She is, we can tell, dispirited as she tries to prevent our barge from sailing on, so that her son and grandson can stay with her. Spring winds, on the other hand, like all spring winds, blow lightly, carefully across the water's surface, laden with the smell of new grass, awakening the name of the martyr Deng Shaoxiang, and I invariably sense the presence of an unfamiliar ghost as it nimbly climbs aboard from the stern and, dripping with water, sits on our barge to gaze tenderly at Father.

I was perplexed. In the autumn I believed what others were saying – that my father was not Deng Shaoxiang's son. But when spring rolled around, I believed *him* when he insisted he was.

Whatever the truth, Father's one-time glory had vanished like smoke in the wind, and all he'd been left with was a sofa he'd once kept in his office. Now he sat on that sofa, a memento of the power he'd once wielded, and slowly grew accustomed to life on the water, treating the barge as if it were the shore and its cabin as his office. The second half of his life was like a rubbish heap, with no place to hide beyond the river and the barge. In his later years, he and the shore parted company, and on those rare occasions when we approached Milltown, he'd stick his head out to take a peek at the shore, but then I'd walk over and close the porthole.

Other people could appreciate the sights of Milltown all they wanted, but not him. He'd get vertiginous and complain about his eyesight, saying that the land was moving, like flowing water. I knew all about his fears. The shore wasn't moving; what moved were his shameful memories. After so many years had passed, his frail, ageing body had split into two halves, one having grudgingly fled to the water, the other remaining for ever on the riverbank, where people no longer punished him yet had forgotten to forgive him; they had tied him to a pillar of shame.

I could not free my father from that pillar of shame, and this brought him his greatest torment and me my greatest heartache.

Separation

AFTER THE incident with the investigative team, Father remained ashore for three months, the first two in the attic of the Spring Breeze Inn, where he was kept in isolation while being checked out. A metal door with three locks separated the attic from the rest of the hotel; the keys were kept by three members of the team, two men and a woman who occupied rooms on the second floor. An endless stream of problems arose for my father, beginning with his education and as much of his work history as could be verified. He gave them the names of two schoolmates who could testify on his behalf, a man and a woman. No one knew the whereabouts of the man, while the woman had suffered a nervous breakdown. As for testimonials from the White Fox Logging Camp, where he'd worked for many years, the two individuals whose names he provided had died in a forest fire. And the person who had vouched for his acceptance into the Party was particularly suspect. A man of considerable renown, his reputation was badly tainted. Known as the most notorious rightist in the provincial capital, he had been sent to a labour-reform farm, where he was generally recalcitrant until the day he mysteriously disappeared.

Even Father was surprised to learn how dubious his own

personal history was. 'Who are you?' the investigative team asked repeatedly. 'Just who are you anyway?'

Eventually, they managed to wear him down. 'Is there some sort of mental illness that can cause a person to remember everything wrong?' he asked earnestly.

They rejected the implication. 'Don't try to turn this into a health issue,' they said. 'No neurologist can solve your problems. Seeing one would be a waste of time. You need to do some serious soul-searching.'

No therapy for him. So the soul-searching began, and over time he began to see the error of his ways. It wasn't his memory that had let him down, it was his fate. A dark path lay in front of him, one with no visible end, and he could no longer validate himself.

As rumours flew around Milltown about how my father had created a false identity to fool the Party, the wall outside our house began to fill up with angry graffiti: 'LIAR . . . ENEMY AGENT . . . SCAB . . . BUFFOON.' Someone even labelled him a secret agent for Chiang Kai-shek and the US imperialists. Mother, who seemed to be on the brink of a nervous breakdown, went to the General Affairs Building to speak with Party leaders. That had the desired effect, for they assured her that she would not be implicated, that even though she and Father shared a bed, they could take divergent political stances. So she was still on safe ground when she returned home. With uncertainty she made the necessary arrangements for my life, while deep down, she was planning her own future. I had a premonition about what her future entailed. I could not be sure if I was included in that future, but I knew that Father was not.

Without telling Mother, I went to see him, but was stopped by the metal door. I knocked, attracting the attention of one of the team members, a middle-aged man in a blue tunic who escorted me out of the hotel. 'Is that what you call solitary confinement?' he screamed at a hotel employee. 'Do you people still not understand what this is all about? Unauthorized people are not allowed in here, period!'

'But it's Ku Wenxuan's son,' the employee said. 'He's just a boy.'

The official scrutinized my face. 'A boy, you say? He's got the start of a beard already. He's unauthorized and is not allowed in!'

During the two months Father spent in the hotel attic, people reported that he began to behave bizarrely. He stubbornly dropped his trousers once a day, regardless of time or occasion, to let the team examine the fish-shaped birthmark on his backside. For humanitarian reasons, they decided to end the solitary confinement early and notified us to come and get him.

So Mother and I waited in the third-floor hallway for the green metal door to swing open. When it did, Father emerged, bent at the waist, carrying a bag in one hand and a chess set in the other. Deprived of sunlight for so long, his face was wan and slightly puffy. At first glance, he seemed relatively healthy, but on closer examination, it was obvious that he bore the look of fatigue. He cast Mother a fervent glance, but when she turned away, fear replaced the fervour in his eyes as his timid gaze fell on me. That gave me goose bumps – he was so humble, so helpless. It was as if I were the father and he the son. Having committed serious errors, he was now trying to ingratiate himself, begging for my forgiveness.

I no more knew how to forgive than how to punish him. So I followed him down the stairs, watching as he stepped cautiously, still bent at the waist, like a doddering old man. After living in the attic, with its low ceiling, for two months, he'd become used to standing in a semi-crouch. 'Dad,' I said, 'you're out of the attic now. Why are you still bent over like that?'

'You're right,' he said. 'I am out of the attic. Am I bent over?'

'Yes,' I said, 'like a shrimp.'

Suddenly aware of his posture, there, on the third-floor stairs of the Spring Breeze Hotel, he raised his head anxiously and jerked his body straight, which induced a painful scream. He dropped the bag as if his body had snapped in two. Then he dropped the chess set and braced himself with his hand on the small of his back. His face was a study in suffering. 'That really hurt!' he said as he stared fearfully at Mother.

Mother bent down to pick up the bag, as if she hadn't heard his scream. 'What's in here?' she asked. 'What's that jingling sound? Why not throw it away? Why take it home?'

I went to give him a hand. He looked at Mother, expecting her to help as well. But she stayed put, bag in hand, and looked away without moving a muscle. So Father composed himself and pushed me away. 'Pick up those chess pieces,' he said. As I did, I watched him bend, little by little, and start downstairs. 'It's all right,' he muttered. 'I'll walk like this. It doesn't hurt as much.'

The investigation was brought to an end, at least for the time being. The team had got half of what they were after. My father refused to admit that he'd created a false identity or that he'd misled the Party, and insisted he was the son of the martyr Deng Shaoxiang. But they'd had more success in another area than they'd expected. After only a few sessions, during which he'd put up strong resistance and argued in his own defence, Father eventually confessed that there were problems with his lifestyle, either because he was being too honest or because he was trying to evade a more serious issue.

There were problems with his lifestyle.

And those problems, I heard, were serious.

Lifestyle

PROBLEMS WITH lifestyle meant sex, everyone knew that. Women were always involved when a man was accused of having lifestyle problems. This was serious, and the more women were involved, the more serious the problem. I was fifteen at the time, still some way from sexual maturity, but I knew that my father – a man, after all – had sex outside of marriage. I didn't know how many women he'd slept with, and had to wonder what was so great about sleeping with lots of women. Since it wasn't something I could talk about, I pondered it silently, stopping only when I got an erection. That was something my mother would not tolerate, calling it a shameful sign of degradation. One morning she awoke me by slapping me with a plastic sandal. Glaring at the little tent I'd made in my underwear, she drove me out of bed with more slaps. 'I'll teach you not to learn such things from him! It's shameful! Degrading!'

My mother made a clean break with my father, but stopped short of going her separate way. I later learned that this was not an act of mercy, but a way to settle scores. She did not intend to come to his rescue. In her eyes, he was little more than a pile of dog shit, and in no need of being rescued. What she wanted was enough time to do something. What, exactly? Punish him. Unwilling to give up the advantage she held, she wanted to make him suffer. At first she concentrated on his mental state, and the unexpected occurred when Father's spirit, like his bent back, was irreparably broken. When there was nothing more she could do to his spirit, all that was left was whatever punishment she could inflict on his body.

Early the next morning, Father pushed Mother's bicycle outside. 'Be careful out there,' he said, 'and take it slowly.'

'It's none of your business how fast or slow I ride,' she said, 'and keep your filthy hands off my bike. Maybe a tractor will come along and put me out of my misery.'

Wisely, Father stepped back, but then said, 'Read the news slowly during the broadcast and don't make any mistakes. With everyone pushing against the wall, it's ready to topple. You don't want to give people any excuse to capitalize on a mistake.'

Mother just sneered. 'At a time like this, how can you pretend to be so caring? With all these daggers in my back, what makes you think they'll let me anywhere near a microphone? Know what I do at the studio? I clip stories from the papers for Zhang Xiaohong.' The mere mention of how she had to serve a co-worker incensed Mother, and she was on the verge of hysteria. Finally, she pointed to the ground. 'Ku Wenxuan, even death would be too good for you! Get down on your knees, you owe me that!'

Hesitant for a moment, Father might have been reflecting on all the terrible things he'd done, and wondering if death would truly be too good for him. He glanced up at the window to my room before he fell to his knees in the gateway and looked up at Mother with a tight smile. 'If death is too good for me, then kneeling is what I deserve.'

'Oh?' she said. 'Then tell me, why do you have to do that here? You want our neighbours to see, is that it? They open their doors, and there you are, on your knees. Maybe you don't care about losing face, but I do.'

Father stood up and muttered, 'Worried about what people

might think, that's good. Where would you like me to kneel?' He glanced around, looking for a good spot, and settled on a stone barbell lying under the date tree. He shuffled over and eased himself down on the stone, gazing helplessly at Mother and hoping for her approval.

She merely snorted and pushed her bike through the gate, crestfallen over the docility of her husband. But then she turned and pointed at him. 'You're kneeling there only because I told you to,' she said contemptuously. 'I tell you, Ku Wenxuan, a man should not kneel too easily; there might be gold under his knees. Know what I mean? We'll see if anyone anywhere will look up to you from now on.'

As he knelt there I spied on him and detected a slight movement. One of his knees rose from the stone, the other one stayed put. He waited for Mother to leave before getting slowly to his feet, and when he spotted me, an embarrassed look flashed briefly on to his face as he brushed the dirt from his knees. 'Just this once,' he said as casually as possible. 'It won't happen again. All in fun. But tell me, Dongliang, why haven't you been lifting the barbell lately?'

'Because it's a waste of time, it doesn't do any good. Lifting things doesn't do any good.'

'What do you mean, it doesn't do any good? It makes you stronger.' He scowled before standing up beneath the date tree, bent at the waist, deep in thought. After a moment he laughed a brief bitter laugh and said, 'Truth is, it won't make any difference. This family is doomed to split up. Sooner or later your mother will leave us.'

I didn't say anything. What could I say? Immaturity and confusion had me swaying from one parent to the other. There were moments when my sympathies lay with my mother, but most of the time I felt sorry for my father. I stared at the smudges on his knees and then let my gaze drift cautiously upward, until I noticed a bulge in the front of his trousers that was sliding disconsolately downward, like a broken farm tool hanging uselessly from a scrawny tree. I didn't know what Father looked like with an erection, nor did I know how many women he'd slept with, or the times, the places, the details, and the sorts of women they were. Deep and complex emotions rose irrepressibly inside me, and the look on my face surprised him. He gazed down at his crotch. 'What are you looking at?' he barked.

'Nothing.'

Father angrily smoothed down the front of his trousers. 'Then what are you thinking?'

'Nothing.'

'Liar. I know there are bad thoughts racing through your mind. You can fool other people, but not me.'

'I'm not thinking anything,' I said, 'so stop trying to get into my head. My head's a *kongpi*, nothing but a *kongpi*.'

'*Kongpi*? What's that?' He gave me a dubious look. '*Kong* is "empty", I got that. And *pi* is "ass". But what do they mean together?'

'Go and ask somebody else. I don't know. That's what they call me now. I used to belong to the Ku family, but now my surname is Empty. And I'm not Dongliang, I'm Ass.'

'Who gave you that terrible nickname? And why?'

'What good would it do to tell you?' I couldn't hold back any longer. 'It's your fault!' I complained. 'It's all because of you! And stop calling me Dongliang. From now on you can call me Kongpi!'

Father stopped and thought for a moment. 'Yes, I know. When the city gate burns, the fish in the moat die. I dragged you into this.' Still bent at the waist, he began to pace around the tree, casting an occasional look my way, but quickly shying away from the loathing in my eyes. Finally he walked over to a clothes line in the yard, on which hung some of Mother's fancy costumes from her youth. She'd held on to them all, preventing them from getting mouldy by airing them each autumn. The sight of them hanging there was like watching birds singing in the spring: a Uighur cap, a black vest with threads of gold, a long emerald-green skirt, a Tibetan blouse with half sleeves, a pair of felt boots, a colourful apron, a traditional Korean robe, white with a red belt, and two pairs of ballet slippers, all hanging from the clothes line with a show of bluster.

Father looked up, and I noticed that he was blinking. Inspired by the costumes, he was recalling the time when Mother had been a beautiful stage performer. He set the ballet slippers in motion, then took down the Uighur cap and brushed the dust off it. He sighed. 'Dongliang,' he said, wanting to make me feel better, 'having a nickname is nothing to worry about. Your mother is the one I've hurt the most. She'll never be allowed back into the drama troupe, and now even broadcasting is closed to her. If she can't be a broadcaster or an actress, her talents will go to waste.'

It was obvious that in his eyes my anguish counted for little next to Mother's, and I felt like saying, 'Well, let me call you Kongpi, and see how you like it.' But I thought better of it. What he said made sense. What does a nickname mean, anyway? What does it prove? The family was breaking up, and I knew I could not cast my lot with him. That left only Mother. If she had a future, so did I. If she was neglected, I would be too. And if she wound up as a nobody, then I'd be a real *kongpi*, and not just in name.

Let me tell you about my mother, Qiao Limin, and her artistic talents.

In her youth she was Milltown's most ravishing beauty, the star of mass literary and arts activities, and known popularly as Milltown's Wang Danfeng. If she hadn't been a bit long in the body, with short legs, she'd have been more beautiful and more exceptional than the famous 1940s movie star. She had upturned, slanted eyes and a straight nose with a slightly bulbous tip, an oval face, and a voice equally comfortable with sweet lyrics and loud, sonorous arias. But singing and dancing aside, her real talent lay in the realm of broadcasting. For Milltown residents, the perfect enunciation and intonation of broadcaster Qiao Limin's voice was like a musical weathervane. Her mid-range notes told them that everything was fine, in China and in the world; her lower register told them that news of battleground victories by workers and peasants was pouring in; her alto tones told them that people's lives were like sesame stalks, whose blossoms grow higher and higher. But the loudest cheers were reserved for her soprano notes, for in them were hidden rare metals with natural powers of penetration and shock. The slogans thundering from her during one open trial actually caused the historical counter-revolutionary Yu Wensun to lose control of his bladder up on the platform. On another occasion, before she'd finished her slogan, a corrupt bookkeeper at the purchasing station by the name of Yao fainted dead away. If you'd been there to hear my mother broadcasting you'd know I'm not exaggerating. Her whole existence was tied up in sloganeering, and her shouts were full of noble aspirations and daring; they pierced the heavens and crackled like magnificent yet graceful thunderclaps in the sky above Milltown, sending chickens flying and ducks leaping, and striking cats and dogs dumb. Below the platform, people's ears rang, and those few individuals with sensitive eardrums were forced to stuff their ears with cotton to withstand the tonal assault.

Father once said that Mother exuded revolutionary romanticism that had a distinct charm. Revolution and romanticism were for her a single-minded pursuit. She'd spent her youth in Horsebridge, where her beauty and artistic flair were first spotted, though the place was too small for her talents to be fully realized. Either out of envy or prejudice, the locals had not held her in high regard, referring to her behind her back as a butcher-shop Wang Danfeng, a nickname that drew attention to her origins and bloodline. My maternal grandfather lived in Horsebridge, but I'd never met him. Why? He was a butcher by trade, a man whose profession called upon him to slaughter pigs. Neither a member of the bourgeoisie nor a landlord or rich peasant, he still could not lay claim to the status of proletarian. Being born into a questionable family was a hindrance to Mother's chances of making a good match. Rumours went round that during the famine Grandfather had sold buns stuffed with human flesh, a scandalous story that was widely publicized when each new campaign was launched, causing Mother unbearable humiliation. And so, over the years, she nurtured a plan to escape from her family, which she carried out soon after her eighteenth birthday. She came home one day, broke open her cherished savings jar and, while she was counting the money, announced gravely that she was making a break with her family.

'And how will you accomplish that?' they asked.

'I'll no longer let you feed or clothe me,' she said. 'I'm going to strike out on my own.'

'How do you, a mere girl, expect to do that, especially on that little bit of money? Have you got a mate in mind? Who is it?'

Angered that her family had underestimated her future prospects, she said, 'Who is my mate? You wouldn't understand even if I told you. My mate is the performing stage! You may think I'm callous, but if I don't make a break with you, you will control my future, and while you may not care about the future, I do!'

After leaving the Horsebridge butcher's shop, Mother's travels took her to many places. She applied for membership of the Beijing Opera Troupe, the Armoured Corps Cultural Troupe, a Shaoxing Opera Troupe, as well as district Beijing Opera troupes. She even applied for an acrobatic troupe. But her hopes were dashed each time – in like a tiger's head, out like a snake's tail, as the saying goes – either because they thought her legs were stumpy or that her family background presented problems. After being refused entry into the traditional cultural troupes, she'd used up all her travel money and had become discouraged. So she lowered her expectations, setting her sights instead on the popular stage, to perform for the masses. By taking a step back, she opened up new vistas and quickly found work at the Harvest Nitrate Fertilizer Factory, which was home to the celebrated Golden Sparrow River Region Cultural Propaganda Troupe. And there she received the recognition she deserved; at last her beauty had caught someone's attention. During the day, workers at the factory packaged fertilizer, but after hours they rehearsed for cultural performances. My mother was either the lead singer or lead dancer in the amateur troupe. When she walked out of the factory door at the end of her shift, her blue uniform reeked of ammonia, but the captivating world of the stage lived beneath her collar.

One day, my father, who worked as a woodsman at the time, went to the factory to buy fertilizer and laid eyes on my mother for the first time. He was surprised to see a bright-red silk jacket under her work clothes, her costume for the red silk dance. He did not know what to think about her costume or how to sum up her singular charm. Their second meeting, which was arranged by a go-between, took place by the fertilizer drainage ditch; he watched as she emerged from the factory's rear door, lithe and graceful, again with a costume under her work clothes, this one a familiar light-green dress, which, he recalled, would be worn in the tea-picker's skit. This time he was prepared. He stirred feelings in her with the first thing he ever said to her: 'Comrade Qiao,' he said, 'your body emanates the spirit of revolutionary romanticism.'

While one could say that my parents fell in love, it would be more accurate to say that they discovered one another at the same moment. My father discovered her beauty and talent; she discovered his bloodline and future prospects. He was half a head shorter than she, which even then made their marriage a mismatch, though there were reasons for them to come together. But then in September, my father's secrets were exposed. Someone, it's not clear who, revealed to Mother that the first thing he habitually said in furtherance of his womanizing was 'Comrade So-and-So, your body emanates the spirit of revolutionary romanticism.'

My mother's lungs felt as if they were about to explode – that was one of *her* favourite expressions. She once described for me the powerful reflex anger caused in her lungs: 'I have trouble breathing,' she said, 'my lungs pound against my chest, and I'm sure that I lose part of them every time that happens.' Anger and hurt led her to a new discovery about Father, that he was what is known as 'cow dung disguised as a flower garden to trick the flowers'. She was one of those flowers, now growing in a pile of cow dung, and the reasons for them to have come together suddenly no longer existed, while reasons for them to part mounted. Mother began folding her clean autumn clothes and packing them away in a camphor chest, storing her treasured stage costumes in a suitcase that itself was a treasure, a relic from her life on the stage. A red seal on top of the suitcase said:

AWARDED TO THE POPULAR
ENTERTAINMENT ACTIVISTS
OF THE HARVEST NITROGEN FERTILIZER
FACTORY

Towards the end, our family life became chaotic and stifling. Mother divided the household chores into three categories. One was reserved for her, and consisted mainly of preparing lunch and dinner for me and for herself. Another was reserved for me, and consisted mainly of sweeping and dusting and taking out the rubbish. The final category was the most arduous: making break-fast for all three of us, cleaning the toilet twice a day, and taking care of all aspects of Father's daily life: food, clothing and what-ever else he needed. Those were his duties. Mother said she'd lost her appetite for washing his socks and underwear, and was ada-mant about not cooking for him. She said she'd suffered so much humiliation she could barely keep from poisoning his food.

My mother followed methods used by organs of the dictatorship in punishing criminals, subjecting Father to the ultimate settling of accounts. She overlooked nothing, from his labour-reform activities in the yard to special examinations in the bedroom. His last days at home were little more than house arrest, with Mother as his inquisitor, and everything centred on problems of lifestyle. Just that, his lifestyle, which of course involved only the area below the waist, not something people liked to talk about. Father, who was easily embarrassed, could not endure the questioning, so he took to keeping out of sight. The minute Mother came home from work, he hid in the toilet and stayed there as long as he could.

Whenever I saw Mother take a pen and her worker's notebook out of a drawer, I knew the interrogation was about to begin. 'Go on, call your father out here.' She wanted me to bang on the toilet door, and if I refused, she did it herself with a broom handle. Father would emerge and pass under the broom, bent at the waist, heading for the yard. But he'd barely make it to the front door before hearing Mother's sarcastic laugh. He'd stop, turn, and come face to face with her broom, pointing at him. 'Go ahead,' she'd say sternly. 'Open the door and go outside, where a crowd of people is waiting to see Ku Wenxuan embarrass himself. Go out there and give them a show. I'm betting you don't have the guts!'

He didn't. After taking a turn around the yard, he'd obediently come back inside and sit opposite her, where he'd beat about the bush instead of answering her questions, or else admit minor transgressions but do whatever he could to avoid the more serious ones. To Mother, this smacked of passive resistance. They never argued in front of me and lowered the curtain to keep me from peeking in at the window, but on one occasion I heard Mother's hysterical shouts tear through the window: 'Ku Wenxuan, leniency to those who confess their crimes and severity to those who refuse!' The shouts emanated from a bedroom confrontation. It sounded comical to me, but scary as well.

The truth is, the more they argued, the less I cared. On the contrary, the quieter and more peaceful they were, the more I worried. Caution piqued my curiosity. They might be able to deceive the neighbours, but not me. One night a deadly silence descended in their room, throwing me into a panic. I climbed the date tree and had an unobstructed view through the transom window. The lamp was lit, so I could see them both. Mother was sitting at her desk, notebook in hand, her cheeks wet with tears; my father was kneeling at her feet like a dog and had pulled down his trousers to show her his honoured fish-shaped birthmark. At it again! He'd brought his sickness home with him. I saw her curse him loudly, glaring at him with contempt and disgust. But he was relentless. His trousers were round his knees, and he was crawling along the floor, moving to wherever Mother turned her face. Sharp light glinted off his pale, bony backside in the darkened room. Then his shouts tore through the night.

'Look! You used to like looking at it. Why won't you look at it now? Take a good look at my birthmark, I'm Deng Shaoxiang's son! That's the truth! I said look, take a good look. It's a fish. I'm Deng Shaoxiang's son. Don't be in such a hurry to make a clean break. If you file for divorce, you'll live to regret it!'

I burst into tears. Was I crying for him or for her? I couldn't say. I climbed down out of the tree and took a long look at my house, then at the blue sky. I dried my eyes and snarled into the sky, 'Go ahead, divorce! If you don't, you're *kongpi*. And if you do, you're still *kongpi*!'

Their divorce went without a hitch. The only problem was me. If I went with him, I'd sail the river; if I went with her, I'd stay on dry land. The river had its appeal, but I was afraid to give up dry land. So I said to Father, 'I'll spend half the year on the barge with you and half the year with Mother. What do you say?'

'Fine with me,' he said. 'But check with your mother. I doubt she'll go along with it.'

So I checked, and was met with boiling anger. 'Absolutely not! If you want me, you can't have him. And if you want him, you can't have me. If the top beam is crooked, the one below can't be straight. How am I supposed to take care of a child he's had a hand in raising?'

So I had to choose. Two sets of inauspicious gifts were arrayed before me. One was Father and a barge, the other was Mother and dry land. There was no way out, I had to choose one over the other. I chose Father. Even now the boat people sometimes talk about my decision. *If Dongliang had stayed with his mother,* they say, *he'd be this or that.* Or, *If he'd stayed with her, Ku Wenxuan would be this or that.* Even, *His mother would be this or that.* But I ignored all the 'this or that' talk. And 'what ifs' bored me. *Kongpi,* all of them. Like water that keeps flowing, or grass that keeps growing, there was no choice involved; it was all up to fate. My father's fate was tied up with a martyr named Deng Shaoxiang, and mine was tied up with him.

At the end of that year, a notice regarding the forced-transfer barge fleet was posted on the door of my house, spelling the end of my time in Milltown. When we boarded the barge, Mother had to move, and she did. But she was in such a hurry that she accidentally left her notebook behind. As she rushed out of the house she tossed a cloth bundle on to my bed, and when I picked it up, I found the notebook inside. She'd made a cover for her cherished notebook out of an illustrated newspaper. The front was graced with the ruddy face of Li Tiemei from the revolutionary opera *The Red Lantern*. The back showed Li's hand, holding a red lantern. With time and opportunity on my side, I took as long as I needed to decide what to do with this special notebook, and wound up making a bold decision. I'd neither hand it over to Father nor give it back to Mother. I'd hide it away for myself.

To this day I can't tell you who I hid that notebook for. Was it for Father or was it for Mother? Maybe it was for me. This secret most likely impacted on the rest of my life. I committed everything Mother had written in it – or should I say, every one of Father's indiscretions – to memory. Even with the hatred she felt as she recorded everything, her handwriting was always neat and pleasing to the eye. The themes and content were unsurprising. She noted Father's infidelities in great detail: numbers, times and locations. In some places she added angry comments: 'Shameless! . . . Obscene! . . . I could die!' To my astonishment, I knew the names of some of the women, including the mother of my schoolmate Li Shengli, and Zhao Chuntang's younger sister, Zhao Chunmei. Even Aunty Sun, who ran the salvage station, was in there. These women had always impressed me as being proper and virtuous. Why were their names in Mother's notebook?

Paradise

HARDLY ANYONE today can relate the history of the Sunnyside Fleet with any degree of accuracy.

Let's start with the tugboat. Owned by a shipping company, it ran on diesel, had twin rudders and plenty of horsepower. Seven or eight workers manned the tug, although they worked only when there were barges that needed to be moved. Each time out counted as a shift, and when that shift was over, they went back to their homes on the banks of the river. Sailors love to drink, and the more the younger ones drank, the meaner they got. They could be having a normal conversation when suddenly fists would fly. I saw one of them jump into the river with the jagged edge of a bottle stuck in his chest and swim to the riverside hospital, cursing the whole way. The older hands were more easy-going and not nearly as volatile when they were drunk. One of them, a man with a full beard, would lie out on the deck and sleep like a log. Another of the older ones – with a face like a monkey – was in the habit of showering on the afterdeck. Stark naked, he would work up a lather and then rinse off with cold water, making eyes at the women and girls on the barges. I didn't think much of that gang.

For that matter, I didn't think much of anyone. The Sunnyside Fleet boasted eleven barges, manned by eleven families, most with shady backgrounds. In that respect, we were all pretty much alike. Since Father's situation was still unsettled, our background was as murky as any of the others. Taking me aboard one of the barges with him could hardly be called exile, nor was it some sort of banishment; rather, it was a reclassification.

The boat people called a spot upriver named Plum Mountain their ancestral home. You can no longer find it on any Golden Sparrow River regional map. During the construction of a reservoir, Plum Mountain township, with its thirteen villages, was flooded, and now the place is marked on maps in blue – Victory Reservoir. Only an idiot would believe that Plum Mountain was really their ancestral home, since their speech was a mish-mash of accents and dialects, with pithy, bizarre ways of saying things. Let's say we were heading upriver towards Horsebridge. They'd say we were heading 'down' to it. They called eating 'nibbling', and relieving themselves was 'snapping it off'. As for sex, which people ashore seldom even mentioned, they were perfectly happy to talk about it any time, any place. The word they used was 'thump'. If several men were sitting around with conspiratorial looks on their faces, all you heard them talking about was thump, thump, thump. Why 'thump'? Because what most people consider to be a serious social issue was just an ordinary thumping to them.

I was generally repelled by the way they lived. They were sloppy dressers. In cold weather they overdressed, with reds and greens and yellows and blues all thrown together and layered collars sticking up around their necks. Then when summer gave way to autumn they were underdressed, sometimes to the point of being half-naked. Barefoot and shirtless, the men were so dark that from a distance they looked like Africans. They wore coarse, homemade white shorts, the material for which came mostly from Great Harvest flour sacks. Wide in the crotch, the tops were rolled over at the waist and tied with drawstrings. The women were slightly better, in a bizarre way. Married women wore their hair in a bun, adorned with a magnolia or a gardenia. Above the waist, they sported a variety of attire: some fancied the faddish Peter Pan blouses, others wore men's white T-shirts, and others still preferred short granny jackets. But below the waist they were more conservative and unified: they wore baggy, knee-length rayon trousers, black or dark blue, sometimes decorated with an embroidered peony on the leg. Owing to frequent childbirth and nursing, and since they were not in the habit of wearing brassieres, their breasts sagged in defeat, large and unwieldy. They swung from side to side when the women walked the decks of the barges, a grumbling badge of honour. I was not impressed. Even when they were exposed, they held no interest for me.

The barge children usually ran around butt naked, both as an economy measure and as a sort of identification mark. There was no fear of their getting lost ashore, for anyone who found them invariably returned them to the piers. Boys, of course, were favoured over girls. They wore little pigtails, bracelets on their wrists, and long-life necklaces around their necks. The girls, on the other hand, went without jewellery, and their mothers cut their hair haphazardly and unevenly, leaving them with little haystacks on their heads. Adolescent girls covered their private parts with belly warmers made of white handkerchiefs sewn together. Older girls wore either their mother's or their father's hand-me-downs, which meant they never fitted. Though they were more or less unloved, that had no effect on their sense of family duty. All day long they ran up and down the decks doing chores, hollering at their mischievous little brothers and sisters.

The only truly pretty girl in the fleet, Yingtao, was so intent on playing the role of a mother that she carried her baby brother strapped to her back with red cloth, day in and day out, going from family to family. She once walked up to the stern of barge number six, where she watched me steely-eyed, like a sentry.

'What are you doing here?' I said. 'Go away.'

'I'm on barge number six,' she said, 'not yours, so mind your own business.'

'I'm not interested in minding anybody's business,' I said. 'I just don't want you watching me.'

'If you weren't looking at me,' she said, 'how'd you know I was watching you?'

'OK, I won't look at you, and you don't talk to me.'

'Who said I want to talk to you?' she replied. 'You spoke to me first.' She was too quick for me, so I just glared at her with the fiercest, most threatening look I could manage. It didn't faze her. Instead, with an enigmatic smile she said, 'Don't act so cocky. I know all about your family. I'll let you see my brother's backside. He's got a birthmark, and it's a fish too!' She untied the cloth holding her brother and exposed his tiny rear end to me. 'See! See that birthmark. It looks just like a fish!' I could hear the pride in her voice, while the boy, who was now in her arms, began to fidget. 'Don't you dare snap it off,' Yingtao said, raising her voice. 'I said, don't you dare! You can go on the potty in a little while.'

Seeing that the child was about to let go, I turned my head so I didn't have to keep looking at his rear end. Angered by the encounter, I headed towards our stern and muttered, 'Thump! Thump your goddamned fish! Thump! Thump your goddamned birthmark!' Just like all the sailors.

My days on the river were unrelievedly lonely, and that loneliness comprised the last thread of my self-respect. There were lots of boys in the fleet, but they were either too old and stupid or too small and disgusting, so I had no friends. How could anyone expect me to make friends with the likes of them? But they were curious about me and as friendly as could be, often dropping by barge number seven to see me, sometimes bringing gifts of mouldy peas or a toy train to tempt me into being their friend. Who did they think I was? I sent them scurrying.

I'm sort of embarrassed to describe my early days aboard the barge. Father wanted me to study, so he started teaching me things I needed to know. He'd let me sit on his favourite sofa as I read from a pile of books that included the notebook that had belonged to my mother; that one I studied on the sly. In recording Father's lifestyle, Mother seemed to have been in a forgiving mood, since the harshest words she used were 'did it'. I counted – she used that phrase more than sixty times – Who he 'did it' with, when he 'did it' with her, as well as where and how many times, plus who initiated it. Had they been caught in the act? As for other details, she settled for thick, heavy exclamation marks and the unhappy comment 'I could just die, my lungs are about to explode!'

I had nothing to die about as I read what she had written, trying to figure out exactly what had gone on. I wound up wallowing in a space between reason and imagination, and was frightened by the outcome. That outcome was a chemical reaction that made a prisoner of my body – I experienced one erection after another from her words. My crotch was on fire. A shameful flame burned out of control in our cabin, and I didn't know what to do about it. I closed the notebook, only to have Li Tiemei rekindle the fire from the notebook's cover. I can't tell you why, but while there was a look of revolutionary fervour in her eyes, the image of her thin, red lips, her long, straight nose and her soft, titillating ears came across to me as flirtatious. Unable to suppress this imaginary flirtatiousness, I hid the notebook in a chest, an action that settled the upheaval in my groin. But my ears remained unsettled. I thought I sensed a red image on the shore: it was my mother, running along the bank, chasing our barge and shouting angrily, 'Give me back my notebook! Give it back! Dongliang, you're shameful and disgusting! If the top beam is crooked, the bottom one can't be straight. I could just die, Dongliang. Thanks to you, my lungs are about to explode!'

Father was the top beam, I was the bottom one. I couldn't deny that the top beam controlled the bottom one, but at the same time, I was convinced that being the bottom beam is better than being the top one. It's easy for the bottom beam to supervise the top beam. I observed Father's lifestyle with a detached eye, centring observations on his relations with women. But even after prolonged observation, I could draw no clear conclusions. I knew that he was a crooked upper beam, but didn't know how it was crooked, and in whose direction it bent.

The Sunnyside Fleet was the grudging home of his last few remaining adoring supporters. Even after he was banished to the river, they kept calling him Secretary Ku, and the women in the fleet felt that they bore a responsibility to come to our aid. Qiao Limin, they said, was heartless. With a wave of her hand, she had banished father and son to a river barge. How would they survive with no women aboard? So they brought their feminine sensibilities and a warmhearted nature to barge number seven, often bringing us bowls of noodles or a pot of tea. Desheng's wife was the kindest of all. On laundry day she'd walk up to the bow of barge number five, carrying her wooden tub like a rice-sprout dancer, and call to my father, 'Come out here, Secretary Ku. Anything you need to wash? Just toss it in my tub.'

I'd stay in the cabin to watch his reaction. Even if he went out empty-handed, courtesy – which was important to him – demanded that he engage Desheng's wife in casual conversation. I scrutinized her carefully from inside the cabin, starting with her bare feet, with their ruddy backs and red toenails – obviously painted with balsam oil. All the boat women painted their toes in the hope that people would look at their feet. My father did not disappoint. He'd comment, 'Desheng's wife, I detect a look of revolutionary romanticism about you.'

She'd just giggle, missing his point altogether. 'I spend all my time on this barge,' she'd say, 'so stop that nonsense about revolutionary romanticism.' I knew this praise from him was filled with danger. I was pretty sure he had his eye on Desheng's wife, and on Sun Ximing's as well. My guess was, he had his eye on lots of women. With my face up against the porthole, I watched with my heart in my mouth, because the minute he got close to a woman, as soon as the two of them began talking, I'd start to worry and the word 'thump' would pop into my head. Based on my experience, I'd send a silent warning: *Careful, be careful, don't get any ideas, keep that thing down*. Nervously, I'd glance at his trousers, not daring to breathe. Joyfully, whether he was with Desheng's wife or Sun Ximing's, the crotch of Father's trousers remained as flat as a placid river. He avoided making a fool of himself, and I guessed that his years as an official had taught him that there were two ways of dealing with people – one to their face and another behind their back.

I couldn't do that. I couldn't control myself. Once, when he was off to one side chatting with Desheng's wife, I stuck my head through the porthole to get a good look at them both. Spotting me, Father picked up a bamboo pole and smacked me on the head. 'What are you looking at, you little sneak? If I tell you to study, you put your head down on your book and sleep. But now your eyes are as big as cowbells!'

I pulled my head back inside, stuck for an excuse. No excuse was possible. An unhealthy adolescence is sewn together by countless unhealthy details. I knew I annoyed people. I was empty-headed, yet weighed down with cares. Someone might assume that nothing bothered me, but I was a sneak. I really was. Father's so-called lifestyle caused no problems on the river, but mine certainly did. I was burdened with a gaunt exterior and dark moods. That was all Father had to see to know that I had begun masturbating. During the daytime he frequently launched surprise inspections of my hands, even sniffing my palms; at night, when I was in bed, to make sure my hands and crotch were apart, he'd wake me up if necessary to keep my hands on top of the covers.

It didn't seem fair that while I never bothered him about his lifestyle, he couldn't stop bothering me about mine. Now that he had lost his leadership position in Milltown, the task of reforming me became his number-one priority. Like a schoolteacher, he transformed our barge into a mobile classroom, starting by cutting out four pieces of red paper and writing a commandment on each of them: UNITY, ANXIETY, SOBRIETY, ENERGY. Then he stuck them up on the cabin walls.

I had no argument with two of his commandments. Anxious? Thanks to all those surprise inspections, I was certainly that. Sober? Day in and day out, nothing good ever happened, and I felt as if the whole world owed me something. But where unity and energy were concerned, all I can say is, I found the former boring, while the latter, though not without its appeal, required certain preconditions. Activities like playing ball or practising with slingshots were things you did on land. I was on the water – how energetic could I be?

So Father handed me a chess set. 'You spend all your time inside, anxious some of the time and energetic at other times, whatever's called for. But you haven't played chess in a long time, so take these outside and find someone to play with.'

'Who? Who knows how to play chess? Tell me that?' I pushed his hand away. 'Barge people are stupider than pigs. All they know how to do is thump!'

'What do you mean, thump? What's that?'

He didn't know what thump meant. 'Thump their pig brains,' I said, 'that's what. They couldn't learn how to play chess if their lives depended on it.'

'I don't want to hear talk like that about labouring folks,' Father said. 'There's nothing wrong with not knowing how to play chess. They know how to work, and that's enough. They may not know how to play, but I do, so let's have a game.'

'No,' I said. 'I'd rather play against a chess manual.'

He went inside to get the chess manual for me. But the sight of all those carriages, steeds, and cannons bored me, so I laid the manual down on the table, picked up our enamel spittoon, undid my trousers and aimed a stream of urine at a peony at the bottom.

'How many times have I told you to go outside and pee over the stern?' Father said. 'Why do you insist on using the spittoon? Boatmen pee over the side. Who hides in a cabin to do his business? You're not a spoiled bourgeois young mistress, are you?'

'Who says a boy can't pee in his cabin?' I argued. 'I don't want people to watch me peeing over the side.'

'Who'd want to watch you? You're not a little girl. Nobody's interested in watching you take a leak. This is more proof of your unhealthy attitude. There you go, looking cross-eyed at me again, and for no reason.' With that, he turned his criticism to my eyes. 'I keep telling you to stop that. No matter what you do, having the right attitude is the most important thing. I don't want you looking at people cross-eyed any more, especially when you're talking to them. Only social misfits do things like that.'

To be honest, I didn't know if I was in the habit of looking cross-eyed at people, and I didn't have a mirror to see if he was telling the truth. But I hated the way he used that excuse to pick on me, so I mumbled, 'So what if I'm looking cross-eyed? That dick of yours is cock-eyed, go and pick on that.'

It was a good thing he didn't hear that last comment. If he had, he'd have known exactly what lay behind it.

I was, as I've said, fifteen. Like a waterlogged branch, I was carried from swell to swell on the river. The wind and water had me under their control, as did Father on a daily basis, but I had no control over myself or my secret. One morning I was startled awake – smacked awake, more like. Still half asleep, I unconsciously covered my crotch with my hands. Sure enough, I saw a little mountain peak down there, thanks to an erotic dream about Li Tiemei from the revolutionary opera. But this time I wasn't going to be punished for having a hard-on, because my father was standing by my bed and he'd discovered my secret. He hit me – in the face – with Mother's notebook. In the process he knocked Li Tiemei and the red lantern off the notebook and on to the floor.

His hair was uncombed and there was sleep in his eyes. His face looked weird – pale white on one side and pig's-liver red on the other, painted anger. 'Where did you get this?' he roared. 'Get up. Get on your feet and tell me why you did this!'

Still not fully awake, I stood up and covered my face. 'I didn't write that,' I said, putting up the only defence that came to me. 'Mama did. I had nothing to do with it.'

'I know she wrote it! You stole it. What I want to know is why you didn't give it to me. Why did you hide it? This is damning evidence against me. What were you planning to do with it?'

Maybe I had a plan and maybe I didn't. But I didn't know why I had hidden it, and since I didn't know, I should have kept silent. But I was not capable of that. So I said something to prove my innocence. 'I hid it for fun,' I said. 'It was just for fun.'

'For fun?' he screamed. 'What kind of fun?' That really set him off. The questions began to pile up. 'You say it was for fun. This is evidence your mother gathered to punish me. How was that supposed to be fun?'

How was it supposed to be fun? What could I to say to that? Nothing. There were flames of anger in his eyes that I'd never seen before, and I knew I was in big trouble. So I scooped up my trousers and burst out of the cabin. He was right on my heels. 'Go on!' he shouted, 'get away from me. Get the hell out of my sight! Go ashore, go and find your mother.'

The fleet was moving downriver that morning. As I stood on the bow of our barge, there was no place I could run to. My eyes roamed over the other barges, now safe havens. But I didn't want to be there. As day was breaking, the barges began to stir, and people emerged to discover that Father had kicked me out of the cabin and up to the bow of barge number seven, where I was holding on to the cable housing for dear life. Desheng was the first to react. 'Secretary Ku,' he shouted, 'what's the matter with Dongliang? I don't know what's made you so angry, but you have to stop now. If you keep this up, he'll be in the water.'

Pretending he hadn't heard, Father pointed a coal shovel at me, like a weapon. 'I told you to leave, you shameless brat! I want you off this barge. Go and find your mother.'

I looked down at the water and, in all truth, I was scared. But I wasn't about to let him know that, so I said, 'I'll leave as soon as you tell the tugboat to stop and let me off.'

'Just who do you think you are?' he replied. 'Do you really think the tug will stop just because a little bastard like you wants it to? Dream on! You won't drown, so get in and swim ashore.'

'No,' I said, 'the water's too cold. I'll wait till there's a sandbar. Do you think this old rust bucket is all I've got? Well, I'm telling you, once I'm off it I'm not coming back. You can live on without me.'

But my threat did not work. 'All right,' he said as he glanced at the riverbank, the coal shovel still in his hand, 'there's the duck farm sandbar. You can get off now.' Then he slipped the shovel under my feet and picked me up. By then, Six-Fingers Wang's daughters had come out on to the deck of barge number six and were giggling stupidly over the scene in front of them. I was mortified. He could have flung me off the barge.

I wasn't a chunk of coal, but that's what he treated me like. With a full-throated roar, he bent at the waist, squatted down, and shovelled me on to the sandbar near the duck farm.

Words

THAT WAS the first time Father ran me off the barge. I went ashore at the duck farm, where there was no one around, just two rows of ducks waddling from side to side on a sandbar – a welcoming committee heralding my return to terra firma. I started walking towards Milltown, with the sensation that the ground beneath me was undulating like river swells, although the waters of the Golden Sparrow River were as still as a glistening roadway. At first glance, the boats' masts looked like houses. As I neared the transformer substation several ducks met me head-on, followed by the idiot Bianjin, who was carrying a duck whistle and prancing proudly down the road. When he saw me he called out excitedly, 'You're Ku Wenxuan's son, aren't you? Want to know something? Go and tell your father that the investigative team is coming soon, and they'll announce that I am Deng Shaoxiang's son, her real son!'

At least I knew how to deal with an idiot. 'Idiot,' I said, 'you're the typical toad that wants to feast on a swan. What makes you think you're worthy of being a martyr's son? I'll tell *you* something. The investigative team is coming soon, and they'll announce that your father is a pig and your mother a duck, which means you were thumped into existence by a pig and a duck!'

He took after me with his duck whistle. He knew what 'thumped' meant, and cursed me angrily. 'You've got a filthy mouth for someone so young. Thumped? Do you know how to thump? Well, I'll show you. I'll thump the shit out of you!'

We raced down the road, and I quickly left him in my dust. But even after I was well out of reach I kept running, something I hadn't done in a long time. I ran like the wind. If I hadn't been living on a barge, running would never have become one of life's little pleasures. I ran until I was standing in front of Milltown's red schoolhouse. No more wind – I was exhausted. I stood in the road, trying to catch my breath, and took a long look at the schoolhouse and playground. All of a sudden, I was struck by crippling sadness – I felt it in my belly and in my heart.

I'd spent only three months in the high-school section before leaving, and at the time I couldn't have been happier. But now, with the passage of time and the change in my circumstances, I discovered that I missed school after all. I skirted the wall and walked up to my former classroom, where through the window I could see a roomful of boys and girls, their heads rising and falling like a field of sorghum stalks. A girl in a colourful jacket was sitting in my old seat. Her lips were moving, as if she were mumbling something. And she was picking her nose. They were repeating as best they could the foreign words their teacher was saying, but pretty much all that came out was a jumble of sounds, none of which I recognized. By standing on my tiptoes I could see the blackboard. They were learning English: NEVER FORGET CLASS STRUGGLE! was written in Chinese, and below that a line of English letters. After listening to them several times, I memorized the sounds: Ne-fu fu-gai-te ke-la-si si-que-ge. Was that how you said 'Never forget class struggle' in English? Without being aware of it, I was already translating the sounds into the local dialect, and a happy discovery nearly made me laugh out loud: in Milltown dialect and the secret language of the Sunnyside Fleet, the sentence meant something like 'Go out and thump all you want.'

Thump. Go ahead and thump. That got me so excited I wrote the slogan on the wall with a piece of chalk I found on the ground. Below that I wanted to write my translation into the local dialect, but I couldn't remember how to write one of the critical characters. So I wrote 'Go out and thump' instead. One missing character affected the whole thing. Then, in sudden inspiration, I erased the word 'NEVER', so that the slogan now read, 'FORGET CLASS STRUGGLE.' Just then a boy's head poked out through the window. I didn't know him, but he knew me. His eyes grew wide. 'Ku Dongliang. What are you doing there?'

I threw down the chalk and ran off.

I was running again, but this time I was running away, and as I ran it dawned on me that since the slogan came from Chairman Mao, changing even one word made it a counter-revolutionary slogan. This was bad, very bad. I ran past the burlap-sack factory and headed towards Workers and Peasants Avenue. But when I reached the intersection, it occurred to me that my home was no longer on that street, so I turned and headed for the Government Affairs Building, which I knew like the back of my hand; my father had occupied an office on the fourth floor and my mother's broadcasting studio was on the second floor. Not until I was standing in front of the building did it dawn on me that she too no longer worked there. I vaguely recalled Father telling me that she'd been transferred, but wasn't sure if she'd been sent to the cooking-oil processing plant or the management office. So I went to inquire at the reception desk, where I saw a clutch of people standing around waiting for the day's newspaper. I spotted several familiar faces, including some people who had been friendly to me in the past. But now they looked at me with blank faces. 'What are you doing here, Dongliang?' one woman asked. 'Your mother no longer works at the broadcasting station.'

They told me she worked at the processing plant and described how to get there. It was far, nearly all the way to Maple Village, and it was getting dark by the time I got there, having walked the whole way. The milling machines had shut down for the day, but the smell of new rice and rapeseed oil hung in the air. Some workers, their shift over, gestured in my direction. I didn't know them. 'Is Qiao Limin here?' I asked.

Mysterious grins appeared on their faces. 'Yes, of course she is. She's waiting for you.'

So I walked inside, where I saw three people in front of a milling machine, their eyes glued to me. One was my mother, the second was Teacher Jiang of the Milltown Middle School, and the third was a uniformed policewoman named Hong. I knew I was in big trouble and that it would have been smart to turn tail and run. But I was too tired to take another step.

My mother walked up – rushed me like a lioness, more like – and slapped me three times – smack, smack, smack. Then she turned to her companions and explained why. I still recall every word: 'The first one was for him; the second for me, Qiao Limin, who's tried to be an upstanding citizen all my life, only to give birth to a son who doesn't know the meaning of the word "upstanding"; and the third was for his father, whose education of the boy has him writing counter-revolutionary slogans after only three months!'

The Pier

AFTER ONLY a few days in Mother's dormitory I was ready to head back.

I don't know if it was her doing or the fact that I'd earned a bad reputation, but the other women in the dormitory steered clear of me. Their attitude influenced the men in the neighbouring tool-repair factory, who scowled if I was around. My only fan was a mangy dog that gave me a fervent welcome. It was begging to be liked. Day in and day out it hung around me, sniffing at my trouser legs and at my crotch – mainly at my crotch. I didn't appreciate the mongrel's attention, and was particularly annoyed by its fascination with my crotch. Even if I had felt more unwelcome than I did, I would still have been unwilling to make friends with a mangy cur. Finally I kicked it, and was surprised that the animal retained a measure of self-respect – it was a good thing I could run fast, or I'd have been bitten for sure.

The dog chased me all the way to Mother's dorm, where it set up a howl that frightened the women inside. Knowing I was the one who'd set the dog off, Mother ran out with a wet mop and drove the barking dog off, then went back inside to tell the women that everything was fine. But someone must have said something unpleasant, because when I went up to her room, she wore a dark, gloomy expression. I plopped down on the bed and began scratching my feet – the wrong thing to do, given her mood. Still holding the wet mop, she turned on me, jabbing the mop at my legs one minute and my arms the next. 'You wicked boy,' she scolded. 'You're isolated from the masses, animals hate you, and a mangy dog chases you! Even a shit-eating dog has no forgiveness in its heart for you!'

I was clever enough to keep my mouth shut, and just let her rant on as I pinched my nose and held my breath. Go ahead, yell at me, I thought. Anything you say goes in one ear and out the other. It's nothing but *kongpi*! I sat down to dinner to a chorus of scolding, and for some reason the word 'exile' popped into my head. Maybe that's what I was, an exile. But one thing I knew for sure was that Mother's cramped dormitory was no home for me; it was just a way station. The words 'mother' and 'son' meant nothing here. I was a guest – and an unwelcome guest at that. Mother supplied me with three meals a day, but every grain of rice was saturated with her sadness, and every vegetable leaf was infused with her disappointment. If I lived with her like that, either she would die and I'd go crazy, or vice versa. And I wasn't alone in feeling that way – she did too.

Mother was on the shore, but I had no home there, and had to head back. Note that by heading back I meant back to the barge, back to the Sunnyside Fleet.

One morning a week later, the fleet was returning from its latest mission and I was on the pier, waiting anxiously for them. I could not say if I was waiting for my father's barge and his home to return to, or if I was waiting for the return of *my* barge and *my* home.

So I stood there, bag in hand. It was wet underfoot after a foggy morning, almost as if it had rained. With a bit of hesitation the sun broke through, lighting up part of the pier and leaving the rest to fend for itself. Fog hung over the mountain of coal, the piled-up commodities and the many cranes. There were spots where the sunlight was nearly blinding and others so dark it was hard to see. I waited in the darkness. Someone was moving near the embankment, but I couldn't tell who it was. The person was heading my way from the transport office, nearly running, and dragging a shimmering white light behind. It had to be a stevedore. When he was close enough to hear, I shouted, 'Do you know when the fleet is expected back?'

As soon as the words were out of my mouth I regretted them, for it was the general affairs typist, Zhao Chunmei. Ah, Zhao Chunmei. She was Zhao Chuntang's younger sister, and her name appeared in Mother's notebook at least ten times. She'd been one of my father's lovers. Some of the words Mother had written after Father had told the truth floated into my head. They did it! They did it on the typing desk. They did it on a window ledge. They did it again and again! The description was particularly detailed in one spot. They were in a room where cleaning gear was kept, doing it, when the caretaker opened the door. Never one to lose control in the face of danger, Father covered himself with a broom and a mop and held the door partially shut with his shoulder. 'You can take the day off,' he said. 'We are doing some voluntary work in here!'

I recalled seeing Zhao Chunmei in the office, and my abiding image of her was how fashionable and haughty she seemed. She wore milky-white high-heeled shoes virtually every day of the week, a sight rarely seen in Milltown, or – rarer still – purplish-red ones. Both made a loud click-clacking sound when she climbed the stairs. The other women in the building hated her, Mother included. They felt that her shoes served two purposes: to show off to the women and to tempt the men. I can still see that come-on look in her eyes, flirtatious as hell.

But no longer. She knew who I was, and the look she gave me was unusually cold, the sort of look a policeman might give a criminal, her eyes glued to my face. Then she looked down at my bag, as if it contained evidence of some crime. At first I was tempted to look away, but that would have been too easy. Then I recalled my father's line about voluntary work, and felt like laughing. Suddenly she shuddered, which surprised me. I swallowed my laughter and kept my eyes on her. She was giving me the most hateful look I'd ever seen. 'He's dead!' she cried. 'My husband, Little Tang, is dead, and Ku Wenxuan killed him!'

That was when I noticed a white flower in Zhao Chunmei's hair. Her shoes were also white – not high heels, but funeral shoes, with hempen ties on the backs and heels. Her puffy cheeks distorted what she was saying. I understood that her husband was dead and that she'd said Father had killed him. But I didn't know why. My father had been on board our barge for a long time now, so how could he have killed Little Tang? I'd always been fascinated with death, so I felt like asking when Little Tang had died and whether he'd committed suicide or was killed by someone else. But Zhao Chunmei was in no mood to say more. She just glowered at me. Finally, she gnashed her teeth and said, 'Ku Wenxuan, you'll repay this blood debt one of these days!'

Her menacing glare frightened me. A woman's face, no matter how pretty, becomes a terrible sight when it shows a thirst for vengeance. The look on Zhao Chunmei's face was so terrifying that I instinctively stepped backwards to get away from her, reversing all the way to the loading dock. When I passed beneath a crane, I glanced up at Master Operator Liu in his cage, who signalled for me to climb up, as if he had something important to tell me. He didn't. He just wasn't a man who could mind his own business. Pointing to Zhao Chunmei, he said, 'Don't upset her. She hasn't been herself for the past few days, ever since her husband killed himself with a pesticide.'

'I didn't do anything,' I said. 'She upset *me*. Besides, it wasn't me who gave her husband the pesticide, so what's it got to do with me?'

'It's got nothing to do with you,' he said, 'but everything to do with your dad. He's the one who made Little Tang wear a green hat – you know, a cuckold. People say that the green hat crushed him.'

'Crushed by a green hat – so what! She let my dad thump her, didn't she? Nobody forced her. Besides, he wore that green hat for years willingly enough, and no one forced him, either. My dad did it with lots of women. How come *he* decided to kill himself? Stop spreading malicious gossip!'

'You don't know a damned thing,' Liu said. 'Willing, you say? Whoever heard of a man willing to wear a green hat? It's not their choice to make. You're right, Little Tang wore that hat for years, but hardly anybody knew. As long as people pretended nothing was wrong, he could do the same. But when your dad fell from power, lots of people started talking. Then the backbiting started, with people saying that Little Tang had handed his wife over to someone in a position of leadership for his own advancement. Out on the street, people whispered things. Could he pretend he was deaf? When he went to the bathhouse, the old-timers laughed at him. When he couldn't take it any longer, he got into a fight, and wound up with a bloody nose. They offered him cotton to stop the bleeding, but he refused. Instead, he threw on his clothes and went straight to the pharmacy, supposedly to buy Mercurochrome. But what he actually bought was a bottle of DDT, which he drank on the way home. People who saw him thought it was alcohol. Now I ask you, the way Little Tang died, wouldn't you say he was crushed by that green hat?'

What Liu said made sense. It wasn't very scientific, but since I didn't know what it felt like to wear a green hat, my opinion didn't count for much. But still I said, 'There are internal and external causes for everything, but the internal causes are the main ones. Most of the responsibility for Little Tang's death lies with him. You can't blame my father for what happened.'

'Don't give me any of that internal and external bullshit,' Liu said. 'Do you think I don't know my Marxism-Leninism? I never said your dad was the internal cause. If he had been, then he'd have been the one drinking the DDT.'

I'd have liked to keep the debate with Liu going, but I glanced down at the pier, where Zhao Chunmei was still looking daggers at me. Thrown off stride, I reacted with foul language. 'What's that cunt up to? Her old man's dead, so that's the end of it. Don't tell me my dad has a blood debt. And even if he did, what's that got to do with me?'

'What kind of gutter talk is that?' Liu said with a frown. 'A comrade who's just lost her husband doesn't deserve to be spoken about like that. Nobody's asking your dad to repay a blood debt. She's backed herself into a corner, and all she can do is come down to the pier to get him to put on mourning attire and pay his respects at Little Tang's grave.'

This was probably the only useful thing Liu said to me up there, because now the sight of Zhao Chunmei down below was more terrifying than ever. I'd have liked to stay up there in the cage, but Liu sent me back down, saying that safety regulations did not permit idlers, though the real reason was his unhappiness over my gutter talk.

As soon as I was back on the ground, Zhao Chunmei walked towards me, taking a strip of white cloth out of her overcoat pocket and waving it in the air. 'Ku Wenxuan's whelp,' she shouted. 'Since your dad's not here, you can wear this.'

I was horrified. She must be crazy to think I'd wear something like that. 'Dream on!' I said, before taking off and running up the mountain of coal. She ran after me for a few steps, but when she realized she'd never catch me, she turned and headed back to the pier to wait for my dad, grumbling to herself and tucking the white sash back into her pocket.

I spent the rest of the morning on top of the coal, waiting for the fleet to return, while Zhao Chunmei waited down below. Two enemies, each with their own thoughts, awaited the return of the same person – my father.

Finally, the sun got up the nerve to climb into the sky, making the piers shimmer. Off in the distance I heard the toot of a tugboat and saw the hazy outlines of the fleet. From where I stood, the string of barges looked like an archipelago, eleven floating islands approaching in an orderly fashion. I assumed they were carrying cargo from the town of Wufu. Goods from most places could be shipped uncovered, making them easy to identify. But Wufu commodities were different. The barges approached the piers, their cargo covered by dark-green tarpaulins, and I knew there would be large sealed crates with no delivery addresses under the tarps. They'd be marked with coded Arabic numerals and foreign lettering. I knew without looking that this cargo was destined to wind up at the Southern Combat Readiness Base.

From where I stood I could see barge number seven, and there was my father. The other barges were shrouded in green tarps, like a secretive collective body; number seven stood out from the others by the way its decks were open to the sky. The forward hold was packed with squirming black and white animals. At first I couldn't tell what they were, but soon I realized it was a boatful of pigs – our barge was transporting thirty or forty pigs! My father, bent at the waist beside the hold, was trying to control a boatload of black, white and spotted pigs. After driving me off the barge, he'd gone off to pick up some honoured guests. Now, days later, he was bringing a boatload of live pigs to Milltown.

It was around eight in the morning. The loudspeakers were blaring callisthenics music that drowned out the tugboat's whistle. The barges were ready to dock, sending water splashing in all directions and galvanizing the crews into action – they dropped anchor and secured the boats with hawsers. I saw my father standing in the bow, not knowing what to do until Desheng ran up and helped him drop anchor. A husky man's voice came over the loudspeaker – 'Limbering exercise: one, two, three, four' – as the boats, matching the callisthenics beat – 'one, two, three, four' – nestled up to the piers.

Dockside cranes swung into action, but not before the stevedores had gathered on the embankment. A cacophony of noise rose all around. I saw Zhao Chunmei race under the arm of a crane, heading for the boats. If I knew anything, it was that no one would let her aboard while she was in mourning garments. Sailors are a superstitious lot, and would never allow that to happen. As I expected, Sun Ximing and his wife came down off barge number one to stop her. Then Six-Fingers Wang and his family blocked her way on to the gangplank. So, with a quick change of tactics, she turned and headed for barge number seven. When the people spotted what she was doing, they grew anxious. 'Go away!' they shouted. 'Don't come any closer!' Desheng and Old Qian even used poles to drive her away. I watched as she ran around avoiding them.

In the end, she gave up. 'Ku Wenxuan, get off that boat!' she shouted, before crumpling to the ground.

Anticipating something like this, I ran down the mountain of coal and saw a crowd of people heading from the General Affairs Building towards the piers. We all reached Zhao Chunmei at the same time. Obviously, they'd been sent by her brother Zhao Chuntang, and they started to carry Chunmei away. She was crying – not keening, but sobbing her heart out. 'I'm not crazy,' she insisted. 'Why are you doing this? I haven't done anything wrong, and you don't have to worry that I'll humiliate you.' She struggled in their arms; first a defiant leg kicked out, then an angry arm flailed in the air. She was desperately trying to get back to the pier, by crawling if necessary, twisting her head to keep the boats in sight. We passed each other, going in opposite directions, and when she spotted me, she turned to get a better look. Glaring at me hatefully through tear-filled eyes, she cried out shrilly, in a desolate tone, 'Go and tell your dad that I don't care about the blood debt. I just want him to visit Little Tang's grave in funeral garb!'

I stood on the pier, bag in hand, and watched them carry Zhao Chunmei away. One of the white sashes fell from around her waist and skimmed the ground behind her. As soon as she was out of sight, my fears were replaced by curiosity. *Do it, do it, thump, thump!* How had she and my father managed so well, and Little Tang wound up dead? I struggled to conjure up an image of the now dead Little Tang, and what came to mind was a fair-skinned, bespectacled man with a kindly face, one of the most cultured men in town. He was in the habit of saying sorry. Always 'Sorry. I'm sorry.' He'd played chess at our house, and each time he took one of Father's men, he'd say sorry. I pondered the relationship between my father and the two of them, and couldn't help feeling that it was all tied up with cheating and ugly schemes. Father did what he did with Zhao Chunmei in the caretaker's cupboard during the day and then invited Little Tang over for a game of chess at night. Was that supposed to be some sort of consolation for the cuckolded man, or was it shitting on his head? Then, for some strange reason, two words Mother used a lot in her notebook – 'active' and 'passive' – came to mind. Who had been the active participant in all this, and who had been the passive one? I couldn't work out how passive Zhao Chunmei had been, or how active Father had been. But my mind was clear on one thing: Little Tang had been totally passive. Seen from this angle, Master Liu had hit the nail on the head: Father had secretly placed a green hat on Little Tang's head, and that hat had crushed him to death.

I turned my anxious gaze to barge number seven and looked for Father, since it was time to unload. I didn't want him to see me. The gangplanks were down on the other boats by now, but not ours. Father was still inside, obviously hiding from Zhao Chunmei. But he was wasting his time. 'You can hide through the first of the month, but not through the fifteenth,' I heard myself grumble, quoting a popular saying. 'Come out of there if you've got the balls. All you know how to do is thump women – thump, thump. Well, come out and take a look where your thumping has led!'

The other boat people, who were watching me pace back and forth, interrupted their discussions about Zhao Chunmei and waved greetings. 'Hey, Dongliang, coming back, are you? That's good. Things always work out when a son obeys his father.' I was in no mood to pay any attention, so they directed their shouts at barge number seven: 'Come on out, Secretary Ku. There's nothing to worry about now, they've taken the woman away. Your son Dongliang's back!'

Still he wouldn't come out, and I refused to go aboard until he did. So I stood there watching a bunch of pigs squeal and squirm in our forward hold, giving off a stench I could smell from here. I wondered why our barge had been chosen to transport the pigs. Was it a sign of trust or just the opposite? Was it intended to show consideration for my father or to make things hard on him? I held my nose and surveyed the goods on the other barges, now that the oilcloth tarps had been removed and the goods were laid out in the open. There was machinery for the Southern Combat Readiness Base in wooden crates with strict warnings not to open them. There were also steel oil drums. Those I found interesting, since they had foreign words printed on them – not English, apparently, some language I'd never seen before. I'm kind of weird in a way – when I encounter words in languages I don't know, I read them to myself. Ne-fo fo-gai-te ke-la-si si-que-ge: Never forget class struggle – a chain reaction. I read and I read, and my thoughts went in a new direction, until I began thinking things I shouldn't.

Barge number seven was the last to unload, which made sense, since livestock is always hard to control. The stevedores, under the supervision of a man from the Pork Association, came aboard with bamboo poles and ropes, and were greeted by terrified squeals. When the first animal was carried off upside-down, its four legs tied to a pole, the others created a major disturbance, causing the barge to rock precariously as if tossed about by high waves. And still my father refused to emerge. Something must be wrong in there. I picked up a piece of coal, aimed at the cabin door, and threw it. 'What are you doing in there, Dad?'

The porthole opened and Father's hand made a brief appearance before vanishing again. Why was he hiding in there? I coughed. Something stirred, but he still wouldn't come out. Busy as he was, Desheng glanced my way and tapped the deck of barge number eight with his foot as a signal for me to come aboard. 'Hurry up,' he said. 'Don't stand there like an idiot. Are you waiting for your dad to send a written invitation?'

I shook my head. 'I can come aboard or not, it makes no difference to me. I will if he wants me to, and I'll stay here if he doesn't.'

Desheng's wife giggled and poked her husband. 'He wants his dad to ask him to come aboard,' she said as she picked up a pole, ran to the bow of her boat and banged on our cabin. 'Come out of there, Chairman Ku,' she shouted. 'Zhao Chunmei is gone, but your son's here. He wants to know if you want him back on the barge.'

Still no sign of him. But the stirrings within grew in intensity. Something hit the deck with a bang, followed by the unmistakable sound of one of Father's throaty moans. Then his head emerged slowly through the porthole. His face was the colour of clay, but his hand, which followed his head out, was covered with blood. He looked at me with a dull expression and waved his bloody hand. 'Come here!' he said. 'Help me! Hurry!'

At first I thought he'd cut his finger, and as I ran across Desheng's barge I shouted for him to get his first-aid kit. But I stopped dead when I got inside. He hadn't cut his finger. I thought my eyes were deceiving me. I could not believe what he'd done.

You won't believe it either. The stench of blood permeated the air, and blood ran between the cracks of the floorboards. A pair of scissors lay on Father's favourite sofa. His trousers were down around his knees and there was so much blood in his crotch that I could barely see his penis. At first it looked whole, but then I saw that the front half was hanging by a thread. Rocking unsteadily, he leaned slowly towards me. 'Help me!' he said. 'Use those scissors. It's my enemy, you must help me get rid of it.'

I was scared witless. Desheng's wife shrieked, but was quickly shouted down by her husband. 'What are you standing around here for? Go on, get out!' With studied calmness he crouched down and examined my father's bloody organ. 'It's still connect-ed!' he exclaimed happily. 'That's a good sign. Let's rush him to the hospital and get it sewn back on.'

I wrapped a blanket around Father's waist and Desheng carried him ashore on his back, watched by all the barge people and stevedores. 'What happened?' they asked as I ran past. 'Who stabbed him? All that blood!'

Desheng's wife was running alongside us, helping by clearing the curious out of our way. 'Haven't you ever seen blood before? This isn't a movie, you damned rubberneckers, so get out of our way.'

'Did Dongliang stab his old man?' someone asked.

'What do you use for a brain?' she said. 'Whoever heard of a son stabbing his father? A demon got to him, and it's all Zhao Chunmei's fault. She brought that demon down on him.'

Desheng ran on to the pier with my father on his back. Patches of bright sunlight dotted the path, and a strange feeling came over me. Father and I seemed to be heeding Zhao Chunmei's call, running down a path she'd laid out in white funeral garb. Though I felt the sticky blood leaking on to me, I was oblivious to his weight as I helped support him – from the waist down he was as light as a feather. All the curses that had been flung his way had been fulfilled. Men's curses, women's curses, curses by family members and mortal enemies – all fulfilled. Father's slightly crooked but extraordinarily vigorous member, a one-time bully, an enemy of the people, of women and of men, and, most significantly, of himself, had at last been subdued by Father himself.

He was unconscious by the time we reached the Milltown Hospital, but he'd managed two sentences to Desheng before he lost consciousness. 'I'm not afraid of Zhao Chunmei, Desheng,' he said. 'Brief pain is better than prolonged suffering, so now I can make amends.' Then he added, 'I guarantee you that I'll never again be unworthy of the spirit of the martyr Deng Shaoxiang.'

The Arrival of the Security Group

Later on I became a deckhand.

On my trips back to town, there were kids who didn't know my name, but who followed me and heard adults call out my nickname, Kongpi. If any of them didn't know who Kongpi was, they said: the fleet's *kongpi*. And if that still didn't do it, they added a footnote: the son of Half-Dick. It was no secret. Everyone in Milltown knew I had a strange and laughable father. He only had half a dick.

I was in good health for the first year or so. But then one day I discovered that I was walking strangely. Following my father's scandalous act with the scissors, every time I went ashore I was careful to avoid traces of red on the ground, afraid they might be drops of his shameful blood, and I averted my eyes from white bits of rubbish, worried they could be strips of Zhao Chunmei's mourning garb. One afternoon, as I was walking along with the sun beating down on me, I found myself staring at my shadow as it moved across the cobblestones. It looked a little like a duck, and at first I thought the distortion was caused by the angle of the sun, so I adjusted my walking style and cocked my head to see what my shadow looked like now. I watched as the outline twisted awkwardly, uglier than ever, now a goose, and suddenly I was aware that I really was walking strangely, my feet splayed outward, just like Desheng and Chunsheng. But I was nothing like those two, who went ashore barefoot. I always wore shoes. Having grown up on the water, they had developed a peculiar walking style that was well adapted to the boat's motion. I'd walked on land for fifteen years, so why were my feet splayed like theirs? I took off my shoes, removed the insoles, shook out the sand and pebbles, and examined them inside and out. Nothing there. So I sat by the side of the road and took a good look at my feet. They were dirty, but that's all. Strange. Why would two good feet suddenly forget how to walk the way they'd done for more than a decade? Why had they started acting as if they belonged to a duck or a goose?

Walking with splayed feet is ugly. For a woman, it's humiliating. What kind of woman walks with her legs and feet spread out like that? Is it supposed to be some sort of come-on? And if a man walks that way, he can't blame anyone for thinking it's because an abnormally heavy penis and testicles get in the way.

So I sat by the side of the road and analysed the differences between my feet and those of Desheng and Chunsheng. I concluded that I was an acute splayed-feet walker who'd been influenced not by other seamen, but by my own father. Ever since his damaged penis had been restored to a degree of functionality, thanks to reconstructive surgery, I'd been burdened with the feeling that the nearly severed half was now attached to my own body, that my underwear was too tight and that my crotch was getting heavier by the day. I also felt as if my brain was affected, that splay-footed manner of walking was determined not by the feet but by the brain. Even an idiot knows the difference between a river and dry land, but my brain had merged the two and sent messages of caution to my feet: *Careful, careful, use as much strength as you need to walk steadily and guard against the ground moving, against the motion of waves and undercurrents and eddies.* Once I obeyed those messages, stepping cautiously on the cobblestones and vaguely noting the shadow my head cast, a mysterious image lit up in my brain, and from then on, every road on the riverbank was either my port or starboard deck, and I trod it carefully. From then on, Milltown was a camouflaged body of water, which I had to navigate slowly.

Eventually I became a true splay-footed walker. My father did not influence my general health, but I became infected with a germ called 'halves'. As I looked at the world of the river around me, I arrived at the bizarre conclusion that only half of my world remained. Birds on the shore danced and sang as the water rushed along, but there were no dancing or singing birds around me, just rushing water, and I found that water disgusting. I rode up and down the river behind a fast-moving tug that towed our barge in a mad dash. The wind, the speed and that mysterious germ came together to launch an assault on my eyes and ears. No matter how stirringly the loudspeaker on the shore blared its messages, I only ever heard the first half, the remainder blown away by the wind. When I stood at the bow trying to take in the sights on both banks, if my eyes focused on the wheat fields to the left, I forgot about the market towns on the right and could not tell the difference between the places we'd just passed. The scenery changed with each successive day, but my hasty glances created a half-baked understanding of the triumphant socialist construction on the banks of the river. When we passed a duck farm, I saw workers laying a foundation and digging a ditch on the sandbar; I didn't know it was the Victory Hydroelectric Station and assumed it was just an extension of the duck farm. I grumbled at the sight, wondering why the ducks were being treated so well when I didn't even have a home on shore. When we sailed past Phoenix, I saw people building a cement pylon to the east, and all I could think was, 'They've just built a hydroelectric station near the duck farm, and now here's Phoenix building another.' Was it a competition? I was oblivious to the fact that an identical pylon was going up on the other bank, and that Phoenix was in fact getting not a hydroelectric station but a new bridge.

The people on shore were all talking about Milltown, my hometown, and how it was undergoing a spectacular transformation and would become a key sector, the most important one in the Golden Sparrow River region. Word had it that a secret combat-readiness facility was to be constructed in Milltown, but since it was all hush-hush, no one knew for sure what sort of facility it would be, which was why everyone – on shore and on the river – was talking about it. Some thought it might be an air-raid shelter, others that it would be a missile-launching site, while some predicted that it would be a petroleum pipeline that served the Southern Combat-Readiness Base. After hearing more and more comments, I finally worked out what they meant by a 'key sector', but had no way of telling whose prediction was more reliable. If Father had still been in office, I'd have been privy to first-hand information. Too bad. As they say, a river flows east for thirty years, then west for the next thirty. Father and I were now the last to hear any news relating to the Golden Sparrow River region.

I never liked asking people for news, and in my personal investigation into signs relating to the military construction, I found none. The General Affairs Building was still the highest authority in Milltown. The skies were bluer than before, the air cleaner, and production on the wharf was being reorganized. The mountain of coal had been pared down; commodity storage, always haphazard, was being systematized; and relatively clean public toilets had appeared, with the smell of disinfectant lying heavy in the air. Other than that, there didn't seem to be any earth-shaking changes or improvements in a town that was the focus of public opinion.

One day I was walking down by the piers when I passed a

chemical warehouse and was surprised to see that it had been newly painted, white with red windows. A sign on the door read: 'Pier Security Group'. I stuck my head through the door and spotted familiar faces: Scabby Five, Baldy Chen and Wang Xiaogai, each sporting a red armband with the words 'You Zhi' printed on them. I quickly figured out that it stood for Milltown *Zhi-an*, or Security Group. After the words came some Arabic numbers in parentheses, evidently their personal numbers. I knew what the armbands meant, but I was in a teasing mood. 'Does that say "Lard-town"? Are you the lard group? If so, you belong in a wok.'

Their expressions hardened when they heard my voice. 'What do you know?' Xiaogai said with a disgruntled look. 'Can't you read? We're the Milltown Security Group.'

'Security group?' I said. 'Under whose authority?'

'The General Affairs Building, pig brain. What do you think?'

But I couldn't let it go. 'Three guys keeping watch over a run-down chemical warehouse, and you call it a security group!'

'At the moment it's just the three of us,' he said, 'but there'll be more of us pretty soon. We might not have a big office, but we've got big-time authority, and we're going to let you see just how big that is.'

With obvious impatience, Scabby Five, my long-time foe, glared at me and cut his colleague off. 'What are you doing, explaining things to someone like him?' he said, making a handcuffing gesture. 'He wrote a counter-revolutionary slogan, and that makes him a target for us! If he doesn't watch his mouth, I'll come down hard on him.'

Nothing but farts came out of Scabby's mouth – empty, stinky talk – and I wasn't about to argue with him. I focused my attention on the sign on the door. '*Zhi-an*,' I said. 'Do you know what that means?'

Blinking furiously, Xiaogai glanced at his two colleagues,

looking for help. But, less well educated even than him, they too were stuck for a response. Having suffered an embarrassing loss of face, he growled, 'You and your goddamn never-ending questions, Kongpi. It means just what it says – *zhi-an*. Don't try any of your tricks on me.'

I wasn't trying to trick him. I knew that the word *an* meant 'safety', but I didn't know if *zhi* meant to take charge of people or to make them suffer, so I said, 'Since you have no authority over the goods or the longshoremen, who are your supposed *zhi*?

Scabby Five was the first to react. 'Good question!' he said hatefully. 'And the answer is you!'

'Not only you,' Baldy said, 'though you're the one we need to watch the closest. We're charged with watching the whole fleet.'

Wang Xiaogai, who had a '2' on his armband, was the group's second-in-command, I later learned, so no wonder he talked like a bureaucrat. 'And not only you people on the barges,' he said as he adjusted his armband. 'These are critical times, and things get busy at the police station, so we're in charge of wharf security – all of it.'

I looked up into the blue sky, with its patches of puffy white clouds, then stood on my tiptoes to gaze at the top of the General Affairs Building – no signs of those so-called critical times, as far as I could see. 'What's all this nonsense about critical times?' I said. 'What's so critical about them? I for one can't see it.'

'If we let a *kongpi* like you see things,' Wang Xiaogai said with a sneer, 'they wouldn't be critical, would they?'

Usually, when we pulled up to a pier, I avoided the other boat people, either by going ashore before or after them. On this occasion I'd been the first person ashore, so after leaving the Security Group office, I headed for Milltown. But I hadn't got far before Wang Xiaogai and the others caught up with me. 'Stop right there,' they called out. 'You have to wait till everyone's ashore, so you can all go into town together.'

'Says who?' I said. 'We're boat people, not soldiers. Why do we have to travel as a unit?'

'Instructions from our superiors,' Xiaogai said. 'A new regulation. Critical times always require new regulations. Otherwise they wouldn't be critical. The regulation takes effect today. Members of the Sunshine Fleet are not permitted to go wherever they damn well please in town.'

I looked over at the distant streets, where people seemed to be going wherever *they* damn well pleased. 'Why do boat people have to travel together,' I said, 'but people in town can go where they damn well please?'

Wang Xiaogai's gaze followed mine. 'Don't worry,' he said with a derisive snort. 'We treat everybody the same, boat people and townspeople. We were just told to deal with signs of trouble – wherever the wind's blowing and the grass is swaying, on land and on water.'

I hated people playing with words, so I said, 'Does that mean you can always tell how the wind's blowing and the grass is swaying? Fine, go and watch the wind and grass if you want, but forget about keeping me under observation. I'm going into town, it's my right.'

Xiaogai pushed me back. 'I'm not going to argue with you,' he warned. 'Your rights don't count during critical times, and I'm telling you not to go anywhere by yourself.'

Baldy walked up and gave me a shove. 'Your boat people are on their way. Wait for them. It won't kill you.'

But Scabby Five was the worst. Taking a red and white truncheon from his waistband, he pointed it at me. 'That loud-mouth of yours isn't going to do you a bit of good,' he said. 'Who said you had any rights? That's one thing people like you don't have.'

I stared at the truncheon in his hand. 'What do you plan to do with that,' I said with a sneer. 'Enter a relay race?'

'Go ahead, laugh,' he said. 'But this is a security group, and if you disturb the peace in Milltown, I'll use it on your head.'

'Come on, then,' I said as I pressed up close to him. 'I just disturbed the peace. Now use that on my head.'

Xiaogai and Baldy Chen rushed up to pull us apart, just as there was a sudden flurry of activity at the pier. The barge crews were coming ashore. Seeing what was happening, the security group sprang into action. Xiaogai pulled a whistle out of his pocket and blew it. Scabby Five and Baldy cast sombre looks at Xiaogai, who draped the whistle around his neck and said, 'Take your positions and get ready for action!'

Action? What was he expecting? To my amazement, I saw that they planned to follow the crews as they disembarked, like a trio of annoying dogs tagging along behind the rag-tag, boisterous gang of boat people. Xiaogai called out numbers that Baldy Chen recorded in his notebook.

At first the boat people didn't realize they were being followed. It was common knowledge that the Sunnyside Fleet – men and women, old and young – came to town in a slovenly group, leaving splayed footprints in the road and bringing all manner of containers with them, including woven baskets and plastic pails. Their joyful expressions belied the sounds of bickering that marked their passage – they were a happy group. So I fell in behind them, adding a morose tail. They turned around. 'I see Dongliang's coming with us today,' one of them commented with a puzzled look. 'He's in a good mood.'

'I thought you went ashore early,' Desheng said. 'What are you hanging around here for?'

I jerked my thumb over my shoulder. They turned and saw what was behind them. 'Hey, it's Scabby Five and Baldy Chen, and there's Xiaogai. What are they doing? They seem burdened by a guilty conscience, whether they've done anything wrong or not.'

Someone, it must have been Six-Fingers Wang, uttered a panicky scream. 'They're going to arrest us!' The women grabbed their kids and scattered, while the men's reactions varied: some bent at the waist, clenched their fists and stood their ground; others wrapped their arms around roadside trees. Chunsheng, timid as always, crouched down and covered his head.

The chaos among the boat people was echoed by chaos among the security group. A flustered Xiaogai blew his whistle madly – with no results – then cupped his hands, gesturing for everyone to come back. 'Don't scatter,' he shouted. 'Stay as a group. Don't pay any attention to Six-Fingers's crazy talk. We're not going to arrest anybody! We're here to supervise people, not arrest them.'

Looks were exchanged, followed by a tentative return to the middle of the street by a few of the boat people, who watched Xiaogai and his friends nervously. 'Close up ranks!' Xiaogai shouted, repeating his gesture. 'Close up ranks, I say! Stay together and keep going. We're not going to arrest anybody.'

'So what?' Sun Ximing said. 'Do you expect thanks for not arresting us? What are you up to? Who said you could supervise us?'

Xiaogai took a sheet of paper out of his pocket. 'Who, you ask? Read this and you'll know who. It's from the General Affairs Building.'

Sun tried to take the paper from Xiaogai, then, barely literate, he called me over. 'Come here, Dongliang, and tell us what this says.'

I walked up and read what was on the pink sheet. It was, as Xiaogai had said, a new regulation: 'Effective immediately, members of the Sunnyside Fleet must travel as a group on shore under the supervision of the security group.' I read it again, this time out loud for the benefit of the people who had gathered around me. The bickering started at once. 'Are we counter-revolutionaries or a labour-reform group?' Desheng shouted to Xiaogai. 'Why should we let you supervise us?'

'You heard what this said.' Xiaogai shook the sheet of paper. 'These are critical times. When that's no longer the case and you can go back to your normal jobs, we'll stop supervising you.'

Baldy Chen glared at Desheng. 'You've got quite a temper, Li Desheng, haven't you? What's so bad about being supervised? Will it give you haemorrhoids? Or cancer?'

Before Desheng could reply, his wife counterattacked: 'No haemorrhoids and no cancer. Just baldness so severe that not a single blade of grass will grow on his head.'

The crowd roared, all except Sun Ximing, who looked glum. 'Go ahead, supervise,' he said, 'but not like this. Anybody who sees us will think you're letting prisoners out for fresh air and exercise.'

'Nobody cares about appearances during critical times,' Xiaogai replied. 'By staying in line you make our job easier.'

Sun didn't know whether to laugh or cry. 'What the hell does that mean? First you say you're going to supervise us, then you want us to do your job for you. When a cat chases a mouse, the mouse doesn't just roll over!'

Apparently, Xiaogai was serious about getting us to cooperate, since he offered Sun a Front Gate cigarette. Sun hesitated before accepting the cigarette, which eased the tension on both sides. The boat people continued to grumble and maintain their dignity as best they could as they silently closed ranks, no one making a reckless move. With the false alarm over, the odd procession moved slowly towards town, its tails still attached. But a subtle change came over the group, as the people rearranged themselves in families. Related men, women and children walked together in tight little units, apprehensive looks on the faces of the adults, who held tightly on to their puzzled children.

Walking a few paces behind Desheng and his wife, I was the

sole straggler. My father had refused to come ashore, so I held my tote bag as if it were his hand. Made of grey leatherette, it was crammed full of oil and soy-sauce bottles and a sack for rice. But the most important contents were in the lining pocket: two letters. Father's letters. One was a petition appealing against the decision of the Martyrs' Orphan Appraisal Team, in which he argued that the team had been swayed by rumours, leading to an unjust decision. The second letter was also an appeal, not on his behalf but on behalf of the spirit of the martyr, criticizing Zhao Chuntang for his passive attitude towards the preservation and maintenance of Deng Shaoxiang's memorial stone. I recall that one was addressed to Comrade Wang Chuan at the District Party History Office, the other to the appropriate person at the Civil Administration Section. My steps that day were heavier and more cautious than those of the other boat people, owing to a feeling that Father was hiding in my bag, vacillating between indignation and terror; I heard his voice emerge from inside: 'Careful,' he was saying nervously. 'Be very careful.'

The boat people passed silently in front of the General Affairs Building, with its sunlit, flower-filled square. A gigantic banner hung horizontally across the top of the building: 'MOBILIZE TO WELCOME THE EAST WIND PROJECT NO. 8!' I tapped Desheng on the shoulder to point it out. 'Ah, so that's what the so-called critical times are all about.' He stopped and gazed at the banner; the others in the group did too. They may have been poorly educated, but they weren't stupid, and they immediately made a connection between their situation and the East Wind Project No. 8, though there was doubt on their faces. Given their level of political consciousness, they did not understand what their journey through town had to do with the project.

Seeing that the procession had stopped and that everyone was looking up at the banner put the security men on their guard. They drew their truncheons and nudged the gawkers. 'What are you stopping for? Loitering in front of government facilities is prohibited.'

Sun Ximing grabbed Scabby Five's truncheon and said, 'Hold on a minute. I can read what that banner says.' He raised his eyes and read it aloud, stumbling over some of the words. When he had finished, he grew animated. 'We enthusiastically support East Wind Project No. 8,' he shouted to Scabby Five, 'and we'll do nothing to interfere with it. So there's no need to keep following us.'

With a sarcastic laugh, Scabby Five said, 'Interfere with East Wind Project No. 8? You wouldn't dare.'

'Since you know that,' Sun said, 'why waste energy following us? Don't you have anything better to do?'

Xiaogai walked up and said softly, 'Pipe down, old Sun. Don't cause a scene. The General Affairs Building has been designated a strategic area. It's where our military experts work these days. The consequences of making any impact on their work would be more than you could deal with.'

'Just where have these military experts come from?' Sun asked with increasing doubt. 'And why would they be here at the General Affairs Building instead of on the front lines?'

Xiaogai snorted. 'Maybe I know and maybe I don't, but I wouldn't tell you even if I did. It's top secret.'

Brandishing his truncheon, Scabby Five tried to get the crowd moving. 'Break it up,' he said. 'We'll get rough if you cause a scene here.'

After weighing up the situation, Sun decided not to say anything more and led the group away from the building, grumbling as he headed to the flowerbeds, followed by the rest of the group, who were grumbling too. When they reached the public toilet on People's Avenue, they stopped and automatically reached for their belts. With a glance at Sun Ximing, they broke the silence. 'Toilet break.'

'OK, no harm in that,' Sun said. 'Who has to go? They can control heaven and earth, but not our bowels or bladders.'

Xiaogai stopped Scabby from interfering. 'Are you all going?' As the official in charge, he mulled over the prospect for a moment before dismissing them with a wave of his hand. 'Go ahead, do your business. But don't forget that these are critical times and that sanitation teams are everywhere. Don't bring Milltown into disrepute by making a mess in there.'

Sun Ximing led the crowd into the toilet. These people habitually stopped at the public toilet every time they walked down People's Avenue. It was, after all, the finest toilet in town, with four taps, at least two of which provided running water all year round. Automatic flushes every five minutes cleared the foul air. Local residents could use the facility daily, but for the boat people it was a rare treat, and they'd have been fools to pass up the opportunity, whether there was a need or not. A bit of symbolic relief was better than nothing. Even washing their hands with running water was enjoyable and free.

Xiaogai waited at the door while we went inside, followed by Scabby Five and Baldy Chen, who stood just inside the doorway, one on each side, like guardian deities. 'Watch where you're peeing, Six-Fingers,' Scabby called out, disgusted by the man's indelicate way of relieving himself. 'Are you a man or a donkey? You're pissing all over the place. You're in town now, not on the boat, so step up to the urinal.'

'What's your interest here?' Six-Fingers replied. 'Security or pissing? Or is pissing part of security?'

'That's enough smart talk from you,' Baldy Chen said. 'You can read, can't you? See that sign on the wall? "ONE SMALL STEP CLOSER TO THE URINAL IS A GIANT LEAP FOR CIVILIZATION." It wouldn't kill you to step up closer to the urinal, would it?'

Six-Fingers didn't move, so Scabby walked up, stuck his security truncheon into the man's back and nudged him forward. 'I'm warning you, Six-Fingers, don't give me any lip. It's not just your pissing attitude I'm concerned about. You have political problems too. Who told you to shout something about arrests back there? I tell you, starting rumours is a political offence!'

The stream from Six-Fingers stopped abruptly, and I had to laugh. Scabby turned his anger on me. 'Go ahead, Kongpi, laugh all you want, but you're a worse case than him. Do you really think we don't know what you did?' He jumped over to the squat-toilet area and pointed to the scribbling on the wall with his truncheon. 'Did you write this scurrilous attack on the leadership?'

I moved up to get a closer look. The words 'ZHAO CHUNTANG IS AN ALIEN CLASS ELEMENT' had been written in crayon. 'Who says I wrote this? I don't even know what an alien class element is. You're the genius, you tell me.'

He obviously didn't know either. 'I know it's nothing good, or it wouldn't have the word "element" in it,' he said. 'You've written counter-revolutionary slogans before, so who are we supposed to suspect if not you?'

Everyone has his Achilles heel, and that was mine. I was too young to have a black mark on my record, that I knew, but I couldn't work out what doing a number two in a public toilet had to do with politics. That added to my discomfort at having our toilet activities so closely monitored. Not knowing how to deal with Scabby, I squatted there to kill time. Keeping those guys holed up in a public toilet was the only tactic available to me in this struggle.

Desheng also squatted a few places away, mumbling to himself. Then he decided to taunt Baldy. 'Why aren't you monitoring what's going on in the women's toilet? With your authority, what's to stop you?'

'Enough of that,' Baldy said. 'Our security group is understaffed at the moment, but there's a female comrade coming.'

Scabby Five appeared at my side and glared at me. 'Kongpi,'

he said, 'is that the best you can come up with, a bit of passive resistance? You're supposed to pull down your pants before you shit. But go ahead, squat there. I'll keep you company.'

As I looked up at the crayoned graffiti on the wall – 'ZHAO CHUNTANG IS AN ALIEN CLASS ELEMENT' – I wrestled with the word 'alien'. 'I'll squat here as long as I want,' I said, 'and I'll get up when I feel like it. You're welcome to stay with me if you can stand the smell.'

'Kongpi, your thoughts stink worse than your shit. You and your anti-socialist hatred.'

'Bullshit,' I said. 'I love socialism, it's you I hate. Your kid brother and sister stole half a buttered bun from me. That's a political issue – why don't you deal with them?'

'You hate the proletariat,' he replied, 'which means you hate me because I'm part of it. Interesting how you can't let go of something as small as half a buttered bun.'

All the time I was arguing with Scabby Five, my eyes were fixed on Zhao Chuntang's name on the wall. Every debt has a debtor, every injustice a perpetrator. With hatred building up inside me, I spat on it. Hatred, Scabby Five had said, and he was half right. I didn't really hate him, or Wang Xiaogai. I no longer hated my childhood enemies, and as I squatted in that public toilet, I began to understand the blind hatred that had risen within me: my number-one enemy was my father's number-one enemy; my father's enemy was my enemy. And that was Zhao Chuntang. I hated him from the bottom of my heart.

And so, finally, I got to my feet, looked at Scabby Five, and said, from memory, one slow word at a time, '"Zhao – Chun – tang – is – an – alien – class – element." How's my pronunciation?'

'I wouldn't be too cocky, if I were you,' he said. 'Sooner or later we'll get to the bottom of that slogan, and whoever wrote it will be punished.'

When I emerged from the public toilet I spotted the green

window of the Milltown Post Office. A postbox stood at the entrance, tall and dignified, mouth open, seemingly waiting there for me. The boat people had no need for the post office, which they had passed on their way to the open-air market. But that postbox and I had an appointment. When I reached it, I considered stuffing in Father's letters while I was being watched by the security group. I delved into the bag, and when my hand touched Father's letters I looked behind me, to see Scabby Five staring at me, his eyes shining. 'Be careful,' Father had said. 'Be very careful.' It was strange, but I felt the letters slip through my fingers, letters that had retained the warmth of Father's hands. But this time they were fearfully cold, as if they wanted to escape. I tucked them back into the lining, and that made me feel that I was keeping Father safe with me.

I followed the boat people to the marketplace. This was the women's domain, and where I too could take care of some small matters. By now the security group had herded the men into the open-air market. 'Do what you've come to do, but do it together,' they said. 'Form lines and don't squabble.'

'Why are you driving all us old men into the market?' Sun Ximing complained. 'What are we supposed to do here?'

'Why can't you boat people shed your feudal ideas?' Baldy Chen replied. 'Will your dicks fall off just because you're in a market?' He pointed to me. 'What about Ku Dongliang? He's here to buy provisions, isn't he? Has his dick fallen off?' He laughed at his own little joke – there was more he wanted to say, and by the way he was looking at me out of the corner of his eye, I could guess what it was, and knew it would be about my father. The one thing I could not tolerate was people saying bad things about my father's injured penis. So I grabbed a knife from the pork counter, walked up to Baldy and said in a low voice that only he could hear, 'Say anything about me you want, I don't care. It's like farting in the wind. But mention my father and this knife will go in white and come out red.'

Unnerved by what I said, he looked down and pointed his truncheon at the knife. 'I said a dick, not half a dick. But go ahead, stab me. We're a martyr's family, too, but a real one, not phoney like yours.'

Baldy Chen had a mouth fouler than mine, and even an idiot would have known what he meant by that. I raised the knife, but didn't have the guts to use it. All I could do was give him a dirty look as I began to shake with anger. Fortunately, Sun Ximing and one of the meat vendors rushed up and snatched the knife out of my hand.

That, in a nutshell, was my problem: I was quick to anger, but incapable of translating that into violent action. I invariably reacted to critical moments with fear. I grumbled as I bought my provisions – grains, vegetables and lamp oil. A potato seller gave me a wary look and backed away, not knowing why I was acting the way I was. 'Buy them or not, it's up to you,' she said. 'But you don't have to grumble like that.'

'I'm grumbling at somebody else,' I said, 'not you.'

'If you're angry at somebody else,' she said, relieved, 'don't take it out on me. Those potatoes may have turned dark, but they're still good.'

'You can't fool me,' I said impatiently. 'How can black potatoes be any good? Don't you have fresh ones?'

'All gone,' she said. 'There's nothing wrong with potatoes as long as they haven't started to sprout. Besides, you boat people aren't the picky type.'

That was the wrong thing to say. 'Thump your mama,' I cursed. 'We boat people are human too. What makes you think you can force us to eat rotten potatoes? You shore people are as rotten as your potatoes. I *was* grumbling at somebody else, but now I'm grumbling at you.'

In truth, she had every reason to discriminate against us boat people, since we didn't enjoy the luxury of fresh meat and vegetables. For the most part, we bought large quantities of potatoes, cabbage, salted pig's head – things like that, since they keep well. With this in mind, the security group staked out certain vendors, getting the men to line up to buy rice, and the women fresh produce. 'Go on, buy it and move on,' they urged. 'Don't be picky. Get what you came for and then form up again.' But the crowd had no sooner entered the market than they dispersed like ducks on the river, way beyond anyone's control. Short-handed to begin with, the security group was helpless to gather them together again.

The women were complaining about the supervision as they quickly made their purchases, looking daggers at the vendors and at what they were selling – rotten goods to go with rotten attitudes. The first argument broke out between Sun Ximing's wife and a corn seller, and it grew in intensity until the two women were sparring with cobs of corn, using some as clubs and others as flying missiles. The security group rushed over to break up the fight, losing sight of the fact that, as Mao had said, a single spark can ignite a prairie fire. Before the waves of discontent had died down at the corn stall, Six-Fingers's mother was embroiled in a tug-of-war with one of the local women over a pig's head. The combatants began to wrestle, leaving the pig's head in peace for the moment, but when the vendor was knocked to the ground, she screamed blue murder.

I was the first to run, but was followed outside by the other men. As always, people were coming and going on the same street, with the same rows of buildings and the same townspeople in the same blue, grey, or black tunics; but on this particular morning, Milltown seemed to hold new significance for the boat people. All that hounding by the security group made us want to recapture the joy of walking freely in town. Weren't those free times going to return? The men looked lost and slightly fearful. 'Run!' I shouted. 'Go and do whatever you want! Run!' Which is exactly what I did. I saw that Desheng was running, too, as were Six-Fingers and Sun Ximing. To outsiders it must have looked like a jailbreak. We made it to the Ironsmith Avenue intersection, where we peeled off in different directions. Out of the corner of my eye I watched Desheng head towards the public bath, his favourite spot in town. Six-Fingers was heading towards the cultural palace, but as far as I knew, air hockey and not culture was what he had in mind. Sun Ximing ran with me for a while, until we reached Broom Alley, where he vanished. I knew where he was going: to see a widow who lived there. That was his business, not mine, so the less said the better.

And me? I wasn't sure how I wanted to spend this precious time. With so many important things to do, I couldn't make up my mind where to start. So I just kept running, heading for the vegetable-oil processing plant. My feet had made up my mind for me – I missed my mother. No matter how badly I had disappointed Qiao Limin, I still missed her. Why? I couldn't say. My feet were doing the talking, so you'll have to ask them.

I ran and I ran, my bag slung over my shoulder. At the plant I wandered through the various sections amid the roar of milling machines, enveloped in air filled with rice dust, its fragrance mixed with the smell of kerosene. Women in white uniforms were busy on the floor, but they were either too tall or too short, too heavy or too slight to be my mother. One of them spotted me and asked who I was looking for. 'You'll have to shout,' she said. 'It's too noisy in here.'

But I refused to shout. *I'm looking for Qiao Limin*, I wanted to say. *My mother.* But I couldn't get the words out.

I left the milling section and walked to the women's dormitory, where I stood beneath the window. I could see Mother's bed and desk. The bed was empty, the exposed slats covered with discarded newspapers. My heart sank. 'She's gone,' I concluded, just as Father had predicted. He'd said she had aspirations and would leave this godforsaken place. 'What was she chasing?' I wondered. The words popped out of my mouth: '*kongpi*.' With a sense of anger, I examined her desk, on which rested an ageing enamel mug; the little bit of tea inside was mouldy, but the mug attested to her glory: 'AWARD OF EXCELLENCE FOR AMATEUR FEMALE CHORUS.' 'It's mouldy,' I said to myself, 'what kind of *excellence* is that?' With my face pressed against the glass, I noticed that one of the desk drawers was half open, and that a faint light glinted off something inside. I pushed the window open and slipped into the room. When I yanked the drawer open, I was greeted by a cockroach, which scared the hell out of me. A framed photograph lay in the drawer; it was a family photo – Father, Mother and me. Our faces had been touched up with colour, giving us a healthy, ruddy glow, sort of cosmetically enhanced. I couldn't recall when it had been taken, though my parents were both much younger and I was a tiny innocent. We were huddled closely together.

So, Mother had left a family portrait behind in her drawer. What did that mean? I wavered, trying to decide if I should take it with me. My right hand, I recall, was in favour, my left opposed, preferring to smash it. So I took it out with my right hand and placed it in my left, then flung it to the floor and stamped on it. The glass shattered, some of the shards flying up and hitting me. I looked down at the broken glass and said, '*Kongpi*.'

I actually did much more than that. As I walked through the gate, my ears were assailed by loudspeakers blaring the melody 'Commune Members Are All Sunflowers'. Mother had once performed this by dressing up as a peasant woman, a scarf over her head, an apron around her waist; she was holding a sunflower and dancing in the yard, hiding her face behind the sunflower. 'Commune members – are all – ' her face emerged from behind the sunflower and she smiled at me, 'sunflowers – ah!' With these thoughts running through my mind, my eyes began to fill with tears. The tears running disobediently down my cheeks reminded me that I could not forgive my mother, that what she deserved from me were curses; and that's what she was going to get, whether she actually heard them or not. I turned and ran back to her workplace, where I bent over, took a deep breath, and shouted at the women working there, 'Commune members aren't sunflowers, and Qiao Limin is a filthy cunt!'

East Wind No. 8

I N MY mind's eye I can still see the grand ceremony that marked the beginning of the project known as East Wind No. 8. An army of labourers was mobilized in Milltown, where the town's enormous sleeping abdomen was split open and cleaned out. Under the leadership of a provisional supervisory authority, the town was given a gullet filled with asphalt, cement intestines, a metallic stomach, and an automated beating heart. Not until later did I learn that the rumoured predictions swirling around the General Affairs Building were right on target: East Wind No. 8 was not an air-raid shelter, but the first petroleum pipeline in the Golden Sparrow River region, a secret wartime project.

As it turned out, that autumn witnessed a hundred-year flood. It was as if someone had ripped open a hole in the sky and let water stored up for a century come cascading down. As the river rose, the surrounding land receded abruptly. Floods began in the mountainous upper reaches and surged downriver, drowning riverside villages on their way. Land transportation came to a halt, leaving only waterways open. With water everywhere and as the Golden Sparrow River overflowed its banks, heroic qualities emerged. I'd never seen so many boats and ships, all headed for Milltown, so numerous they caused a bottleneck on the river. To the distant eye, the masts and sails turned the river into a floating market.

The Sunnyside Fleet was detained on the river for two full days. I found the first day of this watery assembly especially interesting. Standing on the bow of our barge, I gazed at boats in other fleets, most sporting red banners that read 'HONOURED TRANSPORT FLEET'. But not ours. They not only carried cargo, but also transported PLA soldiers and militiamen. We were limited to transporting farm labourers. I mentioned the disparity to Father. 'What do you know?' he said. 'Ours is a complicated fleet politically. The Party is showing its trust in us by letting us transport farm labourers.'

On the second day, I was surprised to see a travelling propaganda troupe. They had converted the cabin roof on one of the barges into a stage, where colourfully dressed women representing workers, peasants, soldiers, students and merchants performed; as rain fell around them they recited the women's anthem, 'Song of Struggle'. I was shocked to see Mother among them; she was the oldest member of the troupe, but was playing the part of a young worker in blue work clothes, with a white towel tied around her neck. The rain had washed away her make-up and obliterated her painted eyebrows to reveal a gaunt, wrinkled face. But she was oblivious, caught up in the drama, putting everything into her role. When others shouted, 'Fight against the heavens!' she raised her arm, brandished a fist, and in the loudest voice she could manage shouted, 'We welcome the fight!'

I'd been denied the chance to see her on shore, and now here she was, out on the river. Sure she was old – old and unattractive, and totally lacking in self-awareness, surrounded as she was by a bunch of girls. I worried that people would laugh at her presumptuousness. This accidental encounter distressed me so much that I headed back into the cabin, where Father was leaning against the porthole, staring at the distant stage.

'That's your mother's voice,' he said. 'It's her voice. I can tell from here. How is she?'

'What do you mean, how is she?'

He paused a moment. 'Everything – no, how she acts, how she looks.'

I nearly said, 'She's disgusting,' but I couldn't. 'About the same,' I said. 'No change.'

'Did she see you?'

'Why should anyone want her to see me? And what if she did, anyway?'

'I haven't seen her in a long time,' he said. 'With all the boats out there, I can hear her, but I can't see her.'

'What good would that do? She wouldn't want to see you, even if you did.'

Lowering his head, he said unhappily, '"What good would that do?" Is that all you can say? What good would anything do? That's how nihilists talk, and it must be challenged.' He took a straw hat down off the wall. 'Would people recognize me if I went out in this?' he asked.

I knew what he was getting at. 'What difference would it make if they did?' I said. 'Lying low in the cabin all day long solves nothing. If you feel like coming out, do it. Nobody out there is going to eat you.'

Father laid down the hat, shaded his eyes with his hand and gazed over at all those boats. With a burst of excitement, he blurted out, 'How stirring! How incredibly stirring! No, I won't go out there. I'll stay here and compose a poem. I've already got a title: I'll call it "A Stirring Autumn"!'

Of course it was a stirring autumn. Hundreds of sailing vessels choked the Golden Sparrow River for two days and nights. Our fleet had never shared the river with so many others, all close together. I'd always thought that the world's barges somehow belonged to the same family, until, that is, I spotted a strange fleet out in the middle of the river. Six boats, all 'manned' by young women, including one at the helm. Bright-red banners fluttering at the bows proclaimed they were the Iron Maiden Fleet, while the sterns were adorned with feminine clothing and underwear, like an array of national flags. No one knew where this unique fleet had come from, including Desheng and his wife, who nearly came to blows over it. She forbade him from gawking at the women on the boats, and punished him with a whack across the back with a bamboo pole when his eyes turned in that direction. That sparked a reaction: 'If you're going to use that pole, try pushing those boats out of the way, if you think you can. Well, I'll tell you, you can't, so don't tell me where I can look and where I can't!' My ears rang from the arguments on Desheng's barge, which continued throughout that day and the next. Fortunately, on the third day, the fleet began to move, slowly opening up a passage down the river. A squad of armed militiamen jumped aboard one of the boats, rifles slung over their left shoulders and bullhorns over their right. An embarkation system had been created, and no ships were to nestle up to the piers – we were all to sail east. The Honoured Transport Fleet led the way, an effective manoeuvre, with as many as three hundred barges sailing downstream through rain and mist until, in the midst of a torrential downpour, we reached the piers at Milltown.

I hardly recognized the place, though I'd only been away a few days. It had been turned into a – into a what? By nature given to confusion and disorder, and deficient at expressing my feelings, I'm incapable of describing the town that autumn. So, if you'll bear with me, I'll borrow a few lines from my father's poem: 'Come on, come on, who's afraid of a flood? Floodwaters open up our way ahead. In this stirring autumn red flags flutter in the wind, songs of triumph rise into the air, as we move forward, forward, racing towards a workers' paradise, a revolutionary advance guard.'

An advance guard, to be sure, but our barges, the Sunnyside Fleet, brought up the rear, so when the drums and cymbals welcomed the flotilla, we could only look on from a distance to where Young Pioneers waited in the rain: the boys lined the road, arms raised in a salute, while the girls flocked to the ships like swallows to present each honoured sailor with a red flower. As the pier-side welcoming ceremony began, a mass campaign was under way in every corner of the town; labourers with farm tools over their shoulders were everywhere, their shouts drowned out by the driving rain. While the barge crews waited to go ashore, our ears were pounded by the voice of an anxious young man coming over the loudspeaker: 'Red Flag Fleet, come ashore, move sharply, come ashore.' The crews made ready, but then rousing music blared from the PA system, followed by static. Then the anxious young man returned: 'Comrade so-and-so, report to the construction site command post. An urgent matter awaits!'

Our crews were standing at the bows awaiting a command from the PA system. But our cargo appeared to be the least important of all. The Great Wall Fleet barges, with their cargo of pork, fresh produce and rice, had received their call, and we were still waiting. Sun Ximing ran to the riverbank to complain to a raincoat-clad man. 'We're carrying human cargo, so why are we lined up behind barges carrying pork?'

The official bellowed his response: 'Have you forgotten what times these are? Do you see this as some sort of competition? All people and cargo coming ashore must be registered, and registering cargo is faster than registering people. With only us few working, of course we register pork first.' That cleared things up.

I heard Desheng's wife say to her husband, 'We're working as hard as anyone else. Will we get red flowers too?'

'Revolution isn't a dinner party,' Desheng replied. 'If it's a flower you want, go and get yourself a water gourd.'

As the rain eased off, the people inside our cabin began to shout, 'It's suffocating in here, give us some air!' So I raised the hatch, and was hit by a blast of sweat-sour air, mixed with the stench of cigarette smoke, urine and vomit. Then the heads of the workers started popping up, more men than women, most of them young. With bed rolls on their backs, they elbowed one another to get their first look at the legendary workers' paradise. Mouths open, they breathed deeply and gawked at the construction scenes on the banks. One of the women shrieked, 'They're turning the earth upside down! They'll work us to death!' She could have chosen a better time to shout – someone shouted back at her: 'What did you think we brought you here to do, loaf around? If you're afraid of hard work you shouldn't have come to Milltown.' The uproar in the cabin died out quickly. A man who looked like a demobilized soldier travelling with the fleet began recording the passengers with a roll call, but he'd only managed a few people when the PA system blared out the name of the Sunnyside Fleet. He hopped down on to the deck and began issuing orders: 'Shock Troops Three over here! Shock Troops Four over there! Gao Village Shock Troops and Li Family Crossing Shock Troops to the rear!'

So that's what they were, shock troops! A barge-load of shock troops was on the move and our spacious forward hold emptied quickly, leaving nothing but two rows of buckets used for toilets, all filled and sending their hot stench straight into my nostrils. Some of them must have been knocked over, since the deck was soiled with puddles of a disgusting liquid. The smell was over-powering.

After changing into rubber boots, I snatched a mop and began cleaning up. But I'd barely begun when I saw that something else had been left behind – a bundle wrapped in an army raincoat had been tossed into a corner. I touched it with my broom; it moved. Then a child's leg kicked out, scaring the hell out of me. The next thing to wriggle out of the raincoat bundle was the head of a woman with hair going every which way, and I heard her complain crisply, 'Why'd you hit my leg with that?'

Two people had taken refuge in the army raincoat: a thirty-year-old woman and a little girl, apparently a mother and daughter. Two pairs of eyes, one dazed, the other lively, both gaped at me sleepily.

I struck the deck with my mop. 'Up!' I said. 'Get up! I have to clean the cabin.'

As soon as they stood up, I saw how weary the woman was. She had a pale, unhealthy face. And there was more inside that raincoat, lots more. She opened it up to expose a bulging knapsack and a rolled-up blanket, plus a netted basket with a wash basin and rice tin, all tied together by the hood and sleeves of the raincoat, which she held in her arms. The girl's arms were just as full: she was hugging a cloth doll and had an olive-green army canteen draped around her neck by its strap. She was also holding a little blackboard on which words had been scrawled in juvenile writing: 'East Wind No. 8,' it said. 'Huixian. Mama.'

'What are you doing here?' I demanded. 'How dare you sleep on while everybody else has left the boat! Who are you?'

'Who are we? We're not going to tell you.' The girl glared at me and put herself between me and her mother to keep her mother from telling me. 'He's mean,' she said. 'Let's ignore him.'

'This is a shock-troop barge,' I said. 'How did you sneak aboard?'

'We didn't sneak aboard,' the girl said provocatively. 'We flew aboard, so you couldn't see us.'

The woman combed her fingers through her tangled hair and glanced eagerly at the shore. 'Huixian!' she scolded. 'Don't talk like that! It's rude.' Then, turning her eyes away from the shore, she smiled, almost apologetically. But she hadn't answered my question. She crawled out of the hold, dragging her bundle and the girl with her. Then she turned and said, 'We're shock troops too. I just overslept. I didn't dare fall asleep at night. I was exhausted.'

From Inside an Army Coat

I CAN'T SAY why, but one look at Huixian and her mother raised doubts in my mind about them.

I'd always been suspicious about people like that. If they were shock troops, my name wasn't Ku Dongliang. I didn't know why they'd boarded our barge and was pretty sure they'd tricked their way on. We'd received strict orders not to allow unknown persons, as well as the old, the weak, the sick and the infirm, to board the barges for the trip to Milltown, and I hadn't seen a single child at the Horsebridge pier. I wondered if they'd slipped aboard barge number seven in all the confusion during the two days when the river was clogged with all those ships. If so, why had the former soldier turned a blind eye when they came aboard, and how had the shock troops let her get away with it? Whatever the reason, they'd made it possible for Huixian and her mother to hide inside an army raincoat for two days and two nights.

Since the woman and her daughter definitely hadn't come to Milltown to work, they'd probably come in search of someone. Announcements of missing persons were broadcast daily, and it usually took only one to locate someone. If the announcement was repeated, the person was truly missing. The announcements for whoever this woman was looking for must have been repeated several times, but the name had made no impression on me. Stuff like that didn't interest me. With so many people travelling, not finding someone wasn't necessarily a bad thing. As far as I was concerned, other people's misfortunes weren't worth more than a tear or two, compared to what my family had gone through.

I had no idea where these two were from. In Milltown, food was supplied at the work sites, and when ration cards were handed out, personal information was dutifully recorded. So if Huixian and her mother had eaten at a public canteen, their details should have been recorded. But there was so much going on at East Wind No. 8 that no one had checked up on Huixian and her mother. Even if they had, who could say whether the data was reliable or not, since it was even rumoured that a murderer had managed to pass himself off as belonging to the shock troops? That made a mockery of recording personal details in the first place.

I watched Huixian and her mother closely, mainly because they must have had a shady background, but also – I forgot to tell you this – because the woman resembled my mother. I know it sounds strange, but I wondered if she might have been my aunt, a Horsebridge woman I'd never met. For three days the Sunnyside Fleet waited at the piers for orders. I had time on my hands while everyone else was busily running around; everything I needed to do had to wait till I was ashore. Until then, I was on my own. So I stood on the bow, hands on my hips, coolly watching the construction work at the piers.

The heavens opened and the sound of rain rose around us. Rudimentary tents popped up, occupied by labourers from the surrounding areas. Some ran up to our barge to borrow firewood or a bucket or bowl. I said no, but Father invariably overruled me, and I had to lend them whatever they wanted. But the borrowed items never made it back to us, and before long we were down to a single bowl, which Father and I were forced to share at mealtimes. When I complained, he criticized me for being small-minded. 'A few bowls, what does that amount to?' he said. 'Sharing a bowl can be our contribution to the success of East Wind No. 8. You're young enough to make a real contribution, so why don't you go ashore instead of standing around looking down at what's going on, as if it's got nothing to do with you? That kind of behaviour will get you into trouble.'

Talk like that from my father went in one ear and out the other. He thought I got a kick out of watching people busily running around, never considering that I might be concerned about the loneliest people down there. I kept searching out the mother and her daughter. With the oversized army raincoat draped around her, from a distance it was hard to tell if she was a man or a woman. But up close she was obviously a woman whose face showed that she was sick. Instead of continuing down the road, she paced back and forth on the riverbank. The weary look on her face could not mask the fact that she was pretty, her eyes exuding a charm and warmth that was tempered by signs of resentment, as if there was an unpaid debt owed her; it was a heart-chilling look. She seemed more emotional than my mother, yet given to bottling things up. Every time she came near the water I felt like asking, 'Are you from Horsebridge? Did your family run a butcher's shop? Is your family name Qiao?' But the looks she gave me, cold and resentful, made me shrink back rather than engage her in a conversation. I could see that the raincoat did more than protect her from the rain, that it had multiple uses, in particular providing a makeshift roof for someone on the move. All her belongings were hidden under that raincoat, not to mention her daughter, the skinny little Huixian, who was never without her grimy little doll; she'd poke her head out every so often and blink once or twice before slipping back inside.

Tents had been thrown up on the school playground, some clearly marked 'women', where women with children were welcome. Maybe because she had her child with her, or maybe because she was just too shy, she walked into one of them and walked right back out again. As I continued my observation, separated from them by a strip of water, I concluded that they had to be looking for someone. But who? And although they were looking, they were not finding that person.

The day before the incident, I watched the woman pace back and forth by the piers, shielding her daughter with the raincoat. If I hadn't known better, I'd have thought she was just out for a walk or checking the lay of the land. And as darkness settled around us, the rain fell harder, swallowing up mother and daughter.

After cooking dinner, I took the food to Father in the cabin. 'Have you ever seen my aunt, the one who lives in Horsebridge?' I asked him.

'Yes, back around the time of our wedding. I'd have liked to see her again after that, but I never did, since the sisters had a falling out.' That's not what I wanted to hear. Apparently, they hadn't come looking for my mother after all. Why I felt bad I couldn't exactly say.

The incident on the pier occurred the following morning. Our barge was loaded with broken bricks and tiles, and we were about to weigh anchor and head downriver when a shrill wail burst from the shore. The voice was crisp and clear, but obviously juvenile and hysterical, and loud enough to drown out the rousing voice coming over the PA system. From aboard the barge I spotted the little girl; she was holding her doll in one hand and dragging the army raincoat in the mud with the other as she ran madly back and forth. Running and bawling, she attracted the attention of everyone within sight and earshot.

Several of the female labourers chased after the girl. 'Stop running!' they shouted. 'Your mother's coming back!' Someone near me recognized the girl and told me she'd cried and made a fuss all night. 'She can't find her mother. At first I thought she'd gone off on some sort of errand, but it's morning now and the girl's still all alone.' That was when we knew that something was wrong. The woman in the raincoat was missing. The labourers, loving mothers all, went up to Huixian with toys, food, even some plastic flowers. She fought off all their pity and heartfelt sympathy and ran towards the barges, biting one woman's hand and spitting in the face of another. She dodged in between the legs of the women trying to catch her, and when she reached the gangplank to barge number one, she stopped in her tracks. Then she came aboard. 'Where are you going?' they shouted. 'Your mama's not on one of those boats. They bring people here, they don't take them away.'

I still recall how Huixian searched for her mother aboard the barge. Stumbling along with terror-filled eyes, she looked everywhere, crying out for her mother the whole time. The tugboat started up its engine, but then shut it off. 'Whose child is she?' people wondered. 'Why is she running around like that?' She'd changed into a red-striped shirt since the last time I'd seen her; her braid had been combed and was tied with a bow. I recognized her right away, though. I noted that she'd not only lost her mother, but that her canteen and little blackboard were also missing.

While some of the crew members ran after her, others shouted across to people on the shore, discussing what might have happened to her mother. Opinions differed on the water and on the shore. The labourers on shore came mostly from farming villages and, given their view that females were next to useless, assumed that the girl's mother had abandoned her. Few of the barge people accepted that, probably because they spent their lives on the water and had seen their share of drownings, many intentional. Their initial reaction was that ill luck had found the woman. I saw Six-Fingers and his mother, one at the bow and the other on the starboard deck, crouching down to look into the water. Looking for what? Everyone knew the answer. The tugboat crew were on the roof of the engine room searching the water, shielding the sun from their eyes with their hands. I knew that everyone on the river was of the same sad but unexpressed opinion that the woman would not be coming back, that she'd taken the easy way out.

Boat people consider it taboo to look for a dead person aboard a sailing vessel. But no one on the Sunnyside barges had encountered anything quite like this before. A taboo is meaningless to a seven- or eight-year-old girl, and nothing can change that. She had her own logic: her mother had brought her to Milltown on a boat, so that's the way she was going to leave. People tried to talk some sense into her: 'Little girl, we bring people here, we don't take them away. Your mother isn't here.' But Huixian would have none of it. Even at her young age she knew adults' weaknesses. 'You're lying!' she said through her tears. 'If a boat can bring people somewhere, it can take them away too.'

She stamped her foot in front of Sun Ximing, convinced that her mother was hiding below deck and trying to get her to come out. Sun Ximing's son tried to get her to stop. 'Don't do that,' he said. 'You'll stamp a hole in our hatch, and you'll have to pay.' But Sun's wife pushed her son aside and opened the hatch to let Huixian see for herself. 'See, little girl? There's no one in there, nothing but bricks.'

Huixian got down on her knees and stuck her head in. 'Are you down there, Mama?' she cried into the darkness. 'Come out, Mama! Please come out!'

The crew exchanged glances. Desheng's wife wiped her moist eyes and glanced at her husband.

'Why look at me?' he said. 'I'm not the Dragon King.'

His wife lowered her eyes and gazed down at the water. Since she couldn't argue with the Dragon King, she took her frustrations out on the water. 'It's all because of this year's floods. Why was there so much water? It's the damned water. Come and stand over here. See how easy it would be to jump in.'

However ridiculous the woman's comments may have sounded,

I was struck by the knowledge that she'd fathomed the river's secrets: it sends the autumn floodwaters downstream, causing the riverbed to lose its temper. The banks slink off, leaving the murky water to rush angrily along and cover the river's cruellest secret. I'd thought about this secret in the past, and I knew what it was. It was whispered in people's ears, two simple words: 'Come down, come down.'

The tugboat blew its whistle, pressing the people on the barges to do something about the little girl. But no one knew what that something should be, so they congregated on Sun Ximing's barge. As he looked down at the tree limbs and leaves floating by, Six-Fingers made a quick calculation of the speed of flow. 'Already past the town of Wufu,' he announced. 'Way past Wufu.' At first they didn't know what he was talking about, but only for a moment. What he meant was, if the woman had jumped into the river, her corpse would already have been carried down below the town of Wufu. No one spoke; they all turned their heads to gaze sadly in the direction of Wufu.

Sun's wife took the girl's hand and raised her voice in angry protest. 'What kind of woman abandons her own daughter? With officials on land and the Dragon King in the water, someone should deal with people like that. I don't care where she's run to, they should tie her up and drag her back.'

Unfortunately, she hadn't considered the effect of her angry denunciation on the girl, who yanked her hand free and began pounding Sun's wife on the arm. 'I'll tie *you* up!' she screamed. 'Tie you up!'

I saw the women trying to pull the girl away, but she'd have none of it. Some of them walked up with open arms, but to no avail. She moved up next to Sun Ximing, which pleased and surprised him; he gestured for the others to watch what they said around her and had his wife go and get the girl some sweets. His normally tight-fisted wife suddenly turned generous, stuffing a sweet into the little girl's mouth, which opened wide to accept the treat. Her eyes lit up as she sucked it, and she spotted me. 'It's him!' she shouted, pointing at me. 'My mama's on his boat!'

Panicked, I turned and ran. But Huixian took off after me. I knew why she was chasing me, but not why I was running away. Whatever the reason, by overreacting I caused a bizarre scene, as people on all the barges started running, turning the fleet into a rocking runway. They were chasing each other up and down the sides of the barges, shouting, 'Don't run! Don't run!' But no one stopped. I kept looking back, afraid that Huixian might fall in. I needn't have worried, for she had an astonishing sense of balance. Like an avenging demon she kept after me, her feet virtually flying on what for her were unfamiliar boats.

I calmed down once I made it back to barge number seven, where I pulled back the tarp and said to the girl, 'Go ahead, look for yourself. Your mama won't be hidden on our boat unless she turned into a brick. If she didn't, she won't be in there.'

The people who had been running after Huixian stopped when they reached our barge and watched as I jumped down into the hold and started tossing the damaged bricks up on deck, one at a time. 'Go ahead, look,' I shouted, 'and tell me which one of those is your mama.'

Dodging the flying bricks, she stamped her foot and yelled, 'Your mama is a brick!'

'Dongliang!' Sun Ximing called out. 'What's going on here? Why was she chasing you?'

By then I was getting angry. 'How the hell should I know? She may think she knows me, but I sure don't know her!'

Amid all the shouting, the tugboat crew ran out of patience and sounded the whistle. Slowly getting under way, the eleven barges turned into a gigantic boa that smelled the arrival of spring, heading out into the river. Startled by the movement, people aboard the barges turned and shouted, 'Stop! The little girl's still aboard!'

The tug crew ran into the cabin, where a burst of garbled shouts emerged from a battery bullhorn. Finally one of the men blew into the bullhorn and said impatiently, 'What's all the fuss? What are you afraid of? She's just a little girl. It's not as if you've taken a class enemy aboard!'

Frightened by the bullhorn, Huixian straightened up and gazed at the tugboat. She burst into tears and shrieked at me, 'Tell me right this minute, where is my mama?'

Given her youth, I saw nothing wrong with her crying and carrying on because she'd lost her mother. But she was staring at me, wanting *me* to produce her mother. That was too much. As for the other crews, instead of coming to my aid, they all just gaped at me, sort of stupefied, as if to force a cruel response out of me. I looked first at the barge, then at the shore, and finally down at the water. If anything, I was more puzzled than they were, and I couldn't help thinking about my own mother. Strangely, the name Qiao Limin popped into my head, but for the life of me, I couldn't conjure up a picture of what my mother looked like. As I looked at Huixian's tear-streaked face, I knew I couldn't tell her the truth, tell her not to keep looking for her mother. *My mother's a kongpi, and it looks like yours is too.* She was too young to understand, I couldn't put it into words. But I was also unable to escape a responsibility I hadn't asked for. Then an idea came to me. 'Look,' I said, 'here's your mama.' I held up a finger and drew a circle in the air under her nose, then pointed mysteriously into the air. That, I figured, was a good way to get her to understand the meaning of *kongpi*. I didn't care whether or not anyone else understood the meaning of my gesture.

Sofa

HUIXIAN SAT on my father's sofa in the cabin, agitated, wilful and gluttonous. She'd gone through all the snacks we had. That's my earliest recollection of her as she began life on the river.

Our fancy sofa was upholstered in blue corduroy with a sunflower pattern. A close look revealed its public-property origin. The wooden armrests were host to many cigarette burns and the back was protected by canvas with the words 'Welcome to the Revolutionary Committee' still legible. Given that members of the Sunnyside Fleet owned no private property, not even a chair, our sofa had long been considered the fleet's most extravagant item. It also symbolized my father's special status. When he was banished to the barge from the General Affairs Building, all he brought with him was his corduroy sofa.

Safeguarding the sovereignty of that sofa took a lot out of me. None of the barge children could restrain their interest in it, and sooner or later every one of them chose a direct or roundabout way of asking to sit in it. 'Let me sit in it just once, OK? Please.'

My response never varied. 'No,' I said, with a vigorous shake of the head. 'Not unless you give me half a yuan.'

Now where would they get that kind of money? Besides, they wouldn't part with it even if they had it, so that kept them out of our cabin. Yingtao's brother, Dayong, tried to sneak inside once, but I dragged him out and wrestled him to the ground, which incurred the wrath of surprised adults on both sides. Embarrassed by the incident, Father invited Dayong inside to sit on the sofa, but the invitation came too late. Before the boy could step into the cabin, his father slapped him.

'What makes you think you can sit on that sofa? A privy is more like it!'

Dayong's mother grabbed him by the arm and dragged him back to their barge, fuming, though not necessarily at her son. 'What gives a useless brat like you the right to sit on a sofa? No wonder you asked me for half a yuan. Half a yuan just to sit on a sofa? Is it sewn with gold threads or something? Think you'll get up with a gold-plated rear end?'

That sofa was the last vestige of family honour in my safe-keeping, and I was not about to give it up. Money had nothing to do with it. Someone came on board our barge one day and complained about my demand for money. Father nearly twisted my ear off my head. I knew he'd be the one to suffer from my actions and that the sofa would exacerbate our estrangement from the other barges, which was a constant worry to Father, who never stopped stressing the importance of our relationship with the masses. Over time, many of the fleet's adults followed the example of Yingtao's mother, forbidding their children from going aboard barge number seven. 'What's so wonderful about a sofa?' they'd say. 'For half a yuan you'd get your rear end squeezed on to it. Children need to develop a strong will. You're not to sit on that sofa even if you're invited to.'

But the unexpected usually changes things. Huixian turned my strict control on its head. She broke all the rules. I still recall how she headed straight for the cabin, where she stuck her little nose up to the glass to see if her mother was there. Ours was the messiest and most mysterious cabin in the fleet. One wall was decorated with a picture of the martyr Deng Shaoxiang cut out of a newspaper. It was just fuzzy enough to lend it a mysterious, ancient quality. Huixian studied it through the window. 'That's my grandma!' she blurted out. Everyone within earshot fought hard not to laugh at her absurd comment, while watching me for a reaction. I disappointed them.

The next thing Huixian spotted was my father, who was sitting on the sofa, a book in his lap, looking back at the girl. He stood up, smiled at her, and pointed humbly to the sofa. 'Want to try it out?' he said. 'Come on.'

The invitation could not have come at a better time. Huixian dried her tears and darted inside. 'Sofa!' she cried out, loudly enough for everyone to hear. 'Sofa! My papa's sofa!'

What nonsense! How could our sofa suddenly become her papa's?

'She says it's her papa's sofa!' A bunch of kids mimicked, hoping to get under my skin.

Not wanting to pick a fight with a little girl, I tried to assess the situation objectively. Her father had probably also sat on a sofa, which meant he might have been an official or someone who lived in the city. I watched as she jumped on to the sofa, like a fledgling returning to its nest. For some reason, the people outside greeted her achievement with applause and a flurry of whispers. They were obviously waiting to see what Father and I would do. His reaction was exactly what they'd expected: he stood close by, hands at his sides, like a doddering old king relinquishing his throne to a little girl. What piqued their curiosity was my reaction. They were eager to see how I'd deal with the girl. I knew that for some of them this would be a test of my fair-mindedness, while for others it was my kindness and decency that were under scrutiny.

I instinctively reached out, just missing grabbing her braid. Before I knew it, she was on the sofa, draping one leg over the armrest as she sank with practised ease into the cushion, a look of satisfaction and gratification spreading across her face. I'll bet her mother was the last thing on her mind at that moment, for I heard her mutter – more like an old woman than a little girl – 'I'm beat!' She looked up at me, then shut her eyes, looked up one more time and then shut her eyes again. This time they stayed shut, thanks to the sleep that had settled in.

'Put your leg down,' I said. 'If you're going to sit there, do it right, and don't get our sofa dirty.'

Past being able to open her eyes, she gave the armrest a little kick, and I noticed that she was wearing red cloth shoes, covered with mud. She was also wearing socks, one of which had slid down into her shoe. I turned to look at Father. 'She's asleep,' he said. 'Let her be.'

I was OK with that, but I said, 'Her shoes are muddy.'

And so Huixian, like a mysterious gift dropped from the heavens, settled on to the river, on our barge. She was a gift that had come out of nowhere, for good or for ill, presented to the members of the Sunnyside Fleet, whose interest in her was all-encompassing; for the moment, however, no one quite knew how to enjoy their gift. When the fleet's women and children were reminded of what awaited them, they ran excitedly to barge number seven and gazed at her through the cabin porthole, jostling for position, like a crowd at a zoo. No longer an object of pity, Huixian slept like a baby on my father's sofa. He gestured to the people to keep the noise down as he covered her with a sweater. It was big enough to cover her from head to toe. Some of the women whispered pleasantly, 'I'd never have guessed that Secretary Ku could be so big-hearted.'

The children, on the other hand, saw this as an opportunity to get even with me. With contempt in their eyes, they stared at me, wanting to say something I'd hate to hear, but not sure what that might be. Only Yingtao, who was still quite small, was too envious to let the opportunity pass. She stuck her head through the cabin door and glared at me. 'I thought you wouldn't let anybody sit on that sofa,' she said, denouncing my hypocrisy. 'How come she can *sleep* on it? How come *she* didn't have to pay?'

Standing in the doorway, I had no time to argue with Yingtao. I was too busy watching Father bustle around like an ant on a heated pan after giving up his sofa for her, relinquishing his sole trusty space. He sat down on my army cot, obviously ill at ease as he stared at the girl sleeping on his sofa, a look of anxiety and embarrassment in his eyes. Then he stood up abruptly, waved to me and said, 'She's worn out. Let's go outside and let her sleep.'

Father carried his journal outside with him. He'd begun keeping a daily journal the year he joined the fleet. He may have lost his official position but not the habits associated with it, and he recorded his thoughts religiously. In the wake of the incident that no one talked about, he seldom came out of his cabin, preferring to stay out of the sunlight. He had, as a result, become pale, presenting a stark contrast to the ruddy complexions of the other barge men. He was always ill at ease, particularly in the company of the other members of the fleet. Remorse filled his eyes when he looked at them. People had a pretty good idea why he was so ill at ease, but only I knew the true source of that remorse. He clearly regretted picking up those scissors and, in one rash moment, destroying what little self-respect he had left.

Outwardly, the barge people maintained a measure of respect towards him. 'Aren't you coming out, Secretary Ku? You need to get some fresh air. Spending all your time in there is bad for your health.' But their eyes gave away their secret. Their concern for his health was concentrated on one spot. No matter who was speaking – men, women, young and old – their gaze invariably travelled to his crotch, with either the purest of intentions or salacious glee, like the needle of a compass pulled by the earth's magnetic field. Father dressed in grey nylon trousers, buttoned up and impeccably creased. But that did not satisfy anyone; their eyes kept roaming to his fly, and they wished they could see through the fabric to learn the secret of the severed penis.

They could not, of course, and that fired their imagination. Six-Fingers Wang and Chunsheng would exchange looks and snigger. The women's train of thought was slightly less vulgar and more veiled. Their gaze would move quickly down past Father's crotch before they instinctively turned towards the shore; a moment later they would turn back again, and I once saw Yingtao's mother stifle a giggle with her hand. Not knowing why she was giggling, Yingtao tugged at her sleeve and asked, 'What are you laughing at?' She received a resounding smack. 'What are you saying? I'm not laughing.'

Father would become even more pale than usual. He was dressed properly, but he might as well not have been wearing a shirt or those nylon trousers. His shameful genitalia were like an exposed target, inviting dart-like gazes from everyone. He could have worn a thousand pairs of trousers and still not have been able to keep his lower body out of sight. He would hold out as long as he could before thrusting his journal into his jacket pocket and, forcing himself to remain as calm as possible, say, 'I haven't seen you comrades for a long time. I hope you're all well.' They'd nod and mumble a response, gazing up and down, looking at him curiously. He knew what it was they cared about, but he lacked the courage to talk about it. So he'd gaze into the cloud-filled sky. 'Nice weather,' he'd say, just as thunder crackled, and the people would look skyward. Then they'd look back at Father with puzzled expressions and mutterings of surprise on their lips.

Dayong, from barge number five, once cackled and said, 'Is he seeing things? It's going to start raining any minute, and he's talking about nice weather!'

That was more than I could take. I pushed Father back towards the cabin. 'Go on inside,' I said, like a father ordering his son.

'Go in and read.' Knowing what I was doing, he went and stood beneath the hatch, an embarrassed look on his face, as I turned my attention to the others. First I shoved Dayong. 'Go on!' I said. 'Get off our barge.' Then I pushed his sister. 'Get off, go back to number five.'

That had the desired effect on the adults, who wisely took their leave. 'Time to go,' they said. 'Let the poor little mite get some sleep.'

But Yingtao's mother was determined to let me know that she was unhappy. She left a mystifying comment in her wake: 'I'd like to know what that boy and his father have in mind, hiding a little girl in their cabin like that.'

That really upset Desheng's wife. 'How can anyone respond to a mean, ugly comment like that?' she said, trying her best to defend us. 'Watch what you're saying, Yingtao's mother, or you might wake up tomorrow with your mouth twisted out of shape from a stroke.'

The fleet's mysterious gift was now under the protection, however temporary, of Father and me. We headed downriver with an unrelated girl aboard. Our corduroy sofa was now a boat within a boat. After we passed the duck farm, the river widened and there was less traffic, the sound of churning water in our wake a potent contrast to the deathly silence aboard the barge, silence that was abruptly shattered by our little passenger, who cried out in her dreams, 'Mama!' Father and I were startled by her shrill cry, but fortunately, she slept on. She rolled over, apparently agitated, but then lay peacefully again. One of her socks had fallen off; her pale toes, which were pointing at me, quivered slightly.

We stood in the doorway keeping watch over the sleeping girl. Father seemed morose as he looked down at the water. I knew how fragile he was; humiliation greeted him each time he emerged from the cabin, and he was wallowing in feelings of shame. But I couldn't keep my eyes off the muted light Huixian's naked foot gave off, and had the sudden feeling that the light somehow broke through the loneliness and depression that never seemed to leave barge number seven. Father and I were each occupied with our own thoughts. For some strange reason, my heart was flooded with happiness, but in the face of Father's dejection, I had to keep that to myself.

Desheng and his wife came over to check on our passenger as we were passing Deer Bridge Village. I can't pin it down, but there was something sneaky about their behaviour. 'Is she being a good girl?' Desheng asked.

'She's still sleeping,' I said. 'How am I supposed to know if she's a good girl or not?'

Desheng looked first at me, then at Father, then nudged his wife conspiratorially. 'Don't you have something to say? There's no one around, now's the time.'

She glared at him. 'I wasn't serious,' she said.

Father looked at Desheng and his wife, not sure what was going on. 'If you've got something to say, say it,' he said. 'We're neighbours, one boat after the other, so don't treat me like a stranger.'

Desheng's wife squirmed bashfully as she pointed to our cabin and smiled. 'It's nothing, really. It's just that when I look at that little girl, for some reason I think about my own childhood, when my parents abandoned me on a pier, and my future mother-in-law took me aboard their barge until I was old enough to marry Desheng. Everyone says she was a wise and benevolent woman whose good deeds earned her a daughter-in-law.'

Desheng urged his wife to say what she'd come to say. 'You're evading the issue.'

'Secretary Ku,' she said, 'please don't think I'm meddling, but you really ought to have a woman aboard your barge. The way I see it, Fate has brought this girl and barge number seven together – or, more to the point, brought her and Dongliang together. I've never seen him be this good to anyone, and if you let her stay, who knows, when she grows up . . .'

Father didn't give her a chance to finish. 'No,' he said, 'that's not going to work. What you're talking about is raising a child bride.' Still smiling, he waved his hands to dismiss the idea. 'I know you mean well, but there's a principle involved. We're capable of overcoming any hardship, we're materialists. We don't believe in Fate and we definitely reject the feudal concept of valuing boys over girls.'

The views of Desheng's wife made me blush. I didn't know what to make of them. She rolled her eyes at her husband. 'You see, I told you Secretary Ku wouldn't go along with it. But you forced me to say it.' She cast a look of pity my way. 'You men know nothing about girls. She's going to grow up to be a real beauty.' She sighed and stuck her head into the cabin to listen to the girl's deep, even breathing. 'Hear that? She's snoring like a little piglet.'

Desheng's wife left a few ears of corn for Huixian, as the sky darkened over the river and night settled in. As the shore turned dark, so did our cabin. The little girl slept on. All of a sudden, a strange feeling arose between Father and me. I sensed that he wanted to explain something, but didn't know where to start, while I felt like making something known, but was too embarrassed to do so. He hung up a lantern and turned up the wick, bringing light to the cabin. He had a worried look on his face as he bent down to get a closer look at the girl. 'No good,' he blurted out. 'This won't work.'

'What do you mean, no good? What won't work?'

'It's dark out, night's coming. We can't keep her on our barge.'

I guessed what was on his mind, and was deeply disappointed. 'Are you still worried that people will talk? She's just a snotty-nosed little girl. Anyone who talks is full of shit!'

In the lamplight I could see he was thinking hard. 'Getting

angry at me doesn't solve anything,' he said. 'We have to go on with our tails between our legs. There's nothing wrong with worrying. She may be little, but she's still a female. She has to go.'

Gossip is a fearful thing. I couldn't see all the possibilities, and knew I had to do as he said, so I put Huixian's sock back on and patted her on the foot. 'Wake up,' I said. 'It's time to go.'

She kicked me and mumbled, 'Don't bother me, I'm sleepy,' before rolling over to go back to sleep.

'No more sleeping,' I said. 'It's dark outside and we have a tiger on board that comes out at night to eat little girls.'

She sat up like a shot and glared at me. 'Liar,' she said. 'You're lying.' She tried to lie back down, but, like a coolie, I picked her up and hoisted her over my shoulder. I felt her struggle briefly against my back, but now that she was awake, her first thoughts were of her mother. 'Then hurry up and help me find my mama,' she demanded.

'I don't know where your mama flew off to,' I said. 'I'm taking you to the authorities. They can find your mama for you.'

Sun Ximing was our fleet commander, so I carried the girl over to his barge, crossing five others along the way and answering the same question at each one: 'Where are you taking her?' 'It's dark out, so I'm taking her to the authorities.' Six-Fingers Wang's daughters tried to block my way, chattering about how cute she was and begging me to leave Huixian with them, at least for the night. 'No,' I said. 'Your barge is noisier than a nest of baby birds. Besides, a bunch of silly girls like you can't be the authorities. I'm taking her to Sun Ximing's.'

The Sun family had just finished dinner on barge number one. Sun's wife was washing the bowls and chopsticks under the muted light of the masthead lantern. When she saw me walk up with the little girl on my back, she bleated out in surprise, 'Why are you carrying her over here? Crossing all those barges in the dark was risky. She was happy sleeping on your sofa – why not let her stay there? She can't hurt it.'

'Don't blame me. My dad wouldn't let her stay.' I could only repeat what he'd said. 'She's a female, my dad says, so she can't spend the night on our barge!'

Sun's wife doubled up laughing. 'That Secretary Ku is really something. A female, he says! She's such a little girl that the tongue of anyone who spread rumours would rot away. Your dad's like the man who was bitten by a snake and shied away from ropes for ten years. A man can be too careful, too guarded. There's no need to be ridiculous.'

I wasn't laughing. I thrust the little girl into Sun's wife's arms just as the rest of the family came up to see what was going on. It looked as if they'd be happy to take her. The children commented excitedly on Huixian's braid and her clothes, until Sun shooed them away. 'Bringing her here was the right thing to do, I guess,' she said. 'Without a woman on board your barge, there's no one to look after her.'

Now that she was no longer lying across my back, Huixian began to cry. But she was too sleepy to keep it up. By then Sun's wife was holding her in her arms, but the girl struggled and fought to get down, and I could see the disdain in her eyes. But then the woman's gold earrings caught her eye. She reached out for one and then the other.

Sun's wife pulled her hands back. 'When you're old enough to be my daughter-in-law,' she said, 'these gold earrings will be yours.'

As I was heading back from barge number one, I crossed five more in my bare feet, each deck colder than the one before. A half moon had risen above the Golden Sparrow River, bringing evening to the water and rousing the frogs on the banks. By now the fleet had got under way, picking up speed in the darkness, the water churning fast beneath my feet. My unburdened back felt lighter, but the girl's warmth remained, and I recall how, as I walked across Six-Fingers Wang's barge, I snapped my fingers casually at his daughter, masking my feeling of loss. My back remained bent under the weight of an imaginary little girl. Freed of my burden for only a moment, I had already begun to miss her.

When I reached our cabin, I saw the flickering light in the cabin. Father had gone back inside. The barge seemed a cheerless place for the very first time. I looked down at my thin shadow and discovered how lonely I was. I also felt the stirrings of love, which were more unfathomable than the water in the river.

Huixian

THE BOAT people planned to deposit the girl on the shore. Since even a found penny must be turned in, a little girl would surely not be an exception to the rule. So when the fleet reached Wufu, Sun Ximing and a group of women took Huixian to the authorities.

Wufu was a town where the social order had broken down. It was overrun with refugees who had thrown up tents on the streets, where they slept, ate and deposited their waste. The government offices and compound had been virtually swallowed up by all the squatters, and the barge delegation only managed with great difficulty to locate the local civil administration office, which had been moved to an old earth god temple. A lot of good *that* did them. They were told to take the child back to where they had found her. 'We're too busy here to worry about Milltown,' they said.

So, their hopes dashed, the delegation headed back, grumbling as they went, 'If we'd offered them a wallet, they wouldn't have given a damn where we'd found it, and would have been only too happy to take it off our hands. I guess a human life isn't as valuable as a wallet.'

The fleet returned to Milltown a few days later, and this time we all believed we'd say our goodbyes to Huixian. To this end, people stuffed all sorts of things into her pockets – an egg, a handkerchief, even a handful of melon seeds – to show how they felt about her. Sun Ximing's wife stuck a red flower in the little girl's hair and pinned another to her chest; Desheng's wife dabbed rouge on her cheeks and lipstick on her mouth. Rather than seeing her off the barges for good, you'd have thought they were preparing her for the stage.

Having failed in our first attempt to have Huixian taken off our hands, this time Sun Ximing made careful plans. He came to barge number seven to talk my father into going ashore with them. 'As a former official,' he said, 'you're familiar with policy and you know what to say, Secretary Ku. You have to come. We don't want to make things difficult for you, but we don't know a thing about the girl's background, and I'm afraid that if we say the wrong thing, we'll be inviting trouble. They all think barge people have too many kids, as it is, and that we kidnap them.'

'Rumours,' my father said. 'Wherever there are people you'll find rumours.'

'But it won't be a rumour if they try to pin a kidnapping on us. Secretary Ku, you have to speak up for us. We'll take the girl, all you have to do is talk to them. What do you say?'

'No. I'm no longer a Party secretary, and no one will listen to anything I say.' My father steadfastly shook his head. 'Don't think I don't want to help, Commander Sun. But you know all about my troubles. I can't go ashore.'

'What I don't understand,' Sun said, 'is how much trouble it can be to go ashore and talk to someone. You've got arms, Old Ku, and you've got legs, so what's to keep you from going ashore?' Sun's anxiety showed in his eyes. His gaze darted downward until he was looking at Father's crotch. The thought of his truncated penis reminded him of Father's ugly nickname. 'Tell me, Secretary Ku, what's the real reason you won't go ashore? Are you afraid of what people will say when they see you? Who cares about a bunch of smart-arse kids, especially a man like you? Come with us, and if I hear an unkind word from anyone, he'll pay with his prick – the whole thing.'

Father's face darkened. 'Old Sun,' he said unappreciatively, 'I don't like to hear that kind of gutter talk from you. You can't have a very high opinion of me if you think I'm worried about a bunch of kids. I've said before that I vowed to the ghost of the martyr Deng Shaoxiang that I'll not step foot on land again until my case has been resolved and the verdict on me overturned.'

With an embarrassed look, Sun Ximing grumbled, 'It's not like you to sulk, Old Ku. You have to tough it out. Even a fish winds up on land when the water rises. Don't tell me you plan to spend the rest of your life on the water.'

'I'm not sulking,' Father said. 'You don't understand me, Old Sun. This isn't sulking, it's dignity.'

Sun blinked as he considered what Father meant by the word dignity. A sneer of disdain accompanied a couple of pats on his leg. 'Dignity, you say? Don't you mean face? Old Ku, if you don't go ashore, it's because you're ashamed to show your face.'

But Father shook his head insistently. 'You're wrong, Old Sun. You really don't understand. Face is face, and dignity is dignity. I've walked a bumpy road in my days and tasted everything life has to offer – sweet, sour, bitter and hot. Face means nothing to me any more, but I've got my dignity, and I'll hold on to it, no matter what it costs. I'm not going ashore until my case is resolved!'

Seeing my father's eyes grow moist, Sun Ximing knew there was nothing more to be said. He was smart enough to leave it at that, so he turned to the next best thing to Father – me. 'Then let Dongliang go in your place. He may not be the best talker, but he's been to school. The authorities will want someone who can write, so he could prove to be of some use.'

With a quick glance at me, Father said, 'What good could he

do? He can't make things right, but he's sure to mess them up. If you want to put your trust in him, I can't be responsible. Ask him if he's willing to go.'

Seeing the hopeful look in Sun Ximing's eyes, I quickly looked away and said, 'I don't care.'

'What do you mean, you don't care?' Sun said doubtfully. 'Do you want to go or not?'

'"I don't care" means he wants to go,' Father said. 'This boy doesn't know how to give a straight answer to anything.' He reached down, took off one of his sandals and smacked me with it. 'Won't you ever change?' he complained. 'I try to bring you up right, but you refuse to do what you're supposed to. Can't you give a straight answer?'

Truth is, Father didn't understand me. All he cared about was his own dignity, not mine. The reason I was being so difficult was because I had mixed feelings. I knew that taking Huixian ashore was the right thing for the boat people to do, but I hated the idea. Winds often blew clothes that were drying on the shore into the water, where the boat people fought to scoop them out, dry them and wear them as their own. And waves often picked up logs from the lumber yard and sent them downriver, where they were pulled up out of the water and hidden in cabins. The boat people would take anything out of the water, it didn't matter what. Now that a lovable little girl had come to them, why wouldn't they keep her? I was angry at Sun and the others, but there was no way I could tell them.

So I stuck a pen into one of my pockets and followed the boat people ashore to give up the girl. She rode on Desheng's shoulders, her face covered in rouge put on by the women, in high spirits as she sucked on a sweet. I knew why she was so happy – they'd told her they were taking her ashore to find her mama.

Now that the floods had passed, much of Milltown was in ruins, with mud everywhere. Amid the dirt and filth, red flags and throngs of people lent the construction project a more exalted air than ever. The land around the piers had been opened up, rice-paddy style, although close-up it looked more like the trenches you see in war movies. There were people down in the trenches and above ground nearby. With shock-troop banners on poles dotting the ground, our delegation had trouble finding its way. One of the banners read 'Sunflower Shock Troop', which reminded me of my mother. Would she be a member of that troop? I climbed up a nearby hill to get a better look into the trenches, but didn't see her down there. A woman was reading a commendation letter over the PA system, extolling the virtues of a labourer who had passed out on his work site. Time after time, he'd lost consciousness, then got up to continue digging, only to pass out again. I listened, not to what the voice was saying, but to how it sounded. Could that be my mother? No, it was the voice of a younger woman, crisp, but lacking the emotion I'd always heard in Mother's voice. No, the PA voice belonged to someone else. A river flows thirty years to the east, then thirty years to the west. Mother's revolutionary voice had been replaced by that of an unknown younger woman.

The security group appeared out of nowhere and rushed towards our delegation, shouting, 'Stop where you are! Stop, I said! You can't come ashore!'

Xiaogai and the others blocked our way next to a stack of drainpipes. They'd been joined by a woman they called Wintersweet. She carried a truncheon like the others, but stood behind the men. She added her voice to theirs: 'Go on back, you can't come ashore.'

The confused boat people, who had been backed up against the small mountain of drainpipes, darted glances all around. 'This construction may be your business,' Sun said, 'but, as they say, well water doesn't stop the flow of river water. Why can't we come ashore?'

'What's all this well-water and river-water business?' Scabby

Five said as he grabbed Sun's sleeve. 'Sooner or later well water flows into the river. Didn't you see the signs? We're in the middle of a mass campaign, and the piers are a construction site, off limits to idlers.'

'After all we've contributed to the project, how dare you call us idlers?' Sun complained, knocking Scabby's hand away. 'We're on our way to see the authorities. How do you expect us to get there – sprout wings and fly?'

'You're nothing but a raucous crowd,' Xiaogai said. 'Why choose this time to go looking for the authorities? And what do you want to see them for?'

Before Sun had a chance to answer, Desheng said, 'To report on a new trend in class struggle. And if you won't let us come ashore, we'll see that you're made responsible for what happens.'

Xiaogai glared at Desheng, then spun around to see if there was any reaction from Sun Ximing. Sun wore an enigmatic smile that indicated he liked what he heard. Xiaogai didn't know whether to believe Desheng or not. 'What trend in class struggle could you boat people have? Have you scooped a Taiwanese secret agent's parachute out of the river or something?' His tone of voice had changed from firm to cautious. Special circumstances called for special handling. 'Come ashore if you have to, but you need to be registered. I'll want names, time of coming ashore, and time of return to your barges.'

'Whatever you say. Start with me,' said Sun Ximing. Careful not to take this too lightly, he turned to the delegation. 'Give him your names,' he said with a wave of his hand.

'I don't need you to tell me. We know all about you people.' Xiaogai looked at his watch. 'Take out your family register, Baldy,' he said. 'The following boat people came ashore at ten-forty a.m.: Sun Ximing and his wife, Gu Desheng and his wife, Six-Fingers, your name is Wang Jinliu, right? Wang Jinliu, and Ku Dongliang. Write that down.'

They missed Huixian, who was in the arms of Desheng's wife, yawning sleepily. Only the sharp-eyed Wintersweet had noticed her. She walked up to get a good look at Huixian, then sniffed her neck. 'Hold it!' she cried. 'There's a stranger among them! This little girl doesn't belong on a barge. I can tell by the smell. She doesn't stink, she's had a bath. Find out where she's from.'

Suddenly wary, Xiaogai and Scabby Five went over to get a good look at Huixian and reached the same conclusion: the girl definitely did not live on a boat. Their eyes lit up. 'Where's this little girl come from?' they said at almost the same time. 'So this is your new trend in class struggle. Where'd you snatch that kid?'

'Trust you people to resort to slander!' Sun Ximing complained. 'What good would it do us to snatch a little girl? We barely have enough to feed our own kids. What would we do with somebody else's – feed her river water?'

'Don't twist things around!' Xiaogai demanded shrilly. 'We're not interested in your stomachs. Our job is to register people. Tell me, whose child is she?'

'Now that's a question we can answer.' Sun scratched his head. 'She came aboard on her own. Her mother . . . what can I say? . . . has disappeared. We want to hand her over to the authorities.'

Scabby Five glared impatiently at Sun. 'You're in charge of this fleet, so I expect straight talk from you. What's the story with her mother? And no lies.'

That's when the girl spoke up. 'I don't know where my mama is. She's gone.'

'What do you mean, gone?' Not sure he'd heard her right, Scabby Five turned back to Sun Ximing. 'For the last time, where's her mother?'

Glancing over at the little girl, Sun swallowed noisily, determined not to say what everyone thought. As Scabby Five's anger mounted, Desheng's wife made a gesture of slapping his face. 'We all know what's in that head of yours, Scabby Five. Talking to you is like serenading a cow with a lute. We're not going to tell you, and that's that.' Now that she'd dealt with him, she turned, took Wintersweet by the arm, and whispered something to her.

Eventually the security group began to get a sense of what had happened to the girl's mother. Lacking experience in situations like this, they huddled together, three concerned men and one woman. Finally, it was Wintersweet who took charge. 'This girl,' she announced, 'is a mystery child.'

Baldy Chen took out his register. 'Should we record her name?' he asked Xiaogai, unsure what to do.

Xiaogai took the book and read out the instructions on the back cover. 'Here it is,' he said. 'Item eight. "Pre-school children need not be entered."' Everyone breathed a sigh of relief.

But Wintersweet wasn't satisfied. She bent down and asked Huixian, 'Have you started school, little girl?'

Ignoring the frantic head-shaking from the delegation, she announced proudly, 'Yes, I have. I know how to write, but I lost my blackboard.'

'That means she's not pre-school,' Baldy Chen said with a frown. 'She's old enough to register.'

Wintersweet took the register from Baldy, pointed to the words on the cover and said to Huixian, 'I know you're a smart little girl. Tell Aunty which of these words you can read.'

Huixian leaned closer and confidently studied the red printed words. Recognizing the words 'people', 'coming', and 'ashore', she read them aloud. 'What does that mean?' she asked.

Her question went unanswered. A simple enough question, its answer was significant. Regardless of how cute and bright she might have been, she was still one of the 'people coming ashore', and had to be registered as such.

The security group and boat people crowded around Huixian, combining all their efforts to help record the girl's information. It was hard work.

'What's your name?'

'Huixian.'

'Your family name?'

She muttered something in a child-like stammer, impossible to understand.

'Is it Zhang, written like this or this?' Baldy asked her. 'Or maybe it's Qiang, like in rifle. Which one is it?'

'I'm not a rifle, *you* are. I'll write it for you.' She squatted down, picked up a lump of coal and wrote her name on the ground. It was Jiang.

'Ah!' those who could read exclaimed. 'Her name is Jiang.'

'Do you remember your date of birth, little comrade?'

'What's that?'

'You don't understand. OK, how old are you? That way we'll know the year you were born.'

'I'm nine. I was eight last year, and I'll be ten next year.'

'I know you're a smart little girl, but you don't need to tell us all that. You're nine, that's enough. Do you know your parents' names? What do they do for a living?'

'My father's name is Jiang Yongsheng, my mother's name is Cui Xia. But they're gone.'

'How'd that happen? Where'd your father go?'

'My mother said he was accused of something he didn't do and some bad people dragged him out of his office.'

'Bad people? Who were the bad people who took him away? And where did they take him?'

'I don't know. Mother said she'd take me to see him, some place with a steel fence and soldiers. But I didn't get to see him, and the soldiers said he's missing. Now my mama's missing too. Have you seen her?'

Everyone who heard her tensed. Not everything she said sounded believable, but they couldn't dismiss it out of hand. The boat people, always alert to such things, assumed that the girl's father had been locked up, either as a criminal or as a counter-revolutionary. Desheng's wife whispered to him, 'I'm telling you, don't let them register her. Nothing good can come of it. Look at their faces. You'd think they'd captured one of Chiang Kai-shek's agents.'

The security group exchanged knowing looks. 'Write down what she said,' Xiaogai said to Baldy. 'All of it, every word.'

Baldy nodded. 'I've got it all, every word.'

Wintersweet took a long, proud look at her colleagues. 'I told you there's a problem with this girl, didn't I?' Her eyes flashed. But then she breathed a sorrowful sigh. 'Too bad it turns out to be a little girl.'

The comment deflated Baldy Chen, who had been writing furiously. 'Are we going to let her come ashore,' he asked Xiaogai, 'with a blot on her record?'

Xiaogai wasn't sure. He looked at the girl, then turned to Baldy. 'Go ahead, register her,' he said as he scratched his head. 'That's what the regulations say.'

The boat people were all talking at once, voicing their doubts about the whole process, as the questioning recommenced. Baldy Chen cleared his throat and, trying his best to sound agreeable, said, 'Don't listen to them, little girl. Pay attention to my questions and you'll be fine. Just be sure to give me straight answers. Now I want you to tell me your address. What is your address? You don't understand that? All right, where's your home?'

'By the railroad tracks. Upstairs. There's a peach tree in the yard. Lots of peaches.'

'That's not an address. An address means the city or town or district or county, things like that. What's the district called? What street? Which commune or production brigade?'

'None of those. There's a rubbish dump at the end of a gravel road in front of our house. My mother goes there every day to dump rubbish.'

'You say your mama dumps rubbish every day?' Baldy's eyes flashed. He clicked his tongue. 'Tell your uncle what's in the rubbish.'

Sun Ximing had heard enough. He rushed up and knocked the register out of Baldy Chen's hand. 'What's in the rubbish! Landlord restoration records, radio transmitters, counter-revolutionary handbills? What the hell kind of security guard are you? What do you expect from a little girl like that? What harm can come of letting her come ashore? You should be ashamed of yourselves, treating her like a class enemy.'

Other members of the delegation expressed their opinions in much more colourful language. Desheng's wife walked up and pulled Huixian into her arms. 'How dare you treat her like that! Don't let them register you. Whatever they ask, just ignore them.'

Desheng and Six-Fingers Wang rolled up their sleeves and placed themselves in front of Desheng's wife and Huixian, shoving Xiaogai and Scabby Five aside. Scabby swung his truncheon and hit Six-Fingers in the face. 'You rotten boat people!' he shouted. 'This is a rebellion!'

I was standing some way off, since I never liked sticking my nose in other people's business. But for some unknown reason, I felt compelled to get involved in what was happening with the girl. The crowd pushed Huixian towards me. She was screaming, frightened and not knowing who to turn to. She reached out to me, and the sight of her little hand seeking help made my blood boil. I grabbed it, pulled her out of the crowd and shouted, 'Run! Run, everybody!'

Running, that was something I'd become good at. Knowing the lie of the land around the piers as well as anyone, I had our escape route mapped out. We'd skirt the mountain of coal and head for the cotton warehouse, which would take us out of Xiaogai's sphere of authority. I hadn't run far with Huixian in tow when I turned to see quite a scene behind us. The delegation had formed a human wall to keep the security group from following us. Scabby Five was swinging his truncheon and Baldy Chen was following his lead, both aiming at the heads of the boat people. Hand-to-hand combat ensued, a wild mêlée of clubs and fists; even the wives of Desheng and Sun Ximing joined the battle. Someone, I couldn't see who, kicked Baldy in the balls, and I watched him jump and run around in obvious pain, screams bursting from his open mouth. Then Xiaogai blew on his whistle – jerky, panicky. 'It's a riot!' he shouted. 'A riot! A counter-revolutionary riot! Go and report this to Secretary Zhao, and do it now!'

By now Huixian and I had reached the foot of the mountain of coal. Scared by what was happening behind us, she asked me, 'Why are they fighting?'

'They're fighting over you, you dope.'

She still didn't get it. 'I never asked them to fight. Fighting's no good, it breaks down discipline.'

I was in no mood to explain things to her. I started up the mountain of coal, but she refused to let me pull her along. 'Why do we have to go up that? All that black coal will get my clothes dirty.' She was too young to appreciate what was going on. Angry and increasingly anxious, I hoisted her up on to my back and started climbing. She fought me at first with her fists and feet, but when she began pretending she was on horseback her excitement led to whoops of joy. She smacked me on my backside. 'Giddy up!' she shouted. 'Giddy up!'

With Huixian still on my back, I made it to the cotton warehouse, as the sound of an avalanche erupted behind me. The boat people were cheering me on, like a revolutionary phalanx, as they clambered proudly down the mountain of coal. Wintersweet's shrill voice carried on the wind from the other side: 'Go ahead, run! Don't think we won't settle the score sooner or later! You can run from the monk, but not from the temple!'

We reassembled at the entrance to the cotton warehouse. Six-Fingers's face was scratched, Sun Ximing's wife used a handkerchief to cover her chest where her shirt was ripped. The delegation had suffered some minor losses, but everyone looked triumphant. They were excited over their easy victory.

The workers inside were understandably unnerved by the tumult at the warehouse entrance; when the iron gate swung open with a clang, two women stepped outside, one middle-aged, the other quite young. They eyed the crowd cautiously. 'What are you people doing here?' one of them asked. 'Are you planning to steal coal, or maybe cotton? You can do what you want with the coal, but if you try to steal our cotton, we'll call the police.'

'How dare you!' Sun Ximing's wife protested. 'Do we look like thieves?'

'Thieves don't paint the word on their foreheads,' the middle-aged woman said enigmatically. 'What difference does it make what you look like?'

'We're not going to argue with you,' the younger woman said as she pointed to the warehouse wall. 'Read that if you can. "STRATEGIC WAREHOUSE: FIRES FORBIDDEN. THEFTS WILL BE PUNISHED!"'

'You have no right to treat us this way,' Desheng's wife said. 'What we're doing has nothing to do with you. I'd have thought you'd have your hands full taking care of the cotton, so leave us alone!'

'You can do your business somewhere else.' The middle-aged woman's eyes swept the crowd, filled with hostility. When she spotted the scratches on Six-Fingers's face, she clicked her tongue. 'Where did you people come from, and how did you get those injuries?'

Embarrassed by the comment, Six-Fingers glared at her and cursed angrily, 'You filthy cunt, I'll thump the life out of you!'

The woman obviously knew what the word 'cunt' meant, and

understood what it was to thump somebody. She rolled her eyes at Six-Fingers and shoved the younger woman back into the warehouse, saying, 'This is none of our business. If they're not gone in two minutes, call the police.'

Her threat had the desired effect, since the delegation moved away docilely, though not without plenty of grumbling. Their timidity was understandable, given their fear of the police. Taking Huixian by the hand, Desheng's wife started heading back to explain things to the women, but was stopped by Sun Ximing. 'We're here to make arrangements for the girl,' he announced with a wave of his hand, 'so forget them. We'll find another spot. Don't tell me there's no place for us to talk things over anywhere in Milltown.'

That sounded good, but there really wasn't any place for us in the town, we knew that. So the discussion resumed as we walked, and in the end, Sun's suggestion carried the day. Rather than go to the Women's Federation, the Civil Administration or the Family Planning Commission, we'd take the child straight to Zhao Chuntang.

The General Affairs Building was at the far northern end of the piers, and we kept running into restricted areas with signs that read, 'DEAD END' and 'DETOUR'. We skirted the construction area by the piers until, with considerable difficulty, we found ourselves in front of the white, four-storey building. I can't say what kind of deterrent power it had, but the moment the boat people arrived at the steps of the building, a sense of fear gripped them; there was no grumbling and no talking, just wide-eyed looks and unconscious backing away.

Desheng's wife managed to remain unflappable. 'I'll bet Xiaogai and his bunch are in there,' she said to Sun Ximing. 'They probably ran over to report us.'

Sun lit a cigarette and took several deep drags. 'We've sustained injuries,' he said at last, 'so let them make their report. We have the girl to worry about, and nothing's going to keep us from doing what we came to do.' He looked first at Huixian, then at me, and finally pointed to the building with his cigarette. 'Dongliang,' he said, 'you grew up around this building, so you must know it well. Go in and have a look around, all right?'

I jumped at the chance. But in order to avoid getting held up by Gimpy Gu in the reception area, I told Sun Ximing and the others to wait by the gate while I circled round and entered through a ground-floor toilet window.

I'd been in every office in the building, and knew them all well. I immediately ran upstairs to the fourth floor, only to discover that we'd chosen a bad day to come, since all the officials were out on their weekly voluntary-work day. The doors were locked, and by rights I should have gone back downstairs to tell the others. But, inexplicably, I forgot what I was there to do and stopped in front of Zhao Chuntang's door. It had once been my father's office. A sign that read 'IDLERS KEEP OUT', in my father's hand, had once decorated the familiar glass door, and I'd become so used to seeing it that I'd ignored it. A sign saying the same thing was still there, but now in Zhao Chuntang's hand, and the familiar words disgusted me. I pushed the door, but it didn't open. The lock jangled. *Keep out! Keep out!* The sound of those words rattling around in my head ignited a destructive desire.

'Fuck you and your keep outs! Change those words, change them or else!' Hanging on the wall was a blackboard with an emergency announcement, ordering all officials to go down to the construction site for manual labour. I picked up a piece of chalk, wiped out the words 'KEEP OUT' on the sign and replaced them with 'PLEASE ENTER'. That took the edge off my indignation, but I was still far from being satisfied or mollified. The image of those profound words scrawled on the wall of the public toilet on People's Avenue came to mind. I still wasn't sure what they meant. I couldn't get my head around the 'alien' accusation, but

I was sure it was a condemnation of Zhao Chuntang. So, chalk in hand, I scribbled the words 'ZHAO CHUNTANG IS AN ALIEN CLASS ELEMENT' on the fourth-floor corridor wall.

I threw down the chalk and ran to the second floor, where I stopped to calm myself down, just as a commotion broke out downstairs. Gimpy Gu had come out of his room and hobbled towards the delegation, railing at them, 'Don't you boat people know anything? These are critical times, and you're not helping things by bringing in a stray kid. There's nobody here to take her from you. All the officials are down at the construction site.'

Wouldn't you know it, on my way downstairs Gimpy Gu stopped me. 'What are you up to? Why were you upstairs when everybody else is downstairs? What were you doing up there?'

I ignored him and waved to the delegation. 'It's the day they do their voluntary work,' I said. 'Let's go down to the construction site.'

Stung by Gimpy Gu's criticism, the boat people turned and left the General Affairs Building, grumbling about their treatment. Desheng's wife handed Huixian to her husband and told him to hold her up in the air so the people at the piers could see her. 'That way they'll know we're coming to turn her in, not to make trouble.'

'She's high enough already,' said Desheng, who had the girl on his shoulders. 'They can't see her, anyway, since they're all working. They're not paying us any attention.'

'Isn't it strange,' Desheng's wife complained, 'how many officials are out there worrying about land and cement, and how many more are concerned with all those tools, but there's no one to give a damn about this little girl?'

I knew that the best way to find someone in authority in that crowd of workers was to look for a red flag. I saw one that said 'PUBLIC SERVANT SHOCK TROOPS', and that is where I headed, along with Sun Ximing and the others, only to find that Xiaogai had got there ahead of us. He was resting on his haunches under the flag, register in hand, and reading from it to someone down in the trench. Reporting on us. We looked down to see who it was. As I guessed, it was Zhao Chuntang. He was wearing a hard hat and knee-high rubber boots and had a whistle around his neck as he supervised the work group digging the trench.

One of the women in our group leaned over and shouted, 'Secretary Zhao, this girl turned up at our fleet, so we're bringing her to you!'

Xiaogai jumped up and pointed angrily at her. 'You've got a nerve coming here to cause trouble! Who kicked Baldy in the balls? They're all swollen, and if he suffers a permanent injury, you'll pay. I've told Secretary Zhao how you came ashore to cause trouble on the pretext of bringing over a child. There's a new trend in class struggle, you know!'

Everyone began talking at once, insisting they hadn't attacked Baldy Chen. Six-Fingers stepped up to the edge of the trench. 'Don't listen to him. Look at my face. See how puffy it is? Who did that? Scabby Five did it. Bringing the child ashore is part of the new trend in class struggle, but can you say the same about a security group that uses its truncheons on the heads of the revolutionary masses?'

Everyone on the ground and in the trench turned to look at Zhao and see his reaction. I watched as he waved three times. The first wave was a more or less polite sign to the people to move on. But the delegation stood its ground. There was an angry edge to the second wave, implying that they were ill informed and were interfering with the work under way. Still they stayed put.

'Don't listen to Wang Xiaogai's false accusations,' Desheng's wife said. 'We're not worthy of any new trend, and we're not here to make trouble. We brought this little girl ashore, a living, breathing child we can't abandon and we can't keep. How can we go home before the authorities have taken responsibility for her?'

At that Zhao Chuntang stuck his shovel in the mud and had a hushed discussion with an official named Four-Eyes Zhang. Then he turned back and waved for the third time, a gesture we found a bit strange. 'Come down here, Sun Ximing,' Four-Eyes explained. 'We want to talk to you.'

Sun was about to take the little girl down into the trench, but one of the women snatched her out of his hands. 'You go on down if you want to,' she said, 'but she stays here.'

'Quieten down, you women,' Four-Eyes said, 'and keep out of this. Bring the girl down and let Secretary Zhao see her before he decides what to do.'

So Sun Ximing took Huixian by the hand to go down into the trench, but she baulked at the sight of it. 'It's muddy down there,' she said. 'My clothes will get dirty.'

'Those people are all officials,' Sun said to reassure her. 'They're rich and powerful, so you don't have to worry if you get dirty. They'll buy you some new clothes.'

So she went down and, with a pout, sized up the people around her. Suddenly her eyes lit up and she ran to Leng Qiuyun, Director of the local Women's Federation. 'Mama!' she shouted. 'Mama!' Everyone froze and stared at the happy little girl. Director Leng, momentarily stunned, threw down her tool and stepped aside just as Huixian stopped, realizing her mistake, and, with disappointment in her eyes, looked up at us. Then she turned back to Director Leng. 'Where's my mother?' she said. 'You people tricked me!' She stamped her foot in anger. 'She isn't here, and she isn't there. I want you to tell me where my mama is!'

The officials all laid down their tools and gaped curiously at Huixian, especially Director Leng, who had regained her composure and took Huixian by the hand. She clicked her tongue. 'My,' she exclaimed, 'what a pretty little girl, and so clever. I'd love it if you were my little girl.'

Zhao Chuntang rested his foot on the blade of his shovel,

pushing it in deeper and deeper. He looked at Huixian closely, like a post-office clerk examining a misaddressed package. Finally he laughed softly, reached out and grabbed her pigtail. 'Where'd you come from, little girl?'

Huixian stared at the three pens in the pocket of his tunic and counted out loud, 'One, two, three,' bringing smiles to the adults' faces.

'She's a lovable little thing,' someone said. 'See, even Secretary Zhao likes her.'

Sun Ximing pushed Huixian's finger down. 'Stop counting and say something,' he urged her. 'Call him Secretary Zhao.'

Huixian hesitated for a moment. 'Uncle Zhao,' she said.

People rushed to correct her: 'Not Uncle Zhao, Secretary Zhao.' But Zhao waved them off. 'She's just a child,' he said. 'Why not Uncle Zhao? Like any good girl, she hasn't learned the art of flattery.' That quietened the people, who waited to see what Secretary Zhao would do next. Not much, it seemed, since he casually tossed a shovelful of dirt out of the trench. Seeing their leader go back to work, the other officials did the same, leaving no room for Sun Ximing and Huixian to stand.

Pulling the girl to one side, Sun said, 'What are you going to do, Secretary Zhao? Where should we take her?'

With a display of indifference, Zhao cast a glance at Sun and said, 'She's a clever little thing. And so cute. Where were you planning to take her? I think whoever wants a little girl aboard should have her.'

That was worse than doing nothing at all. Sun cast a pleading look at the people up on the ground. 'You can't just kick the ball to somebody else, Secretary Zhao,' Six-Fingers said. 'Raising a child isn't like keeping a dog or a cat. She needs to be fed and she needs registering with a household.'

But it was Desheng's wife who came up with the cleverest response. 'We can take her on board and make things easy for the leadership, but not the way you say. If we do it your way, she'll be a blacklisted element, which isn't fair. People will assume we took her from someone, and that isn't fair either. What we need is for you to come up with a fair arrangement and give it to us in writing.'

Zhao Chuntang threw down his shovel with a sneer, his face darkening. He walked up to Sun Ximing, obviously wanting nothing more to do with us, and Sun was his chosen target. 'Sun Ximing, do you know why you've never been accepted into the Party? It's because you've got a pig brain. What kind of leadership have you given to your fleet, a bunch of undisciplined backsliders who have no political consciousness or cultivation? You want me to arrange things and put them in writing when I'm so busy I can't even catch my breath? You want me to make arrangements for the child, but my superiors want me to advance East Wind No. 8. I ask you, which is more important? You tell me. Put it in writing, you say. What leadership role do you play? County Party Committee, local Party Committee? Or maybe the Central Committee in Beijing!'

What could Sun say? The delegation was no help at all. One of the officials came up to Zhao Chuntang to defuse the situation, while another railed at the people above them. 'What kind of political consciousness is this? What qualities are you displaying? Don't you have any idea what times these are? A mass campaign will begin any day now, and you're only making things worse with the issue of this child.'

'We're not here to cause trouble,' Desheng's wife said timidly. 'She's just a little girl. With all you officials down there, you'd think that one of you could come up and make things right for her. Isn't a little girl as important as a shovel?'

Zhao gave Desheng's wife a withering look. 'You're quite a talker,' he said, 'but you listen to me. During these critical times, everything must take a back seat to East Wind No. 8, and that includes this little girl. One shovelful of dirt is more important than any single child!'

Zhao had made his decision, and all we could do was exchange troubled looks. Answering back was out of the question, and no one knew what to do. We could only stand there and watch Sun unwillingly lift the girl out of the trench. Back above ground, he turned and cast a hard look down at the officials, who were engaged in whispered conversations. Four-Eyes Zhang muttered something to Zhao Chuntang before saying, with a wave of his hand, 'Go on, get out of here!' That got Sun Ximing's dander up; he was in no mood to leave. He'd rather wait.

Finally Zhao spoke again. 'Sun Ximing, go and see Director Yao at the grain distribution station and get five *jin* of rice. Then you and the others can take the child back to your barges. We can hang her out there for the time being, and work out something more permanent when we're not so busy.'

Sun froze, his face turning red. 'Five *jin* of rice? What do you take us for, Secretary Zhao, beggars?' His bull-headed nature took over, sparked by disappointment and fierce opposition. 'Hang her out?' he shouted down into the trench. 'What does that mean? A little girl can't be that much trouble. If the authorities won't take care of her, we will! And you can feed your chickens with those five *jin* of rice! We don't need your *generosity*! The eleven barges of the Sunnyside Fleet can manage to look after one little girl!'

The Lottery

I F THIS were a literary narrative, I'd have to admit that the open-ing bears some resemblance to a farce, albeit one that can only sadden the reader. The Sunnyside Fleet had sent a delegation ashore, who were forced to take the long way round, with all its twists and turns, just so that they could talk till they were blue in the face; in the end, curses and flying fists accomplished nothing, and my pen proved useless. Even by pulling together, we had no luck in finding a taker for the little girl. Desheng hoisted her up on his shoulders again and returned wearily to the boats.

At the time, I recall, Six-Fingers Wang's daughters were rinsing out sweaters on the riverbank, and when they spotted Huixian riding high upon Desheng's shoulders, they left their work and rushed up to greet us. 'Dad,' they said to Six-Fingers, 'we thought you were going to leave her there. Why are you bringing her back?'

Six-Fingers covered his face with his hands so his daughters could not see his pained look. Then he growled a response: 'Leave her where? Nowhere! No one was willing to take her, so she's been "hung out" here with the fleet!'

Having grown up in and around the General Affairs Building, I'd heard Father use the term 'hung out' and knew that it implied danger. It was often used as a way to deal with a problem, usually associated with leading officials. So-and-so has been 'hung out', they'd say, meaning that that individual's future looked bleak. But hanging out a little girl made no sense. I couldn't tell if it was a prudent use of the word or a means of avoiding responsibility.

Huixian's status improved upon her return, and the boat people's attitude towards her underwent a modest change. Now that she'd been hung out with the Sunnyside Fleet, we assumed a new responsibility, though there was no talk of whose responsibility it would be.

Huixian also changed. Taken ashore twice, only to be returned each time, she must have known she'd been rejected by the people there, that she wasn't welcome, and that her fate rested with the fleet. She proved to be quick and very smart, realizing that the barge people expected her to do as they asked, so she smoothed out the rough edges of her attitude overnight, abandoning her wilful behaviour. On the afternoon she returned from town I saw that she had wound a silk thread around her fingers as she stood on the bow of barge number one, looking for someone to play a game with. Spotting Yingtao, she crossed to her barge and said, 'Big Sister, would you like me to teach you how to do cat's cradle?'

The unexpected invitation bowled Yingtao over, and after a couple of bashful sways of her hips, she thrust her arms out and the two girls began playing cat's cradle. Yingtao's brother, Dayong, made his way up to them and watched with a foolish grin as the thread changed patterns in their hands, their fingers twisting around it. 'Go away!' Yingtao yelled. 'This is a girls' game. What are you gawking at?' When he refused to leave, she complained to her mother, who dragged him away, then walked back thoughtfully to get a good look at Huixian's face. In a not altogether playful tone, she spoke out about her son's marital prospects. 'You know our son Dayong likes you,' she said, 'so why don't you stay on our barge? That way you can marry him one day. See how big and strong he is? Full of energy.'

Huixian looked first at Yingtao's mother, then at Dayong, and shook her head. 'Lots of people like me,' she said. 'How can I marry them all? No. I say no.'

'I don't mean you have to marry everybody. One girl and one boy. You marry the one who likes you better than most.' Yingtao's mother smothered a giggle. 'Ours is a fine boat, with better conditions than most, and one day it, and everything on it, could be yours.'

With a quick glance at the cabin hatch, Huixian said, 'You don't have a sofa, so how can you call it fine? I'm not going to be his or anybody's wife. I belong on the shore. I won't be here more than a few days.'

'There's only a piece of wood separating the boat from the shore, so what's the difference? You don't think you're better than boat people, do you? Ours is a hard life, and simple, and, like life on shore, is part of the socialist system. The rich bourgeoisie and old bosses were wiped out long ago. No one likes a snob. Who knows when or if you'll be back on shore. Didn't you hear the man say you're being hung out here? Maybe that'll last until the year of the monkey or the month of the horse.[1] It's up to you to choose the best boat to be hung out on.'

With a little grimace, Huixian said, 'I'm not a shirt, you know. How am I supposed to be hung out? I won't hang out on any boat. They put me down in their book as lost, so they'll have to broadcast my name and put up posters. If I can't find my mama, she'll have to find me.'

'They could broadcast a hundred times,' said Dayong, who'd reappeared at some point, 'and it wouldn't make any difference. Your mother's a drowned ghost, and if one of those finds you,

---

[1]There are no such things.

you're in big trouble.' He added fearsomely, 'If your mother finds you, then you'll be a drowned ghost too, with moss growing all over your body.'

All ten of Huixian's fingers, which had been swirling in the air, stopped moving. She knew exactly what Dayong was talking about. Her eyes wide with fear, she stared at him. Dayong's mother knew that this time he'd gone too far. 'Don't say things like that, Dayong,' she said, pushing him towards the cabin.

But not in time. Twirling the ball of silk thread over her head, Huixian stormed after the boy. 'Who are you calling a drowned ghost? *You're* a drowned ghost! With moss growing all over *your* body!' She flayed him with her silk thread as she raged on. Each scream was shriller and angrier than the one before. She was nearly hysterical. The strange thing was, she'd learned how to swear like a boat person, her curses aimed at the whole family: 'I'll thump, I'll thump you, I'll thump your mother, I'll thump everybody in your family!'

Hearing the commotion, Sun Ximing's wife ran up breathlessly and went to Huixian's aid. 'I tell you, that son of yours may not know right from wrong,' she said, pointing at Dayong's mother, 'but what about you? The heavens will deal with anyone who torments this child.'

'What kind of talk is that?' Yingtao's mother rejoined. 'You have no idea what's going on here! My son didn't torment her, she hit him, and he didn't hit back. She's no dummy. Were you listening when she called everyone in our family a drowned ghost? Or when she cursed us with filthy language? The little tramp said she's going to thump us all!'

Sun's wife rolled her eyes at Yingtao's mother and her children. 'Forget it!' she said angrily with a wave of her hands. 'Just let it go. Talking to you people is a waste of time.' Taking Huixian by the hand, she returned to barge number one. 'I told you not to go on to any of these barges just because of how they look,' she said.

'There are good barges, and there are those that just look good. Stay away from the bad ones.'

Yingtao's mother, enraged by these comments, ran after Sun's wife. 'You filthy-mouthed woman,' she bellowed. 'What do you mean by good and bad barges? How dare you put stupid thoughts like that in the head of a little girl! Does she belong to you, just because she spent one night on your barge? That's where she learned all those bad things. Why don't you take a good look at yourself? Your body odour could suffocate a person and you can barely spell three words. What makes you think you'd be a good mama to her?'

Sun Ximing's wife turned back to look at her. 'I may not be able to spell three words, but how many can you spell? And maybe I'm not qualified to be her mama, but you couldn't even be her amah. Don't think I don't know how you and your old man were assigned to this fleet. If the authorities hadn't decided to be lenient, you two—' Her harangue was cut short by a flying broom that struck her on the leg. 'Ouch!' She spun around to see who had thrown it. It was Yingtao, who stood with her hands on her hips, glaring at Sun's wife and at Huixian. This time, Sun's wife knew, she'd gone too far. After kicking the broom into the river, she took Huixian's hand and said, 'Let's go home.'

After she had thrown the broom, Yingtao ran to her mother, whose hands were pressed to her chest, her face a ghostly white; she finally managed to exhale. Aiming a mouthful of spit at the spot where the other woman had stood, she railed, 'Even your underarms don't stink as much as your mouth. Damn you! You've got a nerve, talking about my family like that. Everybody knows the scandalous history of your husband and your little sister, who got an abortion after she began to show. So who do you think you are – a big shot just because your husband muddled his way into the job of fleet commander? I tell you, there's plenty of dirt to go around on the eleven barges of this fleet, but you'll never find ours at the bottom of the heap. If I hear any more rubbish from you, I'll tear your lips off!'

I wasn't shocked by what I was hearing, but it was unexpected. Such matters had always gone unspoken aboard the boats. I'd heard that all the fleet families had stained records, but no one talked about them, even during violent arguments. It was a matter of principle. But with the arrival of Huixian, strange things had begun to happen, and a climate of anxiety now dominated our peaceful lives. Insults flew. I hated squabbles among the boat women. But that day was different, because they were arguing over Huixian. No one had any inkling about my feelings towards her, a protective urge that surprised even me, and that grew stronger every day. I'd experienced a secret torment when we'd taken her ashore, but now, miraculously, she was going to stay with us. And yet that miracle filled me with apprehension. The argument between the two women had resolved nothing. Given the blotted history of all eleven families, which barge should she make her home? Who was good enough to be her mama? I mulled the question over, but couldn't come up with an answer. The world of barges was just too small. Yingtao's mother was certainly not worthy of being her new mother. Sun Ximing's wife treated her well and was, at heart, a good woman. But she was illiterate and had terrible body odour that would create a bad environment for Huixian's daily life. I thought about my own mother, and how she'd often sighed over how good her life would have been if I'd been a daughter instead of a son. She was educated, cleanliness was important to her, and she cared about how she looked; she'd have been a good mother for Huixian. Unfortunately, she'd never get the chance. So who was the best candidate? If I had to select a general among all the pygmies, I guess it would have to be Desheng's wife, though there was talk that she'd abandoned the man she'd just married to run off with Desheng and join him on the barge. But she was the only woman in the fleet who brushed her teeth every day. She was clean, she was smart, and she had a way with words. Some people said that she and her husband lacked the necessary experience, since they had no children of their own, but to my way of thinking that was a virtue. They were the only ones who would treat Huixian as their own daughter.

Desheng and his wife, who were standing on the bow of their ship, had heard the argument. Desheng's wife was partial to Sun's wife, while he found them both equally disagreeable. 'Raising hell like that is stupid,' he said. 'Those shrews won't say what they ought to be saying, and let fly with things that should never be said. Neither of them is worthy of being the girl's mother. If she stayed with them, she'd grow up to be a shrew just like them.'

'What the hell,' I said to Desheng. 'Why don't you take her?'

He and his wife exchanged a hurried glance. 'We like the little girl, we really do,' she said. 'But she was turned over to the fleet, so we should all meet to discuss how best to take care of her.'

'That's not your decision,' Desheng said, cutting his wife off. 'The principle here is democratic centralism, with democracy coming first. We're going to have to draw lots.'

That evening, Sun Ximing's second son, Erfu, ran from boat to boat, notifying people that they would all be drawing lots. 'Each boat must send a representative to barge number one!' he cried at the top of his lungs. 'Everybody must participate.'

When Father heard Erfu's shouts he asked, 'What are we drawing lots for?'

'For the girl,' I told him. 'For Huixian.'

'Ridiculous!' he exclaimed. 'They can't do that!'

'Will we send a representative?'

He paused. 'I guess so, since it's a collective matter. We can't shirk our duty. But they have to know where we stand. If our lot is drawn, they'll have to draw again. You go.'

It didn't take long for the representatives to gather on Sun's boat. Many of them could not sit still, they were so nervous. The reasons varied. Desheng was afraid he wouldn't be lucky enough to draw the winning lot. For Six-Fingers Wang it was the opposite. He tried to steel himself against the possibility that he'd actually be too lucky. 'We already have too many children for our ration of food,' he said. 'If the girl came to us, she'd have to eat from a communal supply.'

Sun Ximing's wife rebuffed this selfish remark. 'You needn't worry that she'd put you in the poor house. Taking care of the girl is a joint responsibility, no matter who she winds up with.'

After cutting a hole in a shoebox lid, Sun wrapped the box in a red cloth. Then he placed it on the bow and stuck in his hand to draw the first lot. After fishing around for a few seconds he pulled out a white slip. With disappointment in his eyes, he turned to his wife. 'I told you to do it, but you said no. Women are luckier than men. You should have drawn it.'

Everyone from barge number one to number six drew out a white slip. Now it was my turn. 'Is number seven supposed to participate?' someone asked. 'What happens if Dongliang draws the winning lot? We can't turn the girl over to him and his dad. They don't know how to bring up a child.'

Disgusted by their attitude, I said, 'What makes you think we can't? I'm drawing, whether you want me to or not.'

Sun's wife stepped up to smooth things over. 'Dongliang,' she said, 'don't bite the hand that feeds you. We're only thinking of what's best for you.'

'Will it count if I draw the winning lot?' I asked.

Placed in an awkward situation, she stared at the box. 'What are the chances, anyway?' she remarked. 'Go ahead, give it a try, since you're here.'

I rolled up my sleeves and thrust my hand into the box. You can guess what happened. To everyone's astonishment, I pulled out a coloured slip with a drawing of a little girl with dark eyes and pigtails tied up with big ribbons. It was signed in a juvenile scrawl: 'Huixian.' I'd won.

I held it high and stared at Sun Ximing. 'Well?' I said excitedly. 'I got it. Now what?'

There was a long moment of silence before someone shouted out, 'No deal! Put it back and let the rest of us draw.'

'Put it back? What kind of lottery is that? I won't do it.'

Everyone stared at me, wondering if I meant what I said. 'You're not serious, Dongliang, are you? Keeping it means you have to take her back to your boat. Is that really what you want?'

I didn't know what to say. For some reason my face felt burning hot. Still holding the slip up in the air, I didn't want to give in, but lacked the courage to proceed. Then I heard some of the women laugh strangely, while the men made their opinions known in a confusion of noise.

Covering his ears with his hands, Sun bellowed, 'Stop the bickering! You're giving me a headache.' Then he looked at me. 'Dongliang,' he said warily, 'why don't you put that back in and draw again.' He made as if to take the slip from me, but I pushed his hand away. He stumbled backward, clearly embarrassed. 'Dongliang,' he said angrily, 'you're holding on to that like it was ten goddamn yuan. This is not something to be taken lightly. In case you haven't noticed, the masses are opposed to your keeping this slip. Besides, the girl deserves a chance to say if she wants to live on your boat.'

So now it was up to Huixian. I recall that she was playing cat's cradle with Xiaofu the whole time. She twirled the thread in her hands, forming beautiful, complicated shapes in the air. 'I don't care,' she announced. 'It makes no difference to me.' The nonchalant manner in which she said it belied her young age, and everyone stopped, even me. I hadn't expected that.

Sun Ximing's wife was the first to gather her wits about

her. 'That's no answer, my little ancestor,' she said. 'This is too important for you to say you don't care.'

Then Desheng's wife sidled up to her, anxiously hoping the girl would prefer her. She held a finger up to her face and rolled her eyes as a sign to the girl. Then I heard Yingtao's mother gloat sarcastically, sensing an opportunity to provoke Sun's wife. 'Now can you tell which boat is a good one,' she pressed her, 'and which one is bad? You thought the girl liked you best because you have a good boat. Well, she doesn't think so, and that makes your boat a bad one.'

A hue and cry erupted on barge number one. The lines were drawn between them and me, and I stood there, half muddle-headed and half alert. I felt a deep sense of gratitude towards the girl, since, sofa or not, she seemed to be the only person in the world who actually liked the people who lived on number seven – the only one. Noting my hesitation, the others began whispering among themselves, trying to figure out what to do.

Sun's wife decided to up the ante. 'If you won't draw a second lot, then go ahead, take her with you. You'll be responsible for bringing her up – food, clothing, hygiene, everything. We'll see how you and your father handle that.'

'Dongliang,' Desheng said, 'this is a time for cool heads. You know how to play chess, don't you? Well, once you move a piece you can't take it back, and if you lose a game you have only your-self to blame.'

As for sly old Six-Fingers Wang, he gave me a friendly slap on the shoulder and said something that was totally out of place: 'I don't know what you have in mind, but it is too soon to take the girl over to your boat. Wait another ten years or so, and we'll happily give our approval.'

People laughed. I pushed Six-Fingers's hand away and waved my slip in the air. 'I drew it, it's mine. Who cares if you approve or not? I'm going to take her with me.' I reached for Huixian's hand and said – commanded, actually – 'Come on, we're going to our boat.'

Huixian, who was by then standing in front of me, put both hands behind her back, but there was a smile on her face, and I knew she was egging me on. It wasn't an overt look of encouragement, but it betrayed a sense of reservation and caution. Then her foot moved towards me, and that told me what was in her heart. She wanted me to take her to number seven.

'Let's go, off to number seven, to the sofa!' I said. It was another command, and this time she obeyed me. She scooted over to the deck and the women knew she'd made up her mind; there was nothing they could do about it now. I watched as she flew across the gangplank like a bird freed from a cage, while the people behind us could only gape at our perfect harmony. Some of them snapped out of it and ran up in surprise. 'Don't go, Huixian! You mustn't go to number seven!'

I turned and shouted, 'Why not? What's wrong with number seven, tell me that!'

By now they'd lined up behind me, tall and short, edgy and fearful. My shout had hit them like a blast of cold air, rendering them speechless. Why not? They didn't have an answer. Desheng was more familiar with our boat than the others were, and for that reason he was relatively calm. 'Don't go after them,' he said. 'Dongliang's just a boy, it's not his boat. It's Secretary Ku's. You can believe me or not, but hear me out. Old Ku is not about to take this girl aboard his boat.'

He was, unfortunately, right. Huixian ran to the stern of number six, but that was as far as she got. For the first time in ages, my father, who had heard the commotion, was standing on our bow, bent at the waist and smiling at her. But it was a strange, forced smile that frightened her so badly she didn't know what to do.

'Little comrade,' he said, 'do as they say. You don't want to come to our boat. We've got a tiger aboard.'

'Liar,' she said. 'Tigers don't live on boats.'

'Maybe not other boats,' he said, 'but they do on ours. This one comes out at night to eat up little girls.'

In a gesture that was both comical and ugly, Father pretended to be a tiger, reaching out his hands like claws, and roared. Huixian shrieked in fright and jumped back. But then she held her ground and looked hatefully into Father's face. 'An old man like you shouldn't do that,' she said. 'You're disgusting.' Pointing contemptuously at him, she said, 'I know you're lying. You just don't like me. Well, I don't care. Lots of other people do. What's so good about your boat anyway?' With that she spun around, and ran back to where I was standing. 'You're disgusting, too. Who said you could take me with you? Who cares about your rotten old boat?'

I tried to block her way, but she slipped between my legs and ran back, straight into the arms of Sun Ximing's wife.

Sighs of relief all around. I looked at my father, who was scowling at me. The anger in his eyes made me shiver, so I turned, just in time to see Huixian move from the arms of Sun's wife into those of Desheng's wife. They were protecting her like a galaxy of stars around the moon as they headed back to number one. I couldn't tell if Huixian was crying or not, but they were fussing over her to make her feel better, all talking at once. There was a tiger on boat number seven. There really was. A tiger, an old tiger.

Father and I stared at each other across the water, boat to boat, exchanging angry glares. *Tiger, tiger, there's a tiger on our boat. You're the tiger.* The vague outline of a large, striped cat took form behind him. The sudden illusion took my breath away! With my head down, I boarded our boat, where I was greeted by a repeat of Six-Fingers Wang's comment. 'What's in that head of yours? How old are you, and how old is she? Don't you think it's a bit early to be bringing her on to our boat?'

I'd never been so disgusted with my father, and that disgust found its way into a careless outburst: 'Why'd you come outside anyway? With only half a dick, why didn't you stay in the cabin where you belong? You shame me by showing your face!'

I turned and walked towards the cabin, with my arms over my head in anticipation of a bamboo staff raining down on me. But I made it all the way to the cabin without Father doing a thing. So I cautiously turned to look behind me, where he was sitting on a coiled hawser on the bow, trembling. They had taken Huixian away by then, and the clamour had left with them. Now all I could see was my father, sitting there trembling as if he'd been struck by lightning.

I'd used the most vicious words I knew to humiliate him, which worried and shamed me. How would he punish me when he was feeling better? I had a guilty conscience, but so did he, and his was worse than mine. I went astern to take a leak off the fantail. Then I opened the slip of paper I'd drawn and looked down at Huixian's juvenile drawing. After folding it into the shape of an arrow, I blew on it and sent it flying, watching as it struggled to stay aloft above the river before it fell silently into the water, where it was swamped by a wave. The only way I knew to express the sense of grief and anger I felt at that moment was to roar at the river, '*Kongpi! Kongpi!*'

Mother

HUIXIAN WAS hung out aboard Sun Ximing's boat during her early days with the fleet. Sun and his wife, her new parents, did not scrimp on food or clothing for her. She dressed better than Dafu and Erfu, and ate better food. With the eyes of people from all eleven barges on them, would they dare do less? No, they treated her like royalty. Both their burden and their glory, she was unimaginably spoiled; her moist eyes shone like diamonds some of the time and were hidden behind a curtain of dark clouds at other times. But a modest degree of happiness could not overcome a troubled heart. Everyone knew why she spent so much time with her eyes fixed on the shore. She was waiting for her mother to show up.

There was always the chance that the woman would appear on the river or in Milltown or Phoenix or Horsebridge. Unfamiliar women did, from time to time, board barges in the fleet to sell used clothing or pumpkins or leeks; there was even a young country woman who came aboard Desheng's barge with a basket of corn over her back, who, perhaps inspired by the gun-running legend of the martyr Deng Shaoxiang, hid a baby girl in the bottom of her basket. After selling the corn, she shook the basket and the baby's head popped into view. 'I hear you people want a little girl, but can't find one. Well, I don't want

this one,' she said to Desheng. 'You can have her for thirty
yuan.'

In shocked disbelief, Desheng drove her off his boat. His wife,
unable even to look at the little girl, berated the woman. 'I've
never seen such a hateful woman,' she said. 'And you call yourself
a mother! You haggle over the price of your corn, but when it
comes to your own flesh and blood, all you want is for someone to
take her off your hands.'

The world is populated by all sorts of mothers, but none of them
was Huixian's. No matter how long she waited, the boat people
– men and women, old and young – knew she was destined to be
disappointed, yet no one spoke of it. The children were warned
to keep such talk to themselves; the secret must be guarded.
Meanwhile, the adults pooled their wisdom and experience to
rescue poor Huixian from her vain dream.

To that end it was necessary to erase all traces of the memories
she held of the woman who had abandoned her. Sun Ximing's
wife, who was responsible for Huixian's day-to-day activities,
agonized over how to remove the army raincoat from the girl's
life. Everyone knew she could not sleep unless she was covered
by it, for, they assumed, it retained her mother's smell. Sun's
wife racked her brains to find a way out of this dilemma. Every
time she put the coat away and covered Huixian with a regular
blanket instead, the girl caused a scene. Sun's wife even bought a
nice woollen blanket embroidered with peonies for her, but that
failed too; Huixian demanded the return of her raincoat to use
along with the blanket. 'My little ancestor,' Sun's wife said in
frustration, 'you're harder to please than the empress herself. If
you keep insisting on covering yourself with that raincoat, people
will talk. They'll say that even impoverished children in the old
society had tattered blankets on their beds, while a little flower of
the motherland like you uses a raincoat. If you insist on covering
yourself with both, the new blanket will pick up the bad smell

of your raincoat. I don't mind, but people will say your adoptive mother doesn't care if you suffocate.'

As if that weren't enough, a dangerous, unwarranted and virtually unstoppable trend persisted. No one was willing to shatter Huixian's dream of seeing her mother again, so the adults made a rule for the children: if she hit them, they were not to hit back, and if she called them names, they were to keep quiet. But in the heat of an argument, children cannot be counted on to avoid saying what mustn't be said. More to the point, in order to keep their secret, the adults and children fabricated a tale that Huixian's mother was still alive and would return for her one day. And so when Huixian was in a bad mood, she would rail defiantly at Sun Ximing and his wife, 'You hate me. I want to go ashore to find my mother.'

The couple willingly took the girl on a pretend search for her mother whenever they went ashore; it was something they had to do, though it was hard to keep the story up. They came to our barge with old newspapers and asked my father to write missing-persons posters, which they then pasted up on street corners, with Dafu responsible for pasting and Erfu for putting them up. Once that was done, they inquired at government offices. If they forgot, Huixian quickly reminded them. 'We can't go back until we've checked with the authorities, can we? Maybe my mother is waiting for me in one of those offices.'

The ruse was hard to maintain, and it was exhausting. But the alternative was never considered. They were afraid Huixian would go ashore on her own and cause trouble, so for some reason they thought of me. One day they brought her over to number seven and said to her, 'How about letting Dongliang take you this time? He can read and knows the bureaucratic ins and outs better than anybody. Since we haven't been able to find your mother, let's give him a try.' Sun Ximing reddened and signalled me not to give anything away.

Having no idea what was in my heart, they wrote me off as hateful and cruel behind my back, and yet the warm feelings I felt towards Huixian never left me. I'd cleverly masked my fondness for her. I welcomed the thought of doing something for her, but Sun must have taken me for an idiot, asking me to go ashore to find a ghost. Not only was it stupid, it was a blow to my self-respect, and I was just about to tell him so when Huixian reached out and took me by the arm. Her little hand was pink and plump, its nails painted a pretty red, thanks to the women, and it looked like a flower blossoming on my arm. Her dark eyes turned to me, not in a pleading fashion, but sort of charitable and proud. 'Let's go,' she said. 'You can relax with me.' Then, assuming the wise, knowing tone of an adult, she said, 'We don't need to rush. It's OK if we don't find her right away.'

Knowing I could not refuse that outstretched hand, I took her to Milltown, a trip that gave me the chance to toughen myself up emotionally. It was important to keep that well-intentioned lie fresh in my mind, and to learn how to look after a little girl. Though younger than I was, Huixian was more cunning and more wilful. She was also a lot worse off. Those were my reasons for wanting to look after her.

All sorts of little problems cropped up on our way from the barge to the shore. First of all, I needed to avoid her hand. She'd got used to holding people's hands, and now she wanted to hold mine. But how was I supposed to walk on shore hand-in-hand with a girl? I started by walking ahead of her, telling her to stay close behind me. Then I thought about what my father always told me, which was to take pleasure in helping others. My primary concern, of course, was her safety. The piers were congested with commodities and crowds of people, and I was afraid she might get lost. So I let her go ahead. 'Turn left, go straight on, halt.' I sounded like a drill sergeant. At first she couldn't distinguish between left and right, but she wasn't stupid, and she got the idea after a few false starts, which made her happy. When we came to a junction, she'd halt, turn to look at me and ask, 'Left or right?'

The sky above Milltown was clear and bright. The 'critical times' seemed to have come to an end, and East Wind No. 8 had apparently been completed, since the trench had been filled in and all the stacked pipes were now buried deep in the ground, along with their accompanying legends and secrets. The grand, seemingly endless construction project had produced early results: red banners flapped in the wind, proclaiming the vigour of the East, and the familiar Milltown now had the air of a boomtown, tinged with a sense of grandeur that infused its residents with veneration. A circular steel tower had been erected near the embankment, like a steel colossus holding up the sky; protected by a chain-link fence, it gave off an acrid odour of tar and metallic paint. I had no idea what it was for, whether it was intended for storing oil or in preparation for battle, but I instinctively knew that it was important. Xiaogai and Wulaizi of the security group no longer cared whether we came ashore or not. Now they stood guard on either side of the single gate in the fence, like a pair of faithful stone lions. A large, prominent sign affixed to the gate read: 'HEIGHTEN VIGILANCE, PROTECT THE MOTHERLAND.'

Handbills for Huixian's lost mother, at odds with their surroundings, were still posted where crowds congregated:

If you have any information regarding the missing mother of Jiang Huixian please leave your contact information here or contact the Sunnyside Fleet.

Some were on propaganda leaflets, others on old newsprint, and all were in my father's handwriting. Huixian knew better than I where they had been posted, so she ignored any commands that would have led her away from those spots, and kept running from place to place. If you're no good at tending cattle, your only choice is to chase after them. I was forced to chase after her. When she walked up to the noticeboard outside the General Affairs Building she shrieked, 'It's gone! My mother must have taken it!' I was still digesting this news when Gimpy Gu emerged from the gatehouse and said to Huixian, 'Go and play somewhere else. This is a government building, not a playground. The officials demand quiet.'

'My mama took the handbill that was here,' Huixian said. 'You're in your guardhouse every day, have you seen her?'

'Your mother didn't take it,' Gu said. 'I did. This is a noticeboard reserved for socialist announcements, not to help you find your mother.'

'But what if she's really lost?' Huixian asked Gimpy Gu.

'How should I know?' he said. 'I lost my mother at the age of five and I'm still here. It doesn't matter if you don't have a mother. All you really need is the Party.' Gimpy was obviously unhappy with the look in my eyes. 'Did I say something wrong?' he demanded. 'How dare you stand there rolling your eyes at me! I know you hate the socialist system. You're forever up to no good. What did you hope to gain by writing on the fourth-floor wall that time? By attacking Secretary Zhao you attacked the Party leadership. Understand? I'd have hauled you up for that long ago if you weren't Qiao Limin's son.'

We had to move on. I had a job to do, and it did not include arguing with Gimpy Gu. 'About turn!' I ordered Huixian. 'Forward march!' But she kept turning back again. 'Hurry up,' I said. 'What do you keep looking at? The old guy said your mama didn't take it, he did.'

With a scowl, she said, 'He makes me so mad I could die! Why's he so mean?' What could I say? But then her thoughts took another leap. And this time she handed me a real hot potato.

'The old man said something about Sister Qiao Li, Qiao Limei. Who's she?'

'There's no Qiao Limei. It's Qiao Limin – my mother.'

With a surprised shriek, she said, 'You've got a mama too? Everybody said you do, but I didn't believe them.'

My head buzzed. 'Why wouldn't I have a mama?' I demanded. 'Did you think I slithered out from between some rocks?'

She knew she'd said the wrong thing. With a wounded look, she whined, 'I never said that. But if you're not trying to find her, that makes you a bad person. Why aren't you looking for her?'

Huixian might have been small, but she was no stranger to resentment. The minute I blew up at her, she stopped obeying my commands. When I told her to start walking, she stopped to rest, and when I told her to speed up, she slowed down. Somehow, we managed to make it to People's Avenue and walked up to the general store, at the entrance to the marketplace, where there was always lots of traffic; that meant plenty of wear and tear. Half of her missing-persons poster was missing, the other half had been covered with writing. Someone had written 'Three Cheers for the Revolutionary Committee', another had written 'Li Caixia is a tattered shoe, a whore', and someone else had written 'Down with Liu Shaoqi', to which someone else had added Scabby Five's name. None of these scrawled comments surprised me; what struck me as odd was that someone had drawn a fish – a very realistic fish – on the poster in chalk. Huixian gawked at the fish in alarm and asked, 'What does that mean? Why did they draw a fish?'

'Some kid,' I said casually. 'It doesn't mean anything.'

'Liar!' she said. 'It has to mean something. I think it's telling me that my mama has turned into a fish!'

Huixian was a lot smarter than I gave her credit for. Thanks to what she'd said, I really did start to wonder what significance that fish held. It must have been hinting at something. Fish live in the water; her mother was in the river and had turned into a fish. I took a long look at the drawing and had a premonition of imminent danger. The truth, which the boat people had conspired to hide, was not mine to reveal. Then I had a flash of inspiration. This was the perfect time for me to apply my skill at altering words and pictures. Reaching into my bag, I took out a ballpoint pen, leaned up against the wall and redrew the picture, neatly turning the fish into a sunflower.

'That's a sunflower!' she shrieked. 'What does it mean?'

'A sunflower brings happiness.'

'What does that mean?'

Never imagining she would ask me what happiness meant, I was stumped for a response. I realized that she was smart only some of the time, and dense the rest. Since I lacked the patience of a schoolteacher and the wisdom of a dictionary, a strange sense of dejection came over me. 'You're driving me crazy,' I said. 'I'll tell you what unhappiness is, and you'll know its opposite. You don't have happiness, and neither do I. Now do you understand?'

That earned me a blank stare. Not feeling like describing happiness in detail, or willing to sully the word, I put it in the simplest terms I knew. 'Happiness is something that will come later; it's what you'll have when you find your mama.' As soon as that comment left my mouth, my heart sank. What a damned lie. I avoided the puzzled look in her eyes, secretly regretting the cruel web of deceit I'd spun for her. Where had her mother gone? Where was her happiness? How could I even have said the word? What nonsense! Here were the two of us, Ku Dongliang and Jiang Huixian, actually discussing happiness!

The noise level around the general store rose suddenly. Somebody riding past us on a bicycle slammed on the brakes, while people across the street pointed at Huixian and me. I turned round, and there was my mother, Qiao Limin, standing on the steps. How weird was that! I was trying to help Huixian find her mother, talking to her about happiness and unhappiness, only to run into my own mother. It had been a long time. After all this time, she and I had accidentally run into each other at the general store.

She was paler than ever, but still dressed like a young woman. She had on an army cap, a red woollen scarf and a black woollen overcoat. Her hair was combed into a shoulder-length braid. From where I stood, she had the revolutionary romantic look Father had talked about. But as she walked up to me, I realized it was all an illusion. She had a debilitated appearance. She was just Qiao Limin, an amateur actress whose professional skills and looks had deteriorated. She reeked of face cream.

'Run!' I ordered Huixian. 'I said run!'

She didn't get the message. She took one step and stopped. 'Why?' she asked, looking wide-eyed at me.

I couldn't think of an answer that made sense. 'It's a tiger!' I blurted out.

She looked around. 'You're lying again,' she said with a stamp of her foot. 'I don't see anything but people. There's no tiger.'

Since she wouldn't listen, I had no choice but to leave her standing there and run straight to the public toilet. I hadn't planned on running away; I just didn't know what else to do. When Mother had first left, I hadn't known what to do, so I'd looked everywhere for her. Now here she was, coming straight towards me, disappointment showing in her eyes. And still I didn't know what to do, so I ran off. I might as well admit it, I wasn't just running, I was running away. My destination? The best place to keep us apart – the men's toilet. At the moment that seemed the safest bet.

Mother was holding a newspaper and had a red nylon bag slung over her shoulder. She started moving the minute I ran off, stuffing the newspaper into her bag and stepping spryly down the general-store steps. Holding the bag tightly, she started running too, her hips swaying. It looked as if she was chasing me while doing a dance with a red silk streamer, and that struck me as comical and depressing at the same time. First she ran up to Huixian, and her streamer stopped moving. I watched as she held up Huixian's face with her fingers and studied it intently. She said something – maybe telling her how pretty she was or maybe asking a question – but I couldn't hear what it was. I was concerned only about myself.

First I stood at a urinal. But a strange thing had happened. The wall beside the urinal, which had been so tall, was now so short that my head showed over the top. What had they done to it? I wondered. My thoughts were interrupted by Scabby Seven, who came out of one of the cubicles, hitching up his trousers. He seemed to have shot up suddenly – he looked like a grown-up! And then it dawned on me. The wall hadn't been shortened – I'd grown taller.

Seven gave me a suspicious look. 'Kongpi,' he said, 'what are you so flustered about? You haven't come in here to write another bad slogan, have you?' I ignored him and rushed into a cubicle, but he followed me in. 'You didn't come in here to do your business,' he said. 'I think you're planning to write something dirty on the wall.'

'I'm here to draw a picture of your dad's prick,' I said. 'And your mum's cunt. Here, let me show you!'

'Big talk,' he said, pointing his finger at me. 'You just wait, I'll get Five to take care of you.' He started out of the toilet, but wasn't through with provoking me. 'You can't do your business with your pants on. Pull them down and let me see. Your dad only has half a prick, let's see what you've got.'

That did it. I grabbed him by the arm and started pushing him out the door. 'Seven,' I said, 'I don't have time to mess around. Another word from you and I'll stuff you down the toilet.'

While I was struggling with Seven, I heard my mother shout from outside, 'No fighting in there, Dongliang. Who are you fighting with? Who's fighting with Dongliang? If you don't stop this minute, I'll call the police.'

Seven ran outside. 'I wasn't fighting,' he said. 'It was Kongpi.'

My mother immediately replied, 'How could he be fighting alone?'

Seven laughed. 'He's Kongpi, and a *kongpi* can fight with himself.'

'Come out of there!' Mother called. 'Is this how you deal with things? Even other kids laugh at you. You must have done something very bad to be so scared of seeing me. You don't have to hide in a toilet just because you're afraid. It's time you acted like a man. Ku Wenxian has been a terrible influence on you. Run away, that's all you know how to do. The lower beam will always be crooked if the upper beam isn't straight.'

'Who's afraid of you?' I shouted out. 'This is the men's toilet, it's where we do our business, not a broadcasting studio!'

I hated it when Mother talked. I admit that I'd missed her when she wasn't around. But now that she was, I'd only have still missed her if she hadn't said anything. Everything changed as soon as she opened her mouth. I became agitated, and when that happened, I started hating her again.

Mother couldn't resist an opportunity to speak. 'It wasn't me who didn't want to take care of you. You chose to go with your father. Your father has strong points, and you should learn from them. He's willing to study hard, which shows in the way he writes, including his calligraphy. But stay clear of his thinking and his character. He cheated on the Party and he cheated on me. You must treat his lifestyle as a negative example. Don't you dare let that happen to you.'

'You can leave now, Qiao Limin. Go on, leave! If people see you broadcasting in front of the men's toilet, they'll think you're crazy!'

'Go ahead, be as nasty as you want, I don't care,' she said. 'All the trouble I've been through has toughened me up. I carried you for nine months, and no matter what your attitude is, you're still the one I'm most concerned about. I have the right to educate you. I used to think I'd have plenty of opportunities to do that, but my job transfer changed all that. I don't know when I'll get another chance to talk some sense into you.'

And that was when I knew what this was all about. I didn't say anything. It was quiet outside, and my agitation turned to melancholy. *Where are you going?* I came so close to asking her that, more than once, but I kept it inside me. I held my breath to listen to the sounds around me. I wanted to hear, but was afraid to at the same time. 'Come out of there, Dongliang!' It was Huixian. 'Come out this minute!'

'I can't, I've got the runs!' I shouted back. I was waiting for Mother to tell me where she was going.

A minute or so later, a man walked in to use the urinal. When he was finished he asked, 'Is that your mother and your sister out there? What's going on? Your mother's crying.'

Truth is, I could hear her sobbing. She hardly ever cried – she'd never had any use for tears. Even when I was a boy she let me know that tears were a sign of weakness, so I found the man's comment hard to believe. She'd been fine just a minute ago, but now, apparently, she'd broken down. My mother was crying outside a men's toilet, and I didn't know what to do. So I stood on my tiptoes to look through the window. I could see them both. Mother was crouching down, Huixian was eating a biscuit with one hand and drying Mother's tears with the other.

The man was a real busybody. He wasn't about to leave, even

after hitching up his trousers. He looked out of the door. 'I've seen your mother somewhere,' he said, 'and your sister's a little beauty. What's up with you people? You should be taking care of family squabbles at home, not in a public toilet.'

Strangely, that comment hit home. Did we really look like a family? Me, my mother and my kid sister? We did. Wouldn't that have been great? But we weren't. The man disgusted me. 'Our family's squabbles are complicated,' I said. 'I don't know you and you don't know me, so mind your own business.'

Mother cleared her throat to start talking again after the man walked out, but her voice was raspy. 'Dongliang,' she said, 'don't come out if you don't want to. But remember this: I'm being sent to the coal mines in Xishan. Propaganda work again, in charge of troupe rehearsals. Xishan's a long way off, too far for me to look after you. From now on you're on your own.'

My heart sank. But what I said was, 'Go ahead, the further the better. Who asked you to look after me?'

The fact that I'd heard the news that she was going to Xishan while I was in the toilet was in itself kind of weird. But what I'm going to tell you now is even weirder. The minute I heard it was propaganda work at the Xishan coal mines, my gut swelled up and out it all came, like an explosion. I squatted down, engulfed in a terrible stench, accompanied by popping sounds from my backside, like a string of firecrackers going off at the wrong time. I felt awful, too awful for words. Between moans I kept saying, 'Go ahead, go ahead. It's just *kongpi*. Xishan, your job, haemorrhoids, everything's *kongpi*.'

Then I heard Huixian crying out there, shrieking angrily. 'Come out, Dongliang! I'll leave if you don't, and if I get lost it'll be your fault.'

Mother was gone by the time I walked out. Huixian was waiting for me across the street, holding the red bag. She was still angry, but didn't say so right away. Then she held up the bag and said, 'You're so ungrateful. Your mother brought you a gift, but all you did was hide in the toilet and argue with her!' She took a pair of cloth sandals out of the bag. 'These are for you.' Then she took out a tin of biscuits and waved it at me. 'Half for you and half for me. She said so.'

When the River Talks

THE RIVER talks. When I divulged this secret to other people, they thought I was crazy. When I first went aboard, I was filled with an exuberant childhood desire to explore the world. Of all the things I spotted floating in the river, tin cans were the ones that really sparked my interest. Every time I saw one, I scooped it out, not just to hold on to, but to use for scooping other things out of the river. I'd poke two holes in them, then string wire through the holes and tie them to the side, dragging them through the water like a trawling net. When we pulled up alongside the piers, I'd yank the cans out of the water, like a fisherman, but they nearly always came up empty – no pleasant surprises. One time I caught a snail, another time it was half a carrot, and yet another time, to my disgust, I dragged up a used condom. I had no luck as a fisherman, but when I shook my tin cans the water inside sounded like me, but duller and more hopeless sounding than my own mantra: *kongpi, kongpi.*

Carrying my water-filled tin cans, I wondered if the river was echoing me. The river was so wide and so deep, how could it write me off with the single word *kongpi*? I didn't believe that was the voice of the river. I wanted to hear something else. So I divided the cans into three groups of five and attached them to both sides of the boat. They filled up with overflowing water, murmuring sounds that reached me in the cabin. I ran to the port side and listened. *Come down*, they were saying, *come down*. That was new, but what did it mean? Who was to come down? Was I supposed to somehow climb into the cans? I didn't believe that was what the river was saying, so I ran to the starboard side, where the five cans had all come together and were saying, in a low but stern voice, *Come down, come down.*

Come down. Come down.

This time I believed what I was hearing, maybe because the voice was so dignified, so stern. *Come down, come down.* After that, it was the sound of the river I trusted most.

In my father's eyes, I was now an adult, and he disapproved of this sort of childish behaviour. I hid all my cans, but he found them and threw them angrily into the river. 'How old are you, Dongliang? I joined the revolution at the age of sixteen. But you? You play with tin cans! Sailing on the river is a lonely life, so spend your time studying. And if that doesn't appeal to you, do some work. When there's nothing else to do, you can swab the deck.'

Once, when I was swabbing the deck up front I saw Huixian and Yingtao playing with a skipping rope on Six-Fingers Wang's boat. Six-Fingers's daughter was counting spiritedly, acting as a referee. Suddenly Yingtao shouted, 'Not fair! How come everybody's siding with her? Anyone could see I did a hundred, but you only said ninety-five, and she only did ninety-five but you gave her a hundred.' Wang's daughter went up to humour her, but it did no good. Yingtao stormed off in anger. I'd stopped working and was waiting for Huixian to come to our boat. It always happened like that – she and Yingtao would have an argument, which would end in her running over to number seven.

That didn't mean she paid any attention to me once she got there. With the skipping rope over her shoulder, she walked towards the cabin as if she owned the boat, her eyes on the sofa.

To her chagrin, this time my father was sitting in it. She stuck out her tongue to show her disappointment, then turned and came back down the other side of the boat.

Maybe she'd heard too many grown-up discussions about us, but the moment she opened her mouth, out came the crucial question: 'Is yours a martyr's family or isn't it?'

'Who've you been talking to?' I said. 'Do you even know what a martyr is? We can't be martyrs because we're all still alive.'

'I haven't been talking to anybody. I've got ears, and I know how to listen,' she said proudly. She pointed to our cabin. 'Deng – Deng Xiangxiang, that's her picture. Is she a martyr?'

'Her name's Deng Shaoxiang, not Deng Xiangxiang. She's a martyr, I'm not.'

'Don't be stupid,' she said. 'She's your grandma, isn't she? So if she's a martyr, then so are you. It's a great honour.'

'I'm a martyr's descendant, not a martyr. My grandma is the honourable one, not me.'

She blinked, still not clear on the distinction between a martyr and a martyr's family. Instead of trying to pretend she understood, she took the skipping rope off her shoulder, shook it at me and said, 'Cleaning the deck is boring. Let's see who's better at skipping.'

'Not me.'

'See, now you look unhappy.' She studied my face. 'Do I make you angry?'

'No. I may be angry, but not because of you.'

Abandoning the idea of getting me to skip, her eyes lit up as she blurted out, 'Has your mama sent you any gifts lately?'

I said, 'No. Who wants her gifts anyway?'

She looked disappointed. 'She'll send you gifts because she's your mother and she cares about you. Animal crackers are my favourites,' she said. 'Giraffes taste great. So do elephants.'

I knew how much she liked to eat, so I said, 'If she sends things to eat, you can have them.'

She blushed and twisted the skipping rope in her hands. 'That's not what I meant. She's your mama, not mine. If you want, you can give me half.'

Any talk of mamas was a taboo that everyone adhered to. I didn't want to talk about my mother, and definitely wasn't about to mention hers, so I decided to tell her my river secret. 'You've been with us a long time. Have you ever heard the river speak?'

She snickered. 'Liar. The river doesn't have a mouth. How can it speak?'

'It doesn't speak because you haven't given it a mouth. Give it one and you'll hear it speak.'

She gave me a blank stare. 'You're lying again. The river's water. Give it a mouth and it still can't speak.'

I probed the surface of the river to find its mouth, spotting a wooden spindle floating downstream that was coming slowly towards our boat. It was barrel-shaped, with hollow ends, and seemed to be the perfect shape for a mouth. 'See that? It could be the water's mouth,' I announced earnestly as I scooped it out of the water with a net pole. 'Now watch while I get the river to speak.'

After drying off the spindle, I carried it to the starboard side, where I lay on the deck. Huixian followed me. 'How come you brought it to this side? Doesn't the river speak on the other side?'

I told her that sunlight affected how the river spoke. 'The sun has lit up the other side of the boat, and the river will only speak over here. It's too bright and too noisy over there. And even if it did speak, it would be lies.'

Only half believing me, Huixian put the spindle up to her ear and lay down on the deck to listen to the sound of the water. 'Liar,' she said. 'The water's flowing along, not speaking.' She tried to get up, but I pushed her back down.

'You've got to get rid of all thoughts of animal crackers and focus on the river. Hold your breath and be patient. Give it time and you'll hear it.'

So she quietened down and listened. 'I heard it!' she cried. 'I did!'

'Good,' I said. 'Now tell me what you heard.'

She looked up, with hesitation and a bit of embarrassment in her eyes. 'It said different things. At first it said, *Eat, eat*. Then it said, *Don't eat, don't eat.*'

Eat? Don't eat? That's what she heard? How disappointing. 'That's all you know – eat, eat!' I snatched the spindle out of her hand, gave her back her skipping rope and said, 'Go and skip. That and eating are just about all you know how to do.'

With a pout and an angry look, she said, 'Then what did you hear? Why won't you tell me that?'

'Why should I? You wouldn't understand.'

That upset her. She hit me with her skipping rope and took off running. 'You're a liar,' she said. 'My new mother told me to stay away from your stinking boat, so I'm not coming over any more.'

River Day

THE GOLDEN Sparrow River was calm and tranquil the following autumn. The riverbed shrank and the banks receded, revealing patches of swamp land overgrown with reeds and water grasses. An occasional egret landed, but only briefly, as wild dogs prowled around and barked enthusiastically at passing ships. There was a sometimes bleak quality to the prosperous scenes on the densely populated shore, with villages big and small dotting the area. I knew all their names, but after the floods had passed, the one called Huage had disappeared; the eight dye mills had moved away, and I no longer saw Huage's blue and white fabric billowing in the wind from the boats. The Fairy Maiden Bridge had sunk into the river, like an old man beaten down by time who could no longer raise his head, while by gazing into the distance at the steel tower and traces of high-voltage wires not far from Li Village, I could see a new marketplace that had exploded into existence on the marshy bank, large clusters of simple structures that had seemingly risen up overnight, with red brick walls and white asbestos tiles. From afar, it looked like a mushroom farm. 'They call that East Wind Villa,' someone told me. 'It's where the East Wind No. 8 construction workers who chose not to return to their homes live.'

As autumn arrived, a rash developed in my groin. It itched like crazy, and I couldn't stop scratching, an inelegant practice my father couldn't help noticing. He told me to drop my pants, which exposed my rash, as well as my genitals, for him to see. I'll never forget the look of shock in his eyes, not from seeing the rash – he asked me what I expected, since I hated taking baths and paid no attention to my personal hygiene – but from the physical changes; maturation had occurred unnoticed. The damned 'helmet', with all its rosy freshness, gave off a cursed, wicked glint; bad for others and bad for me. The sight put a worried scowl on Father's face, and I was so embarrassed I wanted to crawl into a hole. The look of fear in his eyes was unmistakable, for this involved desire and tumult, danger and sin. The devil was on its way, the very devil he had extirpated from his own body had now shown up on mine. Any comparison between us was cruel, and the results were hard to utter. Father took out a bottle of gentian violet. His mood resembled the purple liquid in the bottle – irritable and gloomy – while his gaze remained fixed on my crotch, cold and hostile, mixed with profound misery. His eyes were like a pair of scissors, terrifyingly open. I trembled; my rash mutated into a barely perceptible pain that covered my crotch. I knew that Father hated my 'helmet', and it disgusted me too. But what was I to do? Once a male dons the 'helmet', it's impossible to take it off.

Fortunately, they were eventful days. Father got busy as the twenty-seventh of September, the anniversary of Deng Shaoxiang's martyrdom, neared, and so did I. In order to prepare River Day candles and paper flowers, he sent me into town to buy coloured paper and a jug of rice wine. The wine served two functions: I was to spray half of it on the martyr's memorial and bring the rest back to the boat for him. He never touched alcohol, except on the twenty-seventh of September, when he drank to the spirit of Deng Shaoxiang.

I went first to the stationery shop to buy coloured paper. As she was taking a stack of paper down off the shelf, the shop assistant blurted out, 'You're not from the school, are you? And you're not from the General Affairs Building, so what do you need coloured paper for?'

'Coloured paper isn't rationed,' I said. 'What do you care where I'm from? I'm buying, and you have to sell it to me.'

She gave me a suspicious look. 'Do I have to sell it to you if you're buying it to write counter-revolutionary slogans? Don't roll your eyes at me. I know who you are. You're Ku Wenxian's son, aren't you?'

'Yes,' I said. 'So what? Can't Ku Wenxian's son buy coloured paper?'

She looked at me out of the corner of her eye and snorted. 'Your father owes us money. Back when he was one of the town's big shots, he took lots of our paper – plain white paper, writing paper, coloured paper, even some fine paper for calligraphy. But we never saw any money.'

'That's your problem,' I said. 'You could have made him pay for those things.'

'You're quite the talker,' she said. 'He was a local tyrant who told us to charge it to the General Affairs account. Who'd dare to refuse? Then there's your mother, Qiao Limin. She wasn't in the habit of paying for her purchases either: books, fountain pens, pencils, pencil cases, notebooks. All for official business, she said, so charge it. Oh, we did that all right. It would have been fine, except that Ku Wenxuan fell from power and Zhao Chuntang refused to honour the bill. We're the losers. Our books and inventory never match.'

Telling me about my parents' past deeds embarrassed me and made me angry. 'That's none of my business,' I said, rapping my knuckles on the counter. 'I don't want to talk about what they did. I'm here to buy coloured paper. If you won't sell it to me, I'll just take it.'

'Fat chance,' she replied. 'The son inherits the father's debts.

And what makes you think that you, who owes us money, can act like a little tyrant? Nobody's afraid of you any more. Why should we be? You can buy your paper somewhere else.' When she saw me move closer to the display case, she slammed the door shut. Then she gave me a shrill warning: 'I doubt you'd dare to rob us, but if you did, the police station is right down the street, and they'd come running if they heard me scream.'

The assistant and I were confronting one another across the glass-topped counter when a three-wheeled vehicle loaded with cardboard boxes pulled up in front of the shop. The driver entered carrying a large box and set it down. It was the shopkeeper, Old Yin, a round-faced man with big ears. He'd save the day, since in the past he'd been a frequent guest in our home. Back then he used to rub my head whenever he dropped by. He didn't do that this time, but he hadn't forgotten who I was. 'Dongliang,' he said, 'why the scowl? You're not shopping for a knife to kill someone, are you?'

'That's exactly what he wants,' the assistant said, 'all because I told him to go home and remind his father that he owes us money. What I got was that look in return. With such a long face, someone who didn't know better might think we owed *him* money.'

Old Yin was a man who enjoyed digging up local anecdotes and was thoroughly versed in Milltown's revolutionary history. When he learned that I'd come to buy coloured paper he glanced up at the wall calendar. 'Ah,' he exclaimed. 'Tomorrow's Deng Shaoxiang's memorial day.' With that, he agreed to sell me paper, and even separated it by colour to let me choose the ones I wanted.

'I don't know how to choose,' I said. 'You do it for me.'

So he bent over and began selecting the right colours. 'Your father has a good heart,' he muttered. 'Even after what happened to him, he makes a point of observing September the twenty-seventh. But what I don't understand is, since he refuses to come ashore these days, how will he memorialize the martyr?'

'Water's as good as land,' I said. 'He'll just face Phoenix and toss paper flowers into the river.'

Old Yin raised his head and gave me a dubious look. 'Phoenix, you say? You don't know? You really don't know?'

I gaped at him, having no idea what he was talking about. 'Know what?'

He glanced at me, cleared his throat and spoke in an authoritative, almost callous tone. 'There's new information your father couldn't know about, since he's out of the picture. Go home and tell him not to rely on the almanac. They've discovered that Deng Shaoxiang wasn't from Phoenix after all. That coffin shop was moved to Phoenix from Running Ox Village. You understand what I'm saying? Deng Shaoxiang was born not in Phoenix but in Running Ox Village. Ever hear of it?'

I stood transfixed in front of the counter. I neither shook my head nor nodded. I glared at Old Yin. I'd never heard of Running Ox Village, and people were going to think this was a joke. My father insisted that he was Martyr Deng's son, and that I was her grandson. But neither of us had ever heard of Running Ox Village!

My face reddened with embarrassment. I scooped up the paper and ran out of the shop, followed by the loud voice of the shop assistant. 'Who do you think you are?' she shouted. 'A pretender! Stop being stupid. Father and son – one's a cheat, the other a little hooligan. If Deng Shaoxiang had descendants like you, any commemoration would be a waste of time.'

I walked down the streets of Milltown with the coloured paper under my arm, anger boiling up inside me, not just because of the shop assistant, but also because of the murky nature of Martyr Deng's life. Deng Shaoxiang, your glorious deeds are worthy of song and tears, but why did you lead such a complicated life with so many twists and turns? You are the most famous of martyrs, your name remains with us even after your death. You were not a cloud, so why did you drift from place to place, here one minute, there the next? Where did you actually come from? And who is your real son? When will all the doubts be dispelled? Martyr Deng Shaoxiang, I beg you, won't you show yourself to tell us the truth?

I looked into the sky above the chess pavilion. The people who saw me gave me curious stares. Those who didn't know me asked, 'What's up with him?' Those who knew me said, 'Don't mind him, he's Ku Dongliang. He often walks with his head up, but sometimes he keeps it down. Whatever makes him happy.'

I was walking with my head up because I wasn't happy. But the noise from a crowd of people around the general store calmed me down. I lowered my head, and there on the steps of the store stood a throng of women and children, baskets in hand, lined up to buy sugar. An announcement had been pasted up on the door:

A SUPPLY OF SUGAR IN COMMEMORATION OF NATIONAL DAY HAS ARRIVED. THREE OUNCES OF SUGAR WILL BE SOLD FOR EACH SUGAR COUPON.

Remembering that I was supposed to buy a jug of strong rice wine, I elbowed my way up to the steps, only to be pushed back. 'I don't want any sugar,' I said. 'I need to buy rice wine.'

I was wasting my breath. 'We don't care what you want or need,' someone said. 'Line up.' Then a woman elbowed me out of line and, in a voice dripping with contempt, said, 'You boat people have no manners. Getting you to stand in line is like threatening your existence. What harm can it do to queue up for a change? Are you afraid you'll lose weight, or money? Am I right or aren't I?' Other people in the queue nodded in agreement, looking disgustedly at me. I could have pleaded my case, but it would have been a waste of time. They were there for sugar, I was there for rice wine – two different things. But to them it was all the same. I didn't want to go to the end of the line, but no one was willing to let me go in front of them, so all I could do was step away, fuming at them.

Feeling restless, I stood to one side to watch the queue when I recalled that one of Huixian's handbills about her mother had been pasted up on the wall across the way. I walked over to see if it was still there. Either sanitation workers had torn down most of what remained or the elements had worn it away; except for a tiny fragment, it was obliterated under a fresh coat of whitewash. The stubborn defiance of that fragment evoked in me a sense of mourning. With National Day, the first of October, approaching, the walls of the streets and small lanes had been whitewashed to welcome the holiday. The handbill had died a natural death. I saw no trace of Father's calligraphy, nor of Huixian's name. Not content to leave it at that, I patiently scraped the whitewash off the remaining scrap of paper, and there beneath my fingernail, the sunflower I'd drawn the year before came to life before my eyes, slowly blossoming as I scraped and scraped.

That sunflower brought me a strange sense of elation. So I waited at the corner as the queue in front of the general store grew shorter and eventually disappeared.

As I walked out of the store carrying my jug of wine, I heard a voice behind me. It was Four-Eyes Ma, the store's bookkeeper. 'That's powerful stuff,' he shouted. 'When you get home, tell Old Ku not to drink too much. Tell him Bookkeeper Ma says he'll get even more downcast if he tries to drown his sorrows!'

I couldn't tell if there was some hidden meaning in his comment, but I pretended not to hear him. He and my father had once enjoyed playing chess together, and he had been good at letting Father win by a slim margin. They were on relatively good terms, but no matter how good the terms were, in the end it was nothing but *kongpi*. I refused to believe that Four-Eyes' comment was well-meaning, and suspected that his soft-spoken suggestion was really a ruse to win the respect of the young woman behind the counter. I never passed on people's greetings to Father, because I didn't think they came from the heart. I put my trust in myself alone, his son, since I couldn't think of a single person in Milltown who gave a damn about Ku Wenxuan.

I carried out Father's instruction by taking the jug of rice wine over to the chess pavilion, where a noisy crowd had gathered, and a gaggle of geese filled the air with their honking. My access to the memorial was effectively blocked. But I got as close as possible, and there I spotted the idiot Bianjin, cavorting drunkenly in front of the martyr's memorial, protected by the geese he tended. He was calling out 'Mama!' to the etched likeness of Deng Shaoxiang. 'Mama! Mama!' he said. 'Go and tell Zhao Chuntang to build a shed for my geese. Mama! Mama! Go and tell Little Wang at the general store to marry me. Mama! Mama! Give me five yuan so I can buy a jug for good wine. They look down on me, and won't even drop the price by five fen.'

People tried to stop him, but failed. 'Even an idiot knows how to take advantage of a situation,' someone yelled, 'calling Deng Shaoxiang Mama. You think calling her Mama is going to help you eat and drink well, do you? We'd like to be the chosen one, too. What makes an idiot like you think you can make that claim?'

'I'll tell you why,' Bianjin said. 'I've got a fish on my ass.'

'Be careful, you idiot,' someone warned him. 'Palming yourself off as Deng Shaoxiang's son can get you into serious trouble. Knock it off, or the police will haul you in.'

'I *am* Deng Shaoxiang's son,' Bianjin insisted. 'The police don't scare me. I'm the martyr's son. I scare *them*!'

'Empty talk!' someone else shouted. 'Take down your pants and show us your birthmark. We'll see if it's a fish or not.'

I shouldered my way to the front in time to see Bianjin take down his pants and expose his backside to the crowd. A roar erupted from everyone – men and women, old and young – who gawked incredulously at the idiot's backside. 'A fish!' came a shout of astonishment. 'It's a fish! A perfect little fish! Maybe he *is* Deng Shaoxiang's son, after all!' Taking the uproar as an invitation to put on a show, the idiot stuck out his rear end and danced around the memorial, only to be met with an explosion of joyous laughter. Someone went up and kicked his exposed backside. 'Pull your pants up, idiot, and be quick about it,' the man said. 'If Deng Shaoxiang really was your mother, then she wasn't hanged by the enemy, she died of humiliation over her son.'

The pavilion was in the neighbourhood of the piers, so instead of the police, it was Scabby Five and Baldy Chen who showed up. By then, Bianjin had sobered up enough to know it was time to leave, so he ran off towards the river, followed by his geese. 'The work team is coming back on National Day,' he proclaimed to anyone who would listen, 'and they'll announce the name of Deng Shaoxiang's son. Just you wait, especially all you people who've tormented me!'

Now that the farce had ended, people became aware that I was there in their midst. They exchanged hurried glances and whispered among themselves. I could guess what they were saying. They were ridiculing or trying to humiliate me. I'd arrived at the chess pavilion like a rabbit that has landed in a hunter's sights. The idiot Bianjin could run off, but not me. It was my turn to sprinkle wine on the memorial and tell the residents of Milltown that my father was firm in his belief. I wanted them to know that Ku Wenxuan was Deng Shaoxiang's son, which made me her grandson.

I carried the jug up to the memorial, but before I could open it, Scabby and Baldy walked up. Scabby put his foot on the jug cap and said, 'Just what do you think you're doing, Kongpi?'

'I'm going to sprinkle wine on the martyr's memorial. Isn't that OK?'

'No,' he growled. 'Pick that jug up and take it away from here.'

'Look over there,' Baldy said with a tap on my shoulder. He was pointing to a bulletin tacked up on one of the pavilion posts. 'You do have eyes, don't you? How could you miss seeing that? A new regulation. "Engaging in feudalistic and superstitious behaviours in the name of memorializing the martyr is strictly forbidden." Sprinkling wine is feudalistic and superstitious behaviour, don't you know that?'

I went up close to read the bulletin. There it was, in black and white: 'New Regulation Concerning Memorials to the Martyr Deng Shaoxiang.'

Baldy was telling the truth. The new regulation was intended to stop people from spreading a rumour that Deng Shaoxiang's spirit had the power to heal injuries and rescue the dying, which had been making the rounds recently. Milltown residents were expressly forbidden from devotional displays at the pavilion. There was to be no burning of spirit paper or incense, no calls to the spirits of deceased persons, and no laments by women from neighbouring villages over their mistreatment.

But there were no strictures against sprinkling wine. 'You people must be illiterate,' I said. 'This forbids people from feudalistic and superstitious activities, but says nothing about sprinkling wine. Where does it say that? Show me!'

There was nothing Scabby Five, who was barely literate, could say, so he kept his foot on my jug and glowered at me. Baldy, on the other hand, was surer of himself. With a contemptuous grin, he traced his finger over the words 'feudalistic' and 'superstitious' and stopped at the small print, where it said 'etc'. 'See that? It says "etc". You've been to school, Kongpi. Know what that means? It means that sprinkling wine may not be listed, but it's included in "etc".'

I could only stare helplessly at the words.

'Why are you wasting your breath on him?' Scabby Five yelled at Baldy Chen. 'No sprinkling means no sprinkling!'

As he was bending down for the jug, Baldy glanced up and saw the hard look in my eyes. He dropped his hands and placed them on the small of his back. 'I sprained my back yesterday,' he said, 'so come and pick it up.'

'It's not your back you sprained,' Scabby said angrily. 'It's your guts! Are you afraid of him? I'll pick it up if you won't. Of all the people who scare me, he's not one of them, not Kongpi!'

I fought with Scabby Five over that jug, each of us trying to pull it away from the other, and we wound up outside the pavilion. A loud thud ended the struggle, as the jug fell to the ground and the lid broke, spilling the contents on the ground. The distinctive fragrance of aged wine spread quickly in the air; my feet were quickly drenched. I was enraged; there were several options available to me, and the first was to pick up the bottom half of the jug and fling it at Scabby's head, a sure-fire way to settle scores, old and new. So I picked it up and was just about to throw it when something unexpected occurred. What remained of the wine in the broken jug was sloshing back and forth, reflecting my face, which shifted with the liquid and began to blur. But what really caught me by surprise was the familiar sound that emerged from the jug: *kongpi, kongpi*. Dejection overcame me and my anger dissipated. Utterly deflated, I laid the jug down on the ground and asked Scabby a shameful question: 'If I can't sprinkle the wine, is it OK if I drink it?'

He dipped his finger in the wine and tasted it. 'Do you have all your pubic hair, Kongpi? You want to drink at your age? It's none of my business if you do or not, but you have to do it out here. No drinking in the pavilion. Go ahead, drink it, but that's not going to make a man out of you. You'll still be Kongpi.'

Well, I went ahead and did that shameful thing, which later made the rounds of Milltown: on the eve of Deng Shaoxiang's commemoration, I laid a sheet of coloured paper on the ground,

sat down, and, with everyone's eyes on me, drank half of the wine
in the jug.

I was barely sober when Sun Ximing and Desheng passed by
the pavilion; before they dragged me back to the river I told them
to bring along the rest of the wine for my father. I can't recall how
I made it back aboard the boat; but I do remember how Father
slapped me with the sole of his cloth shoe and roared at me. I have
no idea what he said or what I said to explain myself. I've never
been good at explaining myself when I'm perfectly clear-headed,
so you can imagine what came out of me when I was half drunk.
All I could say was 'Kongpi'. How else could I explain myself?

Most drunks sleep like pigs. I tossed and turned and had terrible
dreams, one of which scared me awake. Suddenly I had the feeling
that our barge wouldn't move. The tug chugged forward, taking
all the other barges with it, but not ours. A strange watery sound
came to me from the stern, so I went back to take a look. Something
weird was happening to our anchor: it was being held by a hand
coming out of the water – not too big but not particularly small,
all five nicely shaped fingers wrapped around the anchor, half of
the back of the hand white, the other half – scary as hell – covered
with dark-green moss. I was reminded of all the Golden Sparrow
water-demon legends. Rice wine, rice wine! Heat up some rice
wine to drive away the demon! I went back to get the jug. It was
empty. In my dream I even recalled my mistake – I'd drunk it all.
Suddenly panicked, I picked up a bamboo pole to dislodge that
hand. It didn't work. I pushed harder, madly, until the pole flew
out of my hands and landed in the river. Then the dark water
under our barge lit up and waves began to crash as the face of a
beautiful woman rose up out of the water – a round face, with
big eyes, a slightly concave nose, and old-fashioned hair cut, ear-
length short; water grass woven into her black hair glistened like
crystal. Her shoulders came into view next, then a basket she
carried on her back. I saw water in the basket; it was silvery, and a

lotus leaf was floating on top of it. The leaf moved, exposing the blurry, wet head of a baby.

I was seeing Deng Shaoxiang, I was privileged to see her heroic spirit. I should have felt honoured, but what I actually felt was dread. Her dignified presence struck fear in me. Now that she had risen out of the water, she fixed her perceptive gaze on me, a look that told me she saw everything I did and heard everything I said. I stood on the stern of our barge trembling, waiting for her to reveal her identity. But she did not talk about herself or about her descendants. I waited for her to educate me, but she neither forgave nor criticized me. No, she raised her moss-covered hand and sternly patted the basket on her back. 'Come down,' she said. 'Come down. I want you to come down here!'

I didn't dare. How could I jump into her basket? The thought frightened me awake. The lamp in the cabin where I slept still shone. Father was asleep on the sofa, traces of his angry outburst imprinted on his old and slightly bloated face. He had kept the lamp on, creating paper flowers that lay in profusion on his knees and on the floor, big and colourful. I picked up several of them and took them out to the stern, where the anchor rested against the side of the barge, as always. It gave off a dull glint and banged softly against the steel hull, a tranquil, felicitous sound.

Deepening night lay over the river. The night breeze rippled the surface, with shadows cast by passing birds and water gourds floating in our wake. I could even hear them knock up against the space between the barges. But the martyr Deng Shaoxiang had come and gone, a magical spirit performing secret tasks. She had come and gone at will, leaving no trace of her clandestine visit.

I couldn't say if I'd had a nightmare or a sweet dream.

Maiden

FOR THE longest time I couldn't wait for Huixian to grow up.
That was my deepest, darkest secret.

But I was afraid that she would develop into an adult too fast.
That was a secret second only to the other.

My unsociable traits and short fuse were linked to the conflict
of those two secrets. Many people keep diaries, in which they
record details of their lives. Not me. Everyone called me Kongpi,
and the life of a *kongpi* does not deserve to be written down. It's
a waste of paper, ink and time. I had enough self-awareness to
know that the only person whose life was worth recording was
Huixian. I used the same kind of notebook that both my father
and mother had used – a worker's handbook with a cardboard
cover. They were on sale at the general store and the stationery
store for eight fen. Sturdy and durable, they had enough pages
to record things for a long time if you wrote small, with concise,
precise words.

I was particularly prudent at first, sticking to the 'dossier'
style of writing and the principle of 'seeking truth through facts',
limiting my entries to practical and realistic considerations: how
tall she was, how much she weighed, how advanced her reading
skills were, how many songs she knew. But gradually, over time, I
loosened up, enhancing my jottings with aspects of her life, such

as who she argued with. Whatever I heard went into my diary. When she was given a bowl of chicken soup, whether it was tasty or not, thick or thin, any comment she made went into my diary. If someone made a jacket or a pair of shoes for her, how they looked and how they fitted all went into my diary. Then later, whenever someone praised Huixian or passed on gossip about her, if I heard it, it went into the diary. Finally, I began entering my own ideas and any number of chaotic, largely inarticulate thoughts, even dreamed-up code words and phrases that only I understood. To illustrate, I began referring to Huixian as Sunflower and to myself as Gourd. My father was Lumber, while the people on shore were Bandit One, Bandit Two, and so on. The boat people became chickens or ducks or cows or sheep, things like that. All this to keep my father in the dark if he tried to read my diary entries. At times, when I was writing or drawing in my notebook, I was conscious of his presence and the suspicious look in his eyes. 'What in the world are you writing?' he'd ask. 'And why won't you let me see it? Keeping a diary is a good idea, but you can get into serious trouble if you're not careful what you put in it. Remember Teacher Zhu from the Milltown Elementary School? Well, he took out his frustrations with the Party and society in general in his diary, and they arrested him.'

'Don't worry, Dad,' I said. 'I'm perfectly happy with the Party and society in general. It's me I'm not happy with. You've heard how people call me Kongpi, haven't you? So that's how you can see my diary – *kongpi.*'

I was lying, of course. I could be *kongpi*, but not my diary. That held my greatest secrets; it was the one thing I could rely upon. By opening it I was able to see Huixian's face and her body; I could tell what her hair smelled like and could detect the delicate fragrance only a young maiden possessed. After so many years had passed the image of Huixian as a little girl to pity existed in my head, but not in my body; I embraced a hard-to-describe love and an uncontrollable desire for her. As I flipped through my diary, my heart was filled with anxieties that weighed me down and threatened my very existence, all because of a girl's maturation. I resisted that process. As she matured, a pair of budding breasts pushed up underneath her red blouse; as she matured, hair sprouted in armpits that were like yellow jade; as she matured, I was burdened with erections. That spelled danger. Though I resisted her maturation, what I really resisted were those erections. I was a healthy young man who could forgive himself for having erections, whether they occurred at night or during the day, whether they were caused by fancily dressed, fashionable girls and women on the shore or by the full-figured, flirtatious daughter of Six-Fingers Wang, with her daringly wild nature. But I could not forgive myself for the dark, gloomy erections over which my mind and body were engaged in a bitter struggle. There were times when I triumphed over them, but I must confess that most of the time they were beyond my control; at those times my wilful genitals overpowered my will and my mind.

Summer, it seemed to me, was the truly dangerous season, and after Huixian came aboard, summers became more dangerous than ever. Each year seemed hotter than the year before, turning our steel-hulled barge into a blast furnace. When the fleet was berthed at the piers, we lay there baked by the sun. Men and boys who knew how to swim stripped naked and dived into the river. That did not include Father and me, not because we tolerated the heat better than the others, but because we shared an aversion to the naked body. I'd stand on the bow keeping watch, not looking at the men and boys in the water but the girls on the barges. They watched the swimmers, I watched them. The other girls were green leaves, Huixian alone was an eye-catching sunflower. I watched her go ashore with a bucket in one hand and wash basin on her hip, and I wondered why she chose to wash clothes on the shore. But when I looked more closely, I figured it out.

Each time she dumped a bucketful of water into the basin, a thin jacket spread out and sank to the bottom; then her flowery pants floated to the top as the water turned red. Why red? I knew why, don't think I didn't. I'd sneaked a look at the *Barefoot Doctor's Handbook* as a youngster, from which I'd learned a thing or two about female physiology. For her it was perfectly normal; I was the abnormal one. With my eyes trained on the shore, my heart cried out with great clarity and abnormal logic, *Don't wash that, don't! Don't grow up, don't!*

Knowing that something was wrong, Father followed me with an almost spectral gaze, from the aft cabin to the forward hold, from bow to stern. Like a trained hound, he homed in on the smell of my desire. As my physiological urges grew stronger, my facial expressions hardened; I tried to hide them, but his gaze sharpened and became ruthless. 'Dongliang,' he said, 'what are you always sneaking looks at?'

'Nothing,' I said.

He just sneered and looked down at the front of my trousers. 'I know what you're looking at,' he said irritably, 'and I'm telling you to watch yourself!'

With his eyes always on me, I had nowhere to hide, so I walked back to the stern at a half crouch, feeling that my crotch was about to catch fire. I needed water. Half the river was in shadow, the other half in sunlight; a clump of grass was spinning mysteriously on the surface, creating a stream of bubbles. Once again I heard the river call to me: *Come down, come down.* The river was trying to save me with its coded message. This time I was ready to obey. Go down, why not? Go down. I stripped off my white vest and dived into the water.

I swam over to the perfect vantage point, the space between our barge and number eight, where I held on to the anchor, which was cold to the touch and slightly sticky. Maybe the ghost of the martyr Deng Shaoxiang had left a secret curse. I wasn't afraid of the martyr's ghost, nor of secret messages. I looked around – it was the ideal spot for me. Why, I wondered, hadn't I understood the water's secret message in the past? *Come down, come down.* Now that I was in the water, I knew what awaited me: freedom. I could not be free on the barge; I could be free only in the river. How good it was in the water, absolutely wonderful. Finally, I'd found a spot where I could be free, a spot where I could escape Father's watchful eye.

I have a hard-on, Dad. I'm having one whether you want me to or not!

I'm firing my pistol, Dad. I'm firing it whether you want me to or not!

I heard Father's anxious footsteps up on deck and experienced the joy of retaliation. In the shadows between the two barges, I availed myself of the water's protection to calm the tumult fomenting inside me. My body was submerged in the water, submerged in darkness; maybe fish could see what I was doing, but they couldn't talk, so I wasn't worried. The men and boys in the water might have spotted me there, but they could only see my head and shoulders, not my hand, and heads and shoulders were incapable of firing a pistol. And even if they discovered what I was doing, I wasn't worried that they'd say anything. The women and girls on the shore were too far away to see me, and I wasn't interested in seeing them, anyway. Huixian was the only one I wanted to see. She was crouching down on the bank, painstakingly washing her clothes. From time to time her glance swept over barge number seven, but my secret was safe. My father was watching me, while I was watching her.

She loved to dress up at that age. She wore a gardenia on her breast and had on a green skirt, which she hitched up over her knees to keep it from getting wet. Her exposed knees were milky white, like a couple of lovely buns fresh from the oven – no, not buns, I mustn't use such common food items to describe any part of Huixian. How about sweet, alluring fruit? But is there a fruit that resembles knees? I racked my brain, trying to come up with something, when all of a sudden a beam of light passed overhead. There in the spot between the two barges, in the narrow space I occupied, the upper half of Father's face appeared, his staring eyes frightening me so much that I couldn't react before I heard him roar, 'Dongliang, what are you doing, hiding down there? Just what are you doing? Get up here, right this minute!'

I ducked my head under the surface. My ears were pounded by water as I tried to find a new secret message. But there was nothing. Trying to keep one step ahead of my father was hard, and the water offered no help. It was hopeless. I could stay in the water for ever, hold my breath until I drowned, and still I couldn't escape Father's watch over me.

I had to come up for air, I had no choice, like a criminal returning to the scene of the crime. I took a quick look around me, fearful that he might spot signs of my crime. The fluids that had escaped from my body were as nothing in a riverful of water. The surface was as before – no joys, no anxieties – nothing had changed, and I had nothing to worry about. 'It was hot,' I said to him, 'and I wanted to cool off. What's wrong with that? How come you're always watching me? Don't I deserve a little freedom?'

With a sneer, he said, 'I know what you want to do with your freedom. Freedom is wasted on a boy like you. OK, you've cooled off, now get up here.'

I pulled myself out of the water, and the moment I was on deck I was drained of energy, and felt dirty. As I sat there without moving I discovered that I looked like one of those legendary water demons, my skin mottled, rust from the anchor on the backs of my hands, and clumps of moss from the bottom of the boat on my thighs; a rotting leaf was tangled in my hair, plus a golden stalk of rice straw, both of which had been floating on the surface. The really strange thing was that a snail was stuck to my shorts;

I picked it off and tossed it back into the river, and when I looked up, Father was standing in front of me, a scowl of disgust on his face. He was holding a bucket in his hand. 'Go up to the bow,' he said as he gave me a shove. 'You're filthy, body and mind. After I wash you down,' he said, 'go into the cabin.'

I was as disgusted with myself as he was, but I couldn't put my feelings into words. While he was washing me down I shot a glance at the riverbank, where girls from the boats had already hung wet clothes on drying poles; colourful cottons, polyesters and rayons sparkled in the sunlight. One bucket of water was all he needed to wash off the dirt, as I scoured the bank for Huixian's flowery blouse. But the boat girls all dressed pretty much alike, and many of them owned flowery blouses with sunflower patterns, so I couldn't tell which one was hers. The wet clothes seemed flecked with gold in the bright sunlight, and to me it looked like a row of sunflowers in bloom, a sight that brightened my mood. But it also instilled a sense of self-reproach, an understanding that I owed Father an apology. So I took the bucket from him. 'That's enough,' I said as cordially as possible, 'I'm clean enough.'

'Your body, yes, but not your mind. It's a shame I can't clean that.'

Not daring to argue, I walked into the cabin, with him right behind me. 'What are you thinking now?' he asked.

'Nothing,' I said. '*Kongpi*, that's what my head is, just *kongpi*.' Actually, if I told him what I was thinking, he wouldn't understand. I was pondering a perplexing matter: how can a water gourd and a sunflower come together? Two diverse things, one at home on the water, the other on land, how could they come together? Could they ever come together?

Red Lantern

NOBODY BUT me ever called Huixian a sunflower. The residents of Milltown all called her Little Tiemei.

When she was fourteen, Huixian and some of the girls on the other boats started playing a type of hopscotch called house-jumping. Crowding around lines of squares drawn in chalk, they giggled as they took turns jumping from square to square, competing to see who could acquire the most houses.

One day the girls encountered Teacher Song of the district's propaganda troupe. Song was travelling from town to town and village to village, searching for an actress to play the part of Li Tiemei, the heroine of the revolutionary opera *Red Lantern*, and to ride in a National Day parade. The authorities had made strict demands: the actress chosen to play Li Tiemei had to be simple, unaffected and in good health; she should be old enough, but not too old; she had to fit the part, physically and in spirit; and her thinking was to be progressive. She would be required to stand in an open vehicle, holding a red lantern, for several hours. A delicate girl would not fit the bill. Song, who was searching the banks of the Golden Sparrow River, could not have come at a better time, for he had just arrived at the Milltown piers when he spotted the girls playing hopscotch. He stood to one side watching, mesmerized.

The girls appealed to him as simple and vigorous. They all had dark skin and heavy thighs, their feet were somewhat splayed, but their eyes were bright, their voices crisp and clear, and they appeared to be in good health. Naturally, he paid particular attention to their faces. He gave only a passing glance to those like Chunhua, Chunsheng's little sister, with pointed mouths and sunken cheeks. People said that Huixian and Yingtao caught his attention at first, and that he kept looking from one to the other, unable to decide. But the attitude of the two girls, each from different boats, towards an obviously cultured man they'd never seen before could not have differed more. Song took a red paper lantern out of his bag and asked Yingtao to hold it up. She was a charming girl, but a bit ill at ease, guarded and shy in the presence of a strange male adult. Nothing he said could get her to hold the lantern up. She even went so far as to mutter, 'Who do you think you are? You must be crazy to want me to hold up a lantern in broad daylight.' Huixian, on the other hand, was not only confident and unaffected, but, thanks to her native intelligence, she sized the man up and knew that he was someone special. Instinctively grasping the opportunity, she straightened out her clothes, smoothed her hair with her hand and a bit of saliva, and held the lantern up high. She smiled at Teacher Song. 'Comrade, is this how Li Tiemei would do it?'

Song's eyes lit up. 'Nice,' he said. 'That's a good pose. A real-life Li Tiemei.'

Yingtao saw her mistake, but too late. The Seagull camera in his hand revealed his identity. He snapped one picture after another of Huixian holding up the lantern in a variety of poses, each meeting with his approval. 'Good,' he said, 'that's the right look and the right pose, just like Li Tiemei.'

I still recall the spectacular National Day parade that year. The theme was the eight revolutionary operas, each represented by a truck fitted with tractor tyres towing a miniature stage up and down the banks of the Golden Sparrow River. The important characters from each opera assumed their signature poses, in full make-up, as they stood in the truck beds. The *Red Lantern* vehicle was given the lead position. Huixian, I recall, was wearing a red padded jacket with a pattern of white flowers; her hair had been combed into a single long braid, her face was resplendent with dark painted eyebrows and heavily rouged cheeks. For a whole day, she stood on her truck, posing motionlessly with a red lantern held high over her head. She seemed somewhat nervous. 'Pay attention to your expression!' Song shouted from the street. He wanted her to open her eyes as wide as possible to display Li Tiemei's determination to revolt. After blinking a couple of times, Huixian opened her eyes until they were as round as the mouth of a bronze bell, and that expression seemed to infuse her with greater strength; she held the lantern as high as her arm would allow, turning it into a torch. 'Watch that lantern!' Song shouted. 'Be careful with it!' This incarnation of Li Tiemei neither sang nor acted, but standing all day on a truck holding a red lantern over her head was no mean task.

I was worried she wouldn't have the strength to strike her pose the next day, but she was up to the challenge. Li Yuhe and Granny Li, played by a strapping young man with a small horse lantern and a woman in a coarse apron, also stood in the truck, clearly at ease. The eyes of everyone along the parade route were on Li Tiemei, on Huixian, who had quickly and cleverly mastered the pose; she looked the part, just like the propaganda poster of Li Tiemei. People cheered her on; my hands were red from clapping wildly, even though I spotted a cold sore at the corner of her mouth that her make-up could not hide. It could have been caused by nerves or simple exhaustion. Worried that the authorities might find that reason to replace her, I shouted to her and pointed to my mouth to call her attention to the cold sore. Did I really think she could hear me? As it turned out, I needn't have been concerned, since someone had been assigned to look after her. The parade route shifted to Horsebridge on the third day, but this time they were to ride in a miniature steamboat. The Sunnyside Fleet docked at the piers, where we watched the performers – male and female, in costume and full make-up – strut their way to the steamboat; we all recognized the skinny girl among them, and excitedly called out Huixian's name. She was too focused on tying her red hair band to respond, so the tugboat crew broadcast her name – Huixian! – over a bullhorn. She lurched and cast a quick glance at the fleet before catching up with Li Yuhe and Granny Li.

This was Huixian's moment. She was an overnight sensation. Throngs of people on the banks of the Golden Sparrow River were witness to the girl's sudden flowering. People up and down the river were talking about a Little Tiemei who rode past them on a truck, saying that a golden phoenix had flown out of a chicken coop. The lovable Little Tiemei had actually grown up under the communal wing of the Sunnyside Fleet. Reactions to this varied on the barges. Sun Ximing and Desheng displayed the smiling air of people who were responsible for her success, while Yingtao and her family held their own wrists in sadness. Yingtao often broke out crying for no apparent reason. But my reaction was unique. I don't know why, but I was deeply troubled. In the days just before and after National Day, we were often kept so busy loading and offloading cargo that we missed our chance to watch the parades, and all we saw was the litter left by the trucks on their joyous passage: banners that hadn't been taken down, rubbish on the ground, and an occasional abandoned shoe. In my eyes, that litter was all a part of Huixian's glory, which was leaving me in its wake. My sunflower had been blown away, chased by the water gourd, which remained on the water and could never catch something on land.

Keeping up my diary was demanding work. Forced to draw on

what little imagination I possessed, I based my understanding of what was happening to Huixian on what I gleaned from open-air movies and newspaper clippings. I sometimes daringly dreamed up magnificent scenes and wrote them down in my notebook: 'A clear, sunny day. People crowded the Milltown piers under the blazing red sun, in a festive, excited mood to greet Chairman Mao in their midst. He warmly asked the sunflower—' What did he ask her? Nothing came to mind, and I didn't dare keep writing, since I'd brought our great leader into it; if I wasn't careful, I might write something that could be interpreted as a counter-revolutionary slogan. So I turned the page and started a new line, asking the single most important question: 'Sunflower, oh, Sunflower, when will you return to the fleet?'

Some time around November, the parades ended and the people playing the roles of Li Yuhe and Granny Li returned to their regular jobs, he to a farm tools plant, where he repaired tractors, and she to a general store, where she sold soy sauce. But Huixian did not return. She had been discovered, like a piece of raw jade that many people wanted to cut and polish to produce a fine jewel. Song, her most ardent promoter, became her teacher, taking on the task of turning her into one of the foremost portrayers of Li Tiemei.

Huixian's early training came with the district revolutionary op-era troupe, where she was taken under the wing of the renowned actress Hao Liping. Mother had mentioned this woman in the past, referring to her as the Golden Sparrow District's version of Comrade Jiang Qing, the Chairman's wife. An acknowledged authority, she was the most influential and talented actress in the troupe, regardless of which heroic role she was cast to sing and dance in; by donning a fake beard, she could even take on the role of Yang Bailao in *The White-Haired Woman*.

This actress, this Hao Liping, was not favourably disposed towards Huixian; her assessment of the girl was diametrically opposed to that of Teacher Song and others. Finding her anything but simple and natural, she criticized her voice as substandard and found her work ethic wanting. She said Huixian butchered every song she attempted, modifying it to suit herself. After trying her best to mould the new student, she took Huixian to see Song and told him to take her back. 'She has plenty of pluck,' she said, 'but not an artistic cell in her body. She's ambitious, but has no future.'

Though not convinced that Hao Liping was being fair, Song was forced to call together a group of artistic individuals in the district to evaluate Huixian's potential. The results were less than ideal. She had, they concluded, a natural talent for striking the right pose, but her flaws became immediately apparent when she began to sing and act. Disappointed but not ready to let that be the end of it, Song transferred Huixian to a travelling propaganda troupe attached to the cultural centre, of which he was in charge. Having her under his direct supervision, he assumed it would be smooth sailing. It was an unmitigated disaster. The other girls had grown up in the troupe and formed a perfect chorus line. If a line of poplar trees was called for, all it took was an eye signal for them to stand tall and straight; if they formed a flower garden, as soon as the plum blossom opened, the apricot and the peach, the Chinese rose, the primrose and the other flowers bloomed in perfect sequence, without a hint of dispute. But not Huixian. On stage, if all the others were poplars, she was a weeping willow; if she was a lotus, she insisted on blooming before the plum blossom. The bad habit of always wanting to do things her way, which we'd fostered in the fleet, resurfaced. In her mind, when she was on stage, she was the only one the audience was watching. The director, knowing she didn't fit in, placed her in the least conspicuous spot in a dance. Predictably unhappy with this arrangement, she would impulsively work her way to the front to show the audience that her role was the most important one.

Her fellow performers quickly ran out of patience, complaining that she was incapable of getting anything right, which then took the shine off their reputation. Whatever they did when she was on stage was a waste of effort; she was ruining their chances of winning prizes in competitions. What could she do, besides hold up a red lantern, they asked. If the leaders of the troupe were interested in training her, they should wait till the next time there was a parade and let her enjoy the limelight by standing there holding her red lantern.

Chairman Mao once said that persistence triumphs. Huixian persisted with her work in the troupe for some time, but in the end, a single blossom stands no chance against the jealousy of a garden of flowers. She persisted, but triumph eluded her in the end.

Snow fell during the New Year's Festival of the third year. A thin layer of ice formed in the shallows of the river, and the air turned cold on the barges. Piles of snow kept the temperature low on the banks. Huixian returned. She was wearing her hair in the style of dancers in the city, with a round bun tied with a sky-blue satin band. An army overcoat hid her developing body from view. Though it was too big for her, it gave her a unique look; it was obvious that the red sweater and white scarf underneath were what she wanted people to notice. The way she was dressed reminded me a little of my mother. Was that the style of revolutionary romanticism? I wasn't sure if I liked it or not, whether it pleased or concerned me. One thing I was sure of was that it was too early for her to have such an affected look.

The impressive manner in which Huixian came home masked the frustration, the dashed hopes we'd heard about. Zhao Chuntang himself went to fetch her in a newly purchased Jeep. She arrived in town not via the piers but via the highway. She stepped down off the Jeep, a girl proudly returning home in glory. But there was an inside story, a behind-the-scenes detail, which became a hot topic of discussion among the population. I heard lots of stories, the most believable of which was that the authorities were especially fond of this Milltown Little Tiemei, who was regularly invited to attend banquets and such. Older comrades doted on her and were reluctant to see her go. But she was simply too young for many of the things required of her, and too inexperienced. Better to send her home to grow and to train out of the limelight. Many of the leading officials, including Bureau Chief Liu, spoke on her behalf, informing people in the General Affairs Building that Huixian had a bright future, and entrusting the grassroots organization not only to look after her, but to mentor and educate her.

So Huixian returned, but not to the Sunnyside Fleet. Milltown was her new home.

I was no fool, I didn't expect her to come back on the barges. But I hoped for the best. No one knew for sure what her plans for the future might be. Maybe Sun Ximing and his wife knew, since they had been her surrogate parents, but I could not get up the nerve to ask them. I went instead to their youngest son, Xiaofu. 'Have you taken down Huixian's bed?' I asked him.

'Not yet,' he said. 'My mother wants to, but my father won't let her.'

'Are her things still on your barge?'

'Yes,' he said. 'She doesn't want them.'

'Why wouldn't she want all that stuff?'

'Are you crazy?' he said. 'Why would she want to hold on to junk when she can wear nice sweaters and leather shoes?'

I couldn't bring myself to ask around about Huixian. Better to seek answers from myself than from anyone else. I experimented with a deck of playing cards. Father watched me from the sofa. 'Fortune-telling?' he asked. 'When did you start believing in that stuff?'

'Not my fortune,' I said. 'The future.'

'Whose future? How can you expect to have any kind of future the way you loaf around all day?'

'Not my future,' I blurted out. 'I'm Kongpi, I can't have a future. But a sunflower can.'

He just stared at me, as if pondering something. Then it dawned on him. 'What sunflower are you talking about? Don't think you're clever enough to play with words with me. Sunflower – you mean Huixian!' He turned and looked ashore, first at the sky, then at the land, and then uttered a wise comment. 'You're wasting your time trying to figure out the sunflower's future. As long as a sunflower keeps its face turned to the sun, it's got a future. But the minute it drops its head and turns away from the sun, it's done for.'

I'll never forget what he said that day, not till the day I die: a sunflower must keep facing the sun. For years after that, whenever I saw Huixian, out of habit I surveyed the scene around her, including the sky overhead and the ground beneath her feet. Huixian, Huixian, who is your sun? Who do you want to face?

I once spent an entire afternoon at the General Affairs Building waiting for Huixian, but could not screw up the courage to go inside and ask for her. It was during the New Year's Festival, so the building was quieter than usual. Gimpy Gu had gone back to his home in the countryside for the holidays, and a young man who had taken his place in the foyer was engrossed in a newspaper. I wasn't worried, since he didn't know who I was. Seeing the Jeep parked next to the flowerbed, I decided to hang around. As long as the Jeep was there, so was Huixian.

At around noon, I heard noise coming from a small room off the dining hall, so I tiptoed up to the window and looked inside, where I saw Huixian surrounded by a bunch of officials. Like a peacock fanning its tail for their entertainment, she was wearing Li Tiemei's Chinese jacket with buttons down the front and had let her hair down so that her jet-black braid rested on her shoulder.

She seemed uncomfortable, shifting in her chair, first to one side and then the other, in a slightly sloppy way. But her broad smile told me she was happy; it was the smile of a spoiled little girl. She'd grown up since I'd last seen her, and seemed almost like a stranger. The men were drinking the whole time. All of a sudden I saw something shocking. Zhao Chuntang, who was sitting next to Huixian, grabbed her braid and gave it a tug. She stood up, held out her glass of orange juice, and toasted her admirers, one after the other. When she'd finished, Zhao tugged her braid a second time and she sat down. To my astonishment, in the short time since she'd returned, Huixian had become Zhao Chuntang's marionette, and that thick braid, of which she had once been so proud, was now the string he pulled to control her.

In that instant I recalled what Father had said about a sunflower. Huixian, what kind of sunflower have you become? Is Zhao Chuntang now your sun? Do you let him order you around these days? You're no longer a sunflower, you're a blade of grass on a wall, bending whichever way the wind blows. Flames of anger burned in my breast. I bent down, picked up a broken brick and stood at the window taking aim, first at Zhao Chuntang. How can I describe my feelings towards Zhao? I hated him with all my heart, but I was too afraid of him to throw that brick. So I took aim at my sunflower, Huixian! All the officials in the dining hall were her suns; she'd smile at one of them, then bow to another, her cheeks flushed as she glanced round the room. But she was my secret sunflower! No matter how many mistakes she made or how badly she acted, I couldn't harm her. So what could I do? In the end, I decided to let words be my weapon. Using the brick as my writing instrument, I wrote on the wall: 'ZHAO CHUNTANG IS AN ALIEN CLASS ELEMENT'.

That same line. But was he? How should I know?

I wondered why I was obsessed with that line. Maybe because it was the most perplexing slogan I'd ever seen on the banks of the Golden Sparrow River, and I was obsessed with its confounding nature, and maybe there was nothing strange about that. My hatred of Zhao itself was confounding, and I was perfectly willing to display it openly. I was not, however, willing to display my love openly. That was the love of a water gourd for a sunflower. It was a love far more confounding than hate, and more bizarre, the sort of love I was incapable of bringing out into the open.

Celebrity

THE TEENAGED Huixian took up residence in Milltown with her tinplate red lantern.

For the first two years after returning, she kept her Li Tiemei-style braid, ready at a moment's notice to join a parade. Word from the General Affairs Building had it that she usually wore it coiled at the back of her head, both on account of how it looked and to protect the braid itself. Some of the women who were close to her reported that she'd often had nightmares in which she was chased by someone with scissors who wanted to snip off her braid. When they asked who that someone was, she wouldn't say. But then the tears would flow, and she'd say, 'Lots of people, like Yingtao, and Chunhua and her sister . . . all the girls on the boats are jealous of me, and they chase me with scissors to cut off my braid. I nearly die of fright!'

Eventually, there were more parades, but now there were changes, in China and around the world. The biggest change was in the number of trucks and their appearance: there were now five festooned trucks with fifteen actors, presenting a unified front of workers, peasants, soldiers, students and merchants – workers carrying hammers, peasants holding wheat stalks, soldiers with rifles on their shoulders, students reading books, and merchants fingering abacuses. Teacher Song brought some of the young directors from the cultural centre to Milltown to search for actors and actresses. No matter which class they were to represent, they all had to exude a commanding presence, the boys with heavy features, the girls displaying a valiant air that made the enemy tremble with fear. Huixian, of course, was a natural. Teacher Song had planned for her to be on the fifth truck, representing a student in the prime of life. He even gave her a pair of non-prescription glasses. But after several rehearsals, although her body was acting the role, her mind was elsewhere, feeling that she'd been given a supporting role as a student. She wanted to be on the first truck. 'The first truck is for a member of the working class,' Song said, 'who holds a hammer. If you had a hammer in your hand, people would mistake it for a comb.'

'I want to be on the first truck,' she replied, 'or no truck at all.'

Song recognized her attitude as the typical vanity of a young girl, and was determined to stick to his guns. He was confident he could talk her round, never anticipating that she would forget the debt of gratitude she owed him and turn wilful. She refused to participate.

Ordinarily, Huixian would have been a student at Milltown's middle school. She did attend for several days, but her mind wandered when she was sitting in class. At first the teachers and the other students treated her like a myriad of stars circling the moon. But it only took a few days for the novelty to wear off. She was well suited to play the part of Li Tiemei, but ill suited to student life; she was much too deeply immersed in the ambience of the stage, feeling that everyone else was a member of her audience. Once the attention wore off, she decided to stop going. But she needed an excuse to do so, and found one in her braid. Combing it out in the morning was so much work she could never make it to school on time. Besides, she said, some of the other girls were so jealous of her that they tucked scissors into their school bags and hoped that one of the boys would be bold enough to cut it off. There was no evidence of this, but people did feel that she had the right to protect her braid, since it was Li Tiemei's mark of distinction. Owing to her unique status in town, there was a consensus among local officials that maybe she should not be in school, after all. If their superiors came to town and wanted Little Tiemei to accompany them during their visit, to banquets, for instance, having to call her out of school didn't seem quite right.

She was Milltown's celebrity. The visits of senior officials were a busy time for her. Dressed in her Li Tiemei costume and holding her prominent braid, she rode around town in a Jeep in the company of the out-of-towners. But most of the time she had no commitments and was not inclined to look for something to do. She could usually be found in or around the offices, wherever there was any activity. She'd blink her eyes as she listened to whoever was talking, and when a senior official's name came up, she'd smile enigmatically and add her voice to the conversation. 'Are you talking about Gramps Li? Is that Uncle Huang? I know them, I've been to their homes.'

Huixian had grown up as a child of the barges. To her no one was a stranger, and she did as she pleased. No door in the General Affairs Building was left unopened by her hand. Not a single drawer escaped her attention. That was especially true of drawers belonging to the women, which she treated like a scavenger. She ate their snacks, she primped in their mirrors, and she dabbed her fingers in their face creams. Some of the less charitable among them kept their drawers locked; if Huixian could not open them, she shook them and complained, 'How stingy can you be! Who'd want to steal your stuff?'

Zhao Chuntang was responsible for seeing that Huixian's demands were met. She ate her meals in the public dining hall, and was free to enjoy her favourites, but had to also have some things she didn't like. One of the cooks, the one responsible for preparing her meals, was not permitted to throw any of her food into the slops bucket. Except on summer days, Huixian wore her Li Tiemei costume – red jacket with white flowers over dark-blue trousers – on Zhao Chuntang's orders. At first she was happy to oblige, but over time she came to realize that the glorious days on festooned trucks had come to an end. She waited and waited, but Teacher Song stayed away; with no news and no summons, she grew impatient, even irritable. How to vent her unhappiness, and to whom, was the question. She settled on her attire. 'Wearing this stuff doesn't make me look like Li Tiemei, it makes me look stupid.' She was too young to have any sexual awareness, but her body was awakening. Most of her costume jackets had split seams or missing buttons and had become tight-fitting in places. So she packed them up and deposited them on the desk at the propaganda section.

'What's this all about, my Little Tiemei?' the surprised official asked. 'What are you going to wear if you don't keep these?'

'Who says I have to wear this stuff?' she said. 'I have plenty to wear.' She reached up and fingered the collar of her pink blouse to show it off. 'Have you seen this blouse? Notice the embroidered plum flower on the collar? It's from Shanghai. Granny Liu at District Headquarters gave it to me.' After showing off her blouse, she rested her foot on a chair so they could see her shoe. 'Know what this is? It's what they call a T-strap. You can't buy them anywhere in Milltown. Guess who gave them to me. They were a gift from Gramps Liu.'

She was not an indifferent, heartless girl. Often, when she heard the sound of the tugboat whistle, she ran down to the piers to see the people who had cared for her as a child. But they found her behaviour hard to accept: she tossed fruit drops to each of the barges, and when they were gone, she turned and ran off, disregarding all the questions about her health and ignoring her childhood playmates. They could not decide whether she had thrown the sweets as a charitable act, as an expression of gratitude, or in an attempt to maintain ties of friendship. Some of the children looked forward to the sweets and nothing more; others refused to be swayed by her sugar-coated assault. Yingtao, for instance, grabbed the treats out of her little brother's hand and flung them hatefully into the river. 'What's so wonderful about that?' she'd ask. 'We don't eat her stinking candy!'

Everyone knew that Yingtao was jealous of Huixian. But so was her mother, who regularly reminded anyone who would listen that her daughter too had had a chance to ride in one of the festooned trucks, but had let her obstinacy deprive her of a bright future. While bemoaning Yingtao's shyness, she did not hesitate to criticize Huixian maliciously. 'How can a girl like her know how to deal with grown men?' she wondered aloud. 'A little seductress is what she is.'

That was more than Desheng's wife could take. 'Not everybody can be a seductress,' she said pointedly. 'Every girl has her fate, so there's no need to compete. Your Yingtao doesn't have what it takes to seduce anybody.'

Sun Ximing's wife used bloodlines in her defence of Huixian. 'Dragons beget dragons,' she said to Yingtao's mother, 'and phoenixes bear phoenixes. It's Yingtao's bad luck to have emerged from your womb. Huixian, on the other hand, is graced with a better fate. She came to us from the shore, and her return to the shore was preordained. She spent time with us because she had no choice. It's what they call falling on hard times. You know what that means, don't you? Did you really think that our golden phoenix was going to spend the rest of her life in this chicken coop?'

These women's exchange might have seemed laden with feudal ideas and superstitions, even a degree of prejudice, but that did nothing to contradict the truth in their arguments. Huixian had not only returned to the shore, but was now living in the General Affairs Building.

The authorities had arranged for her to share a room with the Director of the Women's Federation, Leng Qiuyun, who, by mutual agreement, became her surrogate mother. Leng was told to look after and mentor their Little Tiemei. Leng Qiuyun, a military dependant with no children of her own, looked after the young orphan with motherly passion – at first. She threw herself into the assigned task, laying out a regimen of study that included reading the daily newspaper to Huixian. But she had an inattentive listener, who nibbled on melon seeds throughout the reading. That infuriated Leng, who complained that Huixian ignored even the fundamental principle of respect for one's elders. 'I'm listening,' Huixian defended herself. 'I listen with my ears, not my mouth. Cracking a few melon seeds doesn't affect your reading, so how can that be disrespectful?' It was clear to Leng that she had her hands full with this girl. Given her background, she ought not to be so wilful. But she was. And there was no reason for her to be haughty. But she was. She could be more mature than other girls her age, but she could also be ridiculously juvenile. Before too long, Leng could not stand the sight of Huixian, as hostility triumphed over reason. She could only look askance at her charge. When she reached breaking point, she went to see Zhao Chuntang, to whom she reported Huixian's behaviour and gave her opinion of the girl. She wanted nothing more than to bow out of her assignment and leave Huixian to someone else. But Zhao had other ideas. 'You must do it,' he said. 'My superiors have made that clear. Can't you see that she's a valuable piece of baggage that's being kept in Milltown for safekeeping until it's delivered to higher authority?' The more people exaggerated the promising future awaiting Huixian, the more Director Leng tried to refute the idea. 'You male comrades only see the girl's exterior. All she wants to do is eat and lie around. How am I supposed to mentor someone who has so little political consciousness? And why should I try? I tell you, heed my words, this girl has no future!'

Everyone knew that Zhao Chuntang was Huixian's protective umbrella, held carefully over her head as he waited for a signal. A year went by, and though signal flares rose from time to time, no decision was forthcoming. Another year passed, and still the signals were mixed. Then a series of personnel changes at local and county level broke the chain of connection, leaving Huixian like a chess piece without a board. Where to put her now became Zhao's dilemma. A directive came down to send Huixian to the provincial Young Female Cadre Study Team for training. But a few days later, a new directive indicated that selections for the study team had changed, thus contradicting the earlier directive. Huixian packed and unpacked her bag several times, but wound up staying put. She became a true idler, spending nearly all her time in and around the General Affairs Building porch, gazing out at the piers and nibbling melon seeds. Having nothing else to do, she had learned the skill of opening and eating melon seeds without using her hands. Compressing her lips slightly, she'd bite down, producing a cracking sound, and neatly spit out two halves of the husk, leaving a hillock of them on the ground wherever she was.

Huixian had plenty of melon seeds, and plenty of free time. The seeds and time were her companions as she waited for her future to appear out of the haze.

Bureau Chief Liu's grandson, Little Liu, came to town one day, ostensibly on business, but actually to see Huixian. Tall and lanky, he had fair skin, long hair, and was wearing a checked shirt. He wasn't very old – in his thirties, by the look of it – but he had all the airs of a fashionable young man from the big city. Huixian was drawn to him immediately. She went up to the fourth-floor meeting room to serve tea, and before she got there she straightened her hair in a small hand mirror and adjusted her clothes, even powdered her face lightly. She brought in two cups of tea, one for Zhao Chuntang, the other for Little Liu, who, instead of taking the cup, just looked at Huixian, starting with her face. She stood there holding the cup and let him look. Obviously someone used to taking liberties, Little Liu let his gaze drift downward, stopping halfway. Huixian put her hand to her chest. 'What are you looking at?' She raised the cup, as if she wanted to throw it at him but lacked the courage. As her face reddened, she handed the cup to Zhao and ran out of the room.

All her preparations were wasted. She ran into the hallway, where women stuck their heads out of their offices to look, which greatly upset her. Straightening her clothes again, she turned and headed back, reaching the door in time to hear Little Liu utter a vile comment. 'The little cunt,' he said, 'belongs on a boat. You don't put dog meat on a dining table!' Then he gave Zhao Chuntang his impression of her looks and her temperament. 'Her face is nice enough, and she's got a good body. But she's vulgar and small-minded. What I find most peculiar is how her figure could have changed so much since leaving her red-lantern days behind. Why does she hunch over like that? She walks like an old woman.'

Angry as this made Huixian, it puzzled her as well. Had she started walking like an old woman after leaving the red lantern? She'd never have thought that Bureau Chief Liu's grandson would see her that way, so critical, as if he were talking about an animal or a toy. He hadn't shown her a shred of respect, and she found him shameless, cocky and obscene, in a smug, superior way. She did not like him, not least because he instilled in her a strange sense of self-loathing. Her mind a tangle of emotions, Huixian ran back to her room, holding both hands over her chest.

Little Liu's visit was a short one. After seeing him off, Zhao Chuntang went straight to Huixian's room, where he tossed a notebook with a plastic cover on to her bed. 'He said you don't put dog meat on a dining table, then he handed me this to give to you – a gift from Bureau Chief Liu. Little Liu came with an

armload of gifts for you, but has taken them all back with him.'
Zhao stood in the doorway staring at her, displeasure in his eyes.
'Aren't you the queen!' he said. 'What harm can a look do? Well,
you've done it this time. No more talk of Gramps Liu. Now that
you've offended his grandson, he's no longer your "gramps".'

Huixian opened the notebook Bureau Chief Liu had sent.
There on the first page he'd written, 'For Comrade Huixian.
Wishing you progress in your studies and your work.' Progress?
A meaningless greeting, nothing more. She knew how significant
Little Liu's visit and her behaviour had been, but what she didn't
understand was why he'd said that thing about dog meat. And
what about that comment about hunching over? Don't tell me,
she was thinking, that a girl's supposed to walk with her chest
thrown out as far as it'll go!

With Little Liu's departure, her future had become hazier than
ever. Huixian sat on her bed, wishing she could cry, but afraid that
Leng Qiuyun would laugh at her. Besides, Little Liu wasn't worth
the tears. So she turned her attention to Chief Liu's notebook, and
suddenly she knew how to express her feelings about the paltry
gift: she wrote 'shit' after the word 'progress'. That made her feel
better, good enough to try throwing her chest out and see how
that looked. But all that did was rearrange the wrinkles in her
blouse. But she wasn't through. Now was a good time to examine
her own breasts, so she locked the door and opened her blouse to
get a good look at herself in the mirror.

What is it about jutting breasts that makes a girl beautiful
and desirable? That had always puzzled her. For small-town
girls, well-developed breasts were considered shameful by most
people. She'd felt the same way until today, when she saw herself
in the mirror and, for the first time, thought she understood.
Her breasts, she discovered, were neither especially large nor
too small, but when she threw out her chest, a mysterious arc
shot out in the mirror. They were so much better looking jutting

out than concealed. Still looking in the mirror, she stood up and moved around, examining herself from all angles, in profile and full on, to see which was the best view of her changing figure. But having no mother or sisters to guide her, she could not judge, nothing suggested itself. That left it up to her own reckoning and imagination. Thinking back to her experiences in the public bath house, she tried to recall what the older, good-looking women's breasts looked like, their size and shape, but failed. Then she remembered something: all those women wore brassieres. Why were her breasts so unappealing? Because she didn't wear a brassiere. Why didn't she own one? Because she'd grown up on a Sunnyside Fleet barge, where none of the women did. She had an idea. Opening a drawer in Director Leng's dresser, she took out three brassieres and tried them on, one after the other. She detected the feminine smell clinging to the material as the cups gently covered her breasts. The image in the mirror, now in a brassiere, was enhanced, but at the same time produced a feeling of unease, of ferment, of coquettishness. The brassiere carried a subtle fragrance.

Huixian decided to start wearing a brassiere. For other girls in Milltown, buying one was something that had to be kept a secret and was entrusted to mothers. But Huixian was motherless. None of her many surrogate mothers could be bothered with this task, so it was up to Huixian to buy her own. Once her mind was made up, she approached the situation with what could be termed fanaticism, an opportunity to do something for herself. She went to the department store determined to buy whatever style and colour she wanted, without a hint of embarrassment, making her selection with a hostile expression. The clerk was visibly intimidated. 'This bra is too big,' she said. 'You want it to be unattractive, do you?'

'What's it to you. If it's unattractive, that's my business!'

Huixian began observing the chests of other girls and women, comparing herself to them and eyeing them critically. She was guided by curiosity, not malice. But the looks created a degree of pressure, and comparisons were inevitable. Between her and me, whose breasts are fuller and more attractive?

Back in their room, she paid particular attention to Leng Qiyun, her eyes glued to her when she got changed. Hurriedly covering her breasts, Leng demanded angrily, 'What are you looking at?'

Huixian stifled a laugh. 'I'm not a man,' she said, 'so what's wrong with looking?'

Still angry, but now somewhat embarrassed as well, Leng replied, 'You're not a man, but that doesn't mean you can look at me like that. What are you thinking?'

Huixian repeated what Zhao Chuntang had said: 'I'm not thinking anything, but aren't you the queen? What harm can a look do?'

Along with Leng's responsibility came the authority to examine Huixian's personal belongings. So when Huixian was out of the room, Leng opened Huixian's chest, to find a number of racy brassieres hidden at the bottom, all exuding a worrisome air of sexuality. To Leng, this was clear evidence of the girl's degeneration, but it was not something she could go to Zhao Chuntang to lodge a complaint about. Instead, she told the female officials, some of whom openly defended Huixian. 'So what?' they said. 'She can buy all the brassieres she wants. No one can see them under her clothes.'

'What about her motive?' Leng said with a derisive snort. 'Have you thought about that? No one can see them now, but sooner or later someone will. You just wait. If you let this go on, one day you might see her in one of those decadent miniskirts. She's an accident waiting to happen!'

Little Liu's visit had forced Huixian to put her disorienting girlhood behind her; she said goodbye with a brassiere, although it was a parting that brought her little joy. The decorations on

Milltown's once gaudy parade trucks had turned black in the farm tools factory warehouse, their treads missing, their wheels scattered on the floor. Teacher Song's propaganda poster for the *Red Lantern* team still hung on the wall; the family in the drama now lived on a warehouse wall, three generations of revolutionaries staring down at abandoned objects, and left with nothing but cherished memories of past glory. The picture, locked away in this cold 'palace', attracted not the eyes of the masses, but mildew, dust and cobwebs. While Li Yuhe and Granny Li's faces were covered with a layer of dust, Li Tiemei's rosy cheeks and bright, staring eyes showed below her defiantly raised red lantern, which fought for space with cobwebs and struggled against the dust.

Whenever Huixian passed the warehouse, she hoisted herself up on to a windowsill to look through the glass at the poster, focusing on the fate of the poster's Li Tiemei as if to somehow determine her own future. She cried on her windowsill perch one day, after seeing her disfigured face on the poster, half of it obscured by soot-like dust, while her lantern was losing its battle against a small spider that had circled its gleam with a web. The more she cried, the sadder she grew, and soon she attracted the attention of the factory workers. 'Little Tiemei,' the surprised workers asked, 'what are you doing up there?' How could they understand? She hurriedly dried her eyes, hopped down from the windowsill and ran off. Her heart ached, thanks to the factory, though she in fact already knew that it had all ended, whether or not she ever looked at what was stored inside. Li Tiemei would never again put on her make-up. Her glory had come out of the blue and then evaporated. It was over, all of it.

She was not Li Tiemei. She was Jiang Huixian, that's all.

What to do about her waist-length braid caused her much anxiety. First she untied it and weaved it into a pair of braids, but after a while she didn't like the way that made her look like a country girl. So she decided to coil her hair again, but instead of wearing it the old-fashioned way, at the back, she piled it up on top. That made her taller, and somehow fashionable, and brought her plenty of scrutiny. Her new hair-style caused a stir around town. Leng Qiuyun said it looked like a pile of horse dung, but no one could deny that after shedding her Li Tiemei appearance, Huixian continued to be someone to watch. Her sudden glow and new image, while gaudy and slightly frivolous, was uniquely hers. With her new stacked hairdo, she came and went at the General Affairs Building, the freshness of youth in full view; like a peacock fanning its feathers with blatant self-assurance, she elicited sighs of admiration from some, reproaches from others, and from one segment of the population, worry and unease.

Zhao Chuntang was particularly worried. A self-possessed man, his face never betrayed his emotions, but a good many occupants of the General Affairs Building could see that he disapproved of Huixian's new hair-style. He had grown used to tugging on her braid. It had become a means of exercising leadership, whether in the building's conference room or in the dining hall when he entertained guests. He made his instructions known by how he tugged the braid – to the side, downward, from the middle, or at the tip. But now that Huixian's braid was stacked atop her head, when he reached behind her out of habit, what he held was not her braid but her lower back, an unintentionally inelegant and easily misconstrued action. Officials in the building frequently noticed a frown on Zhao's face. 'Take it down,' he'd say to Huixian, point-ing at her hair. 'It looks like a pile of horse dung. You don't really think it's attractive, do you? It's brazen and it's ugly!'

Not daring to defy Zhao in public, Huixian would unclip the braid and let it hang down her back. As soon as he wasn't around, she'd coil it back up on top again and complain to anyone who would listen, 'What does he know about beauty? Besides, my braid isn't public property. I don't need him to tell me what to do with it. That's my business.'

It was apparent that Zhao Chuntang was beginning to fold his protective umbrella. International and domestic conditions are in constant flux, and plans for Huixian's cultivation were no different. Her case had become an intricate mystery, now that Zhao's hand was growing tired of holding his umbrella. A desk that had been set up in the General Affairs Building intended for Huixian's studies, complete with books and notebooks, was now covered with a layer of dust. The books had disappeared, and Huixian's drawer was filled with junk: a hand mirror, face cream, a hair band, socks and toilet paper, not to mention her collection of sweet wrappers. That desk represented Huixian's status in the building, and moving it out would signal the loss of her patron's backing. She was in the midst of a transition that would be reflected by the descent of her desk. Transitions for some people have an upward trajectory; hers would go in the opposite direction, from the fourth floor to the ground floor. Her desk had occupied space on the fourth floor for a long time, just outside Zhao's office door. Also on the fourth floor were an office for confidential matters, another for archives, and a small conference room. That in itself demonstrated a determination to invest heavily in Huixian's development. When he was talking to her from his office one day, Zhao noticed that she'd stopped responding. He stepped out into the corridor. No Huixian. When he asked his typist where she had gone, she took a quick look around before saying, 'Oh, I heard her cracking melon seeds just a moment ago, so now where's she gone? Probably downstairs to get more.'

Zhao went over and opened Huixian's desk drawer, which was overflowing with seed husks, some of which fell on to his shoes. Smoke seemed to shoot from his eyes and ears. With an angry stamp of his foot, he yanked the drawer out and flung its contents to the floor. 'The sight of this desk infuriates me!' he barked at the typist. 'Have someone from Logistics come up here and take it downstairs. Get it out of here!'

First stop, the third-floor offices of the Women's Federation. But Director Leng would not let them move it in. 'Aren't I supposed to be mentoring her? Well, then, wait till she's Director of the Women's Federation, and she can have her desk in here.'

So the movers were standing out in the hall, not knowing what to do with the desk, when Huixian walked upstairs with a fresh bag of melon seeds, to find her way blocked by the desk. She cast an icy glare at the two removal men. Making room for them, she said, 'What are you standing around for? Go ahead, move it downstairs. I have no quarrel with you two.' Neither wanting to argue with the removal men nor daring to go upstairs to face Zhao Chuntang, she found an outlet for her anger when Leng Qiuyun stuck her head out of the door to see what was going on. 'What are you peeking at?' she said. 'Chairman Mao tells us to be open and above board and not to plot and scheme!' Leng pretended she hadn't heard the comment, calculating the damage that would be done to her reputation by arguing with a young girl, and slammed the door shut. With a look of contempt, Huixian turned to the removal men. 'She must think that federation of hers is something special, but she doesn't do anything important. Disgusting! Who wants to be in that office anyway? I have to share a room in the dorm with her, but if I had to be in the same office too, she'd drive me mad. I wouldn't work in there if she begged me to. Go ahead, move it downstairs, some place where there's always something going on, like your rooms on the second floor.'

So Huixian's desk wound up in the Logistics department, the messiest, least dignified spot in the building. People were always coming and going in an office where things were strewn all over the place. The so-called officials ran errands day in and day out, which is why there was a carefree attitude throughout the section. Most of the time was spent playing chess or cards or having long conversations about everything under the sun.

Now that her desk had been relocated, Huixian finally began

to use it. It was hard to tell if she'd come to her senses or not, but there was no question that she found that the Logistics department was the place for her. In no time, she began acting as if she was in charge. She fell in love with the game of cards, though she never got good at it. The players tried to help her, telling her to stand behind them and watch and learn, but that wasn't for her. Taking a seat and grabbing the deck, she was relentless, forcing them to coach her in the rules of the game. They had not taken her self-absorption into consideration, and she rebuffed all their good intentions, showing neither gratitude nor the slightest bit of humility. If she played the wrong card, she became hostile, blaming everyone but herself. At first they let her have her way, but over time their patience began to wear thin. No longer Little Tiemei, she had been demoted from the fourth floor to the second, so what reason did anyone have to spoil or protect her? Now, when she came up to the table, they nudged her away. 'Get out of here,' they said with a wave of the hand. 'Go away. You don't know the first thing about cards. Anyone who plays with you is in for a bad time. You're working in the Logistics department now, so go and get us some tea!'

Huixian was smart enough to discern how some people in the department felt towards her and she knew that petulance and hell-raising would do her no good. Getting tea for them was out of the question, so she chose to walk away and play cards by herself. She could be sensible, but they wouldn't appreciate that. After a while, someone – it wasn't clear who – intentionally or not, placed a carton of light bulbs on her desk, where it stayed for several days. She asked for someone to take it away, but when no one responded, she finally picked it up and angrily dropped it on the floor, where a series of crisp explosions brought the others running. They yelled at her, all at the same time. 'You wild little tramp, how dare you smash a caseful of light bulbs! This will cost you plenty!'

One of them said, 'Trying to mentor this girl is a waste of time. She was born for the unruly life on a boat. She can't change, she's absolutely undisciplined.'

One of the others pointed at her and said, 'You think you're still Little Tiemei, don't you? Well, you're not. There's no place in this building for your hell-raising!'

Under such a withering attack, she just stood there, stunned. She was outnumbered, and she knew it, so she ran upstairs to get Zhao Chuntang to come to her aid. But Zhao, who had already been informed of the light-bulb incident, drove her out of his office. 'Where do you get the nerve to come looking for me?' he demanded. 'Go to your room and write a self-criticism, a detailed, heartfelt criticism, and bring it to me tomorrow!'

Huixian sat down on the fourth-floor landing and bawled, but she was wasting her time. So she wrote a self-criticism and handed it over. It was pasted up on the reception-room wall, where she passed it every day, keeping her head low. Growing increasingly afraid of the General Affairs Building, and hot one minute and cold the next, Huixian holed up in her dormitory room all day long. Now, she thought, was a good time to turn to her studies. So she dug out an armful of books and stacked them by her bed. But when she found it impossible to read any of them, from *On Practice* to *The Art of Embroidery*, she put them aside and spent her time at the window, gazing out at the scenery and, though she tried to stop, nibbling melon seeds. But the minute she heard someone at her door she ran to her bed and picked up a book. No one was fooled. The pile of seed husks on the windowsill was irrefutable evidence that she was frittering away her time.

Huixian was clear that being Leng Qiuyun's enemy was not in her best interest. So she made an attempt to mend the relationship. First she placed pumpkin seeds on Leng's desk, then she put a tin of biscuits on her bed and laid a pair of Kapulong socks beside her pillow. A good try, but too late. Leng sneered at the sight of the gifts and said, 'Trying to buy me off, is that it? What for? I'm not your Gramps Liu, nor your Uncle Zhao.' She picked up the pumpkin seeds and biscuits and threw them out of the window, just as Gimpy Gu was walking by. Both falling objects hit him. He picked up the pumpkin seeds and threw them in the rubbish, then picked up the tin of biscuits and took it home with him.

Milltown occupied a large area, but to Huixian it seemed small and confining. There were many places she dared not go, and many others she wouldn't deign to go. Sometimes she went out, only to be met by whispers, and she returned home wishing she hadn't gone out. One day she went to the embankment, nibbling on melon seeds along the way. She saw that the eleven barges of the Sunnyside Fleet were tied up at the piers to unload their cargo of oilseed. On an impulse, she hopped on to the gangplank of barge number one, a packet of melon seeds in her hand, and was immediately spotted by Sun Ximing's wife. 'Hey, it's Huixian, you found your way back!'

The surprised and happy shout, coarse and loud, scared Huixian, who dropped her packet of melon seeds into the river. People ran out of their cabins to see her bending over, watching the river take her seeds away. Everyone was shouting: 'Huixian, come to our place! Huixian, come over to our barge!'

On barge number one, Xiaofu, afraid that the others would snatch her away, jumped on to the gangplank and reached out to take her hand. 'Come on over, Sis, hurry!'

But the movement of the gangplank drew a shriek from Huixian, who wobbled and looked up, her face ghostly white. Instead of taking the boy's hand, she pointed to her own forehead and forced a smile for his benefit. 'I feel dizzy, I don't think I can manage the gangplank. I'll come back another time.' She turned and waved to Sun Ximing and his family, spun around and ran off.

Huixian's trip home had ended before it really began, to the disappointment of the Sunnyside Fleet families. She didn't miss them, it seemed, but they missed her. She didn't care about them, but they were always asking people how she was doing and what the future held for her. Why not, that wasn't confidential information, was it? Inevitably, they learned that she had lost her benefactor and protector at the General Affairs Building, which drew a cloud over her future. No one would have predicted anything like that, and they were anxious to learn what would happen next. When they asked Sun Ximing, he sighed and said, 'I don't know what the future holds for her either, but I hear she's been "hung out" by Zhao Chuntang.'

They knew what that meant. Hearing the words 'hung out' had them thinking back to the girl's unusual background, and many of them could hardly believe their ears. Talk swirled in the air. 'Impossible,' they said. 'Who would dare hang her out these days? She's not a little girl any more. Huixian's grown so pretty, and she has a patron. For the sake of argument, let's say that Zhao Chuntang wants to bring his mentoring project to an end. The people above him won't let that happen.'

Sun Ximing was sick of hearing the chatter of his ill-informed neighbours. 'You people don't know what you're talking about,' he said. 'Don't you listen to news broadcasts? You know what "circumstances" means, don't you? Well, circumstances have changed. They've changed at the top and they've changed in Milltown. And with a change in circumstances, Huixian's prospects have changed as well. When all is said and done, her fate has been "hung out". As a little girl she was hung out on the barges, where we could raise and look after her. But now she's hung out on the shore, beyond our reach. What happens from now on depends on her fate.'

The People's Barbershop

HUIXIAN BEGAN spending every day at the People's Barbershop just north of the General Affairs Building.

The barbershop was Milltown's style centre. It was where the faddish young men and chic young women, or those who aspired to that status, went to exchange the latest news on fashion and hair-styles. They not only accepted Huixian into their circle, but welcomed her. Needless to say, she thrived in the lively atmosphere, enjoying a cordial relationship with barbers like Old Cui. Speaking the same language, they were a perfect match. In the barbershop she was in her element; it was a place where she found contentment.

Surrounded by mirrors and fashionable women, she gazed at her reflection and watched as hair-stylists worked on clients, possibly seeing the light of freedom in the styles they chose. One day, without warning, she stood up from her chair and removed all her hair clips to let her hair down. She walked up to Old Cui, holding on to her braid, and said, 'Cut this off, Old Cui, I'm sick of it. No more braid for me.'

He wouldn't dare. Since he refused to do what she asked, she picked up a pair of scissors, turned to the mirror and was about to do it herself. 'Don't do that!' an alarmed Old Cui said. 'It's

Li Tiemei's braid. How could you think of losing it? Use those scissors, and you'll stop being Li Tiemei.'

Defiantly, she held the scissors in one hand and her braid in the other. 'I'm sick of being Li Tiemei!' she cried out shrilly, staring at Old Cui with a destructive look in her eyes.

To him it sounded like a threat. 'Your braid is public property,' he said. 'The only way I'll cut it off is with Zhao Chuntang's permission.'

'Whose braid is it?' she said. 'Mine or his? I can cut it off if I want to. Go and ask him, I don't care. I'll cut it off myself.'

In the end, Old Cui agreed to do it for her. After discussing several styles that were popular in the big cities, they decided to start a new trend by copying the style seen on Ke Xiang, the heroine of the model opera *Azalea Mountain*. Owing to the pressure he was under, Old Cui's hand shook when he tried to cut off the braid, and he had to stop and call over Little Chen to do it for him. Chen, young and somewhat scatterbrained, made a clicking sound with his tongue as he grabbed the braid and dug in. Huixian's thick, black braid fell to the floor with a dull thud. She shrieked, scaring Old Cui, who thought that Chen had snipped off part of her ear. 'What's wrong?' he asked Huixian, whose eyes filled with tears.

'Nothing,' she said, shaking her head. 'I feel a little light-headed, that's all, something I'm not used to. Now it's your turn. Go ahead and start cutting. There's no going back now.'

For Old Cui, this was an experiment, since he'd never done this style for anyone else. He snipped a bit, then stopped and studied the photo of Ke Xiang in the magazine before continuing. All talk had stopped in the shop, everyone's eyes were glued to Huixian as she sat in the barber's chair. It was a replay of the surprised encounter with a beauty they'd experienced years before at the sight of the girl with the red lantern on the festooned truck. Their mouths hung slack from curiosity at the sight, except this time they were witness not to her glory, but to the risk she was taking.

Huixian covered her face with a newspaper, lacking the courage to watch Old Cui as he plied the scissors. 'Go ahead,' she said to encourage him. 'Do what you have to do. I can live with however it turns out. I won't blame you even if it's terrible.'

People gathered around to get a closer look. They watched and watched until suddenly they started clapping. 'It's lovely!' they shouted. 'Terrific! She'd look great with any hair-do. Goodbye Li Tiemei, hello Ke Xiang!'

Still holding the newspaper over her face, Huixian sneered, 'What do you mean, Ke Xiang? I'm not that old.' When it was finished, she lowered the newspaper and looked at herself in the mirror. 'Not bad,' she said after a long pause. 'Maybe a little old for me, but so what?' She got out of the chair, walked over and kicked the braid, which rolled across the slick tiled floor until it finally came to rest. There was a smile on her face, but tears glistening in her eyes. Refusing to embarrass herself by crying, she covered her mouth with her hand and said, 'Did you see how that braid crawled across the floor? Looked like a snake, didn't it?'

The atmosphere became strained; no one knew what to say as they gaped at the braid on the floor, somewhat stunned. Deep down they felt that Old Cui's scissors had shortened more than Huixian's hair, maybe even her destiny, and they didn't know what to do to console her. The grain-distribution-centre book-keeper had a sudden flash of inspiration. 'Pick that up, Huixian. You can sell it at the purchasing station. A fine braid like that will fetch a good price.'

Without giving it so much as a second look, Huixian said, 'Who'd want it? Nothing you can sell at the purchasing station is worth anything.'

*　　*　　*

Huixian was 'hung out' for half a year or more, during which she spent all her time at the barbershop, which was fine with her, until she was assigned a job by the General Affairs Building. She went out early in the morning and returned to the dormitory after nightfall, almost as if she worked in the barbershop. Then one day Leng Qiuyun changed the lock on their door, and Huixian had to force it open, leading to a violent argument. The confrontation worsened the next day, when Huixian found her chest and bedding out in the hall. Her tin lantern rested atop the chest. She raised the roof outside the room, but Leng Qiuyun had gone off somewhere after hanging a sign on the door, indicating they'd fight another day. Occupants of nearby rooms rushed into the hallway to calm Huixian down, telling her that Leng's husband was coming to visit, and that Huixian's presence in the room would make it awkward for the couple. 'Awkward for her,' Huixian insisted. 'What about me? We share the room, half each, and unless I agree, her husband can go somewhere else!'

'It doesn't matter if you agree or not,' they said. 'The Party Secretary has given the OK, so you have to give up the room for now. Leng Qiuyun talked to Zhao Chuntang, who said you can sleep in the third-floor conference room.'

'What does he take me for?' Huixian shouted. 'Tables and chairs live in the conference room, and I'm neither. I won't sleep there!'

Her face was white with rage as she looked through her things, one item at a time, getting angrier by the minute. She stamped her foot and uttered every dirty epithet she could think of: 'Leng Qiuyun, you rotten cunt, I'll thump you, thump you to death, just see if I don't thump that cunt of yours!'

The officials standing nearby all knew exactly what she meant. These were all swear words used by the boat people. Struck dumb at first, they quickly gathered their wits about them and launched an angry attack from all sides: 'Go to hell, Little Tiemei! The organization wasted its time trying to educate you, mentored you for nothing! How could you fall so low so easily? When there are disputes between comrades, you don't settle them with filthy low-class language you learned on the boats.'

Huixian knew she'd caused a public outrage, but she said, 'Why are you all taking her side? She had it coming. If people left me alone I'd leave them alone, but if they won't, I won't stand by and take it. Chairman Mao said that!'

She could see people looking at her in disgust as a result of her using one of Chairman Mao's sayings to defend herself. One of them sneered and said sarcastically, 'See that? Who said she neglects her studies? She's learned the art of distortion.'

Lantern in hand, Huixian went up to the fourth floor to see Zhao Chuntang, who was well aware that she and Leng Qiuyun were at loggerheads. In the past, Huixian had started most of the arguments, but as her protector, he'd backed her up. This time, while there was no denying that Leng had tossed Huixian's things out into the hall, he placed the blame squarely on Huixian. Before she even stepped into his office, she heard him bellow, 'What are you, a spoiled mistress of the bourgeois class? You've got a nerve, coming here to lodge a complaint! A husband and wife belong together, so what's wrong with sleeping in the conference room for a few nights?'

Unaware of the current situation, Huixian stood in the doorway with her lantern and railed at Zhao, 'You're not being fair! Why can't they sleep in the conference room?'

'He's a soldier, and she's a soldier's wife. It's policy to give them special treatment. Who do you think you are, anyway? Don't you think I've treated you well enough?' Zhao glanced down at the red lantern. 'What are you trying to prove by holding on to that? Just look at you. Do you really think you're qualified to raise a red lantern? Wearing your hair like a disgusting mass of noodles. Go and take a look at yourself in a mirror and tell me if you see even a trace of Li Tiemei!'

The withering criticism rendered Huixian speechless. She raised the lantern and took a look at it, then let her hand drop, causing the lantern to bump against her leg. 'Why do I have to look like Li Tiemei?' she mumbled. 'I'm not her, and that's not my fault. Do I have to be Li Tiemei to bed down in the dormitory?'

'When you're not Li Tiemei,' Zhao said, 'you're nothing. Now stand aside, treat a soldier's dependant the way she deserves and take your things up to the conference room.'

'I'll stand aside, all right, but I won't treat her the way you say. I'm supposed to go to the conference room just because she says so, is that right? Well, I'm not going to do it. She tossed my chest out, so tomorrow I'm going to toss her blanket out!'

'You do that and I'll toss you out, all the way back to the Sunnyside Fleet. Think I won't?' Zhao banged his hand on the table and glared at her. 'Do you want to go back to the fleet? Well, do you? No? Then do as I say, and bed down in the conference room.'

'Why does it have to be the conference room? I could stay somewhere else, like Li Ling's dorm or Little Yao's.'

'You could, but they don't want you. You think you've won over the masses, don't you? You're not the Little Tiemei you once were. Who do you think your friends are now? Not one person in all four dormitories wants you as a room mate.'

'So what? I don't care if they don't like me. I don't care if I never see them again. But I'm not going to sleep in the conference room. It's not safe for a girl to be alone, and it's inconvenient too.'

'What do you mean, safe? And inconvenient? You're haughty, you're wilful, and you're more trouble than you're worth.' His patience exhausted, Zhao turned and gazed out of the window. Suddenly, a look of steely determination filled his eyes. 'Why don't you move out of the General Affairs Building altogether and take up residence in the People's Barbershop. You spend every day there anyway, learning what you can about how the bourgeoisie live, so move in. You'll be safe there, and it couldn't be more convenient.'

Huixian was dumbfounded. Zhao's suggestion caught her completely by surprise. At first it took her breath away, but shock quickly turned to anger. Her lips quivered. Flinging her red lantern to the floor, she said, 'Then that's where I'll go. But I'm going to write a letter to the district authorities and tell them how you people have been treating me. Don't be surprised when Bureau Chief Liu comes asking about me.'

Zhao laughed. 'So, the girl has learned how to play politics. You think you can put pressure on me with Chief Liu, do you? Come here, I want to show you something.' He took a newspaper out of his drawer and opened it up to show Huixian. 'You never read the paper and you won't study, so you're clueless. Your Gramps Liu suffered a heart attack and went up to report to Karl Marx.'

Huixian saw the obituary. The familiar, white-haired old man who had once looked kindly at her across a banqueting table and had watched over her behind the scenes had been reduced to a tiny black-and-white photograph, looking up at her from the pages of a newspaper. Only the kindness and admiration in his gaze remained.

'Gramps Liu, you can't die! None of you care about me,' she shouted. 'What am I going to do?' With that, she crouched down, covered her face with both hands, and wept.

That same day she carried her chest and her red lantern over to the People's Barbershop. Her face was still tear-stained when she walked in and hung the 'closed' sign on the glass door as if she ran the place. Fortunately, the work day had nearly ended and all the clients had gone, so there were no witnesses to her shabby entrance. Old Cui noticed she'd been crying, but was shocked to see that she'd brought her things along. 'No!' he said, waving her back with both hands. 'You can't do that! We don't dare stick our noses into your arguments with the officials. You can't move into a barbershop, not Little Tiemei. What would that look like?'

'Little Tiemei, you say? I count for nothing now, only good for living in a barbershop.'

'You have to control your temper, Huixian. Put your things anywhere you want, but you mustn't move out of the General Affairs Building. If you can't get along with Leng Qiuyun, move in with someone else. Don't tell me they can't find a room for you in that great big building.'

'Who cares about the General Affairs Building? I don't like anybody who lives there. They're all terrible people. No, this is the best place for me. Don't you want me here, Old Cui?'

Suddenly apprehensive, Old Cui picked up Huixian's things to take them outside. 'People say you have an intelligent face but a foolish mind. I don't believe that. I just think you've been spoiled. Everybody gets mad at people sometimes. With all your contacts, you have a bright future, but you mustn't be wilful. Don't throw away your future, like smashing a pot just because it's cracked.'

That comment from Old Cui caused the last bit of Huixian's reserve, which she had been struggling to maintain, to crumble. She burst into tears and placed her foot on the chest on the floor. 'Future?' she sobbed as she dried her tears. 'Future, you say? I've got no future! Gramps Liu is dead, he has been reassigned, and Zhao Chuntang is mad at me. There's no one left. I have no one to rely on.'

Unable to talk Huixian out of staying with him, Old Cui made space for her in the tiny boiler room at the back of the shop, which would have the added advantage of keeping her warm in cold weather. He told the young barber Little Chen to move two benches into the room and put them together to make a bed. 'It's only for the time being,' he whispered to Chen. 'She can stay here a few days, and then we'll improvise. She's Zhao Chuntang's protégée, after all, and he won't give up on her.'

Huixian walked into the boiler room as they were getting it ready for her. The first thing she did was hang a couple of white smocks over the window. 'What are we going to use as smocks tomorrow if you use those as curtains?' Old Cui remarked.

She turned and glared at him. 'How can you be so selfish? Do you expect me to sleep in here without curtains? The situation in town is complicated, as you very well know. There are people who put up a good front but are capable of doing bad things, like peeping at me through the window.'

For Old Cui, the arrangement was makeshift and temporary, at least at first. Everyone in town had heard about the unusual life the girl had led; to them she was a mysterious package, constantly being hung out here and there. For now, she'd been hung out at the barbershop. But a few days passed, and though she went out from time to time, no one from the General Affairs Building had a plan for her, and Old Cui knew that this was bad news. Things had changed, and her future had been revealed, which made the situation suddenly grim; Milltown's celebrity was living in a barbershop!

Four days later, Zhao Chuntang came to the People's Barbershop. When he walked in, everyone, including Huixian, stood up. They wondered if he'd come for a haircut or to rescue Huixian. He sat in the barber's chair. 'I've let my hair get long,' he said. 'How about a trim, Master Cui?'

With a quick glance at Huixian, Old Cui picked up his comb and scissors and walked up to the chair with a strange feeling of trepidation. 'Has the Secretary come on official business?' he asked Zhao.

'Official and personal, I need to attend to both.'

So, with great care, Old Cui cut Zhao's hair, urging Huixian out of the corner of his eye to make amends with Zhao. She merely turned her head, with a look that said 'I'd rather keep a piece of broken jade than an undamaged tile,' and began filing her nails. Old Cui laid down his comb and picked up a razor. 'How about a shave, Secretary Zhao?'

Zhao made no response, but Huixian, audacious as ever, made another of her unseemly comments. 'Hah!' she said. 'Zhao Chuntang doesn't have a beard, so there's nothing to shave.'

Zhao tensed, and Old Cui felt it. Slightly unnerved, he barely stopped himself from holding Zhao down in the chair. But all Zhao did was turn and say, 'Could I ask you all to give Old Cui and me a few minutes to speak in private? It's work-related.'

A few of the other customers, haircuts still in progress, demurred momentarily, but then followed the barbers, towels still draped around their necks, and stood outside the door. One of them, unaware of what was going on, wondered aloud, 'What work-related issue could Zhao Chuntang have with Old Cui?' One of the others, equally in the dark but wanting to give the impression of being well informed, said, 'Work-related? That's just an excuse. Huixian's living in the barbershop these days, and I wouldn't be surprised if something's going on between her and Old Cui.' Little Chen reacted to that comment by cursing, 'If anything's going on, it's between Old Cui and your mother! You must have sperm swimming around your brain the way you see everything through your crotch! You really don't get it, do you? Huixian is taking refuge here for the time being.'

As promised, a few minutes later Old Cui opened the door to let Zhao Chuntang, whose hair reeked of Phoenix hair tonic, leave. He looked relaxed but sort of sad. The customers poured back into the shop, where they saw a red-faced Huixian with a comb in one hand and a pair of clippers in the other, banging the two together over and over and shouting, 'Who wants their hair cut? Come on, don't try to shame me. I'll shave your heads, all of you!'

Anyone could see that she was hysterical, but no one had any idea what had caused it. It was left to Old Cui to rush up, snatch the tools out of Huixian's hands and force her into the boiler room. 'Settle down, Huixian,' he said loudly, before shutting the door and locking it from the outside.

The shop customers peppered Old Cui with questions. 'What's wrong with her?'

Ignoring their questions, Old Cui muttered, 'Me, mentor her? I'm a barber, how am I supposed to do that? Orders from the organization, he says. All we do in the barbershop is cut and wash and shave and blow-dry, what kind of mentoring is that? So she can go to Zhongnanhai to shave the heads of the Central Committee?'

Little Chen would have gone in to console Huixian if he'd known how, but all he could do was cast a perplexed look at Old Cui, who covertly gestured in the direction of the boiler room. 'Zhao Chuntang was here to hang out Huixian,' he said softly. 'Starting tomorrow, the barbershop is where she'll hang out officially. Zhao's idea is to bring people of a kind together, so from tomorrow, we three are officially comrades-in-arms.'

Little Chen could hardly believe his ears. 'You're joking, right? No matter how far she's fallen, she can't come here to be a barber, can she?'

'Don't look at me like that,' Old Cui said. 'What makes you think I'd joke about something as important as this? I didn't believe it myself at first. Who'd have thought that the grand Little Tiemei would wind up working with us?'

News of Huixian's downfall spread faster than a racehorse. The crews of the Sunnyside Fleet had all heard by the next day that Huixian had been hung out by Zhao Chuntang. People disregard Fate at their peril. Over the course of several years, Huixian had not been able to escape her fate. The boat people's expectations regarding the direction her life would take had run the gamut from county to district, even to the provincial capital; as for her workplace, a broadcasting station or propaganda team had been mentioned, as had the possibility of her becoming a member of the Women's Federation or County Committee. Not a negative thought had ever emerged, and since they had seen her heading in only one direction – up – who could have guessed that she'd wind up in the People's Barbershop? Huixian, Huixian, the pride of the Sunnyside Fleet; her proud figure would from now on be seen only through the glass of the People's Barbershop window, continuously under the critical gaze of men and women of all ages. Her proud hands would repay the residents of Milltown and the nurturing people of the Sunnyside Fleet. Huixian, Huixian, from now on, she would serve the people by shaving their beards and cutting their hair.

That year Huixian turned eighteen.

PART TWO

Haircut

IN MY eleven years aboard the barge I never posted a letter of my own. But I stopped by the post office every time I went ashore to post letters for my father. I was his postman.

A large wooden box had been nailed to the wall outside the Milltown Post Office, put there for the use of the boat people. Year in and year out, it remained empty, which is understandable when you consider that most of the boat people were illiterate. When their sons and daughters reached adulthood and started their own families, they continued their lives aboard the barges. If they didn't meet on the Golden Sparrow River, they met on the piers, and so asking someone to write a letter and attach an eight-fen postage stamp was more than merely a matter of dropping one's pants to fart, it was a waste of money and energy. For a long time, the only users of the fleet postbox were the occupants of barge number seven. Once every month or two I received a letter from Mother. In it she urged me to study hard, reminding me that though I was living in less than ideal circumstances it was my duty to work hard. She insisted that I set up long-term goals, the mere thought of which gave me a headache. Sure, I had goals, all of them were related to Huixian, but I couldn't say so. If I did, I'd either become the butt of people's jokes or a sinner in their eyes. How could I tell Mother? I couldn't, so I didn't reply to her letters, which came less and less frequently. Eventually Father's letters were the only things that ever showed up in the postbox, where they waited for me to go ashore. Everyone knew that my father was an orphan with no siblings, no relatives and no friends. At first he wrote to the leadership of the County Party Committee, but kept going higher, to district Party and governmental offices: the civil administration, the organization bureau, the commission for inspecting discipline, the history office, the office for complaint letters and calls, even the family-planning commission. Throughout my eleven years on the barge, Father sent appeals to leading Party bureaus and offices regarding his status as the son of a martyr, demanding a definitive ruling and an official certificate that recognized his martyr-family status. Unfortunately, the red-lined envelopes I received in reply were invariably thin and light, and I never saw one of those certificates, which Father had described to me as being red with gold print. Instead they were standard-issue letters with a series of dotted lines. Sometimes Father's name was filled in, sometimes not. 'Comrade so-and-so,' they read, 'your request is very important to us. At a future date we will give it careful attention and scrutiny. Revolutionary greetings to you.'

More than once he told me that the only inheritance he could leave me was one of those martyr-family certificates. I was no fool, I knew the value of one of those things, and on this matter we were in rare agreement. He diligently wrote his letters aboard the barge, and I diligently posted them for him. I never went into Milltown without performing the same task: I went into the post office, bought a stamp, pasted it on to the envelope, and dropped it into the big green postbox. It became as mechanical and as fruitless a routine as scooping ladlefuls of water into the river – not even a tiny splash was made.

On my way to the post office one day I saw a scowling, uniformed man emerge with a drawerful of keys, which clattered as he walked. He dropped the drawer on the ground in front of the green postbox, which he opened with one of the keys, releasing an avalanche of white envelopes into the drawer. I stepped up and looked at the drawer, but all I saw were envelopes piled on top of one another, with no discernible names or addresses, and, of course, no return addresses. I instinctively followed the drawer on its trip back, until the man became aware of my presence. He spun around and shouted angrily, 'What the hell are you up to?'

'Nothing,' I said. 'I'm just posting a letter.'

He looked at me suspiciously. 'You're from the Sunnyside Fleet, aren't you? Aren't you Ku Wenxuan's son?' He shook the drawer in his hands. 'You came at the right time. Toss your letter in here.'

I took another look at the drawer, then glanced back at him, with his gloomy face and crafty eyes, and wondered if I was being taken in. Why should I trust him, or that drawer of his? I waved him off and walked back to the postbox, whose dark, gaping mouth seemed to draw me to it. The lock on its side was still swinging back and forth. Was it taking me in too? Why should I trust that postbox? It was, after all, Milltown's postbox, in a town where people said even the sky belonged to Zhao Chuntang. That had to include the postbox. Be careful, I told myself, be very careful. So I stuck Father's letter into my bag; better to forgo the one close at hand in favour of the more distant one. I could go to Wufu to post my letter, or, for that matter, Phoenix. It didn't matter where I went, but I knew I wasn't going to commit my father's future to the Milltown postbox.

After that, on my trips to Milltown, in addition to buying provisions, there was another thing I needed to do – some might have seen it as important, others might not have. It was something I did for myself, something I couldn't talk about.

I went to the People's Barbershop, where the walls on both sides of the entrance had been opened to install display windows.

Three plastic mannequin heads were arrayed in the window to the left, each adorned with a woman's wig, and each with a sign in front that stated the wave length: long, medium and short. That threw me. This wasn't the Golden Sparrow River, and there was no wind, so why did women want waves in their hair? I stepped over to the other window, where illustrations torn out of magazines were displayed. The print quality was poor, but good enough to see city girls from somewhere or other trying to outdo each other with their bizarre new hair-styles. One of the illustrations was both clear and familiar. It was Huixian. She did not shy from showing herself to her best advantage, letting herself be seen with the others. She was turned sideways and looking off at an angle, her eyes bright, and she wore her hair coiled weirdly on top of her head, so that it looked to me like a stack of oil fritters.

I looked at her hair-do from every angle, and didn't like what I saw, though I wouldn't say it was ugly. I was reminded of something my father had said: when a sunflower turns away from the sun, it droops, bringing an end to its future. I knew that Huixian, my own sunflower, had turned away from the sun. By leaving the General Affairs Building, she was, I felt, closer to me. But that didn't mean I'd been given a chance to get closer to her. She was now a barber, yet people continued to treat her as if she were the moon and the stars aligned around her. Local girls who wanted to look as pretty as possible were allowed to get close to her, Old Cui and Little Chen ate and worked alongside her every day, and drooling, audacious boys around town never missed a chance to draw up near her. I wasn't that brazen, nor was I that audacious, and if I didn't need a haircut, I couldn't force myself to go inside.

My hair, which grew slowly, still wasn't long enough, and that was a nuisance. So I sat in the doorway of a cotton-fluffing workshop across the street from the People's Barbershop, laying my bag next to me so people would think I was taking a rest, open and above board. The people inside were hard at work on the cotton; the clamour of the wires fluffing cotton – *peng, peng, peng* – echoed my heartbeat. I couldn't pace back and forth in front of the barbershop, since that would attract the attention of the people inside, and I definitely couldn't press my face up against one of the windows to get a good look; only an idiot would do something like that. No, I had to sit across the street and watch the people come and go, creating pangs of jealousy, whether I knew them or not.

Xiaogai from the security group went in several times, with obvious evil intentions towards Huixian. He had a special talent for looking respectable when he walked through the door, even when he was harbouring those evil intentions. He walked out again, talking and laughing.

Among the boat people, Desheng's wife was the shop's most frequent client. Her appearance was especially important to her, and her husband doted on her. The other boat people, more money conscious, had their hair done by street vendors. But for Desheng's wife money wasn't as important as having the latest hair-style, and she and Huixian were closer than ever. She'd sit in her chair and chat away while she was having her hair done, looking around at the local girls' fashionable hair-styles. With so much to see and do, it'd be a while before she left. On those days when she came by, I went inside the workshop to watch the cotton being fluffed, not knowing what I'd say if the woman, a notorious busybody, asked me why I spent my days sitting outside doing nothing.

At times my body felt hot all over as I sat there guarding my secret, and at other times I turned cold and stiff. The barbershop was open to the public, so why couldn't I saunter in like everybody else? I had no answer. I was sitting there because of Huixian, gentler than anyone could imagine, but also gloomier. For eleven years I'd fallen under the constant scrutiny of my father, and the shore was the only place where I could escape his radar-like vision. These were the times when I tasted true freedom, and I put this precious time to good use, keeping a supervisory eye on Huixian – no, supervisory isn't the right word. 'Guarding' is more like it, or, even better, 'watching over'. Neither job, of course, was by rights mine, but for some strange reason it had become second nature.

Men were always entering and leaving the barbershop, and I could easily spot those who had something other than a haircut in mind. But was I any different? Maybe not. Probably not. I'd started going ashore wearing two pairs of underwear as a hedge against an ill-timed erection. That proves that I did have something in mind, and it was a worrisome thought. Wearing two pairs of underwear was proof of my sinful nature, and timidity and restlessness were a by-product of impure thoughts. Sometimes I got a fortuitous glance through the display window of Huixian standing behind her barber's chair. More frequently, all I saw was her white moving image. Near her, I yet remained far away, and that was an ideal distance to lure me into dreaming up scenarios which frightened me yet brought me great pleasure: I imagined the conversations she had with the people in the shop, what made her frown and what made her smile; I imagined why she treated X with such warmth and Y with such aloofness; when she was at rest, I imagined what she was thinking; on those occasions when she was moving, I imagined the shape of her legs and buttocks; and when she was working on a client's hair, I imagined the swift, agile movements of her fingers on the clippers. The one thing I would not let myself imagine was her body, though that was sometimes beyond my control, and then I limited my visualizations to the areas above her neck and below her knees. When even that was impossible, I forced myself to go over and stare at a dustbin on which someone had written the word *kongpi*. Could that have been a warning to me? If so, it was an effective sign. I read the word aloud three times – *kongpi, kongpi, kongpi* – lowering the temperature of my sex organ. An embarrassing sense of excitement mysteriously evaporated.

Spring arrived in May, with warm temperatures and flowers blooming at the base of the walls that lined the streets: Chinese roses, cockscombs and evening primrose. Even the sunflowers by the entrance to the People's Barbershop were in full bloom. As I walked past the entrance, one of the big golden flowers actually struck me in the leg – lightly, to be sure, but it got me thinking about the past; since it was a sunflower, I had to believe this was either a hint or an invitation. How could I be unmoved? Unprecedented courage dropped on to me out of the sky. I got up, picked up my bag and decisively pushed open the glass door.

Every seat in the barbershop was taken, and no one took any notice of my entrance. The men cutting hair were too busy to greet me. Huixian, whose back was to me, was washing a client's hair. But I could see her face in the mirror, and there our eyes met. A light flashed in her eyes, but only for an instant before they darkened again; she turned slightly, as if to see me clearly, but didn't follow through as she slowly turned back again. She might have seen it was me, but she might also have thought she was mistaken.

I spotted a newspaper rack by the door, where a days-old copy of the *People's Daily* hung crumpled, dog-eared and enervated. Just what I needed to keep anyone from seeing my face. I sat in a corner, trying to arrange the angle and distance between my head and the newspaper, but failed miserably. It seemed to me that Huixian kept looking at me in the mirror, and the stronger my feelings became, the more uncomfortable they made me. To be honest, I had no idea how to go about establishing a friendship with Huixian. I hadn't known back then, and I still didn't know. Hell, I didn't even know what I should call her. Back on the boat I'd never called her by her name, and I'd never used the word 'sunflower'. It was always 'hey'. I'd yell 'hey' and she'd come running, expecting to get something good to eat. But she'd changed; so had I, and I couldn't figure out how to talk to her. I thought hard about that, finally deciding to let nature take its course. If she spoke to me first, I'd count myself lucky. If she chose not to speak to me, it was no big deal, since I wasn't there to chat her up. I was there to keep watch over her.

Women love to talk, and that was especially true of the women who came to have their hair done. Curious about Huixian's stylistic talents, they were even more curious about her precipitous fall from grace. Dressed in a white smock, like a doctor, and wearing rubber medical gloves, she was washing the hair of Wintersweet, the female member of the security group. Buried in the sink, Wintersweet's head was covered with soapy water, but that did not stop her from asking questions. 'Huixian,' she said, 'I thought you were supposed to be studying in the provincial capital. What's our famous Little Tiemei doing in a barbershop?'

By this time, Huixian had a ready answer for such questions. 'I'm afraid that Little Tiemei has become Old Tiemei. What's wrong with a barbershop? Do you think that someone working in a barbershop is inferior to other people? Aren't we all serving the people?'

With a worldly look, Wintersweet snorted contemptuously and said, 'You so-called artistes don't know how to give an honest answer to anything. But I'm on to you people, don't think I'm not. All you do is dance and sing and wear stage make-up. Have you planted a rice seedling or made a single screw nut even once in your life? Serve the people, you say? The people are serving you!'

'Go and make that speech to somebody else,' Huixian said. 'You're barking up the wrong tree with me. I gave up that life long ago. I'm washing your hair now, aren't I? You're sitting and I'm standing, so who's serving whom? Tell me that.'

That shut up Wintersweet, but just for a moment. Suddenly her eyes flashed as she looked up at Huixian. 'Those are fine-sounding words, Little Tiemei, but you'll never be happy serving people like us. I know why you're working in the barbershop, you're practising for the day when they send you to cut the hair of high-ranking officials.'

Huixian had been getting angry, but she had to laugh at this last comment. 'You certainly do know how to say stupid things,' she said. 'I've seen my share of high-ranking officials, with their cooks, their bodyguards and their secretaries. But I've never heard of one having his own barber.'

Another snort from Wintersweet. 'Don't get it into your head that you're a woman of the world. You're still a novice, and I'm telling you that a woman who survives by working with her hands is fated to live on gruel, but a woman who gets by thanks to her good looks or who has a powerful backer will eat and drink well.'

'Now you're making sense,' Huixian said. 'I'm not good-looking and I don't have a backer, which is why I'm serving you.'

Making clicking sounds with her tongue, Wintersweet thought for a moment before replying, 'That's strange, I heard you had lots of backers. There's Zhao Chuntang in town, Secretary He at the county level, and Bureau Chief Liu in the district government. Don't tell me they've all suddenly stopped backing you.'

Clearly annoyed, Huixian said with a sneer, 'Are you here to have your hair done or to cook up stories? Front or back, I've got nobody, not even a mother and father. Where would I get a backer? People like you may yearn for a backer, but not me.'

That rebuff silenced Wintersweet, but her mind kept racing. In the end, she was incapable of controlling her tongue. 'I know why you're here, Little Tiemei. You've been hung out at the grass-roots level. For how long? Six months? A year or two? I advise you to ask the leadership for a timescale. Listen to me when I say that even a young girl grows old one day, like a pearl that turns yellow, and there's no future for anyone who's old and ugly.'

Huixian's tolerance ended at that moment. I saw anger and loathing in her eyes. She dug her fingers into Wintersweet's scalp, snatched a towel off the rack and jammed it down on the woman's head. 'I'll hang out as long as it takes – until the day I die if necessary. Don't you worry about me. I've been hung out all my life, I'm used to it by now.'

I don't know why, but I couldn't hide my head any longer. I lowered the newspaper and cast a ferocious glare Wintersweet's way. 'If you can't hold your tongue, you cunt, I hope you choke to death!' I spoke so softly the target of my curse could not possibly have heard me as she followed Huixian back to the chair, her hair dripping wet.

'Why get mad at me, Little Tiemei?' she said. 'I'm just giving you advice. It's for your own good.'

But Little Chen had heard what I'd said. He turned and glared at me. 'Who are you calling a cunt? And who's supposed to choke to death? What's a big boy like you doing sounding off just because a couple of women are bickering?'

'I didn't say anything,' I said. 'I'm reading the paper.'

'What are you here for?' he said. 'Why squeeze your way into a busy shop just to read the paper? This is a barbershop, not a reading room.'

'I'm waiting for a haircut, what's wrong with that?'

'Are you sure you didn't come to read the paper? I'll bet you're not interested in reading the paper *or* getting a haircut. You're sneaking around like a US Chiang Kai-shek agent. Who are you and where are you from?'

Now the people took notice of me, and I saw Huixian glance my way. She hadn't got over her anger, not completely; it was a lazy, casual glance. But then her eyes lit up. She recognized me, I

could tell. Pointing her comb at me, she said, 'It's you, you're that
. . . something Liang.'

She smiled, and I saw in her smile that she was pleasantly
surprised, if somewhat puzzled, racking her brains to come up
with a name. How depressing. How could she have forgotten
my name? Ku Dongliang would have worked, or Elder Brother
Dongliang, or even my nickname, Kongpi. She pointed at me,
then dropped her hand and said with obvious embarrassment,
'What a rotten memory I've got. It's on the tip of my tongue,
but it won't come out. It's something Liang. You're from one of
the barges of the Sunnyside Fleet, aren't you? Now I remember –
there's a sofa on yours.'

That was the sum total of her memories, the sofa on our boat,
and I was reminded of how Yingtao had tried to stir up trouble
between Huixian and me after they'd had an argument. Yingtao
had come looking for me and said, 'Go on, be her lackey if that
makes you feel good. But I'm telling you, Huixian doesn't like
you, she likes your sofa and the treats your mother sends. She's
bourgeois through and through, a girl who wants the good life.'

'Don't look at me like that,' she said. 'I've forgotten your name,
but only for the moment.' Seeing how disappointed I was, she cast
a guilty smile my way before turning to the people in the shop.
'What's his name? Remind me, someone. All I need is one word
to jog my memory.'

A young man in a checked sports shirt, a crane operator, knew
me. He was standing there with a peculiar smile. In a pinched
voice he said, 'Kong. You know, Empty.'

'What do you mean, Kong? Stop playing around. Empty isn't a
family name,' Huixian said. 'Who are you, Mr Full?'

'I thought you said all you needed was one word. I know his
nickname, it's Kongpi.'

Aha! Now she had it. Either she was embarrassed or she was
oversensitive, but I saw a change come over her. Her cheeks

reddened as she rolled up her client's smock and hit me on the shoulder with it. Then she covered her face and giggled. 'Me and my rotten memory! You're Ku Dongliang, aren't you? I pretty much survived on the snacks you gave me when we were kids.'

What could I say? I heard a whispering sound as a gentle breeze redolent with the smell of Glory soap swept past my ear. She was shaking the barber's smock in my direction. 'Ku Dongliang,' she said in a pretend commanding voice, 'come on, I'll cut your hair.'

Quickly putting my hands on top of my head, I said, 'It's not long enough to cut today. Besides, I have to get back to the barge.'

'You'll have to get it cut some time, if not today.' She inspected my hair. 'What do you use on it, a comb or a broom? That's not a head of hair, it's a bird's nest. Are you waiting for a bird to lay an egg in that?' Putting her smock to work flicking loose hair off the chair, she said, 'What are you waiting for? Quit stalling and sit down.'

Now what? I couldn't make up my mind. Huixian nudged the chair with her foot, swivelling it around towards me and creating a gust of wind that made the hem of her smock flutter enough to let me see that she was wearing a blue knee-length skirt underneath. It too was caught by the gust of wind, revealing her knees, her knees, those knees, two lovable little bun-like mounds, two alluring, fruit-fresh knees. The scene had a dream-like quality. Be careful, I heard a voice whisper sternly, be very careful. It sounded like my father, but could have been my own voice. I didn't move and didn't know which way to look. A person's gaze can be dangerous, it can give away your secrets. Whenever I sensed this danger in the air, I reminded myself: Above the neck and below the knees. But I didn't have the nerve to look at her neck *or* her knees, so I kept my eyes on the floor, where there were clumps of dark hair, some long, some short, like an archipelago of dark islands. Huixian was standing on one of those dirty islands with her white half-heeled shoes and flesh-coloured nylons, on which a tuft of hair – man's or woman's, no way to tell – hung precariously.

'What's wrong with you? You look like a frightened criminal.' She studied me, as doubt crept into her eyes. 'Ku Dongliang,' she said playfully, 'you haven't changed. You're as peculiar as ever. Why did you come to a barbershop if you don't want a haircut?'

What could I tell her? Nothing. 'Not today,' I stammered. 'Maybe next time. It's getting late. My dad's in poor health, so I have to go and get dinner ready for him.'

She uttered a gasp, probably reminded of my father and his famous genital mutilation. She clearly felt like laughing, but not wanting to embarrass me, she covered her mouth. When she saw what I was gazing at, she looked down and spotted the tuft of hair on her stocking. 'Damn,' she said, 'no wonder I felt an itch. So that's why you're looking down there.' With a stamp of her foot, the hair fell to the floor, then she looked up at me and, out of the blue, asked, 'How are my surrogate parents? I asked Desheng's wife to invite them to come and see me, but they never have. They must be unhappy with me.'

She had a cold side, but she also had her impulsive moments, and I could tell she wanted me to smooth things over for her with Sun Ximing and his wife. 'Why would they be unhappy with you?' I said. 'They think a haircut here costs too much. They don't part with their money easily.'

'Costs too much? How much can a haircut cost at the People's Barbershop? Go and tell them to bring the whole family. I'll shampoo, cut, blow-dry and perm, and I won't charge them anything. I'm here to serve the people.'

I told her I would, then went over to retrieve my bag from the corner, with a roomful of curious eyes on me. Their expressions varied, but you could hear the wheels turning in their heads. I had no idea what they were thinking, but Huixian's display of friendliness towards me had upset them, especially the fellow in the checked sports shirt, who was sitting in one of the chairs. He stuck out his foot and kicked my bag. 'What are you hiding in there, Kongpi?' he said. 'You bring it with you every time you come ashore. If I was in that security group, you can bet I'd want to search it.'

I glared at him and unzipped my bag. 'You want to search it? Go ahead, I dare you.'

He gave it a quick glance, but before he could say another word, Little Chen nudged me on the shoulder. 'Go on, get out of here,' he said. 'This is no place for you to be showing off. Don't come back unless you need a haircut. This is a barbershop, not a public park.'

If he hadn't been one of Huixian's fellow barbers, I wouldn't have stood for that kind of nasty treatment. I turned and walked to the door. Huixian came up and patted my bag. 'You can't blame people for being suspicious. Why do you have to bring a big bag like that with you when you come ashore?' She squeezed it once, then a second time, a habit I knew well. Ever since she was a little girl she had been in the habit of squeezing people's bags. Mine was obviously filled with cans and other stuff which was of no interest to her. She pulled her hand back, reached into the pocket of her smock and brought out a stick of chewing gum, which she handed to me. 'Give this to Xiaofu for me, would you? He asked me for a stick of gum when we met on the street once. I told him I'd get one for him, and a promise is a promise.'

I tossed the gum into my bag.

'How's Yingtao doing? Thinking of getting married?'

She'd forgotten my name, but not Yingtao, her mortal enemy, and that really made me mad. 'How should I know? Who cares if she's getting married or not?'

'I just asked. What are you so stressed about?' Then, with a hint of mischief, she pointed at me and said, 'I'm not trying to be your matchmaker or anything.'

Apparently, her animosity towards Yingtao hadn't faded, and I waited to hear what she'd say next. I didn't have long to wait. 'When you get back, tell her to stop talking behind my back. I'm a nobody now, a barber, so there's nothing for her to be envious about, and nothing to talk about.'

It was not a welcome assignment, and as I walked out of the barbershop, my mind was a welter of confused thoughts. After not seeing her for so long, I'd had a friendlier reception than I'd imagined. She seemed open and approachable, which gave me a warm feeling. But even more, I felt a sense of loss. How could she have forgotten my name? Or had it all been an act? Not finding an answer, my mood soured. She had asked me about everyone but me, and maybe all she could recall about me was that I was Kongpi. I walked quickly out on to the street, then turned for another look at the barbershop. The sunflower by the door had opened happily to greet the bright sun. What a great thing a sunflower is! As I stared at the flower, I could imagine Huixian wishfully planting a seed outside the barbershop door and watering it each morning. That made me feel better.

Now that I'd left the barbershop and Huixian, my imagination took hold, and my enthusiasm returned with a vengeance. I imagined a conversation with Huixian. She was interested in me. 'How old are you, Ku Dongliang, twenty something? How come you're still single? Can't get a girl?' What do I say to that? 'Don't look at me like you're unworthy, like you're seeing me through a crack in the door. I could get one if I wanted. Six-Fingers Wang's oldest daughter could come into my cabin on her own, but I wouldn't thump her. I don't want to thump anybody, believe it or not. Didn't you once say that Chunsheng's little sister will change into a beauty when she's eighteen? Well, she flirts with me day in and day out, but believe me, she's wasting her time. I'm not one of those guys who'll say anything to make himself look good. Have I ever lied to you? If you want to know, there's a girl on shore who likes me too. You know Li Juhua, who runs the oil pump on the pier, don't you? Well, the only thing that mars her good looks is that white patch of skin on her neck. I came ashore in the rain one day, and she offered me an umbrella without my having to ask for it. I don't need to tell you why she did that, do I? Nor do I have to tell you what it meant when I turned her offer down.' I imagined Huixian's reaction to hearing this: 'You have high standards,' she'd say. 'So what kind of girl do you like? Want me to introduce you to someone?' How do I answer that? That's my deepest, darkest secret, and I have to be prepared to reveal it. It would take considerable skill to do it right. I definitely wouldn't say, 'My standards aren't all that high. Someone like you would do just fine.' That would be humbling myself. And I definitely wouldn't say, 'I'm waiting for the right person. I won't marry anybody but her.' However veiled this comment might be, it could easily earn me a strong rebuff: 'You're waiting for the right person, but what if she's not waiting for you? Wouldn't you just be wasting your time?' If forced to say something, the safest solution would be to hide my meaning behind code words, like I did in my diary: 'The water gourd loves only the sunflower. The water gourd is waiting for the sunflower.'

Water gourd. Sunflower. I'm sure she forgot that agreement long ago. I can imagine the belly laugh with which she'd greet this explanation. 'You're weird, Ku Dongliang,' she'd say. 'That's a stupid limerick, it doesn't make sense, like a fart in the wind. A water gourd loves water, a sunflower loves the sun. Not only that, but a water gourd lives on the river, a sunflower lives on the shore, so how could they ever come together?'

I'd stand there and take her mockery. Would it anger me? Sure. But mainly it would break my heart, the sadness emanating from both my rational nature and my inferiority complex. Only a deranged water gourd would fall in love with a sunflower. A water gourd that waits for a sunflower has lost its grip on reality. For me, this was the final pipe dream of my youth. My ruminations concealed my timidity, my obstinacy obscured my despair. I, Ku Dongliang, was a twenty-six-year-old man of average intelligence, with a well-developed body, a decent appearance and a fiery libido, yet I lacked the courage to tell a girl I was waiting for her. Kongpi, Kongpi, Kongpi, Kongpi! My life was enshrouded by that nickname, and I needed no one to waken me from that dream of mine. I was alert to the fact that waiting was, for me, *kongpi*.

Having grown used to that pointless waiting, I had gone to the barbershop to see a girl with love and sadness in my heart. That love and that sadness were simply *kongpi*. So too was my secret, since it could not be revealed. I certainly didn't have the right to reveal it, but *kongpi* has the right to drift along. And it was this incredibly base right that I exercised on shore in the People's Barbershop, waiting for and watching over Huixian.

I wasn't conscious of my abnormal behaviour until one day when Desheng's wife quietly summoned me to the stern of our barge. From where she stood on the bow of barge number eight, she said, giving me a strange look, 'Did you go to the barbershop again today?'

'I'm no counter-revolutionary,' I said, 'so I can go where I want. Is going to a barbershop against the law?'

With a grim smile, she said, 'It's not against the law, it's just repugnant!' Then she blasted me: 'What crazy thoughts are running through that head of yours, Dongliang? What is Huixian to you? And what are you to her? As soon as you go ashore you run over to spy on her. Why?'

I was speechless. Spy? Yes, I was spying on her. Desheng's wife had laid bare my secret with a single remark. Though I was in no mood to admit she was right, I realized the nature of the right that I had been exercising. It was to spy, that and only that. There was nothing false about her accusation. I'd been spying on Huixian.

Everyone said that Huixian had a secret, and I longed to find out what it was. My waiting may well have been *kongpi*, but I wanted to know the nature of hers; who was she waiting for? The fleet was a hotbed of rumours regarding her marriage prospects. Some views were based on gossip overheard on the shore, others sprang from the rumour-mongers' own baseless thoughts. Some of what I heard was fine-sounding and utterly fantastic talk: Huixian was waiting for a singer in Beijing who had been her voice coach when she was with the district artistic propaganda team. Their relationship had developed to the point where the artist was waiting for Huixian's twentieth birthday, when he would return and take her back to Beijing.

One of the other stories seemed credible. It also happened to be vulgar and sordid. Bureau Chief Liu's grandson, the story went, had returned to Milltown and gone to see Huixian at the barbershop. A life of luxury had fattened him up and turned him so sluggish that she did not recognize him until halfway through the haircut she was giving him. How? Not visually, and not by smell, but with her breasts. All the time she was cutting his hair he kept brushing his arm against her full breasts. Finally, she grabbed his arm and said, 'I know who you are. Everyone else may have forgotten me after all these years, but not you. You haven't given up your desire for my breasts.'

Realizing what was happening, the people waiting their turn jumped up and surrounded Little Liu. 'Chief Liu has been dead a long time,' Old Cui said, grabbing Little Liu by the collar, 'so there's no reason to worry about offending him. The last time Chief Liu came to town, I gave him a shave, and not only did he refuse to exploit his authority, but he gave me a cigarette in thanks. How could a wonderful leader like him have a prick like you for a grandson?' Together they hustled him out of the barbershop.

But before he was out of the door, his head half shaved, he apologized to Huixian and pleaded with them to let her finish the job. 'I can't go out looking like this,' he said.

But Huixian stood by the door and said, 'That's exactly how you're going out! Now you'll know how it feels to be outside with half your head shaved. You people never gave me a thought when you treated me the same way – my life was in the same disarray as your head. Didn't I go out into the world and keep on living?'

I recorded every rumour about Huixian in my diary. But rumours are just rumours. So I wrote them down in pencil, and rewrote them in pen and ink only when they proved to be true. Dark pencil, blue ink, even an occasional entry in red – a mix of colours that enhanced each other's beauty. But that wasn't why I did it. I owed it to Huixian, and I owed it to myself.

What I needed was facts, the truth. But I lived on a barge and she lived on the shore. How could a ship's mast observe flowing water? And how could flowing water keep watch over the banks of a river?

I continued to observe Huixian, but I did not learn any of her secrets.

Secrets

B ECAUSE OF Huixian, though I lived on a boat, my heart was on the shore.

I refused to let Father witness my suffering, half of which came from the secret buried in my soul, the other half from the secret my body held. As far back as my youth, erections had been a constant worry. Maybe it was the enduring loneliness of being aboard a barge, or maybe I was simply oversexed, but my genitals were like a volcano about to erupt. Day or night, it made no difference: if I let down my guard even for a moment, the volcano erupted. I had observed Chunsheng and Dayong when they were looking at girls on the shore. Their eyes blazed as unhealthy thoughts ran through their minds, but the front of their trousers stayed flat. Not me. I dreaded the summer, when Huixian dressed in skirts that exposed her knees; one look and I lost control. I wondered if I had a sickness. I know Father thought so. But he did not think it was physical; as he saw it, it was a character flaw.

Was my character flawed? I didn't know. But for years I fought off the erections, for my benefit and for Father's. By now everyone knew how he had suffered over his erections, and how he'd come up with a unique way of dealing with the problem – in essence, cut the weeds and dig up the roots. With one snip of his scissors, he had eradicated the evil at its source, thus atoning for his sins. It had also afforded him plenty of moral capital. By overseeing what went on in my head and how that affected my crotch, he was able to exercise control over me. He considered this to be a lifelong mission.

I was stuck. Why did he have to be my father? He forced me to study Marxist-Leninist texts, believing it was for my own good. Guarding against and forbidding erections was also for my own good. I knew that he was not like other people, and that his rules of discipline differed from theirs. Sometimes I humoured him, as if I were the father. If he told me to read something, I pretended to read it, even though it was all an act and I was actually doing something else as I held the book in my hands. I'd become very good at that. But what angered and shamed me was his scrutiny of the front of my trousers. No matter where or when he did this, it put me on edge. If, on a sunny day, Chunsheng called me over to his barge to play cards, I'd only make it halfway there before I heard my father shout, 'You should know better. Don't go over there in shorts. Come back and change your clothes.' Or I'd wake up on a cold night to discover that he'd pulled back my quilt and, by the light of a lantern in his hand, was examining my face and my crotch. 'What were you dreaming? That's all you think about, day and night. Look at you, and look at this mess on your quilt! Don't tell me you weren't having one of your sordid dreams.'

My genitals were a constant worry. Genitals have no brain, no knowledge and no ability to pretend. God, how I hated my hand! Its assistance was the reason why I left evidence of my genital crimes on my quilt. I tried everything. I made it a point not to let my hand come into contact with my genitals. They had to be kept apart, and the best way to do that was to give up some of the comforts of sleep. So I began wearing long trousers and a belt to bed; I got into the habit of slipping under the covers each night wearing a pair of work trousers over my underpants, and prayed to the image of Deng Shaoxiang to help me get through the night without incident. I lay stiffly on my army cot, not relaxing until I heard the martyr's stern command – *Come down, come down* – and fell asleep. The habit served me well. Granted, the stink of sweat rose from my bedding, but my dreams were clean and pure. All I had was an infrequent nightmare. I'd wake up out of fright, drenched in sweat. I had one particular bad dream I never told my father about. In it I saw Huixian standing on the shore, calling my name over and over again. I stayed in the cabin, unable to move, since many people had conspired to tie me up and get Father to repeat a ritual over me. He was crying as he snipped off half my penis with a pair of scissors. As he wiped the blood off the scissors he said to me with fatherly concern, 'Try to bear the pain, Dongliang, it's for your own good. Now you're just like me, we're the same, and I don't have to worry about you any longer.'

On the river and on the shore, I was a captive of Father's shadow. My trips ashore were tightly controlled, my freedom severely restricted. He limited the time I could spend off the boat to two hours, one of which was for buying provisions, taking a bath, getting a haircut and visiting the public toilet. The remaining hour was to be devoted to carrying out his instructions: checking the fleet postbox, and going to the General Affairs Building to see if any political work teams were coming to town from the district headquarters. The arrival of one of those teams was a special occasion that required special arrangements, and I was to head back to the barge and tell him without delay if one came. He would then break his own rule by going ashore. If a team arrived in Milltown, he'd hand over eleven years' worth of reports on his ideological progress and detail the unjust treatment and misfortunes he'd suffered during that period.

Before going ashore I'd put whatever I needed in my bag, then take pains to make myself as presentable as possible. Father reminded me to wear my wristwatch. 'I see you've polished your shoes. Well, keep your eyes off your shoes and on your wristwatch.'

Then he pointed to the alarm clock in the cabin and re-stated his rule. 'I'll be watching that clock,' he said. 'Two hours, no more. Last time you were fifteen minutes late coming back. Don't let it happen again.' I climbed out of the cabin, bag in hand, but stopped in the hatchway and turned for one more instruction: 'Let me see you,' he said.

I knew what he meant by that. Sucking in my gut, I shook my trousers and said, 'OK, take a good look. See anything out of order?'

With concern in his eyes, he looked at my crotch. 'What kind of attitude is that? It's for your own good. Be careful out there. Don't go anywhere you're not supposed to go or do anything you shouldn't.' That left only the final ritual. I raised my eyes towards the image of the martyr hanging on the wall, as he said in a sombre voice, 'Whatever you do, always remember your lineage. Shaming me doesn't count for much, but don't you dare besmirch the reputation of Deng Shaoxiang!'

Over our eleven years on that barge, people – me included – had pretty much forgotten Father's and my status. Except for on River Day, the twenty-seventh of September each year, and the infrequent occasions when I walked past Milltown's chess pavilion, I had all but forgotten that I'd once had the honour of being Deng Shaoxiang's grandson and that we'd enjoyed the status of being a revolutionary martyr's descendants. Father defended his glorious bloodline like a drowning man vainly clutching a leaky life-raft. I was baffled by my bloodline. Father had been registering appeals over the bloodline issue for eleven years, but I had no place to appeal to. I was Ku Dongliang, and Ku Dongliang was Ku Wenxuan's son. If he was not Deng Shaoxiang's son, then I was not her grandson. And if somebody like me was not the descendant of a martyr, I was a *kongpi*. And if I was a *kongpi*, what relationship could I ever have with Deng Shaoxiang? That being the case, what could I possibly do to vilify her name?

My bloodline held no fascination for me. I was too caught up in my concern for Huixian, and that constituted the greatest betrayal of my father's wishes from my youth onwards. That betrayal brought me no rewards. Huixian's attitude towards me bounced back and forth from cold to hot. Maybe she wasn't interested in me – I could deal with that. But I had to know who she *was* interested in.

As I was going ashore I saw Six-Fingers Wang's daughters Big and Little Phoenix on the deck of their barge, drying mustard plants. Big Phoenix was standing with an armload of plants and looking at me with fire in her eyes. 'Look at you, all dressed up. Off to find a bride?'

Regardless of how bold Six-Fingers's daughters were, or what they said to sound me out, or whether they were wearing shorts and revealing vests, you have my word that I would never have given either of them a second look. Big Phoenix took being ignored in her stride, but Little Phoenix felt a need to take up the fight on behalf of her sister. 'If you haven't got anything to do,' she said, 'go and talk to the river, but don't waste your breath on him. Everybody knows what he does over there. He hangs out at the barbershop like a moron waiting to snag a wife, or like a toad wanting to feast on swan!'

No question about it, Desheng's wife had not been able to keep her mouth shut, and my secret was now public knowledge. Sooner or later it was bound to reach Father's ears, and maybe sooner than I imagined, if he was within earshot of Little Phoenix's shouts.

Suddenly laden with worries, I walked faster, in case Father came out and called me back. I hustled past the piers, where I heard Li Juhua reciting poems inside the oil-pumping station. 'Youth, ah, youth, you are a flame that burns for Communism! Burn on!' On my way past, she burst through the door, just like a flame, and nearly crashed into me. 'What's your hurry?' she said. Where's the fire?'

I smiled. 'You're reciting poetry. Is there going to be a theatrical festival?'

Apparently, she didn't want me to know why she was reciting poetry, so she shook her head, sending her pigtails in motion, and said, 'Ku Dongliang, how about going to the general store and buying a couple of rubber bands for me. Mine are about to snap.'

'No time,' I said, 'can't do it.'

She snorted. 'No time? You, Ku Dongliang? Except to spend a couple of hours sitting in the barbershop. You ought to take advantage of your trip to read a paper or shoot some hoops, do something healthy for a change. Is there a circus troupe living in the barbershop? Aren't you afraid people will talk if that's the only place you ever go?'

Though that bothered me, I kept my cool and said, 'People will talk? What do you think I do there? I get a haircut. That's not against the law, is it?'

I went to the People's Barbershop for a haircut, but I wouldn't let Huixian do it. Old Cui cut my hair, and in his chair I felt as if I were the sunflower and Huixian the sun. I turned to face her, wherever she was. 'Sit still,' Old Cui would say as he turned my head back, 'and quit looking where you're not supposed to. Keep your eyes on the mirror.' So I looked at the mirror, and my gaze was transformed into a sunflower that struggled to turn to the sun, usually squinting at Huixian out of the corner of my eye, which gave me a strange, ugly appearance. When Old Cui glanced in the mirror and saw what I was looking at, he thumped me on the shoulder. 'Watch out, Kongpi, or your eyes will fall out of their sockets.'

Ah, the mirror had revealed my secret, so I went over to get a newspaper and covered my eyes with it. Running short of patience, Cui tore the paper out of my hands and tossed it to the floor. 'High officials can read the newspaper when they're getting their hair cut, not you.' Knowing what was on my mind, he didn't like it one bit, and he took his disgust out on my scalp. He cut everybody else's hair with tender concern, but not mine. To him my head was a dark, bleak patch of ground, which he attacked with scissors in one hand and clippers in the other, like a reaping machine. And there was nothing I could do about it, because when I complained that it hurt, he stopped, turned to Huixian, and said, 'Here, take over. The people from the Sunnyside Fleet are too much trouble. I'm turning them all over to you.'

Huixian would shoot me a quick glance before smiling ambiguously at Old Cui and saying, deftly masking her attempt to get out of it, 'You're a model worker, Old Cui. No one can compete with you, so you go ahead. Besides, he won't let me work on him anyway.'

Why wouldn't I? She should have been curious, should have wondered what that was all about, but she wasn't curious about an eccentric like me, and not interested in asking. I actually felt OK about that, since I didn't have to make up a story. But disappointment took over as I tried to imagine what place, if any, I held in her heart. Maybe to her I was a *kongpi*, and the thoughts of a *kongpi* are *kongpi*, as are the eccentricities of a *kongpi*, so there was no need to give me another thought.

At the People's Barbershop I was able to probe the rumours I'd heard about Huixian. Given the infrequency of my trips ashore, the accuracy of my research was about one in ten thousand. There were times when I wished I were one of those swivelling chairs, so I could be with Huixian morning, noon and night. Or I wished I were her scissors, always in the vicinity of people's heads, wondering who they were and if they'd really come for a haircut, or were just pretending. Why did some people keep dawdling until they could get her to cut their hair? They talked about anything and everything, and they could well have been flirting. I needed to keep a close eye on them. My eyes were a camera focused only on Huixian. My ears were a phonograph, with the same intent. Too bad my time ashore was so limited, and my camera and phono-graph had such restricted functions. When I was there, Huixian was so close, but still I was unable to glean any secrets of her heart.

The women who came to the barbershop talked mostly of romance and marriage. I found their wagging tongues valuable, but they could never stay on one topic long enough. They were eager to pry into her private life. Did she have a mate picked out, they wondered aloud. Is the boy you've chosen really in Beijing? That'd get my antennae twitching. But when they saw she wasn't interested in talking to them, they'd switch to the weather, or ask about the latest hair-styles. What would look best for my face, Huixian? I had to bite my tongue to keep from reminding them that no hair-style could improve their looks. Ask more questions, go on, ask her who the boy is. They couldn't hear me, of course, and they only wanted to talk about hair-styles. The camera in my eyes was secretly aimed at Huixian, the phonograph in my ears went on strike, and I angrily shut it down.

I once ran into Zhao Chunmei at the barbershop. She was wearing white high-heels and holding a white handbag as she sat in one of the barber's chairs, waiting for Old Cui to do her hair. She'd aged a bit, but had lost neither her charm nor her spite and resentment. I didn't recognize her at first, but she knew who I was right away. 'What's *he* doing here?' she demanded.

Before Old Cui could reply, Huixian laughed. 'What's he doing here? Good question. This is the People's Barbershop. He counts as "people", and he's here to have his hair cut.'

Zhao Chunmei snorted. 'The people – him? If he is, then there are no class enemies. Do you know that he writes counter-revolutionary slogans? Mostly targeting my brother!'

Enemies are bound to meet on narrow roads. It was an awkward encounter. Coming face to face with women who'd had relationships with my father not only made me blush, but threw my heart into turmoil. I still recalled their names, those few people who had been instrumental in my sexual initiation. Now those ageing faces, thickening waists and limbs, and cellulite-laden buttocks brought shame on those wonderful, moving, desirable, tantalizing names. I was ashamed to let my mind dwell on thoughts of their sexual encounters with Father, but then his reminder was confirmed: my crotch underwent an unexpected occurrence, as my wayward organ broke loose from my underwear and subtle changes appeared in the creases of my trousers. All of a sudden, I had trouble breathing. I thought I could see my father's bizarre penis; after surgery, it had sort of regained its original appearance, but it was still ugly, comical even. Why had this mark of shame been transplanted on to my body? Crushed by unimaginable terror, I held tightly to the smock and could not hold up my head. I heard Huixian's voice – she was defending me. 'Don't get involved in class struggle and political issues,' she was saying. 'Opposing Chairman Mao or the Communist Party, now that's counter-revolutionary. He was opposing Secretary Zhao, an ordinary section chief, so nothing written about him can be considered counter-revolutionary.'

With a click of her tongue, Zhao Chunmei turned and attacked Huixian. 'What are you to him?' she demanded. 'Who are you to defend him? An official? What sort of political stance do you call that? Writing about my brother isn't counter-revolutionary, is that what you're saying? Are you trying to stir up the masses in opposition to leaders of the Party?'

'Don't try to stick that label on to me! Your brother is not the Party, and opposing him is not opposing the Party.' There was anger in Huixian's voice as she picked up a brush and began tapping it against the back of her chair. 'Why take your anger out on me? Who am I to him? Who is he to me? I've got no mother and no father, so who is anybody to me? Nobody! But you can't stop me from saying what's fair. Chairman Mao has said the masses have the right to state their opinions, so who is Secretary Zhao to keep the masses from voicing theirs?'

'That's not opinion, that's rumour!' Knowing she was not going to win an argument with Huixian, Zhao Chunmei turned back to me. 'No, it wasn't a rumour,' she shouted, 'it was a venomous attack. All the time, that's what he did, write lies all over the place, like: "Zhao Chuntang is an alien class element", which had a widespread pernicious effect. Even grammar-school children were asking, "What's an alien class element?"'

The shop went quiet, as people pondered the meaning of alien class element.

I saw that slogan everywhere too, but still didn't know what it meant. Little Chen was the first to voice his confusion. 'What does alien mean?' he asked me. 'How about explaining it to us.'

I refused his request. 'Who am I to explain anything? Besides, I didn't write it, so why should I be the one to explain?'

'If you didn't write it, who did?' Zhao Chunmei bellowed. 'You haven't got the guts to own up to your own deeds! You're like your father, hiding in dark corners to spread rumours, sling mud and act like a hooligan.'

I sat there affecting the 'a real man doesn't fight with a woman' pose. Old Cui considered alien class elements on a par with morally bankrupt elements, while Teacher Qian from the Milltown high school announced authoritatively that alien class elements were the same as degenerates. You could have heard a pin drop. But Little Chen wasn't quite finished. 'What do you say, Kongpi? Does it mean the same as degenerate?'

'Sort of,' I replied ambiguously, 'but not quite. Alien class element is a more serious label, I think.'

Before I could elaborate on my vague comment, Zhao Chunmei jumped out of her chair and rushed over, blind with anger. 'What do you mean, morally bankrupt and degenerate? My brother is a good and decent man and an upright official. Your father is the morally bankrupt and degenerate one. Go back and tell him that cutting off half his dick means nothing, and even if he'd cut it all off and turned himself into a eunuch, that wouldn't mean anything either. He's a sex fiend, a liar, a bastard, and a criminal who will never hold his head up in society again! Listen, everyone, here's the latest news. Ku Wenxuan palmed himself off as the descendant of a martyr for decades, but now we know that he is not Deng Shaoxiang's son, he's the son of the river pirate Old Qiu. The woman they call Rotten Rapeseed was his mother, not Deng Shaoxiang. Before Liberation she was a riverboat prostitute.'

Silence settled over the shop. Customers and barbers alike were tongue-tied. But only momentarily. Like oil popping in a pan, one person spun around in his swivel chair, while others tried but failed to stifle giggles as a frenzy of whispering began. Huixian was the first to come to my defence. 'Have you gone mad, Zhao Chunmei?' she demanded. 'Your mouth is going to get you into trouble. Even if their whole family are your mortal enemies, you still don't have the right to say whatever you want about their ancestors. You could bring the wrath of the heavens down on your head.'

'Did I say anything about their ancestors?' Zhao shot back. 'I don't have time to waste on that, even if could. I'm telling you, people, it's confidential information, but my brother says that the next time Ku tries to file an appeal, my brother will go public with it.'

It took Old Cui and Little Chen, plus some of the customers, to keep me from charging at Zhao Chunmei. 'Calm down,' they said. 'Don't fly off the handle. Don't demean yourself by reacting to a woman's empty-headed talk. If it's confidential information, it could be true, it could be false. We're the only ones who heard it, and it won't go any further. You're OK with that, aren't you?'

Working together, they managed to bundle me out of the shop, followed by Zhao Chunmei's shrewish comments. 'Where are you taking him?' she said. 'Bring him back in here. I want him here, so I can settle things with him once and for all. And if he lays a hand on me, I'll see him punished by law.'

There was no calming me down. I fired off a stream of filthy, almost hysterical curses, which drew the attention of passers-by on the street. Holding my arm with all his might, Old Cui shouted to Huixian, 'Come out here, I can't hold him. He'll listen to you.'

She ran out and glared at me. 'Do you think that kind of filthy talk makes you a man? Why provoke her? You can't win with a woman like that, especially with what your father owes her. So leave now before a crowd starts to gather and she goes into broadcast mode, blaring the news to anyone who'll listen. Put yourself in your father's position. Do you think he could stand it if this news reached him?'

Huixian's advice calmed me down, and I decided to avoid further conflict. I walked across the street to the cotton-fluffing shop to wait for Zhao Chunmei to come outside. I hated her with a passion. The shop's proprietor came out to ask what was going on, but the look in my eyes sent her scurrying back inside, afraid of what I might do.

I waited a long time, but no Zhao Chunmei. Huixian came out with a kettle. 'Still here? What fiendish plan are you cooking up? Are you going to confront her alone out here? I tell you, calm down. A real man would not fight with a woman. So what does that make you?'

I shook my head. 'You water your flowers and don't worry about me.' To be honest, I wasn't sure why I was waiting for Zhao Chunmei. What was I going to say to her? I hadn't decided. What did I plan to do to her? Nothing, given my timid nature. I watched Huixian water her plants; a new sunflower bloomed, its golden petals having burst open so it could stand tall, fresh and tender.

It was velvety soft and immature, and I saw Huixian smile as she looked at it.

My gaze was fixed on a young woman and a single sun-flower, so when Zhao Chunmei came out of the barbershop, I didn't know what to do. She was several metres away when she turned and spat on the ground. For me that was like waking from a dream.

I made up my mind to follow her. Not to retaliate or scare her – the loathing I felt for her took a new direction. I resolved to make her tell me everything, so I could learn the true secret of Father's legacy once and for all.

It didn't take long for Zhao Chunmei to realize that I was following her, and she took that as a threat. At first she kept turning around and rolling her eyes at me, a sign of contempt, but as the distance between us narrowed, fear crept in, and she grabbed a mop that was drying in the sun outside a house and pointed it at me. 'What's made you so bold all of a sudden? Why are you following me in broad daylight? Come on,' she said, 'I don't care what you're planning, just come on.'

I gestured for her to calm down. 'What's got you so worked up? I just want to ask you something.'

'I've seen lots of people like you,' she said. 'I'm not worked up. If you've got something to say, spit it out; if you've got gas, let it out.'

'Not here,' I said. 'Let's go somewhere where there aren't so many people.'

Once again she got the wrong idea. Her eyes blazed as she raised the dripping mop over her head and was about to hit me in the face. 'Somewhere where there aren't so many people? It'll still belong to the Communist Party, even if there's nobody there. You think I'm afraid you'll try to kill me?'

I had to keep moving to stay out of range of the mop. 'Why don't you put that down? Don't worry, I won't touch you. I just want to clarify something. You said my father is Rotten Rapeseed's son. Where's your proof?'

'I don't need proof, my brother is Zhao Chuntang, a Party leader. Whatever he says is all the proof anyone needs.'

'Maybe, maybe not,' I said. 'If he spouts nonsense in his sleep, is that proof? I'm asking you, how does Zhao Chuntang know that my father is Rotten Rapeseed's son? Can he prove it?'

She blinked and pondered my question for a moment before laughing smugly and saying, 'He's a leading official, so of course he can prove it. He read it in a top-secret document.'

Zhao Chunmei's expression told me everything I needed to know: that what she said was not an empty rumour. My heart fell as I imagined Zhao Chuntang opening a manila envelope with 'Top Secret' stamped mysteriously in red. I imagined what the document said: *Upon investigation, it has been revealed that Ku Wenxuan is the son of the river pirate Old Qiu and the prostitute Rotten Rapeseed. Effective immediately, make appropriate changes in all the materials in Ku Wenxuan's dossier and terminate all financial benefits for a martyr's family member.* Then an almost paralysing fear and boiling anger hit me, and I began to quake. Top-secret document? That's not what it was; it was a death-dealing document, and I didn't believe it. Could they change an orphan's parentage so easily? – a martyr one day and a prostitute or a bandit the next? I didn't believe a ridiculous document like that existed. At that moment I was reminded of the birthmark on Father's backside. Maybe it had never been a mark of glory, but of sin! Could he ever atone for his sin? My poor father, my self-confident father, my atoning father, all that remained to him in this world was a single barge. He had gone into hiding on the river, and if this shameful news were ever to reach him, where could he hide then?

I despaired for my father and, lacking any other course of action, decided to negotiate with Zhao Chunmei. 'Aunty Zhao

– ' Hearing my own voice, soft, supplicating, ingratiating, I was incredulous. Was that me?

She looked as surprised as I was, her eyes big and round. 'So now you're calling me Aunty, are you? Sounds strange to my ears.' She snorted and produced a little sarcastic smile. 'Well, it won't do you any good. I can't save your father, and wouldn't if I could.'

'I'm begging you, Aunty Zhao. You have to leave him a reason to live. You're driving him to his death.'

'Who is? Don't you put that on me! You never heard me say that pretending to be a martyr's son or being the son of Rotten Rapeseed was a death sentence. Take my word for it, the organization has treated him as well as he deserves, and my brother has showered him with kindness. Even after committing a crime of that magnitude, he still draws his pay and receives his food rations. And don't forget, he has a barge, so you have no reason to be dissatisfied with your lot.'

'I'm begging you, Aunty Zhao, please don't lump Old Qiu and Rotten Rapeseed together with my father, and please don't go spreading this around.'

'I've spread nothing. It's confidential information, and if you hadn't forced me, I wouldn't have brought it up.'

'Please, Aunty Zhao, go to Zhao Chuntang and, if this top-secret document really exists, ask him not to go public with it.'

'I can't do that. I'm not my brother's superior. What makes you think he'd listen to me?' She rested the mop against the wall, enjoying the taste of victory. I heard her breathe a sigh. 'I hear you're a dutiful son,' she said. 'Too bad you have to be dutiful to a father like him!'

She walked away and I fell in behind her. She wasn't getting rid of me that easily, and was obviously growing anxious. She turned into Cotton Print Lane and sort of jogged in the direction of the Milltown police station. 'You're worse than your father,' she said without slowing down. 'Come on, follow me – I'll even let you catch up – all the way to the police station, where we'll see what they have to say about all this.'

That worked. The last place I wanted to be was a police station, so I stopped following her. Standing in the entrance to Cotton Print Lane, I saw several old men sitting on stools at a table they'd set up in the sunlight next to a water-boiling tiger oven. They were drinking tea and passing the time of day. Spotting me and knowing at once who I was, they began talking in hushed voices. 'That's Ku's son,' one of them said. 'He used to swagger around town, but no longer. Now he walks with his tail between his legs.' The other oldster, who gossiped like a woman, was passing judgement on my appearance. 'As a boy he looked like Qiao Limin, but the older he gets, the more he takes after Ku Wenxuan, with that hang-dog look.' I'd forgotten their names, but I knew who their sons and daughters were. The one with the bulging growth on his neck was Scabby Five's father. A retired blacksmith, he kept spitting on the ground and smearing his spit with the sole of his shoe. The other man was the father of Little Chen, the barber. He'd worked at the public baths, where he was in charge of cleaning bathers' ears and trimming their corns, until he managed to pull the right strings to get a transfer to the piers as a longshoreman, although he still plied his old trade, clearing the ears and trimming the corns of high officials after hours. I recalled the days when he'd show up at our place with a little wooden box to perform his services on my father.

I took a good hard look at them, trying to guess how old they were and see if they were ageing faster than my father. But then it hit me – they were the winners in this drama. They might have been old and slovenly, but they were more carefree than my father. There were no crimes or sins associated with their names, so they were spared the need to reform themselves. Ordinary citizens all their lives, they'd never had much of anything, which meant they had nothing to lose. They were in good shape; so were their sons. A bizarre thought struck me: wouldn't it be interesting if everyone's lineage was as easy to change as my father's? And if I hadn't been the son of Ku Wenxuan, but instead called the old black-smith or the professional ear-cleaner father, would I have turned out like Scabby Five or Little Chen? How would I feel about that? I stood there thinking for a long time, until I was brought up short by the beating of my own heart. I was actually envious of that bastard Scabby Five, actually willing to trade places with Little Chen the barber. I had answered my own question: I'd be just fine with that.

It was noon, and Father's going-ashore plan called for me to be at the clinic by one thirty and then return to the barge to make lunch. As I passed by the tiger oven, golden flecks of rice chaff fell from its ledge on to my shoes. There were piles of the stuff up there. The operator of the stove, Old Mu, stripped to the waist, was shovelling it into the oven. I couldn't see the flames, but I heard them crackle. Pop! Pop! Burn, burn, burn. My heart echoed the beat of the flames, and I suddenly felt hot all over. There was a stabbing pain in my foot, and when I bent down to look, I saw a rice husk embedded in the space between two toes. I picked it out and saw that it had the world's tiniest and most abject little face; the inevitable progression from a piece of grain to fuel for a fire gave it a fearful and terribly sad expression. I rolled it around in the palm of my hand. The rice paddy had been plundered until there was nothing left. The next thing I felt was the hot sun on my scalp, and then I saw my father's face in the shrivelled rice husk, his look of fear and sadness greater even than the solitary husk in my hand. I heard the subdued sound of his pleas: Save me, please save me!

I knew I had to save Father.

But who could I find to help me?

All of Milltown, in my mind a great metropolis, had once been my playground; now it was alien territory. There was no one on whom I could rely; then I thought of someone – Huixian. She owed us, and she remained a celebrity. I placed my hopes on her, but what could I say to convince her to come to my father's aid? I couldn't begin to guess if she'd be willing to do so. I passed a bakery stall on the eastern edge of town, its fragrance reminding me that I was hungry. I bought a baked flatbread and immediately sank my teeth into it. Just then I heard my name shouted in a crisp voice. It was Desheng's wife, who was gaping at me in complete surprise. 'Why aren't you back on the barge, Dongliang? Your father is waiting for his lunch.'

'So what? I'm not his personal servant, you know. He's got two hands, and there's a pot in the kitchen and rice in the pantry. What's keeping him from making his own lunch?'

She gave me a bewildered look. 'Why is a dutiful son like you saying things like that? Have you fought with your father again?'

I waved her off and started walking. I hadn't fought with my father. It was the rest of the world that was fighting with him.

I returned to the barbershop, where, amid the smells of food and Glory soap, the barbers were eating on a makeshift table made of two stools pulled together. Their surprise at seeing me again was matched by my surprise at what I saw: since when had Wang Xiaogai of the security group started eating with this lot? There he was, sitting in the middle, stuffing a fried egg into his mouth.

Old Cui stared at me uncertainly. 'What are you doing here? You've had your haircut.'

I'd come to help my father, after pondering what I'd say to Huixian on the way over. But one look at Wang Xiaogai drove that thought out of my mind. What was he doing, enjoying a meal with the barbers? I glared at him – his hair, his new grey jacket, and the area around his crotch – and was immediately reminded of the talk I'd been hearing about Huixian, especially the rumour that Xiaogai had the hots for her. I'd laughed it off as crazy talk. Could it possibly be true?

Huixian laid down her bowl and looked me up and down. 'Did you fight it out with Zhao Chunmei? How come you look like you've lost your best friend?' She could see I was staring at Xiaogai. 'Who are you looking for? Wang Xiaogai?'

I knew what I must have looked like, so I turned away from Xiaogai and said to her, 'I want to talk to you about something. Can you come outside?'

'Why do we have to talk outside?' There was a guarded look in her eyes. 'I don't like that sneaky expression of yours. Who do you want to talk about? You? Me?'

'N—neither,' I stammered, beginning to lose my composure. 'What's got you so uppity?' I said. 'All I'm asking is for you to step outside. It won't take long. What do you say?'

'I say no.' She shook her head, showing she meant what she said. 'I'm not afraid to step outside, but I'm not a girl who shares sweet nothings with just anybody.'

The men around the table exchanged knowing looks. With a grin, Little Chen smacked his chopsticks against his lunch box. 'You heard her. She doesn't go for that kind of talk. If you've brought a love letter along, read it for us. We'd love to hear it.'

Wang Xiaogai hadn't taken his eyes off me. I was his enemy, and he was ready for anything. But then he sneered and pointed to the mirror. 'If you've written a love letter, go and take a look at yourself and see if you're fit to read it.'

I sneered back. 'That's enough of that talk, Xiaogai,' I said. 'I may not be fit to read a love letter, but you're not even fit to write one. You're not educated enough to write one even if you wanted to.'

Being put down in front of his friends infuriated him. He threw his spoon at me. 'Kongpi,' he snarled, 'maybe you can write love letters, but you're still a *kongpi*. I may be dumb, but I'm a hell of a lot better than you!' He stood up and pointed to me threateningly, his eyes blazing. 'I told you to take a look in the mirror, but since you won't, I'll tell you what you look like: you look like a parasite. Who've you come here to feast upon, that's what I want to know. Who is Huixian to you? And what does she owe you? Do you think you own her just because she had a few meals on your boat? What do you want to talk to her about? Everybody knows what's on your mind. You're like the toad that wants to feast on a swan.'

I responded to the thrown spoon by picking up a pair of clippers and throwing them at him, hitting him on the leg. 'My new clippers!' Old Cui shouted. 'You'll buy a new pair if you've broken them. Now get out, all of you! I'm not going to have you two fighting over a woman in my shop!'

The veil of motives was broken by that shout. No one in the shop spoke. Boiling with rage, I glared at Xiaogai. My anger stemmed in part from his aggressive behaviour, but also because the words had hit home. I glanced at Huixian, hoping she'd come to my aid, but she bent over to pick up the clippers, her expression giving away nothing of what she felt. The hint of a vacant smile appeared on her lips. She tested the clippers. 'Do me a favour,' she said. 'I don't want you fighting over me here. If word got out, people would be thrilled to place the blame squarely on me.' She walked over to the washbasin, then turned and beckoned me over. 'Come on, Ku Dongliang, I'll wash your hair for you. Since you don't want them to hear what you say, come here and let me wash your hair, and they won't hear a word.'

I hesitated as I saw Huixian turn on the water and test the temperature on the back of her hand. 'Sit down,' she said. 'You said there's something you want to talk about. Well, everything's open and above board here. You can talk while I run the water, then stop and leave after I've turned it off.'

As they say, riding a tiger is easy, getting off is hard. So, under the mocking gazes of Xiaogai and the others, I stumbled nervously over to the washbasin. 'Put your bag down,' she said. I didn't. Instead, I laid it on my knees after I'd sat down on the stool. 'What do you have in there, gold ingots? No one's going to steal your stuff.' She took it from me and laid it to one side.

Warm water flowed from the hose, and I was encircled by an unfamiliar but rich fragrance, one I couldn't begin to describe. It came not only from Huixian's jasmine face powder, but drifted over from somewhere else as well, and I wondered if it might be her natural smell, the faint aroma of sunflowers. I know it sounds far-fetched, but her body gave off the aroma of sunflowers. 'My dad . . . my dad, he . . .' I couldn't say what I wanted to say and felt as if I were suffocating.

'What about your dad?' she said. 'Is that what you want to talk about, your dad?'

'I mean, you helped my dad . . .' I felt her fingers moving between my scalp and the tap and swallowed the rest of the words. 'I mean, my dad . . . he's actually a good man, someone who's suffered a lot.'

'That's something you should talk to the authorities about. Why tell me?' She kept massaging my scalp. 'What's wrong with your head, why's it so stiff? Lower it for me.'

I did, and I felt her push it down further, her fingers gently massaging. Then she put one finger into each of my ears and made two full circles. My memory is clear on that, two full circles, and my old problem returned: I forgot what it was I wanted to talk to her about as a mysterious current shot down from the top of my head through my body, all the way to my crotch, where an erection sprang up. Now the feeling of suffocation intensified. Danger! Danger! My brain was sending a warning, stronger and stronger. The tap was turned off and no more water ran through the hose. The sound was replaced by my father's raspy shout: 'Leave, get out of there, come back to the boat!'

I jumped down off the stool, flustered, picked up my bag and held it in front of me to hide the bulge in my trousers. I fled from the People's Barbershop before anyone knew what was happening. 'What got into him?' someone shouted. 'Did he say something?'

I looked behind me. Huixian had run to the door. I'd really offended her this time. Her face was flushed. She raised her fist; she was still holding the bar of soap. 'Ku Dongliang!' she shouted. 'You're crazy. People kept telling me you were, but I didn't believe them. Now I do! And you said you wanted to talk! I tell you, go to Horsebridge, that's where the lunatic asylum is!'

I ran like an escaped convict, all the way to the public toilet on People's Avenue. I'd shamed myself, and every time I did that on the shore, that's where I went. I was a sick young man, and this was my remedy. But, just my luck, the toilet offered no aid this time, had no place for me. A skinny monkey of a man was standing in front of the only cubicle, impatiently trying to undo a knot in his trouser sash. I couldn't get him to hurry, and was forced to stand there and wait. And as I watched him getting ready to urinate, I found myself envying him. What a good life people like him had, with a home to return to when the need to vent his desire came upon him, able to relieve himself in the toilet, pull up his pants, and leave without a care, unlike me, who had a different need for a public toilet. The stink inside got stronger, so I edged closer to the urinals. But the smell was strong there too, forcing me to hold my nose.

Outside, either a gust of wind or a passer-by kicked up the sand on the ground and called out to me. 'Danger, Dongliang, danger!' It sounded so familiar. It was my mother's voice. I went out and looked around, but there was not a trace of Qiao Limin, who had been gone from Milltown for years. I was puzzled. What special talents did she have? After all this time, being so far away, how and why had she returned now to interfere with my private life? I was in control of my own body, and yet her voice could come on the wind to remind me that I was twenty-six years old and ought to have a sense of shame and propriety, that I must keep up the struggle against erections and must not continually seek that remedy; I must stop acting rashly and find a new solution. A determination to mend my ways arose as I headed back inside and stood in front of the urinals, head down. I could sense Qiao Limin's shadow floating in the air outside, forcing me to develop a new remedy, but nothing suggested itself. And so I shouted my nickname to myself – 'Kongpi, Kongpi, Kongpi' – seven or eight times, and a small miracle occurred: my erection finally listened to me and subsided. With some difficulty, I pissed into the urinal, feeling a great sense of accomplishment, and then, like all the local residents, strode guiltlessly out of the toilet.

I felt suddenly weary. I checked my watch; it was already gone one o'clock, well past the time my father had told me to be back onboard. Time to leave. I took a shortcut behind the steel warehouse and headed to the piers. It was a secluded path. I didn't know if I should count myself lucky or unlucky, but I spotted several kids from the barges under the rear window of the warehouse; Sun Ximing's younger son, Xiaofu, had climbed up on to the ledge and was prising the window open with a piece of wood. I knew they were up to no good. 'What are you doing?' I shouted.

With a wink, Xiaofu said, 'Stealing iron to sell for scrap.'

'I'm going to tell your father,' I said. 'You and your stealing! You little bastards are ruining the fleet's good name.'

But my threat went in one ear and out the other, as he made a contemptuous gesture and said, 'Mind your own business, Kongpi. What have you been up to? Ku Wenxuan is waiting for you with a rolling pin. You're going to get a beating!'

Now I realized the trouble I was in. He wasn't lying. I knew my father well enough to realize that coming home so late meant big trouble. So I left the kids to their own devices and turned back towards the piers, head down, my steps heavier than usual. But I hadn't gone far before I turned and went back, thinking, I'm twenty-six years old, too old to stand on the bow of our barge and get a beating from my father. No way was I going to lose face in front of all those people. I'd be punished whether I got home an hour late or three hours late, so why not go ahead and smash the cracked pot – hang out ashore for as long as I wanted to?

The boat people went ashore for a haircut about once a month. I went to the People's Barbershop every day. If the barge people had known that, they'd have said I'd lost my head over Huixian and that I deserved to be driven away by her.

I was the last person to understand what possessed me, but I knew that I'd lost my soul in the barbershop. When I was hurrying there, I sometimes heard the things in my bag bang against each other; those objects had more self-respect than I did, as they voiced their resistance. Don't go, they said, don't go. What do you plan to do? Who are you to her? Her brother? Her father? Her intended? No, you're nothing, just a *kongpi*, that's exactly what you are in her eyes.

That's right, I was nothing but a *kongpi*, and that made me unhappy. There was so much I wanted to say to her, so why did nothing come out of my mouth the minute I laid eyes on her? I didn't want that to be so. Why was I filled with affection each time I stepped into the barbershop, but left feeling angry and resentful? How could love so easily turn into hate? I didn't want that to be so. And since I didn't, I kept returning to the People's Barbershop like a moth to a flame.

Thoughts thronged my mind as I walked along, including memories of the time years before when I had helped poor little Huixian put up posters in Milltown looking for her mother. I passed the general store, where the intersection was flooded with sunlight, and I was taken back in time. I conjured up an image of a little girl carrying a jar of glue and heard her childish voice as she said urgently, 'Over here, Brother Dongliang. Come here!' I felt myself being pushed along, despite my weariness. It might have been the wind propelling me on, but probably it was my memories. My gaze wandered to the wall across the street from the general store; a large blackboard, recently mounted on the wall, was filled with drawings and clippings promoting family planning. A coloured propaganda image in the centre caught my eye with the words

BOYS OR GIRLS, IT MAKES NO DIFFERENCE:
JUST HAVE ONE CHILD!

printed above a drawing of a young mother standing in a bed of flowers, a baby girl in her arms. Possibly because the artist wasn't particularly talented, the smile on the face of the rosy-cheeked mother was stiff and unnatural. As for her baby, either the elements or the mischievous actions of some child had reduced her head to a pair of pigtails – the face was gone. The poster alarmed me. Could that be Huixian? Fanciful thoughts swirled in my head. Was that her missing mother? What a strange day it had been, with all these missing mothers suddenly returning. The memory of a name I'd all but forgotten formed in my head: Cui Xia. Was Cui Xia her name? The woman who had paced the shore in the rain way back then, now hidden among the crowds in the town's streets, her dripping-wet spirit now bright and dry, with no hope of being set free. She poured out her heart to me from the blackboard, nudging me to go and look for her daughter. *My daughter has forgotten her mother. My daughter, she's lost.* My attention was focused on a water mark running down the blackboard, unbroken tears from a mother's departed spirit. *Don't forget that my daughter is an orphan. She has grown into a beautiful, alluring young woman, but she remains an orphan. She is like a precious gem, picked up, discarded and picked up again; but she'll wind up being discarded again, and I ask one of you kind-hearted people to come to her aid!*

I received a flash of mystical inspiration there in front of the general store, which rocked me to my core and made my feet feel as if they were made of lead.

The sound of cotton-fluffing filled the air around the barbershop – *peng, peng, peng* – a happy, monotonous sound that reminded me to see if I had enough money to buy Father new cotton stuffing for his quilt, since that would give me an excuse for staying away so long. So I went into the cotton-fluffing shop and told the proprietor what I wanted. 'New cotton is very expensive,' she said. 'You're better off bringing in your own used cotton.'

'I don't have any.'

'How about making some out of your lightest and cheapest cotton?' They asked how soon I needed it.

'Not too soon, but not too late either. I'll wait in front of the barbershop.'

She gave me an ambiguous look. 'I know what you're thinking,' she blurted out. 'Were you and that Huixian across the street betrothed as children?'

That shocked me. 'Where did you hear that?'

'I didn't hear it, I guessed it. You were together on one of those barges, weren't you? That's something you boat people do all the time.'

The man in the shop stopped beating cotton and brushed off the fluff that nearly covered his body. With a silly grin, he said, 'Child engagements don't count, and I suggest you put those thoughts out of your head. That Huixian is a lovely flower that blooms on a high branch, way beyond the reach of any lowly boat person.'

Struck with a sudden panic attack, I blurted out what was in my heart: 'I don't want to pluck the flower, I want to protect it.'

*　　　*　　　*

My heart had been in my mouth the last time I'd visited the People's Barbershop. I pushed open the glass door, but stopped before going in. 'Kongpi!' they shouted as I stood in the door-way. 'Kongpi's back!' It was immediately obvious that the barbers had begun to see me as a strange creature, and I noticed the look in Huixian's eyes, both fear and disgust, mixed with a degree of pity.

After a brief, whispered exchange with Little Chen, Old Cui jumped down off his stool, came to the doorway and gave me a shove. 'What the hell do you want, Kongpi?' he asked, using uncouth Milltown slang. 'You're here every day. Do your balls itch or something? You look like a damned debt collector, and I want to know what the hell Huixian owes you. Is it money? Food? How much? Give me a number.'

I was stunned that Huixian would ask him to settle up with me. What did she take me for? I pushed him away and said, 'It's none of your damned business! If she wants to settle accounts, let her tell me to my face.'

'You make her sick. If it's money you want, she'll give it to you. Or food. But if it's anything else, dream on.'

I saw Huixian's reflection in the glass; she was clearly agitated. She moved from one chair to the next, then went into the boiler room. I felt like shouting to her, 'Go over to the general store, your mother's waiting there, she's looking for you!' But in the end, that was a secret I had to keep to myself. If it was disclosed it would become laughable, and I'd become a lunatic in her eyes. I can't describe the dejection I felt. I set down my bag, pointed across the street, and said, 'You've got it all wrong. I'm waiting for them to make the cotton stuffing for a quilt.'

'Then wait for it over there. Why come here? Every day you come here to cause trouble.'

'He hasn't got the guts. He's like a bitch in heat.' A man walked out of the boiler room. It was Wang Xiaogai. What a shock! He picked up a pair of scissors to trim his nose hair. 'You can fool other people, Kongpi, but not me. I know what's on your mind. The next time you come here like a bitch in heat, you'll wind up exactly like your old man.' He sneered and pointed at my crotch with his scissors. 'That thing of yours likes to act up, and you don't know how to control it, right? Well, I can take care of that. I'll take half of it for you!'

This time my lungs felt as if they were about to explode. I stormed into the shop and headed straight for Xiaogai. Seeing trouble, Little Chen and Old Cui intercepted me, one holding my arm, the other wrapping his arms around my waist to stop me. 'He was just kidding, it was a joke. He didn't mean it, Kongpi.' But Xiaogai, who was holding a stool in front of himself as protection, was not finished. 'Cutting that off would remove a scourge to the people. Don't think I wouldn't do it. I'd be helping you out. With half a dick, you could stand in for your old man!'

The blood rushed to my head. Spoiling for a fight, I started to take off my belt. 'Come on,' I said, 'you and your scissors. If you don't you're a fucking coward. Just you try, and see if I don't cut off your dog dick!'

Our anger had a comical effect. Little Chen let go of me and bent over in side-splitting laughter. Old Cui grabbed my hand to stop me from taking off my belt. 'Leave that alone!' he demanded. 'I'm telling you to cool down, Kongpi. If you don't stop taking off your trousers, we'll treat you like a common hooligan.'

Huixian came out of the boiler room. 'What's all the fighting about?' The sight of my trousers on their way down gave her a momentary fright. But then she rolled her eyes and said, 'You ugly clown, you're disgusting!' I couldn't blame her for calling me that, given the way things must have looked. I'd have felt the same way, but it was all Xiaogai's fault. I hitched up my trousers, waiting for her to work out what was going on, but then I saw the cold look in her eyes and watched as she banged a comb against the table.

'Haven't you disgraced yourself enough?' she said. 'If you have, then get out of here. Just get out!'

Nothing could have hurt me more than that demand. She should have been able to see that it hadn't been my fault, so why was she telling me to get out? I lost control. 'I've disgraced myself for over twenty years!' I bellowed. 'So what! I'm not leaving until he comes over and cuts off my dick!'

That stopped her. 'If he won't go, Xiaogai, you leave. It's time for you to go to work, anyway.'

But Xiaogai surprised us all by staying put. 'I'm not leaving till he does,' he said. 'I'm responsible for keeping order, and it's my job to watch him.'

With her hands on her hips and a frown on her face, Huixian sized up me and Xiaogai in turn before turning on her heel and saying, 'This makes me sick. If neither of you will leave, I will.'

Everyone watched silently as she took off her white smock and hung it on a peg. Underneath she was as fashionable as ever, in a cream-coloured turtleneck sweater over a pair of black bell-bottomed trousers. A string of pearls completed the outfit. Even though she had suffered setbacks in her life, there was no denying that she had a lovely figure, with full breasts, a slim waist and nice long legs. My gaze slid timidly down and down, stopping just above her knees. But of course I couldn't see those lovely, alluring knees, the mere thought of which gave me a case of the nerves. Lowering my head, I had a feeling that her flaring trouser legs had floated over to me, just as I heard her say in a flat tone of voice, 'Wait here for me, Ku Dongliang. I'll be right back.'

What was that all about? Even Xiaogai and the others gave her a puzzled look. Xiaogai broke the silence. 'What do you think you're doing?' Huixian ignored the question. She pushed open the door and walked out. I watched as she paused by the flower-bed and gently brushed the sunflowers with her hand. Then she walked off without a backward glance.

Xiaogai started after her, but I wasn't going to let that happen. I picked up the scissors and blocked his way. Unfortunately, Old Cui and Little Chen were on his side, and I was outnumbered. I could only stand and watch Xiaogai walk outside. He turned, pointed at me threateningly and said, 'Just you wait, Kongpi. Don't think I won't use those things on you. And if I don't, somebody else will. Get ready to go into mourning for that dick of yours. You're full of big talk now, but you'll be begging for mercy before long.'

I stayed in the barbershop, waiting for Huixian to return. Waiting, too, for Xiaogai to return, and that made me uncomfortable. I sat in the corner from two in the afternoon, reading a newspaper. It was a new edition, but the contents hardly differed from days before: 'News of victories on the labour front continue to pour in' or 'Unprecedented harvests in the agricultural, forestry, and fishery industries,' stuff like that. All I had to do was read the first paragraph to know what the entire article said. Old Cui and Little Chen left me alone, and I ignored them.

Customers started showing up before long, under my watchful eye. A middle-aged woman with a youthful, seductive voice came in and sat down. She and Old Cui seemed to be on close terms. The flirting between barber and customer began. I didn't like what I was seeing. Didn't he know that this work environment had a bad influence on Huixian? Next through the door was a young dandy in fancy clothes, an official at the General Affairs Building called Little Zheng. He was obviously looking for Huixian, since he glanced around and poked his head in the boiler room. When he saw that she wasn't there, he patted Little Chen on the shoulder and left. He hadn't said a word the whole time. That put me on my guard. 'What did Little Zheng want?' I asked Little Chen.

He just looked at me out of the corner of his eye and snorted contemptuously. 'That's funny, you asking about other people. What is it *you* want?'

What could I say? 'I'm waiting for Huixian,' I said once I'd gathered my wits. 'She told me to.'

'You think she likes you, don't you? She says wait, and you wait. Maybe she wants you to take in a movie. Or maybe have a wedding picture taken at the photographer's shop. Dream on!'

'Say what you like, I'm not leaving. I'm waiting for Xiaogai to come back and cut off my dick.'

He sneered. 'This is no place for you to be showing off, Kongpi. We know all about you. You're no match for Wang Xiaogai, so I'd steer clear of trouble, if I were you, and head back to the fleet now, before it's too late.'

The clock on the wall said it was nearly four o'clock. It was beginning to get dark outside. I spotted Chunsheng and his sister walking past the barbershop shouldering a bag of rice. Fortunately, they didn't see me on the other side of the glass door; that would have meant trouble for sure. The waiting was beginning to get to me, and in my mind's eye I could see Father, eyes glued to the shore, rolling pin in hand, and his worry had turned to anger; he was willing me to return to the barge. Tired of sulking, I decided to go across the street to pick up the quilt stuffing, but I'd only made it as far as the door when a familiar figure appeared. It was Huixian; she'd come back.

She was loaded down with purchases, and I wondered what that was all about. A green nylon mesh bag over her shoulder was crammed full of sweets, biscuits and bottles of orange soda, while in her hands she was holding a thermos flask and a sack of apples. I stepped aside and held the door open for her. She smiled; I returned the smile. As we looked at each other, her smile froze. One after the other, she laid her purchases on the floor by my feet. Not sure what was coming, I stepped over the vacuum bottle and bag, but she grabbed hold of my shirt to stop me.

'Let's settle our accounts.' It sounded like a casual comment, but the look in her eyes was anything but casual. 'You said you didn't want money or ration chits, right? Well, I broke one of your thermos flasks when I was a little girl, and I ate a lot of your food – biscuits, sweets, orange soda, things like that. I'm paying you back now. These are the only things I remember, but if I've forgotten anything, just tell me.'

Who'd have thought this would be how she'd decided to call it quits with me? I was on the verge of tears as I looked down at all those things. What could I say?

'I know I'm acting like a spoiled child. Go ahead, take this home with you. Now we're even.' She walked away, heading towards the boiler room, but stopped after a couple of steps and said, 'Are we quits now, or aren't we? I don't want to make you mad, Ku Dongliang. I haven't forgotten where I came from. You may not care about the future, but I do, so please stop coming here to pester me. If word gets out, it'll look bad for me.'

The tension in the shop was palpable. The twisted expression on my face must have frightened them. I picked up the flask and flung it to the floor; the glass lining shattered with a bang, sending the plastic case rolling on the floor as broken glass spread quickly. Then I picked up a soft-drink bottle and aimed it at Huixian. 'Don't you dare!' she shrieked.

That stopped me, but only for a moment. I spun around and aimed it first at Old Cui and the woman he was working on, then at Little Chen. They'd never shown me any respect, but none of this was their fault, so I turned again and flung the bottle at the shop's mirror. 'We're quits!' I shouted. 'That makes us quits!' The mirror shattered. Then I aimed at the second mirror, which merely cracked. So I threw a third bottle. 'We're quits!' I was crying by the time the third bottle was in the air. Hot tears ran down my face. Old Cui and Little Chen rushed up to grab me. Raising another bottle over my head, I swung at Old Cui's face. Little Chen grabbed my left hand, so I hit him in the head with a bottle in my other hand.

Chaos ensued. Huixian and the woman in the chair screamed, blood and orange soda stained Old Cui's face, who glared at me with disbelieving pain in his eyes.

'Are you out of your mind, Kongpi?' A trickle of blood oozed from Little Chen's scalp. Boiling with rage, he picked the last bottle of soda out of the nylon bag and flung it at me. Dropping whatever was in my hand, I turned and ran, but too late. I'd barely made it to the door before I was stopped by people who had quietly sealed off my escape route. I felt like a ball that had banged into a wall, as fists and feet slammed into me, driving me back inside the shop.

A trio of young men surrounded me like three gloomy bombs. One was a powerful fellow with a goatee who went by the name of Old Seven of Li Village; a distant relative of Wang Xiaogai, he'd killed a man during his youth. I knew that Xiaogai had sent them to the barbershop; what I didn't know was what they planned to do.

At first I just stood there to get a good look at them. They were all younger than me, in their late teens, and were dressed alike, with white bell-bottomed trousers and similar checked shirts. They wore fashionable digital watches, and Old Seven had a leather pouch hanging from his belt; something gleaming was sticking out of the top – an electrician's knife. I wasn't scared, not at first, because they merely had mischievous looks in their eyes; I even saw them wink at the barbers. But then Old Seven did something that put me on my guard: he spat in his hand and reached down towards my crotch. I jumped back and shoved him. 'What do you think you're doing?'

He responded with a sinister grin. 'What am I doing? I hear you've been a bad boy, letting that thing act up in public. Well, we're here to see it doesn't happen any more.' Now I knew what they had in mind, and I broke for the door, but again not in time. One of them grabbed me around the waist, another held my legs, and I heard Old Seven shout, 'Pull his trousers off!' All three bombs exploded at once. They were stronger than I'd given them credit for. Suddenly, I felt like a sack of rubbish being thrown to the floor.

As they were taking off my belt, I looked through their legs and saw Old Cui standing against the wall, covering his face with a towel. I wanted to yell for him to come and help me, but I couldn't, not after hitting him in the face with a bottle. Besides, it wouldn't have done any good, not with those three ganging up on me. So I sought out Little Chen, who was sitting to one side, enjoying the show. When our eyes met, he jerked his head away and I saw the blood where my bottle had hit him. As I lay there, the person I really wanted to help me was Huixian, but I couldn't see her anywhere. Someone was choking me, so I couldn't even call out her name. I lay there, unable to move. I was like a pig under the butcher's knife.

I saw a glint from Old Seven's electrician's knife, which was moving back and forth in front of my privates. 'Get hard! Stick up! Hurry up, so we can carry out the procedure!' There in front of everyone in the barbershop he began teasing my genitals with his knife. I felt a sharp, cold pain. I forgot that I was lying on the floor, and saw myself lying in my bed on the boat. The faces of my three tormenters swayed in front of my eyes, all a blur, but the face of my father appeared in the space behind them, the crows' feet at the corners of his eyes and the age spots on his cheeks clearly discernible. There were tears in his eyes, but the trace of a smile floated on to his aged face. 'Go ahead and cut it. Then I won't have to worry any more.'

I was paralysed with fear. Who were these men? And who had sent them? Was it Wang Xiaogai? Or was it my father? With my eyes opened wide in despair, I waited for my salvation. Now it was all up to Fate. I couldn't stop them from molesting me, couldn't keep them from humiliating me. 'Can't get it up, is that it? You can't get it up when you ought to and can't keep it down when should. Without a hard-on, you lose big time. If we can't get a good measure, we might remove the whole thing, and then you'll be worse off than your old man, who at least has half a dick.' Then, with rising excitement, he said, 'Bring Little Tiemei over here. That'll give him a hard-on for sure!'

A hush fell over the barbershop. The hands and legs that were pinning me to the floor went slack as Huixian emerged from somewhere, angry as a hen. I heard a string of vile curses burst from her mouth, mixed with tearful howls. 'Here I am! I'll give you all a hard-on! Get it up, get it up!' She swung a hairdryer at Old Seven's head. He ducked, and the dryer hit one of the other men in the arm. 'What do you think I am, a sow, a bitch, a whore? Don't you dare think I've fallen so low that the likes of you can take advantage of me! The person who can do that hasn't been born. I know who you are. You might feel like hot shit today, but tomorrow I'll call Commander Wang at Division Headquarters and have him send a squad of riflemen to take care of all three of you!'

Huixian's anger stunned Old Seven and his friends. They backed off, grinning, and said, 'What's got into our Little Tiemei to make her so mad? We're doing this for you. Once we take care of him, he won't come around to bother you ever again.'

'Don't you try to toss me on to a manure pile. I don't even know you. If you want to do something for me, then get the hell out of here!' Then she turned and hit me with her hairdryer. 'Why are you still lying there, stupid? Nobody on the shore likes you or wants to help you. For that you need the people in the fleet, so get yourself back on your boat.'

I tried to get up, but couldn't, so she reached down, took my hand and pulled me to my feet. Old Seven came over to stop her. 'Little Tiemei, you're a miserable little bitch,' he cursed. 'We come to your aid, just so you can help him. He's not the good little boy you think he is. How'd you like him to rape you?'

Huixian spat in his face, then spun around and said, 'Old Cui, Little Chen, are you men or aren't you? How can you stand there watching at a time like this. Get over here and help him. Help me!'

I took advantage of the confusion to run out of the door. Old Seven ran after me and kicked me on the hip. I couldn't get out of the way fast enough. One of his friends picked up a cut-throat razor and ran outside, then threw it at me; luckily, it whizzed past my ear. By then I was in the middle of the street. The old man and woman from across the street were standing in front of their shop. 'Three against one, what kind of—' she swallowed the rest, clearly frightened by the looks of the men. Then I heard the old man trying to get them to stop. 'Let him go,' he said. 'You don't have to get involved with the likes of him, he's not right in the head.'

I still hadn't got over my terrible fright, but there was nothing wrong with my head, which was clear enough to recall the adage that a wise man doesn't fight against impossible odds. But strange as it may sound, in the midst of the fix I had found myself in, I had suddenly longed to see my mother. I'd be safe if she were here. I ran through the intersection and past the general store, followed by curious stares from everyone who saw me. Some even attempted to stop me. 'What's wrong, Ku Dongliang? What are you running from?' *Kongpi*. All those voices at once, just a jumble of noise. I turned and saw the propaganda poster on a wall and conjured up the image of another mother, a deeply anxious mother holding a faceless child. As I passed the public toilet on People's Avenue, I caught a glimpse of my mother, Qiao Limin, standing beneath a parasol tree, which she was hitting with the sole of a plastic sandal. 'You useless son, you see what's happened to you? You're just like your father. Why aren't you running? Run as fast as you can, and come home!'

I ran down the path behind the steel warehouse and instinctively headed for the piers. And when I looked up again, my mother appeared on the path ahead. She had emerged abruptly from the dark recesses of the warehouse gateway. 'Where are you going?' she demanded, shaking her sandal in my face. 'Don't go back to the boat, not after disobeying him and causing all that trouble. He'll kill you if he lays hands on you. Go home instead! Go home!'

I stumbled to a stop, and, strangely, my mother faded away. *Go home instead! Go home!* I wanted nothing more. But where was home? I had no home on the Milltown shore. After eleven years on the river, no home remained on land. All those familiar streets and houses and gates and windows belonged to other people; they had homes, I didn't.

This was the first time I was willing to do as Mother wanted. Too bad I couldn't make sense of what she was saying. With nowhere to go, I loitered in the warehouse area until I heard the sound of a bell off to the northwest, telling me that school had finished, and that sound triggered a memory of my childhood and the path I'd taken home at the end of the school day. With no clear purpose in mind, I headed for the scrap-metal heap beside the warehouse. That had been my shortcut. I walked past stacks of prefabricated concrete slabs and wove my way in and around piles of discarded sheet metal and oil drums, until the path opened up on to a familiar street. There it was, Number 9 Workers and Peasants Avenue, my childhood home.

Twilight accentuated the most peaceful street in the heart of Milltown. Workers and Peasants Avenue was no longer worthy of the name. Ordinary residents had moved away, effectively handing the street over to officials. A Jeep and a Shanghai sedan parked in front of houses were testimony to the neighbourhood's exclusive nature. The cobblestone road had been paved over, and the tightly shut doors were accentuated by the shade of parasol trees, a sign of the elite families inside. The roof and walls of Number 9, my childhood home, had been refurbished – no more birds' nests and mossy eaves. The red roof tiles were brand new, the walls had recently been whitewashed and were covered by lush loofah gourd vines. The roses my mother had planted were gone.

My childhood home had changed hands several times. The new occupant, I knew, was Director Ji of the General Affairs Building. He had been transferred from the military, where it was said he'd been a regiment vice-commander. He was the head of a large, prosperous and flourishing family. There was a small plaque nailed to the green gate: 'Five Good Family', it read, referring to the family virtues of respect for the old and concern for the young, gender equality, marital harmony, household economy and neigh-bourly solidarity. Was Director Ji's family really that wonderful? I couldn't say if the plaque gave me a warm feeling or made me feel hostile. The date tree still standing in the yard dropped a leaf on my head, and when I shook it off, it landed on my shoulder. The leaf alone knew who I was and was welcoming me back. I hadn't set foot on the street in years. I felt like a stray dog lingering in the ruins of a former dog house.

A youngster rolling an iron hoop came walking by. 'Did you bring a gift for Director Ji?' he asked me. 'There's no one at home, they're all at work.'

'No, I didn't bring a gift,' I said. 'I'm from the Housing Office. Just looking the place over.'

After eleven years on the river, my childhood home was just a reminder of the past. I walked alongside the wall and I spotted the rabbit warren I'd built back then. The Ji family was using it as a rubbish dump. I went up to the window on the eastern wall. It was protected by an iron grille. A curtain on the other side kept out all the light; I couldn't see inside, but that had been my room. My metal-framed cot had been placed right under the window.

I'd like to have seen if it was still there, but I could only pace back and forth outside. I did notice a paper-cut window decoration, a pair of butterflies, so maybe that was now the bedroom of Director Ji's daughter. I purposefully turned and walked off.

A tall parasol tree stood on the other side of the street, and as I gazed at the shade it provided, I had an idea: that would be an ideal hiding place, a safe spot for me to keep an eye on my childhood home. I started climbing, and the view opened up in front of me. The date tree was still growing; the shade from its canopy covered half the yard. Drying racks had been set up all over the other half, and I was shocked to see all the duck and chicken and fish and meat drying in the sun, more than most families could ever consume. Preserved chicken and duck, pigs' heads and fish, all in separate groups in the sunlight. I remembered the flowerbed beneath the date tree, where Mother had tended her Chinese rose bushes for years. But unlike other people's gardens, her roses hadn't bloomed until the spring we moved away; several flowers, scrawny pink buds, appeared that year for the first time. I'd got up in the middle of the night to relieve myself and had seen her sitting by the flowerbed in the moonlight, reflecting upon her life. 'This is my fate,' she'd said. 'The sins of your father. The roses are about to bloom, just when I'm leaving. I won't be around to see them.'

But today my mother's image followed me relentlessly. It reappeared at Number 9 Workers and Peasants Avenue, and beneath the date tree. Her indignant gaze crossed the wall and glared at me, filled with disappointment that I hadn't improved over the years. 'I don't want you climbing that tree. Get down here and come home. Come home!' I was clear-headed, and knew I could not do as she wanted. The home was within reach, but, unhappily, it was no longer mine. I couldn't go back.

As I sat in the tree, my hip began to ache, the effect of Old Seven's vicious kick. It could turn out to be a permanent injury. I rubbed and rubbed, and suddenly a flood of unconnected thoughts came together. For the first time I was actually thinking about my life. Father and Mother: why had I chosen him over her? If I hadn't fled from her side, would my future have been brighter? Who would have offered me the better education? By staying with her I'd have missed out on the barge and the river, but at least I'd have had a home on the shore. The shore or the river: which life would have been better? Then I heard myself reply forlornly, It's all *kongpi*, yes, *kongpi*. Neither life offered anything good. The shore, the river – both bad. I'd be better off staying here, up a tree.

The higher I climbed, the more entranced I became with the branches and leaves. A brown dog spotted me and walked to the base of the tree, where it barked ferociously, startling me and disturbing the stillness on Workers and Peasants Avenue. I thought that Old Seven and his pals had caught up with me, so I climbed even higher. When I looked down, I saw someone open his door and stick his grey head out to see where the noise was coming from. Seeing nothing, he pulled his head back and closed the door.

The dog's barking had also attracted the attention of the boy with the iron hoop, who stopped at the foot of the tree, looked up and spotted me. 'What's somebody your age doing climbing a tree?' he shouted, surprised by what he saw.

'Nothing,' I said. 'I was tired, so I came up here to get some sleep.'

'Liar,' he said. 'Only birds sleep in trees. You're no bird.'

'No,' I said. 'I'm worse off than a bird, because I don't have a home on the shore and must sleep in trees.'

He didn't know whether to believe me or not. But then he shouted, 'You're lying. You said you were from the Housing Office. You people fix houses, not trees, so what are you doing up there? Planning a burglary?'

'Is that what you think people who climb trees do? Who do you think you are, you little bastard? You listen to me – when I lived here you were still in your mama's belly!'

The boy picked up his hoop and dashed over to a nearby gate. I knew he'd gone to fetch an adult, so I scrambled down the tree. I couldn't keep hiding up a tree. It dawned on me as I jumped down that my hands were empty. I didn't have my bag; I must have left it in the barbershop. Also, my quilt stuffing should be ready by now.

Keeping my eyes peeled the whole time, I made my way back to the barbershop door, where I carefully surveyed the surrounding area. I didn't see anything out of the ordinary, except for glinting shards of glass on a rubbish pile. All my doing. I could distinguish the pieces of mirror from the shattered soft-drink bottles. The shop had closed early. The barber's pole had been turned off, and the sunflowers, seemingly shaken by what had happened, were hiding behind their big leaves, no longer interested in showing their faces. The front door was closed and locked, and there was no one inside. A sign stuck up on the glass door piqued my curiosity, so I went over to see what it said. It took my breath away. Every word slammed into my chest like a bullet.

STARTING TODAY, KU DONGLIANG OF THE SUNNYSIDE FLEET IS BANNED FROM THIS SHOP.
SIGNED: EMPLOYEES OF THE PEOPLE'S BARBERSHOP, MAY 1977

Banned! They'd banned me from the barbershop! What right did they have to keep me from entering a public establishment? I pounded on the door. There was no one inside, but the noise brought out the cotton-fluffing couple across the street, who were covered from head to toe with cotton fuzz. The man had my bag in his hand, his wife was holding the rolled-up quilt stuffing. 'You ran off just in time,' said the old man, smacking his lips at my good fortune. 'There were actually four of them, but the one called Yama went to buy cigarettes. If he'd stuck around, you'd have been in worse trouble. You've heard of him, haven't you? He's cut the arms off five men in Phoenix. I personally witnessed two of them.'

The woman stopped her husband from saying more and handed me my bag and the cotton stuffing. 'You've read that announcement,' she said, pointing to the barbershop. 'They asked me to tell you to stay away from now on. They don't want you in there any more.'

I took my bag and felt around inside. My diary was missing, which proved something my father often said: You're sure to lose anything you don't want to lose. All the jars and cans were still there, everything but my diary. 'Where's my diary?' I blurted out in alarm. 'Who took my diary?'

My panicky shout gave them a fright. The man crouched down to help me rummage through the bag, while his wife, obviously upset, frowned and headed back into the shop, muttering unhappily, 'This town's full of bad people. We were being nice, keeping your bag for you, just so you can accuse us of stealing your stuff. We may be poor, but we're not so poor we'd take your diary!'

Punishment

FATHER'S PUNISHMENT was unavoidable.
Someone in the fleet must have heard about the scandal I'd caused in the barbershop or had seen the announcement on the door. Either way, they couldn't keep it to themselves and just had to tell my father. Standing on the bow, rolling pin in one hand and a coil of rope in the other, he was waiting for me.

Everyone could see that he was fuming. 'What's the rope for, Old Ku?' someone asked, probably already knowing the answer.

'I'm waiting for Dongliang. Have you seen him?' No one had. 'Don't worry about it,' Father said. 'I think I know where he is.'

'But what's the rope for?' they asked. He was about to say something, but stopped, reluctant to publicize a family scandal.

Sun Ximing, having heard that Father hadn't had anything to eat, brought over some food. 'Dongliang will be back soon to make dinner,' he said to comfort Father. 'This will tide you over for now.'

Father rejected the overture. 'I've got too much anger in me to eat. I'm not waiting here for lunch. The audacity of that boy – he's five hours late.'

'Dongliang's not a boy any more,' Sun said. 'Something must have come up to keep him ashore. Maybe he had a date. He'll be back sooner or later, so what's the problem? You're not thinking of tying him up, are you?'

'You may not know this, Old Sun, but minor errors often grow into major ones. There are rules for a country and rules for a family. His thinking and his moral character are flawed, and if national laws don't apply, domestic law has to. He must be tied up!'

Bag and cotton stuffing in hand, I arrived at the piers where the barges were moored. The first thing I saw was Father standing on the bow with the coil of rope in his hand. Some people on the other barges had gloating looks on their faces, others were waving to keep me from going aboard. Father was fuming. I'd done the one thing he could not tolerate: I'd defied his authority. I was five and a half hours late, and I knew I was in for a punishment. Five slaps in the face, maybe, or five hours on my knees. Maybe he'd make me write a five-thousand-word self-criticism. It all depended on my degree of contrition. I'd never even considered the possibility that he'd actually be planning to tie me up. I was twenty-six years old. Six-Fingers Wang's daughters were watching me, so was Chunsheng's sister. Li Juhua could have been peeking at me out of the oil-pumping station for all I knew. My hip was sore, I was tired, and he was planning to tie me up! If I let him do that in front of all those people, I'd be ashamed to show my face anywhere after that. I'd be better off tying myself to a rock and jumping into the river.

I decided to stay where I was until he'd cooled down enough to put down the rope. I called Xiaofu over to take the quilt stuffing on to our barge. But then I changed my mind. What if he wouldn't let me come aboard? The stuffing would come in handy. So I decided to hand him my bag instead. But then I thought, what if he wouldn't let me go aboard ever again, and I had to start a new life on the shore? I'd need the bag on my travels, by train or bus, so I decided to keep it with me for the time being.

My abnormally hesitant behaviour began to unnerve Xiaofu, who complained, 'What do you want me to help you with? You're driving me crazy.' So I took the jars and cans out of the bag for him. He picked up the soy sauce and vinegar bottles and took them up on to the barge, laying them at my father's feet.

'Thank you, Xiaofu,' Father said politely. 'You're a good boy.' He didn't seem so angry, after all, but the moment Xiaofu turned back to me, Father picked up the bottles and flung them back on the shore. 'You coward!' he shouted. 'What is it you don't have – legs or guts? Why don't you come aboard instead of having somebody else act as your porter?'

The soy-sauce bottle shattered at my feet, spilling its contents on the ground and splattering my trouser legs. Now I was the angry one, as I wiped it off. 'You've got legs, haven't you? If you want to tie me up, come over here and do it if you can!'

I regretted the provocation the moment the words were out of my mouth. It only made things worse. Father's face turned almost green with rage. 'You think I won't come after you, is that it? I haven't turned into a fish, not yet, so dry land doesn't scare me. I'll come down there, all right, and I'll tie you up.'

He'd been on the barge so long he'd forgotten how to use the gangplank. He rested one foot tentatively on the edge to see how springy it was, then the other foot. But that's as far as he dared go. He stood there, looking strangely awkward as the gangplank bounced up and down. 'Careful!' I shouted. Straining to keep his balance, and gasping for breath, he pointed at me. 'Don't give me that,' he said. 'If I fell into the river and drowned, you'd be free. Too bad for you, I'm not going to die that easily. I'm still your father.'

Desheng jumped aboard our barge and pulled my father off the gangplank. 'Don't get worked up, Old Ku. Don't try it. You're not used to it any more. If you try walking on it, you'll be in the river for sure.'

'What do you mean, not used to it? I used to walk on it all the time, even carrying a sack of rice.'

'I know that,' Desheng said, 'but you haven't done it in years. Even if you made it across, you'd get motion sickness on land.'

The fear in Father's eyes was unmistakable as he looked nervously at Desheng. 'What do you mean by that? You're making that up. Why would I be unsteady on land?'

Desheng began to sway, holding his head in his hands and rocking it back and forth. 'Being unsteady on land and on the water are the same. People not used to being on a boat get motion sickness on water, just like people who aren't used to walking on land are unsteady on the riverbank. You've been on the river so long the barge is your land and the land is your barge. That's why you won't be able to walk on the shore.'

I could see that Father's mind had begun to wander. He cast a wary eye to the shore, blinking rapidly as he pondered what Desheng said. But then his gaze bounced back to where I was standing. 'Are you coming here or not? Are you waiting for me to wobble on the gangplank or on the ground?' He twisted the rope around his hand and shouted, 'You're acting awfully brave, putting up a desperate struggle with your back to the wall.'

'And I'll keep struggling if you're set on tying me up,' I said. 'Hand the rope to Desheng, and I'll come up.'

'Why should I? He doesn't represent the government, and he's not your dad. I am. You've done a terrible thing today, and I'm going to punish you by tying you up.'

While the two of us, father and son, faced each other, one on the river, the other on the shore, Desheng's wife joined her husband on our barge and asked Father to give her the rope. 'You two are causing a scene. Dongliang's a grown man,' she said, 'old enough to be a father himself. He's stronger than you, and you can't tie him up unless he lets you. And even if he did, because he's a dutiful son, it'd be such a loss of face for him he'd never be able to live it down.' She was right. The people who were watching us nodded in agreement.

But not Father. He shook his head. 'I don't want him to be dutiful, I want him to be better than he is. You don't understand how hard it is to get him to improve himself. I teach him, but he doesn't get any better. But if I stop teaching him, he'll just get worse. And if I simply leave him alone, he'll break every rule there is. He's a disgrace, and I have to treat him like a little tyrant, because that's the only thing he responds to.'

'All this talk about getting better or worse doesn't mean anything aboard these barges,' Desheng's wife said with a scowl. 'All we want is to get by and live a peaceful life. I'll talk to him, tell him to come up and admit he was wrong. I'll make him promise to stop doing things that make you angry.'

'Who cares if he admits he was wrong or not?' Father said. 'He's the type who refuses to mend his ways.'

Desheng's wife was first to notice the pained look on my face. She pointed to me. 'Take a good look at Dongliang,' she said. 'His face is as white as a sheet. He can't stand the way he makes you mad. Put the rope down, Old Ku, or take it into the cabin. You can use what you want, national laws or family law, there's no loss of face if no one sees. But you can start by letting Dongliang come aboard.'

Desheng and his wife both tried to take the rope away from Father, but he tightened his grip and refused to let go. But he looked a bit less angry, which Desheng noticed. This time he gave the rope a hard tug and wrenched it out of Father's hand.

Now that he was no longer holding the rope, Father's face showed how weary he was. 'All right,' he said, 'I'm not going to tie you up. Don't come aboard today, stay where you are. Lead as degenerate a life as you want. Go ahead, stir up plenty of trouble and break all the rules. I won't need to use family law; I'll let national laws do their job. Sooner or later you'll be handed over to the dictatorship of the proletariat.'

Thinking he was beginning to give in, I started up the gang-plank, and barely avoided getting hit by a flying rolling pin. 'Who said you could come up here?' he shouted. 'Get your ass back on the shore!'

My hip really hurt from twisting my body to get out of the way of the rolling pin, and that only fuelled my anger. 'Are you going to let me come aboard today or aren't you?' I gave him my final ultimatum. 'If you won't, then I'll never step foot on that barge again.'

'Is that a threat? Do you think I'm afraid of your threats? Go on,' he said with a wave of his hand, 'get back on the shore. From this day on I have no son!'

'Who wants to be your son anyway? Who needs a father like you?' The blood had rushed to my head and stoked my courage. A stream of ugly curses gushed from my mouth, washing over Father like a raging torrent. 'Take off your trousers, Ku Wenxuan, and show everybody. Who wants a father like you? Everybody else's father has a whole dick. How come you only have half of one? Where do you get the nerve to try to educate me with only half a dick? And you wanted to tie me up! Half a dick. I tell you, I'm like I am today all because of that dick of yours!'

My cries hit the boat people within earshot like a thunderclap and provoked more shouting. 'Ku Dongliang is rebelling, he's rebelling!' My father blanched and began to sway. The gaze in his eyes was very peculiar. What I saw wasn't panic or terror, it was despair. A glob of phlegm caught in his throat, and when he tried to bring it up to spit it out, he was racked by a coughing fit.

Desheng and his wife, who were still aboard our barge, rushed up to help him into the cabin. Desheng glared at me as he propped my father up. 'Dongliang, are you possessed by a demon or something? Your father isn't a class enemy, but you might as well kill him as talk to him that way.'

His wife patted Father on the shoulder. 'Don't let it get to you,' she said to him. 'Someone in town ran into a demon recently, in broad daylight. It scared them out of their wits. I'm sure that's what has happened to Dongliang.'

'No, it didn't!' I shouted. 'I've suffered for eleven years, and I've had enough. Now I'm rebelling!'

On the barges and on the shore, people were looking at me, shocked. 'I'm rebelling!' I yelled. 'I'm rebelling!' Tossing the quilt stuffing over my back and slinging my bag over my shoulder, I turned and headed back down the pier.

Sun Ximing and his wife ran after me; one of them grabbed my bag, the other held on to the cotton. 'Where are you going, Dongliang?' Sun asked. 'What makes you think you can just leave? Where will you go?'

With a wave of my hand, I said, 'Where I go is none of your business. It's a big world, and there has to be a place for me in it.'

'The world may be big,' Sun said, 'but it doesn't belong to you. It belongs to the Party and to socialism.'

'What's wrong with you today, Dongliang?' Sun's wife said, stamping her foot and waving her arms. 'Everybody's always talking about your bad points, but you're a dutiful son. I told my husband that when the fleet chooses its most civilized family this year, it has to be barge number seven.'

'Our barge isn't civilized,' I said, 'but you choose whatever barge you want, I don't care.'

Sun grabbed hold of my bag again and said, 'Dongliang, you can't abandon your father. How's he going to live if you leave?'

'He's got arms and legs,' I said. 'He can take care of himself.'

'OK,' Sun said, 'forget about him if you want, that's your business. But shipping goods is my business, and how is your barge going to keep working if you leave? Tomorrow we're taking on a load of oilseed. Your father doesn't know a thing about how these barges work, and I can't let you affect production.'

'What do I care about oilseed? Or about production? From now on, the only thing I care about is me. I'm a free man!'

I started running, and didn't stop till I'd left Sun Ximing and his wife far behind. But a couple of kids from other barges quickly overtook me. 'They're saying you almost lost your dick today,' Xiaofu said. 'Is that true?'

Chungeng sneaked a look down at my crotch. 'Are you running away to keep from getting punished?' he asked. 'Wang Xiaogai says you go to the barbershop in town every day, and that you went there to harass Huixian. Have you already thumped her? Have you?' Their questions pissed me off, but I was in no mood to wrangle with a bunch of kids, so I kicked Chungeng and started running again. He grabbed his knee where I'd kicked him, and started to scream, 'You're a moron, Dongliang, an ugly toad that wants to thump a swan. You deserve to have your dick cut off!'

As I was passing the oil-pumping station, a crumpled piece of paper flew in the air and landed at my feet. Li Juhua was standing in the doorway in her blue work clothes, watching me, her severe demeanour mocking me.

'What have I ever done to offend you, Li Juhua?' I said. 'Why are you looking at me like that?'

'You've never offended me,' she said. 'It's just that I've been thinking that you know everything about someone except what's in his heart. On the surface you look all right, so how could you have such a filthy mind?'

I just stared at her, stunned by her comment. 'What do you mean, a filthy mind?'

She brushed some dust off her sleeve and said, 'I don't have an appetite for such things. Why do I need to tell you what you've done?' Seeing the blank look on my face, she sneered, 'Don't act dumb with me. Do I have to remind you what you did to Little Tiemei in the barbershop?'

Now I understood. A frightful rumour about me had already begun to spread, thanks to Wang Xiaogai – the guilty one taking a bite out of the victim. I stood there in front of the oil-pumping station in a daze, so angry my limbs felt cold. Li Juhua's words buzzed in my ears. 'Go ahead, be as decadent as you want, it's none of my business. You and I have nothing in common, and I don't care if you wind up in prison.'

I had no desire to engage Li Juhua in a debate about the false accusation. Instead, I headed angrily to the security-group office to settle scores with Xiaogai. But when I got there, I could see through the window that he was out; Baldy Chen and Scabby Five were in the cluttered office playing a game of chess, head to head and cursing up a storm. A blackboard on the wall above them read: 'Current security situation report.' My name appeared below the heading: 'Ku Dongliang of the Sunnyside Fleet took liberties with a woman at the People's Barbershop.' The sight of those scrawled words nearly blew the top off my head. Ignoring the door, I pushed open the window and all but jumped through it. 'Erase that!' I shouted. 'Erase my name!'

Jerking their heads up, they both screamed. Wasting no time, Scabby Five picked his truncheon up off the table and dashed over to me. 'Well, Kongpi, we don't have the time to take care of you, so you are on your own!'

I flung my quilt stuffing at Wulaizi, but he ducked, and Baldy Chen rushed up. He was holding a rifle with a glinting bayonet fixed to the barrel. Blinking ferociously, he charged at me. I jumped down off the window ledge and ran all the way to the cotton warehouse, where I stopped and looked back to see Baldy Chen and Scabby Five in the doorway, yelling something I couldn't hear. Maybe they had decided not to chase me so they could continue with their game of chess. After a quick survey of my surroundings, I picked up an enamel tea cup left on a stool by the gate watchman and took a drink, then wiped my face with a tattered towel. Since I couldn't hang around here, I decided to go to the chess pavilion.

The area around the pavilion was like a black-market communication hub, where oil truckers pulled off the highway to unload and rest and pick up hitchhikers, taking them as far as Horsebridge or Wufu for fifty or sixty cents. It was an open secret.

I went up to the pavilion, my first visit in years, and was shocked by what I saw. The hexagonal structure now had only three sides, the swallow-tail eaves were gone, and striped plastic sheeting was wrapped around the six stone pillars, their tips peeking through the top to remind passers-by that this had once been Milltown's grandest spot. This was possibly the most significant event on the banks of the river, and I knew nothing about it. Who was responsible? It had to be Zhao Chuntang. But why? My attention shifted from the pavilion to a slovenly worker crouching on the ground drinking tea and eating a steamed bun; a sledgehammer lay at his feet. I ran over to confront him.

'Who authorized you to tear down the pavilion? Was it Zhao Chuntang?' In between bites, he said, 'It's not my call, and not Zhao Chuntang's. The order came from above.'

'Why would anyone want to tear it down?' I asked.

'This is valuable property,' he said, and I hear they're going to build a car park. There are so many vehicles in Milltown these days – oil trucks, agricultural transports, even military vehicles – so parking is at a premium.'

'What's more important,' I demanded, 'a car park or a memorial to a revolutionary martyr?' It was a delicate question, but I was asking the wrong person. So I softened my tone and asked, 'What about the memorial stone? Where did they tell you to move it to?'

'It's only a stone marker,' he said, 'and a tomb with some personal effects. Easy to move. I'm told it's going to the revolutionary museum in Phoenix.'

My distress mystified the worker. He looked me over carefully, taking in my bag, my clothes and my leather shoes, but he couldn't figure out who I might be. 'Who are you, anyway?' he asked.

I nearly blurted out, 'I'm the martyr Deng Shaoxiang's grandson!' But I bit my tongue. The river flows east for thirty years, then west for thirty more. Now I couldn't say whose grandson I was. With a sigh I said, 'I'm nobody, nobody at all. Just a rank-and-file citizen. I was curious, that's all.'

'After raising such a stink, now you tell me.' The worker breathed a sigh of relief. 'Why'd you get so angry with me? We're both rank-and-file citizens, so you shouldn't be asking me questions like that. Go and ask one of the big shots.'

He was right, this was a matter for the big shots. That excluded me, and I had no reason to make trouble for an ordinary worker. I walked back to the pavilion and pulled back part of the plastic to look inside. The smell of alcohol hit me in the face. The man wasn't alone. Two other workers were asleep on the floor. The remains of a meal lay on an old newspaper, and a pair of geese were picking their way through the lunch boxes and drink bottles. Then I caught sight of a man watching the geese – it was the idiot Bianjin, sitting in a corner, holding a baby goose in his arms as he gnawed on a pig's foot.

The sight of Bianjin called to mind his backside, and that reminded me of my father's backside, with its fish-shaped birthmark. He had to contend for his birthright with an idiot, a bizarre struggle that had gone on for years and that could only be classified as humiliation. I had no interest in being around Bianjin. My fear of being subjected to comparative scrutiny was like a conditioned reflex. There were plenty of muddle-headed people on the shore and on the barges who would be thrilled at the prospect of discussing our relative appearance and bloodlines if they saw me together with Bianjin. Who were the real descendants of Deng Shaoxiang – Ku Wenxuan and his son, or the idiot Bianjin? Most of the boat people leaned towards us, while people on the shore tended to favour the underdog by insisting that the idiot's birthmark more closely resembled a fish. And there were even people who passionately argued that they'd prefer an idiot to be the martyr's descendant than the degenerate Ku Wenxuan, who would smear the legacy of Deng Shaoxiang.

I stood outside the pavilion observing Bianjin, while several townspeople watched me from a nearby tea stall. The sight of me and the idiot in the same place had them virtually jumping for joy. 'Look!' they said. 'There's the idiot, and there's Ku Dongliang!' They were all talking at once, the topic of discussion, believe it or not, my backside. Some of them were unable to contain their desire to have a peek; their eyes were nearly burning a hole in the seat of my pants. Baldy Chen's cousin, Four-Eyes Chen, who wore glasses, appeared to be cultured and educated, but he came up, grabbed my arm and made a presumptuous request: 'Ku Dongliang, your father never comes down off his barge, so his backside is off limits. Why don't you show what you're made of by dropping your pants and letting us compare your birthmark with the idiot's? That way the masses can fairly judge whether you are Deng Shaoxiang's grandson.'

Four-Eyes was courting disaster. He was no match for me in an argument or in a fight, but I had no desire to get tangled up with this bunch. 'Get the hell out of here, Four-Eyes, and send your wife over. I'll give her a look, front and back. She can tell you what she sees.' My parting shot. A foreboding chill swirling in the early-evening air above Milltown gave me the feeling that this was not the place for me. I had to leave, and leave fast.

A number of oil transports were parked by the side of the road, one of which had just started up. The driver, assuming I was looking for a ride, waved at me from the cab. 'Where you headed? Hurry up, jump in.' I ran over and jumped on to the running board. 'I'm going to Xingfu,' the driver said. 'I can drop you off on the way if that's where you're headed. It'll cost you fifty cents.'

I didn't know exactly where Xingfu was, whether it was a rural village or a market town. But so what! Xingfu – Happiness – a nice name. 'Xingfu it is. Let's go.'

The driver opened the passenger door and stretched out his hand. 'Fifty cents, up front.'

I was digging in my pocket for the money when a strange voice whistled past my ear. There was a commotion at the intersection, with several people calling my name. 'Stay there, Ku Dongliang! Don't leave, don't go anywhere!' Some kids who'd come running over from the Sunnyside Fleet were calling my name, and they surrounded me like a swarm of hornets. One of them wrapped his arms around my legs, another grabbed my bag. Xiaofu stamped his foot and yelled at me, 'Ku Dongliang, while you've been having a carefree time out here, your dad swallowed some pesticide. They've taken him to hospital.'

I had a dim image of Baldy Chen and his rifle, a delayed bullet emerging from the barrel and hitting me in the chest, the bad news arriving mercilessly. I shuddered, jumped down off the running board and ran as fast as I could towards the hospital, arms flailing. I thought I was flying down the road, but then my hip started aching, my legs felt rubbery and I started gasping for breath. I slowed down in spite of myself.

Xiaofu, who was off to my left, yelled, 'Come on, run! Your dad's in hospital fighting for his life, and you're moving like a fat old pig.'

Chungeng, to my right, joined in. 'It's all your fault. A real man has the guts to take the heat for what he's done. What kind of man are you? Are you scared now? You drove your own dad to suicide, but you're like a turtle that pulls in its head. A turtle runs faster than you!'

Six-Fingers Wang's youngest daughter, Little Four, was urging me on from behind by smacking my rear end with a switch, as if she was whipping a horse. 'Get moving!' she said. 'You have to do something to atone for your crimes.' She was panting and cursing at the same time. 'Ku Dongliang, no matter what you think of him, he's still your dad. People only have one father and one mother, and when they're gone, they're gone. But you abandoned your dad and ran off! If my mother hadn't swallowed pesticide once and my father didn't have such a good nose, your dad would have died in his cabin without anybody knowing anything about it.'

Her words hit me hard. I was crying like a baby as I ran. Those kids had never seen me cry, and it stopped them in their tracks. I covered my face with my hands so they wouldn't see my tears. They thought it was their scolding and pressure that had brought on the tears, so they stopped. 'Don't cry,' Little Four said, 'we won't say any more. So you were wrong this time. Next time you'll do better.'

With a frown, Chungeng said, 'What good does it do to cry? The harder you cry, the slower you run.'

People out on the street gaped curiously at this contingent on the run. 'Hey!' they said. 'What's the hurry? Has someone in the fleet died?'

'People are dying in town all the time,' Little Four shrieked, 'but not in the fleet.'

Xiaofu shoved the busybodies out of the way as he pushed me along. 'What business is it of yours if we run? Go ahead, get an eyeful, we're training for a long-distance race. Haven't you ever seen one of those?'

Desheng and Sun Ximing's wives were waiting for me at the hospital entrance. They exchanged relieved looks. 'Dongliang, you didn't leave after all, that's good,' one of them said.

'My Xiaofu knows how to get things done,' said the other. 'He managed to bring Dongliang here.'

I was on the verge of collapse. 'My dad, is he OK?' I managed to shout before falling at their feet. I couldn't stand up; I felt the women try to pull me to my feet by my arms. I didn't resist, but my body and my soul lay fearfully on the ground, refusing to get up. I was shaking uncontrollably.

'There's nothing to be afraid of,' Desheng's wife said. 'Your dad's going to be OK. He's got us to take care of him. Now stand up, come on, stand up.'

But Sun Ximing's wife kept pointing to my head and giving me a good scolding. 'Now you know what it means to be afraid. Why didn't you listen to us earlier? It's OK not to trust the people on the shore, but have you stopped trusting us too? You call yourself a rebel. Well, you nearly rebelled your father to death!'

They walked me into the hospital's intensive-care unit. I have no recollection of the hospital's layout or facilities, but I'll never forget the smell of the room he was in. It stank of dirty feet and blood, along with the acrid smell of iodine and the aroma of food. Father had forced me into a relationship with that place: the first time as a result of his severed penis, and this time in an effort to save his life. I couldn't escape a measure of responsibility for either. Standing in the doorway, I suddenly felt as if my stomach was about to betray me. Afraid that I was going to throw up, I crouched down in front of a spittoon.

'What's wrong with you, Dongliang?' Sun's wife said. 'Your father's lying there in the corner, what are you doing down there?'

I rubbed my belly. 'Hold on,' I said, 'wait a minute.'

When she saw my ashen face, Desheng's wife said, 'Yes, let's wait a minute. He looks as if he's going to throw up, probably from hunger, or fright.'

I strained to raise my head from the spittoon to search for Father. Most of the beds in Intensive Care were occupied. He was lying on a bench in the corner, surrounded by oxygen tanks, IV racks and lots of people. It was obvious that his condition was critical from the way two nurses were bouncing around beside him and the doctor was pumping his stomach. It looked like a slaughterhouse or meat-processing plant. Father was a feeble but stubborn old ox that refused to be led to the slaughter, and was upsetting the nurses.

Since they didn't dare vent their frustrations on him, they took them out on the people standing nearby. 'How can you be so inept? You men, with all that strength, and you can't even hold an old man down. Look how he's thrown up all over me!'

The boat people shuttled back and forth beside the bench until they finally settled into place. Six-Fingers Wang pressed down on Father's body, with Sun Ximing and Desheng in position on either side of the bench, one holding a spittoon, the other holding up an IV bottle. That was when Sun Ximing saw me. He glowered. 'What are you standing around for? Get over here and help Six-Fingers hold him down. Your stubborn dad refuses to let them pump his stomach.'

So I rushed across and pushed down on my father's midsection. He looked up at me and tried to say something, but the tube in his mouth made that impossible. Next best was to push me away, but Six-Fingers was holding his arms down at his sides. Obviously he wanted me out of there, and that was probably a good idea, since my stomach was churning and I felt like throwing up. But I had to force it down. He was the one who needed to throw up. I pushed down hard. 'Throw up, Dad, get rid of it.' But he was determined not to. He was breathing as hard as he could, trying to expel the tube from his throat.

'Empty your stomach, Dad, forget about the tube. Get rid of the pesticide and you'll be fine.'

I looked into his eyes and saw that the anger had given way to torment, just before a geyser of foul liquid burst from his mouth and hit me full in the face. I didn't even try to get out of the way, strangely enough. I just emptied the contents of my stomach right after he did.

An Orphaned Barge

T HE FLEET had left town by the time Father got out of hospital.

I carried him on my back down to the piers, from where we could see barge number seven tied up beside the embankment some distance away, an abandoned vessel seemingly floating at the edge of the world. In my eleven years on the river this was the first time our barge had not been part of the fleet, and it seemed quite alien, as did the shore and even the Golden Sparrow River. Normally, the river flowed so rapidly it could be heard at a distance, with floating objects just about everywhere you looked: brightly coloured or steel-grey patches of grease, dead branches and leaves, and the rotting corpses of drowned animals. But that afternoon the river was so implausibly unspoiled that it spread out before me like a timeworn piece of dark-blue satin, perfectly still and beautiful. Yes, beautiful, but bleakly so.

Father stank after three days in the hospital. I smelled his fetid breath, the dried sweat in his hair and the acrid stench of his clothing. All combined, he gave off a strong fishy odour. Why, I wondered, did he smell like that? Bringing him back that way was like carrying a large marinated fish.

Father was wide awake the whole time, but he refused to speak to me – his last remaining display of authority. He was mired in silence, the only punishment he could think of. Except for an occasional glimpse of his swaying feet, he was hidden from me, especially his eyes, but I knew that the hostility was gone, and that, except for glimmers of suffering, only a blank, empty gaze remained – fish eyes. As we were leaving the hospital, a doctor had recommended that I talk to Father more often, telling me that it was common among rescued suicides, especially older ones, to descend into dementia.

I wanted to talk to Father, but didn't know what to say, how to start or end a conversation with him. His shrivelled body rested against me, but I knew that our hearts and minds were miles apart. While I couldn't see his mouth, that was not the case with the frothy bubbles that emerged from it. I don't know if they were caused by the treatment he had received or by what his body had experienced, but the result of the stomach-pumping was dark- and light-brown bubbles at first, followed by transparent and, I must admit, enticing bubbles.

Sunlight glinted off the river as we approached the piers, with a light breeze caressing Father's face to dislodge the last of the bubbles, which first landed on my shoulder and then fell to the ground at my feet. I was surprised to see them change colour to a glistening rainbow of hues, and the sight made me laugh for the first time in ages. Unfortunately but predictably, Father misinterpreted my laughter. I felt him move and heard him speak for the first time: 'Go ahead, laugh, I know why you're laughing. I'm going to die soon, and you'll get your freedom.'

A trio of longshoremen stood on the pier smoking. 'What's the story with number seven barge?' Master Liu shouted. 'The others have all left, so what are you doing strolling around here?' Then they spotted Father on my back, and that got them animated. The local labourers had long been curious about my father, and this was a rare opportunity to get some answers. They crowded around to get a good look at Father's face and body, before retreating to a nearby crane to exchange opinions. I heard one of them say, 'He's as strange as they say. He's blowing bubbles like a fish.' I detected a sympathetic note in Master Liu's voice as he said with a sigh, 'It's only been ten years or so since I saw him last. How did he get so old so fast? He's had a tough life.' I didn't like what I heard from the third man, who was younger than the others; he contrasted my father's appearance with what he'd heard of the life of Deng Shaoxiang, and, thinking himself quite clever, concluded, 'No, this old-timer can't be the one, he has to be a fraud. No way he's Deng Shaoxiang's son. Think back to when Deng Shaoxiang was martyred, and the baby was in her basket. He wouldn't be this old, not now.'

I felt Father stir on my back and was hit by a dose of foul breath; he'd opened his mouth, probably to defend himself by giving his age. But the second thing he said was also directed at me. 'Just keep walking a bit further, and you can deposit me on the barge. Then you can leave. I haven't got long to live, and I won't be around to run your life any more. You can have your freedom.'

A stray cat that had prowled around the piers for years was crouched on the bow of our barge, watching the river flow past. It might have recognized me. Seeing its master return, it jumped on to the gangplank and skittered past my legs to the shore.

The first thing I saw after carrying Father on deck was a gift the cat had left us: its droppings. Then I noticed that someone had pulled back the hatch of the forward hold, which was now empty, half in sunlight and half in darkness. Echoes of the flowing river emerged, now that there was nothing in there for us to ship. I was remarkably sensitive to the sound of the river, and that afternoon I distinctly heard the faithful echo of its call in the forward hold: *Come down, come down.* There was no question that Father heard it too, for I felt his head rise weakly from my shoulder. 'What's that sound?' he asked. 'Are they shipping oilseed?'

'It's too late for that, Dad, the hold is empty. There's nothing on our barge except some cat droppings.'

We went aft into the cabin, where I put him down on the sofa. He collapsed with a contented sigh. 'We're home, Dad,' I said. 'Everything's going to be all right.'

'I'm fine now,' he said. 'You can go.' I asked him if he wanted to take a bath. After a brief hesitation, he said, 'Yes, that's what I need. After that you can go.' So I got up and started to boil some water, accompanied by his mutterings. 'Don't worry about me, and I won't worry about you.'

'You might not worry about me,' I said loudly, 'but I'm worried about you. Not because I want to be, but because you're my father and I'm your son.'

Everyone in the fleet knew it was a chore for my father to take a bath, and you had to be on your toes. I moved our wooden tub into the cabin and made sure the window was closed to keep nosy people from peeking in at us. He may well have been the most unique man on either bank of the Golden Sparrow River. Other men wouldn't bat an eye if they were asked to do the sorcerer's dance nude, but my father's naked body was a true curiosity for almost everyone. If the front was exposed, he was deeply shamed by his restored penis, but the rear view, with its fish-shaped birthmark, was a source of great pride to him, and both were of considerable interest to all sorts of people. I knew that he had struggled for years to avoid exposing himself to the shame or horror of public viewing. Even I had had no opportunity to see his uncovered penis. In the past, whenever he took a bath, it was my job to patrol the decks outside the cabin to keep out the prying eyes of curious children. But now the other barges were gone, so there was no need for that. After closing the window, I saw that the look in Father's eyes was one of trepidation. Darting glances to one side and the other, he said, 'What's that buzzing in my ears? Who's out there?'

'The fleet's gone,' I said. 'Ours is the only boat left, so there's no one to make any noise.'

With a watchful glance at the door, he said, 'That's not safe, not safe at all. Shut the door.'

So I did, and the cabin got stuffy. After filling the tub with hot water, I helped Father out of his filthy clothes, but only as far as his underpants. 'Those stay on,' he said. 'I'll take them off when I'm in the tub.' I helped him in and watched as he slowly sat down by leaning to one side, like a stroke victim. 'Don't look,' he said. 'There's nothing to see. You didn't listen, and nearly suffered the same fate. Hand me the towel and turn around.'

I did as he asked, and stared at the poster of Deng Shaoxiang on the wall. Then something came over me, and I thought I saw the slumbering martyr come to life. Turning her head slightly, she gazed down at the naked body in the tub. *Ku Wenxuan*, she said, *are you my son? If not, whose son are you?* The sounds of splashing rose behind me. 'Can you manage, Dad?' I asked. 'I don't want you to tire yourself out.'

'I'm not dead yet,' he said. 'I can manage the front, but you'll have to wash my back.' A few moments later, he said, 'The front's done, so now you can do my back. It must be filthy. It won't stop itching.'

Crouching down beside the tub, I had a clear view of his birthmark. The fish's head and body had faded until they were hardly recognizable. But the tail remained stubbornly imprinted on the sagging skin. I was shocked. 'Dad!' I blurted out. 'What happened to your birthmark? Everything but the tail has almost disappeared.'

He shuddered. 'What do you mean? What kind of crazy talk is that?' Straining to twist his neck so he could see, he said, 'Stop scaring me like that. My birthmark is different from other people's, it'll never fade.'

'But it has, Dad! It used to be a whole fish, but now there's only the tail.'

Again he tried to see behind him, but failed, and in his anxiety to turn his head around, he lurched from side to side. 'Crazy,' he said. 'That's crazy talk!' He began thumping me with his hand. 'Let me see for myself.'

'Have you lost your mind, Dad? It's on your backside, where you can't see. But I'm not lying, it's faded. Why would I lie about something that important?'

But he wouldn't stop thrashing in the tub. I leaned to the side to see him from the front. He was trembling and tears were running down his sunken cheeks, though suspicion blazed in his eyes. 'I know what happened, the doctors rubbed it off. No wonder the itch has been driving me crazy over the past few days. It's a conspiracy. Pretending they were saving my life, they were actually destroying my birthmark, removing the evidence so they could sever the relationship between me and your grandmother!'

'Don't try to pin it on the doctors, Dad. I was there every day, and I saw what they did. They pumped your stomach three times, but never laid a hand on your backside.'

'Don't be naive. You watched them pump my stomach, but they wouldn't let you see them carry out their conspiracy. Zhao Chuntang runs things on the shore, and the doctors do his bidding. It was all planned. Why did you people send me to hospital to have my stomach pumped? It was an evil plan. Why did you take me ashore? You delivered me into their hands. You might as well have taken me straight to the morgue.'

His face twisted into a sad grimace. A frantic series of tiny bubbles emerged from his mouth and popped in the air, releasing a fishy smell. Why had I said anything? So what if it had faded, he couldn't see it! Me and my big mouth! I hadn't been forgiven yet for my earlier behaviour, and now I'd caused a new problem. I didn't know what to do, and, with a deep sense of self-recrimination, missed the people in the fleet as never before. How wonderful it would have been if they had still been around. Desheng's wife, with her glib tongue, could have smoothed things over with Father by being sympathetic. Sun Ximing could have talked him around from a political angle, while Six-Fingers Wang, who was usually more negative and passive, could have done some good with a more threatening attitude. It was a critical moment, and none of them were around. They'd sailed off and left Father to me, and me alone.

'You're just starting to get well, Dad, you mustn't get over-excited.' Lacking the gift of the gab, I had to try something to calm him down and make him feel better. 'No matter what, Dad, the tail's still there, and even if it was gone, you'd still be Deng Shaoxiang's son. Truth is truth, and lies are lies, that can't be changed. People who engage in conspiracies wind up dropping rocks on their own feet. Yesterday I heard some doctors say that another investigative team is coming to overturn the other verdict.'

'Overturn it? I doubt that I'll live to see that day. I've got it all figured out. I don't need them to overturn anything. If they'll issue a martyr's family certificate, I'm ready to go and report to Karl Marx.' As he sat in the tub, he began sobbing like a little boy. 'I think about my life, and there's no way I can be happy. How could I be?' Grasping my hand, he said between sobs, 'I've held out for eleven long years, waited all that time, and I ask you, for what? Where's the good news I've waited for?'

'It hasn't come,' I replied, my head down.

'Only bad news. Rumours, slander and conspiracies!' He dried his eyes with his hands and pointed to me. 'You haven't made anything of yourself. Day in and day out I hear how degenerate you've become.'

'I'll make something of myself from now on, Dad, for you. You need to hold on, to persevere, and good news will come sooner or later.'

'I'm not made of steel, you know. I'm not sure I can hold on.' His sobs became weaker, maybe because they were taking too much out of him physically, but his head fell back hard against my shoulder. Then he said in a small, raspy voice, 'Tell me the truth, Dongliang, what do I have to live for? Shouldn't I just die?'

Unable to say a word, I wrapped my arms around his emaciated body. He squirmed instinctively, but I held him tight. My despairing father was wrapped up in my arms, as if our roles had been reversed. To me he felt more like a dried fish than a man, his spine thin and brittle, with fish-like scales suddenly appearing all over his back. The fragrance of the Glory bath soap wasn't strong enough to mask the strange fishy smell of his body. Father, my father, where have you come from? And where will you go? I felt lost. Suddenly a scene from half a century earlier, of a boundless Golden Sparrow River, flashed before my eyes. The bamboo basket left behind by the martyr Deng Shaoxiang was floating down the river, the child and fish inside tossed by the rapid swells. I watched as the water swallowed up the child, leaving only the fish. A fish. A solitary fish. The image frightened me. Was that really what happened? A fish. If my father wasn't that child, could he have been that fish?

Father, who had seemingly fallen asleep in my arms, abruptly opened his eyes and said uncertainly, 'It's so noisy outside. That doesn't sound like people. Is the river speaking? Why has the river started speaking?'

I was amazed by the sharpness of his hearing. Even with his body in such a weak state, he had actually heard the river reveal its secret. 'What did you hear, Dad?' I asked. 'What's the river saying?'

He held his breath to listen closely. 'It's telling me, come down, come down.'

I fell silent. Even after the shock had passed, I didn't know what to say. This was not a good sign. I'd always believed I was the only one who understood the river's secret, but now he had heard it too, and if one day the river revealed all its secrets, why would barges continue to stay in its waters? I felt the steel hull of our barge start to rock, along with my father's life and my home on the water. *Come down, come down.* The river's secret became clearer and clearer, and it was beyond my power to jump in and stop up its mouth. River, ah, river, why are you so impatient? Are you summoning my father or a fish to your depths?

There was nothing I could do. Then my eye was caught by a length of rope under my cot. It was the same rope that had nearly been used to tie me up. As I stared at it, I had an idea that made my heart pound. I hurriedly lifted Father out of the wooden tub and laid him on my cot. 'No!' he shouted. 'Not on your cot! Put me on the sofa.'

'Do as I say, just this once, Dad,' I said to him. 'The cot is sturdier. From now on, this is where you'll sleep.'

I began dressing him in clean clothes, and as I was putting on his socks, I bent down and took the rope out from under the cot. First I looped it around his feet, without his realizing what I was doing. Until, that is, he noticed that my hands were shaking. He shouted and began to struggle. 'What are you doing? What? You're tying me up? My own son! You've gone crazy! Is this how you get your revenge?'

'This isn't revenge, Dad. I'm trying to save you.' In my anxiety, I wrapped the rope around him speedily and indiscriminately. 'Bear with me, Dad, I'll be finished in a minute, and I won't let you go down. You can't go down there. I'm here, and I'll keep death away!'

Father kept struggling until his strength ran out. 'Go ahead,' he said, 'tie me up. I raised you to adulthood and taught you all those years, and this is what it's all come to.' A bleak smile creased the corners of his mouth, releasing a crystalline bubble that fell to the floor and disappeared. He gave me a cold look. 'You're too late,' he said. 'The river wants me. I don't care if you're a dutiful son or an unworthy one, you're too late. Me tying you or you tying me, it makes no difference. It's too late for anything.'

The hopelessness I saw in him scared and saddened me. I felt the blood rush to my head. 'It's not too late, Dad, it's not. You have to wait.' I tied his hands to the sides of the cot as I prepared a vow. 'Don't fight me, Dad, don't be stubborn. You have to wait. I'm going ashore in a minute and I'm going to make sure that bastard Zhao Chuntang comes aboard our barge to give you the apology you deserve.'

'Don't do anything stupid,' Father cried out. 'Even if you drag him aboard and force him to tell me he's sorry, I won't accept his apology. You mustn't go. If you do, I'll find a way to die before you get back.'

But my mind was made up, and I wasn't about to let my trussed-up father interfere with my plan. I picked up the wooden tub, took it out on deck and dumped the dirty water into the river. Not wanting the rope to cut into Father's flesh, I checked all the knots to make sure they were tight but not too tight. I placed two steamed buns and a glass of water next to his head. 'Dad,' I said, 'I don't know how long I'll be gone, so if you're hungry there's food, and water if you're thirsty.' I put the bedpan down by his hip, but then it dawned on me that he could not relieve himself tied up like that. So I reached down to take off his trousers, to which he reacted by curling up and angrily spitting in my face. What I was doing, I knew, was taboo. We needed to talk this out. 'I have to take them off, Dad. How else are you going to relieve yourself? Someone like you, so insistent on cleanliness, doesn't want to pee in his trousers.'

I saw a trickle of murky tears snake down his cheeks. Then he turned his face away and I heard him say, 'Go ahead, take them off, but don't look. Promise me you won't look.'

I promised, but when I pulled down his underpants, I couldn't stop myself from looking down. What I saw shocked me. His penis looked like a discarded silkworm cocoon, shrivelled and ugly, lying partially hidden in a clump of grass. I'd imagined it to be ugly, but not that ugly or that shrivelled. It looked miserable and sad. Instinctively I covered my eyes and ran to the door, not taking my hands away until I was at the bottom of the ladder. I didn't realize I was crying until the palms of my hands felt wet. I looked down at them – there were fresh tears falling through my fingers.

Memorial Stone

I WENT ASHORE.

The sunset had begun to lose its brilliance at the far end of the Golden Sparrow River when I stepped off the gangplank, and in no time, empty, dark clouds had taken its place. This was normally the time when I'd be returning home from a visit to the shore, but everything was different now. As night began to fall, I left the barge with a plan.

The lights had already come on around the piers, including the searchlights at the oil-pumping station, their snow-white beams lighting up the loading docks and the sky above, then creeping across the embankment. Half of our barge was in the light, the other half lay in the water, brooding. The stray cat leaped out of the darkness as soon as I stepped on land and scurried up to the bow of our barge, and I let it be. With Father all alone in the cabin, having a stray cat watch over him was better than nothing.

The evening wind chilled me as my sweat-soaked cotton jersey stuck to my chest and back. Having forgotten to put on shoes, I walked down the newly paved street barefoot, as if prowling the decks of the barge. The soft, slightly tacky surface seemed to be taking pity on the soles of my feet. There was no one to disturb the peace from the embankment to the loading dock. Li Juhua and her co-workers had turned off the machinery at the pumping station when their workday ended. The longshoremen had all gone home. A towering hoist and several light cranes sat quietly in the twilight like strange sleeping beasts. Cargo unloaded during the day had all been taken away, leaving the piers uncannily spacious and quiet.

Too quiet for me. Ghosts are drawn to stillness. As I passed the office of the security group, where a dim light shone through the window, I heard someone intoning a verse or reciting a piece of prose. But that stopped abruptly, and was followed by raucous laughter. Baldy Chen and Scabby Five's laughter was especially loud, while the woman, Wintersweet, was laughing so hard she could barely breathe. 'Stop,' she begged between bursts of laughter, 'don't read any more, or I'll laugh myself sick!'

I tiptoed up to the window, where I listened to what was going on inside. When the laughter died down, Scabby Five recommenced his intonation, and this time I heard a familiar phrase: 'The water gourd will love the sunflower till the seas dry up and rocks turn to dust!'

My head buzzed as I pressed my hands against my ears. No one was more familiar with that lyrical passage than I. Ah, 'The water gourd will love the sunflower till the seas dry up and rocks turn to dust!' It was from page 34 or 35 of my diary, where I wrote down my feelings about Huixian when she was singing with the district opera troupe. Now I knew that my diary had fallen into Wang Xiaogai's hands. They were reciting passages from it. It was too late for regrets. I'd hidden my diary in the lining of my bag so Father wouldn't find it. I'd managed to keep it out of Father's hands, but not theirs, and they were reciting passages from it for their entertainment!

As I stood outside the security-office window, I was both ashamed and angry. 'Don't stop, Xiaogai,' Wintersweet said. 'Read the juicy passages for us.'

'These are the only pages I could get my hands on,' Xiaogai

said. 'Old Cui got some of the others, and Little Chen tore out a few for himself. Huixian got the rest, and nobody wanted to take them from her, since she is the sunflower, and just about everything in that thick little book is about her.'

Break up their little gathering or not? I couldn't decide. In the end, lacking the courage to burst in on them, all I could do was mutter, 'We'll settle scores when this is all over. The time will come. But settle scores with whom? Xiaogai? Old Cui? Little Chen? Or Huixian? Or maybe I should get my revenge on Old Seven of Li Village. I looked up into the sky, then turned to face the riverbank, where barge number seven lay all alone in the deepening twilight. That snapped me out of it. Father was more important than me, and my vow to him took precedence over my lost diary. There was no time to waste, I had to find Zhao Chuntang and bring him back to the barge with me. Every debt has its debtor, and every injustice its perpetrator. I had to get him to apologize to my father.

I headed for the General Affairs Building, but when I got there I realized that my plan had been a case of wishful thinking. I'd arrived too late – all the officials had left for the day. Other than the reception office and a few windows here and there, the lights were all off, including those on the fourth floor. I looked for Zhao Chuntang's private car, and found it. The Jeep, which had seemed so impressive for a while, had been left idle, sitting dejected in a corner, while its original parking space was occupied by a brand-new, black and very distinguished Volga sedan.

The driver, Little Jia, was washing the car with a hose, turning the ground around him to mud. Skirting the puddles, I went up and asked, 'Are you waiting for Secretary Zhao to leave the office? Is he upstairs?'

He looked at me askance and said, 'Who do you think you are, asking after him, and what do you want?'

'Nothing in particular,' I said. 'I just want to report something to him.'

He scowled and continued washing the car. 'You can tell me what it is,' he said arrogantly, 'and I'll decide if it's important enough to tell Secretary Zhao. Besides, what could you have to report? Still making trouble over the business of being a martyr's descendant?'

I was savvy enough about doing business in Milltown to know that cigarettes were a door opener, so I handed one to Little Jia. He took it reluctantly, checked the brand and said, 'Flying Horse? I don't smoke those. I only smoke Front Gates.' He tossed the cigarette on to the front seat. 'Hah, Flying Horse. You boat people are the only ones who think those are any good.'

But I could see that he'd softened his expression a little, so I said, 'I promise you, I'm not here to make trouble. It's nothing important, so please tell me if Zhao has left to go home.'

Another frown. 'Kongpi, that's a good name for you. You talk like a *kongpi*. If it's nothing important, why do you need to see Zhao Chuntang? He puts in sixteen hours a day in the office, and then entertains guests after work. You should know that investigative teams have been sent down here just about every day, and Secretary Zhao has to go out drinking with his guests.'

He'd piqued my interest. 'What guests are those? What are the teams here to investigate?'

Again he looked at me out of the corner of his eye; his lips were curled into a hostile grin. 'Calm down,' he said. 'It's family planning, including vasectomies. This has been a headache for Secretary Zhao. If there are three men in town without vasectomies, Milltown won't be considered progressive. Since that thing of yours isn't doing anything, why don't you get one and perform a service for Milltown?'

I ignored him. Little Jia had given enough information for me to guess that Zhao Chuntang was in the dining hall having dinner with guests, so I walked around to the side of the building and went up to the dining-hall window. In the dim light I saw that there were only two unfamiliar officials sitting opposite one another beneath the window, either eating dinner or talking.

'No need to look over there,' Little Jia shouted. 'Milltown has exchanged its shotguns for cannons. Rank plays a role in entertaining guests these days. High-ranking officials are entertained at the Spring Breeze Inn. I doubt you've heard that the inn has private rooms. But you'd be wasting your time going there, because they won't let you in.'

I took my leave of Little Jia and rushed over to the Spring Breeze Inn, meeting a tall, skinny fellow on the way. He was wearing glasses and had sloping shoulders; he was carrying books under his arms, heading home from school. I knew who he was – Old Cui's grandson, a local high-school student. Old Cui was forever boasting that the boy was a top-notch student with a bright future. Since people with bright futures generally stayed clear of those with no future, I had no interest in stopping to talk to him.

He walked past me with a haughty air and then spun around and fell in behind me. 'You're Ku Dongliang, aren't you?' he said. 'Let me ask you a historical question. Do you know when Chairman Mao came to Milltown?' I immediately sensed that this out-of-nowhere question had something to do with my diary, so I pretended I hadn't heard him and started walking faster. I never imagined that getting away would be so difficult. He kept coming after me. Starting to breathe hard, he said, 'Then let me ask you a common-sense question. Why would Chairman Mao meet with a sunflower and not Milltown's masses? Is it really possible that the great man would stoop to meet with something planted in the ground? Why are you creating a false history, Ku Dongliang?'

Obviously, my diary was being read by people all over town, including Old Cui's grandson. How could a bookworm like him be in on my secrets? I wasn't interested in having a historical debate with the boy and was not obliged to reveal any of my youthful secrets. 'How much history does a little bastard like you understand?' I roared, glaring at him. 'Get away from me!'

I felt sheepish after chasing the youngster away, and as I walked the streets of Milltown at twilight, it seemed to me that my private affairs were like streetlamps lighting up the little town and its residents' lonely lives. I had the feeling that the laughter emerging from windows along the way was directed at me and at my diary. Keeping to the dark side of the streets, I continued on to Spring Breeze Inn, taking pains to avoid meeting up with anyone else. Profound doubts filled my mind. How many more pages of my diary remained, I wondered, and how many of those were with Huixian?

I stopped at the entrance to the inn, with its lanterns that heralded a May Day celebration. The spot was deserted; there was no trace of any vehicles. I glanced up at the third-floor windows of the concrete building, with its isolated 'penthouse'. The purple curtains were shut, making it impossible to determine whether or not the investigative teams were up there. I breathed in deeply, but couldn't smell food; when I held my breath, I heard nothing that sounded like people at a dinner table. Feeling dejected, I went up and tried the front door. It was locked. But by looking through the glass door, I could see someone asleep at the reception desk. I knocked, then knocked again, but the head didn't move. 'Who's there?' It was a woman's listless voice. 'You need permission from the police station to stay here.'

'I'm not a guest,' I replied. 'I'm looking for somebody.'

'Who?' she said. 'You can't do that without permission either. Who are you? And who are you looking for?'

I wouldn't tell her my name. 'You have a private room,' I said. 'Is Zhao Chuntang in there with dinner guests?'

The sleepy-eyed woman stood up and strained to see who I

was. Her tone of voice was guarded. 'I asked you who you are. Who told you we have a private room?'

I decided to try being clever. 'Secretary Zhao,' I said. 'He told me I'd find him here.'

Still she wouldn't open the door for me. She squinted to get a good look. 'I don't know you,' she said. 'You're not an official.' She sat down and laid her head back down on the desk. 'Go and look for the Party Secretary at the General Affairs Building,' she snarled. 'There's no Party Secretary here, only paying guests.'

Assuming that Little Jia had lied to me, I felt my anger rise. I just wanted to talk to Zhao Chuntang, not commit violence against him. 'Why did you lie to me, Little Jia, you son of a bitch?' Cursing him under my breath, I sat down on the steps of the inn, suddenly weary beyond imagining. When you're overly tired, all your aches and pains start acting up. My hip began throbbing so badly I couldn't get to my feet.

The lights in Pock-faced Li's bean-curd shop, which was next door to the inn, came on, as Li and his wife busied themselves emptying bags of soy beans that were piled up at their door on to their millstone. Father had always liked the bean curd from this shop, and since you could buy it without ration coupons, I figured this was too good an opportunity to pass up. Father could use some nutritious food. 'Two cakes of bean curd!' I called out. 'I'll buy two cakes.'

The response was immediate. Li's wife stepped outside with two cakes, but when she didn't see anyone at the door, she cried out, 'Who's that shouting? A ghost?'

'Over here,' I said with a wave of my hand. 'It's me.'

Seeing me sitting on the steps of the inn, she said with obvious displeasure, 'You must think you're some kind of big shot, buying bean curd with the airs of an official! Rather than take a few steps, you expect me to deliver it to you.'

I tried to stand up, but couldn't, and was reminded that buying the bean curd would stop me from doing what I'd come to do. How would it look if I went searching for Zhao Chuntang with two cakes of bean curd in my hands? I changed my mind. 'Forget it,' I said to Li's wife. 'I don't want it after all. I'll just rest here a while.'

'How am I supposed to trust anything you say?' she grumbled. 'First one thing, then another. Are you going to rest or do you want this bean curd? Don't play games with me. There are plenty of customers for bean curd from our shop.'

I muttered an apology, then changed the subject. 'Do you know where Zhao Chuntang moved to, Aunty?'

Something clicked when she heard my question. Still holding the two cakes of bean curd, she gave me a long look, her eyes lighting up, and exclaimed, 'Aha, you're Ku something-or-other Liang, aren't you? I know you, you're Ku Wenxuan's son. Still running around pleading your father's case, are you? Well, you can stop running. They've located the martyr Deng Shaoxiang's son. It isn't your dad and it isn't the idiot Bianjin. The ordained descendant is a one-time schoolteacher in Wufu with a bright future. He used to be a middle-school headteacher, but has been promoted to chief of the Education Bureau.'

About halfway through her rant, she noticed the pained grimace on my face, and a note of fear crept into her voice. 'Why are you looking at me like that?' she demanded. 'You look as if you'd eat me alive if you could. Well, I'm not the one who determined that you're not the descendants of the martyr. I heard that from Aunty Wang at the inn, who heard it from some comrades in the investigative team.'

Just then Pock-faced Li walked outside in his apron, looking angry, and without so much as a glance at me railed at his wife, 'You blabbermouth, what are you doing out here – selling bean curd or selling information? And if you're a spy selling information, you're supposed to ask how much they're paying and who you're selling it to. A dog's got a better memory than you. Have you forgotten how his dad once sent people over to chop off our capitalist's tail, how they confiscated three bags of beans and our millstone? I guess you don't remember how you screamed and wailed. But now the scar is healed and the pain's a distant memory, is that it? Don't you dare answer his questions till they give us back our three bags of beans!'

Pock-faced Li's hatred of my father took me by surprise, since I had no idea that Father and this couple had a past grievance. But then I was reminded of Li Yuhe's song in the opera *Red Lantern*: 'Plant a peach tree and you get peaches, sow rose seeds and roses bloom.' That, in a word, summed up the failure of my father's political career. I gritted my teeth and walked over to People's Avenue under the withering stares of Li and his wife. Once I was out of view I breathed a sigh of relief. Night had fallen and the streetlamps were lit, leaving one side of Milltown's streets in darkness. The town's main street looked cleaner than ever, in contrast to the lanes, which appeared even dirtier than before. Oily smoke from kitchens filled the air with the tempting smells of pork and spicy greens. My stomach began to grumble as I wondered where to go now. Li's wife hadn't produced any evidence to back up what she'd told me, but the news that a new descendant of Deng Shaoxiang had been chosen must have already been making the rounds in town. Father's long wait was about to end in a crushing defeat. He wouldn't believe it, of course, but that no longer mattered.

As I passed the darkened culture hall I noticed shadowy objects on the remains of the open-air stage. Someone had tossed a broken chair on to the stage, and in my mind's eye I saw a pair of shamed figures being pushed up on to the stage: my father and me. I was standing, hands tied behind my back; Father, naked, was sitting in the tilting chair, head bowed as he revealed his disfigured penis to the crowd below. 'I'm not guilty of anything,' he said, his grey head bowed. Wind passing my ears carried the people's angry shouts. 'Yes, you are, you're guilty!' Then a barrage of arrows flew at him from all directions, and I saw my dying father, his body impaled by arrows, terror filling his eyes, turn to me and say, 'Tell them, son, tell them whose son I am. Tell them I'm Deng Shaoxiang's son!'

I couldn't look at that stage or the chair any longer, so I turned and trotted over to the chess pavilion. I didn't have anything particular in mind, but that was a place where people gathered and rumours spread, and I decided to find out from someone where Zhao Chuntang's new home was. I was intent on rescuing Father. When I reached the pavilion, I was surprised to find the place deserted. Widow Fang had left with her stall and so had the people who had once gathered around it. I saw several oil transporters and cargo trucks in the car park, and some of the drivers playing poker on a tarpaulin they'd spread out on the ground. A man with a full beard waved to me from the cab of his truck. 'Want a ride? Come on up, I'm getting ready to shove off. I'll take you to Xingfu for fifty cents.'

Fifty cents to Xingfu. Xingfu again. Too bad I couldn't go this time.

I paced the area around the pavilion, watching my shadow shrink and lengthen under a streetlamp. I was wavering. Suddenly I doubted the wisdom of coming ashore in the first place. *Kongpi*, that's what my vow to Father was, *kongpi*! I couldn't find Zhao Chuntang, but even if I could, what could I say to get him to go aboard our barge and apologize to Father? Nothing, unless I had a gun or happened to be his superior. I had nothing. I *was* nothing. Nothing but a *kongpi*.

I stared blankly at the partially demolished pavilion; it was hardly more than rubble. A gust of wind blew open a corner of the plastic wrapping, releasing a weird triangle of dim light that nonetheless hurt my eyes. The light unexpectedly drew me to it; I crept inside.

Workers' tools were strewn all over the floor – hammers, pick-axes and some small jacks – but their owners were not there; nor was the idiot Bianjin. I did, however, see a pair of his geese, one of which was perched cockily on one of the hammers; the other one unforgivably stood atop the martyr's memorial stone and was soiling it with its excrement.

It was that stone that had sent the dim light my way, present-ing me with the greatest inspiration I'd ever had. It was lying on its side, secured by thick ropes, which could only mean that they would be moving it within the next few days, and when it left it would take the martyr's spirit with it. Would they go to Phoenix in the upper reaches, or to Wufu, some forty li up the road? At that moment, a light went on in my head and I felt my blood begin to churn as a splendid, almost manic idea was born. I wanted that memorial stone. I'd make it mine by moving it to our barge. I was going to return Deng Shaoxiang's martyr spirit to my father!

There was no time like the present. I knew I'd do it. First I kicked off the goose and wiped away some of the excrement. Then, before I started, I didn't forget to bow respectfully. Moving something that heavy was child's play to a boat person. Calmly and in complete control, I grasped the rope with both hands and pulled with all my might. The stone obediently righted itself and stood at the right angle for me to lift it with my arms and hip. Slowly it began to move, and it seemed to me to weigh at least two hundred *jin*. Experience told me that it was too heavy for one man to move, but it gave me a tremendous surprise: it was help-ing me along, dispensing good will and a warm feeling. The heavy stone slid easily along the cement floor, never wavering, with no doubt or hesitation, and by pulling hard, it didn't take me long to drag it free of the pavilion. Bianjin's geese reacted with panicky honks, which attracted the attention of the truck drivers in the car park. Thinking I was a thief, one of them stood up and, with a grin, shouted to me, 'I knew you were a three-handed sort, the way you slinked around there. But a memorial stone? What are you going to do with that? Take it home and build a house to win a bride?'

It was a lucky break. Those truckers were all outsiders, and Milltown meant nothing to them. But their laughter brought me out in a cold sweat. This was Milltown, where everyone was on the lookout for something, and my risky adventure could be over before it really began. I had to move fast. Move fast! Fast! I kept telling myself. Fast! Move fast! I urged the stone, but, seemingly offended, it chose this moment to make a display of its dignity and flaunt its weight. Now pulling it behind me was like dragging a mountain along, and by the time I reached the path by the cotton warehouse, my arms felt as if they were about to fall off and I was gasping for breath. I had to stop. When I turned to look behind me, the first group of followers was catching up. A pair of white geese and three ducks were waddling my way, raising the alarm with their honks and quacks. Then the second wave came into view: the geese's master, idiot Bianjin. He was brandishing a duck whistle. 'Stop right there, Ku Dongliang!' he shouted. 'Kongpi, I said stop!' His enraged shouts ripped through the night. 'You've got guts, Kongpi. What are you dragging there? I told you to stop! Where do you think you're going?'

He blew his duck whistle, which drew more geese and ducks from around the piers, and before I knew it I was surrounded by them. Everyone – man and fowl – was talking at once. The ducks' and geese's incomprehensible complaints fell on deaf ears, but not the idiot's angry shouts. 'How dare you, Ku Dongliang! I thought somebody was stealing a hammer or a jack, but no, you're stealing the memorial stone! I never thought you'd have the guts to actually steal the martyr Deng Shaoxiang's spirit!'

'Stop the crazy talk, idiot. I'm not stealing her spirit, I'm taking the stone to show my father. He's in terrible health, but this'll cure him.'

'You're the idiot! That stone isn't some magic elixir, how can it cure your dad?' With one hand on his hip and the other pointing to his own nose, he said, 'You've certainly got guts. Do you know what you've done? You're an active counter-revolutionary. You can be shot for that.'

'What do you know about active counter-revolutionaries?' I asked. 'Or historical ones, for that matter? With my own eyes I saw one of your geese shit on the martyr's memorial. Come and look for yourself. If that's not goose shit, what is it? What kind of counter-revolutionary is that goose of yours, huh? Should they take it out and shoot it?'

One look at the mess on the memorial stone and his nerves began to betray him. He looked at his flock. 'Which one was it? Tell me. He won't get away with it.'

'All your geese look alike. How am I supposed to know which one it was? But if one of them shit on the memorial stone, I'm sure the others did too. They're all counter-revolutionaries, and they'll have to be taken out and shot.'

'Stop trying to scare me.' After glowering at me, he turned back to his flock and thought for a minute. Then he came up with a smart comment. 'The goose shouldn't have shit on it, but it's an animal and it doesn't know any better. Are you an animal too? Don't you know any better?'

He stumped me. Not having anything to say, I gave him a shove. 'You really are an idiot. I can't argue with an idiot. If they shoot me, they shoot me, and it's none of your business. Get out of my sight.' I kicked a goose and two ducks out of my way and continued dragging the stone towards the embankment.

Bianjin grabbed a handful of my clothes. 'Where do you think you're going? I'm in charge of the pavilion. I can't let you take anything out of it.'

I'd underestimated his intelligence and his physical skills. With a shout he jumped on to the stone, and the added weight nearly broke my arms. I immediately let go of the rope. Seeing that I'd given up, his next move was to take control of the rope. We went for it at the same time, four hands grasping at the same spot. We bumped heads, hard, and I saw stars. That enraged me, so I grabbed hold of his tattered shirt and pushed him to the side of the road. 'Good dogs stay out of the way, idiot, so be a good dog and get out of my way. If you don't, I'll twist that dog's head of yours off.'

But I had underestimated Bianjin's courage. He surprised me by sticking his head right up to my chest. 'Go ahead,' he said. 'Twist it off. If you don't, then you're the dog.'

Bianjin and I grappled atop the memorial. He was no pushover, and as the struggle raged, I fought to stay on top. But that proved to be an unwise tactic: if I couldn't control Bianjin, I wouldn't be able to move the stone. In the end, I abandoned it, ran around and jumped on to Bianjin's back, pinning his arms to his sides and holding on tight. He was not a young man, after all, and couldn't get out of my bear hug, though he stamped around as best he could and screamed in distress, 'Help! Someone come and catch Ku Dongliang! Catch a counter-revolutionary!'

The screams brought Old Qin, night watchman at the cotton warehouse, running, lunch box in hand. But when he saw who it was, he lost interest and continued shovelling food into his mouth. 'So it's you two,' he said finally. 'What's all this about a counter-revolutionary? It's just an idiot and a *kongpi*. Counter-revolutionary? That's above both of your ranks. Don't waste my time.'

'He's stealing the martyr's memorial stone,' Bianjin cried out desperately. 'He's a counter-revolutionary, an active counter-revolutionary. Get the police!'

Old Qin ignored Bianjin's pleas. Instead, he walked up to the

stone, still holding his lunch box, and gave me a quizzical look.
'Come to think of it, this is strange. What do you want this for?
A souvenir for your dad or something? But it's only a memorial.
Why bother to drag it around like that? As far as I'm concerned,
your dad's head is filled with mush. What difference does it make
if he's descended from a martyr or not? What matters is getting
by the best you can in good health.'

Old Qin's admonition fell on deaf ears – mine and Bianjin's.
Bianjin looked up and vented his anger and frustration on Old
Qin. 'Why don't you get the police instead of standing around
talking like a fool? You're abetting a criminal, and that's a crime
punishable by three years in prison!'

Old Qin lost his temper and kicked Bianjin in the rear.
'You stinking idiot!' he cursed. 'I tried to teach you how to do
arithmetic, but you were too dumb to learn. The only way you
could count six geese is by using your fingers, so what's all that
talk about three years in prison? Lucky for me you're an idiot, or
you'd sentence me to three hundred years! If you weren't an idiot,
you'd have lined everyone up along the Golden Sparrow River
and shot them!' His anger growing, he kicked Bianjin a second
time.

Bianjin screeched. 'Where is everybody? Is everybody dead?
Where are the revolutionary masses?' By then he was nearly
crying, so I grabbed him by the collar, and he went limp. I thought
he'd given up, and was about to let him go, when two people
emerged from behind the warehouse. Seeing that his rescue was
at hand, he shouted, 'Grab the counter-revolutionary! You'll be
rewarded for your efforts.'

It was a young couple who'd been up to something behind the
warehouse. He heeded the call, she vanished. In his twenties, he
had bushy eyebrows and large eyes, neatly combed hair, and was
wearing a tunic with three pens in his breast pocket. He looked
familiar, but I couldn't recall his name. But he obviously knew

who we were. He looked down at the memorial stone, then up at the two of us and smiled. With an enigmatic expression, he said, 'So, it's you two. What are you doing, fighting over this stone? One's fighting over Deng Shaoxiang's son, the other over her grandson. Well, you can stop fighting, since you're both out of the running. The latest news is that a school headteacher in Wufu is her son, but that's not true either. You're all fakes! I'll tell you what my research has turned up, but it can't be made public. Here's what happened. Deng Shaoxiang was married, but didn't get along with her husband and had no children. The boy in that basket wasn't her child. She'd borrowed a baby as a cover for her mission.'

The young woman suddenly appeared by the side of the road, and since the young official's mind was still on her, after disclosing his news, he took off after her. Then it dawned on me that he was a college student newly assigned to the General Affairs Building, specializing in revolutionary history. His astonishing news dumbfounded both Bianjin and me, but I quickly gathered my senses and shouted at his back, 'Bullshit!'

Bianjin, who was also watching him, gnashed his teeth and shouted, 'You're spreading false rumours!'

Rare though it was for Bianjin and me to see eye to eye, it wasn't enough to turn a pair of enemies into friends. We both held our ground, one crouching, the other kneeling, eyeing one another suspiciously, and we were soon at it again, fighting over the memorial stone and the rope. 'Stop trying to take this away from me, idiot. Didn't you hear what he said? Deng Shaoxiang didn't have a son, which means my dad has no claim, and neither do you. It's time to stop daydreaming. You've got no right to block my way, and if you keep it up, I'm going to get rough with you.'

'I don't care about that other stuff, but I've vowed to protect the memorial stone with my life, and that's what I'll do, even if I lose my head in the process. You want to get rough with me, well let's see what you're made of. Kill me, and you can take the stone, how's that? But if you can't do it, then turn yourself in at the police station.'

'Don't push me, idiot,' I said. 'I could do that if I wanted, but there's no glory in killing an idiot.'

He responded by kicking me and running off. Glaring defiantly, he yelled, 'Come on, hit me! Think I care? Beat me, beat me to death. I don't care if I lose my head. They'll shoot you, and the glory will be mine. I'll be a martyr.'

I turned to look at the embankment, where the water shimmered in the darkness. But I couldn't see our barge, and I was reminded that I'd left Father tied up on my cot, waiting wide-eyed for my return. But instead of returning with what I'd promised, I was hung up with an idiot on the shore, which enraged me. Raising my fist in the air, the wind brushed against it like kindling lighting a burning torch. *Beat him, beat him to death, he's an idiot, hit him all you want, stop wasting your time.* The mysterious and sinister sound came on the wind, and made me lose my senses. I knew it was wrong to hit someone in the face, that when other people fought, they always punched in places that were hard to see. But I made up my mind to hit him in the face. I grabbed his collar and jerked his head back. He had a flat face with a protruding nose, and that's where I aimed. He turned his face, I jerked my hand back, took aim and swung. His nose seemed to explode, sending snot and blood flying. I turned my head, afraid to look. 'Idiot,' I said in spite of myself, 'your nose is bleeding. Now are you going to get out of my way or not?'

He had such a solemn look I doubt he even felt the pain. With a look of stern righteousness, he said, 'No. A bloody nose doesn't bother me. I'm not afraid to lose my head over this. Go ahead, hit me again, beat me into martyrdom. Then they'll shoot you, a life for a life, and I'm the winner.'

The sight of Bianjin standing there with blood flowing from

his nose nearly had me in tears. The wind returned to my fist, and I heard the sinister voice again. *Hit him, go ahead. He's an orphan, after all, no parents and no friends, kill him and no one will care.* It was a strange, evil voice, forcing me on, making me feel like crying. My fist danced around Bianjin's face, which was like a child's face – dirty, gaunt and innocent. He wore the bleak but inexplicably pure expression common to orphans. My fist stopped before it smashed into his cheekbone. 'Oh, to hell with it!' I said. 'You're a pitiful creature, and I can't keep hitting you. If I killed you, no one would even claim your body.'

'You're done, but I'm not,' he said through clenched teeth. 'We'll settle up later. This debt will be paid.'

His threat rekindled the flames and stoked a nameless fire that had smouldered in my heart for eleven years. Hatred and loathing, old and new, came together in fists that were infused with the power of savage vengeance. 'We'll settle up later. This debt will be paid!' I roared as my fists rained down on his face. 'This debt will be paid! You people on the shore owe a debt to my father and to me. Yes, it will be paid – paid by you. That's how it will be paid!'

The next thing I heard were Bianjin's shrieks, 'My eyes! You hit me in the eyes!' He was in such a state he'd begun to stammer slightly. 'Don't . . . don't hit me in the eyes, don't do that. Hit me anywhere but my eyes. Kill me, but not my eyes. I can't tend my geese if I'm blind. What'll happen to my geese and my ducks?'

He was covering his eyes with his hands, and I saw trickles of blood seep through his fingers, which snapped me back to my senses. I unclenched my fists and looked closely at Bianjin, whose aching head hung low. Now, finally, he jumped down off the stone and, still covering his eyes, began to cry.

In the dim light of the streetlamps I saw someone running towards us with a club. 'Who's fighting out there? Fighting around the piers is not allowed.' It was the security guard, late as always.

The light glinted off his head; it could only be Baldy Chen, who was a stickler for enforcing the law. Without a word, he put his truncheon to use, hitting me on the shoulder and Bianjin on the arm. Bianjin dropped his hands and grabbed his own arm with one of them. He wailed like an abused child. 'You hit me! Why did you hit me? You're in charge of security. Can't you tell friend from foe?'

Baldy gasped when he saw Bianjin's bloody face. 'Did you do this to him, Ku Dongliang? You're too damned wild for your own good. Other people bully you, so you bully the idiot, is that it?' He crouched down to look at Bianjin's injuries. 'Look what you've done to his nose,' he said. 'This spells big trouble for you, Kongpi. What if it's broken?'

'He had it coming,' I said. 'I'll make amends if it's broken.'

Then Bianjin showed Baldy Chen his eyes. 'I can't see,' he sobbed. 'He blinded me.'

Baldy lifted the man's chin with his truncheon to get a closer look at his eyes. Again he gasped. 'Kongpi, you've really done it this time. You're worse than the Fascists. How could you do that? What if he really is blind?'

'He had it coming,' I repeated. 'I'll make amends if he's blind.'

'Make amends, make amends! Talk's cheap. How the hell many eyes do you have to make amends for?' Baldy took out a filthy handkerchief to wrap around the idiot's eyes. 'What the hell's got into you, Kongpi?' he said as he poked me with his truncheon. 'This time you've gone too far. What are you standing around for, when you should be rushing him to the hospital? If he dies, you're done for!'

'I'm not going to take him. He's the one who insisted on a life for a life. Besides, neither of our lives is worth a damned thing. If he dies, I'll make amends with mine.'

I could no longer hold back my tears. Nor could my body stand the stress. Slowly I fell to my knees in front of the stone, my face pressed against its cold surface, which sharply chilled my cheek as if cold water had been poured over it. Whose tears were they, mine or Deng Shaoxiang's? The martyr's spirit was judging me, making its presence known. Overcome with profound regret for what I'd done to Bianjin, I punished myself for my unconscionable behaviour by slapping myself across the face, which was hardly sufficient to absolve myself. Self-pity and grief, the likes of which I'd never experienced, filled my heart. I slapped myself again even harder, as punishment for feeling sorry for myself. Then, like Bianjin, I buried my face in my hands and wept.

As I wept before the memorial stone, Baldy Chen kept poking me with his truncheon. 'You've got a nerve, crying like that,' he said. 'You reduced him to this condition, so you have to take him to hospital, and I mean now. What good does crying do? You don't expect me to take him, do you?'

Speaking almost incoherently between sobs, I said, 'Tomorrow, I'll do it tomorrow.'

'Are you out of your mind? Look at his injuries. His eyes might not make it till tomorrow.'

He could prod or tug me as much as he liked, but I was staying on my knees. I wasn't getting up, and through the mist of my tears I watched Baldy leave with Bianjin for the hospital, followed by a cluster of ducks. The two geese, on the other hand, stuck around to avenge their guardian. They attacked, one of them going after one of my feet.

Night's darkness was deepening and the air brought a strange smell to me. Not a fishy odour, nor rotting grass, and definitely not the smell of chemical fertilizer from Maple Village. Whatever it was, it caught my attention. I stopped crying and sniffed the air to see where it was coming from. Then I discovered a pool of congealed blood the size of a mulberry leaf between the fingers of my right hand. And there was blood on my sleeve, a stain the size of a willow leaf. The knees of my trousers were also stained.

Bianjin's blood was all over me; no wonder the smell was so strong. I remembered when my father had bled all over the cabin of our barge, several years before; Bianjin's blood had a much stronger smell than Father's. Worrying that the stone might be spattered with the idiot's blood, I stood up. I was right. A pool of still-wet blood where his head had rested gave off a reddish glow. I picked up a sheet of newspaper and, after scrubbing the stone three times, wiped it clean.

Now that they were gone and I had stopped crying, I regained my composure and looked down at the memorial stone lying on the ground in the moonlight. I wasn't about to abandon it, but would it abandon me? I got up, grabbed hold of the rope and pulled; there was a moment of resistance before it started moving again, and it seemed to me as if it had raised its head and had its sights trained on barge number seven. Then it began to slide along the ground. It was a miracle, a true miracle. Deep down, I believed that the stone had eyes that I could not see and an unfathomably compassionate heart. I wasn't stealing it, I was taking it where it wanted to go; it was determined to meet my father. That had to be a miracle.

I took a look around; the piers were encased in silence. It was like a dream. The searchlight in front of the oil-pumping station lit up a corner of the embankment wall, allowing me a view of our barge nestled quietly up against the bank. The bank and the river, the barge and my father were all neatly and quietly immersed in a happy dream. Mustering all my strength, I dragged the stone towards the river, listening to it slide across the ground: move, keep moving. When I reached our boat, I looked behind me and saw the piers in their pristine brightness, uncommonly quiet, illuminated in turn by the moonlight and the searchlight. They had let me pass; the moon was not after me, nor were the searchlight or any people. The stray cat was there, all alone, slinking back and forth and watching me with its shining eyes.

I had no time to ponder why this night, which had started out with such bitterness, had ended so sweetly, why luck had been with me in the end, for I now had a problem. How was I going to move such a heavy object on to the boat? Our gangplank wasn't up to the task, and I couldn't borrow anyone else's. Now what? Could I make a ladder out of bamboo? As I anxiously considered tactics for moving heavy objects, I shouted out happily, a note of triumph in my voice, 'Dad, I'm back! I'm home! Come and see what I've brought you!'

Come Down

M Y GREATEST regret during the eleven years I spent on the river was tying my father up. I still recall that night. 'Easy,' he said as I worked to loosen the ropes. A rare expression of fatherly concern emanated from his weary, bloodshot eyes. He'd forgiven me. I led him to the gangplank to show him the memorial stone I'd left on the riverbank. Holding on to my clothes, he followed me on shaky legs, like an obedient son. Fear, I knew, was one of the reasons, but the sight of Deng Shaoxiang's memorial lit up his soul, as if the light of a nameless deity shone down on it. All his misgivings and fear fell away. 'Good,' he said with a smile. 'Wonderful. You've brought your grandmother home.'

To get the stone up on to the barge, I'd need to use one of the cranes, and this was the perfect time, since there was no one around. I climbed into the cab of one of them by removing a window, and though I had no experience of operating the machine, the instrument panel seemed almost magically familiar that night, and everything went without a hitch. The crane picked up the stone and, after one uncontrolled and somewhat dangerous swing, lowered it on to the bow, where Father helped me bring it down. 'Careful now, be careful.' The excitement in his voice was unmistakable, and I wasn't sure if he was talking to me or to the stone.

I'd brought a heavy gift home to Father and he accepted it happily.

Father wanted the stone up next to the sofa in the cabin, facing aft. But the door was too narrow, which disappointed him, though we gave it our all, with me pushing and him giving directions. So, with the stone halfway in and halfway out of the cabin, he sat next to it, stroking it lovingly. 'You'll just have to stay here,' he said, 'which is actually better, since the cabin is stuffy. The air out here is better, and so is the scenery. This way you can enjoy the sights of the river, Mama.'

By then it was very late. The freshly washed moon shone down on the Golden Sparrow River. I lit all four of our lanterns and hung them strategically to shine their warm light on Father and his martyr's stone. After gazing at the inscription for a long while, he said he wanted to see the relief image on the back. So I mustered up the strength to turn it around for him. 'Gone!' he shouted in alarm. 'I'm gone!'

That gave me such a fright I didn't know what to do. Again he said, 'I'm gone, I'm gone!' His hand rested forlornly on the carved basket, shaking uncontrollably. As soon as I went over to look I knew what had happened: the infant's head was missing from the top of the basket.

'How can it be empty? My little head, where did it go?'

'Dad, you must be seeing things. How could something carved in stone be missing?' Flustered, I grabbed one of the lanterns to get a better look, and what I saw flabbergasted me. The basket carved in the stone showed up clearly in the light, but the head of the infant that had once been there was now gone.

'They've wiped me out,' Father said. 'My birthmark's gone, and now so is my head.'

Even when I examined the carving closely, I saw no signs that it had been altered, nothing that would lead me to believe that human hands had done this. But when I traced the area with my finger I felt a slight outcropping above the basket where the head had once been. The spot was cold to the touch. 'Dad,' I said, 'touch it here. You can feel the little round head with your finger.'

He'd already turned away in despair to gaze at the river. So I took his hand and traced his finger over the raised carving. 'You can feel it,' I repeated. 'It's still there.'

He closed his eyes and let me move his finger around; after a moment, he covered the spot with his hand and gently rubbed the barely distinct little head. 'Is that all that's left? Is it really my head? I don't think so,' he mumbled as a shadowy fear came over his face. 'It's not me. I'm no longer there. I only left the shore eleven years ago, and not even calligraphy in ink should fade away in that short a time. That little head in the basket, how did it just disappear?'

His hand slid weakly down the memorial stone and rested on his knee, still shaking. A damp pale light seemed etched on that hand. He shut his eyes; he'd grown tired, and I thought he should rest. 'Dad,' I said as I tried to get him to stand, 'we can't see it in the dark. We'll try again tomorrow in the daylight. It's late. You need your sleep.' But he lay his head against the stone and left it there. 'Don't do that, Dad,' I said as I tried to pull him back. 'It's too cold, you'll come down with something.'

When he looked up at me I saw tears criss-crossing his face. 'I heard it,' he said. 'I heard your grandmother's voice. I no longer blame Zhao Chuntang. Your grandmother doesn't like me, I heard her. Eleven years trying to reform myself, all wasted. I've failed to earn your grandmother's forgiveness. She doesn't want me.'

I wrapped my arms around his emaciated form; it was like a decaying tree trunk that had stubbornly warded off the elements for eleven years, only to topple during a storm. I desperately wanted to comfort him, but tears were filling my eyes and I was so choked up I couldn't say anything. And when I read the words 'Martyred Deng Shaoxiang Lives Forever in Our Hearts' I was suddenly fearful. I'd worked so hard to bring the memorial stone aboard our boat, but had it brought Father happiness or a crushing defeat?

Pale morning light was beginning to show through the darkness at the far end of the Golden Sparrow River. As I glanced at sleepy Milltown I ran to the bow, knowing that dawn would bring people to the piers and that the memorial stone would no longer belong to Father and me. My first thought was to go aft, weigh anchor at once and take the stone away from Milltown. My strength returned as I worked on getting under way, all was normal. But when I ran back up to the bow to take in the hawsers tying us to the pier, my hands became weak and I had trouble keeping my eyes open. The lack of sleep had suddenly caught up to me. I lay down on the deck and fell asleep.

Father came up and shook me. 'We can't run away,' he said. 'There's no place for us, even if we run to the ends of the earth.'

I got up and, in a daze, went back to the hawsers. 'We'll go out on the river, that's where we belong.'

'The river isn't ours,' he said. 'Even this boat isn't ours. We're not going anywhere, we're staying here. Go and get some sleep, Dongliang. I'll keep watch over the memorial.'

I knew there was no sense in arguing with him, and I was in no condition to fight the weariness that had come over me. Father nudged me into the cabin. Eleven years it had taken for me to finally luxuriate in the loving care of my father. He made up the cot and covered me with an old blanket, leaving a small corner open for me, and I vaguely sensed that this was what it would feel like to be wrapped in his arms, arms that had been closed to me for so long. At first the blanket felt strangely prickly, but that gave way to warmth, as if I was in the embrace of Father's affection. I wanted him to get some sleep as well, but I was too tired to resist; I fell asleep almost immediately.

As dawn was breaking I was in the middle of a dream about

the river and our boat. I could hear the churning of the water off the fantail, creating transparent bubbles. Our anchor was banging against the hull – once, twice, three times – and in the wake caused by our passage, an old-fashioned woman appeared, translucent pearls of water dripping from her hair, which was cut short; drops of water shimmered on her face, and the same secret message emerged from her reddened lips: *Come down, come down, come down now.* The fact that I was dreaming did nothing to lessen the reverence I felt towards her. I held my breath so I could hear her clearly: *Come down, come down, come down now.* The martyr was holding on to the swaying anchor, which caused the barge to roll from side to side. *Come down, come down, come down now.* She was so close I could see moss growing on the backs of her hands. I stared in awe at her face and at her hair as it swished back and forth above her ears. Watery pearls fell into the river and revealed the anxious face of a mother. *Come down,* she said, *come down. You can both be saved.*

That startled me awake. The cabin was suffused with soft blue early-morning light. Day was breaking. I got up and went to the door to look outside. Father was still keeping watch over the memorial stone. Two of the lanterns hanging from the canopy had gone out. As I went on deck I was hit by the potent fishy smell of Father's body. His head was resting against the stone, a homemade plywood chessboard on his knees. A few of the chess men remained on the board; the rest were scattered on the deck around him.

Father was half asleep, his forehead furrowed with shadows whose origins were a mystery. 'Dongliang,' he said, 'can you hear that strange sound coming from the river?'

I didn't dare tell him about my dream. 'Your hearing isn't as good as it once was, Dad,' I said. 'That's the anchor hitting the hull.'

'No,' he said, 'not the anchor. Actually, it's not really so strange. The river is saying, *Come down, come down.*'

I lifted him to his feet to force him to go inside, but he pushed me away. 'There's no time to sleep, they'll be here soon.' He pointed to the shore, where people were beginning to stir. An odd smile floated on to his face. 'The sun's out, and they'll be here soon. The battle over the memorial stone is about to start.'

I was puzzled by his casual tone and his smile, and wondered if he had passed a sleepless night reminiscing or planning for what was to come. Daylight filled the sky, and the piers were waking up. The PA system crackled to life, blaring a choral work that extolled the virtues of the labouring masses. 'We workers have power as we work, day and night.' From the mountain of coal to the oil-pumping station, machinery that had slept through the night awakened, motors roaring. Cranes in the dock area creaked and moaned as their arms limbered up, skip cars emptied their loads of bags of cement, which thudded on to the open ground, sending sand up into the air, only to settle to the ground like falling rain. Chunks of coal complained shrilly, like the shrieks of women, as they landed, while boulders roared like rocky avalanches. I saw a strange tubular oil tower, formed, thanks to the morning light, into what appeared to be a blue metal stage. Birds circled it. Why, I didn't know, but flocks of sparrows had flown over Maple Village, on the far side of the river, and brazenly gathered on top of the tent, where they filled the air with a chorus of mysterious, shrill cries, competing with the PA system.

They came, just as he'd said.

Four men were the first to arrive: Wang Xiaogai, Scabby Five and Baldy Chen of the security group appeared on the embankment, along with the head of the Milltown police department, all of them looking very businesslike. I saw that Baldy was holding his rifle, a glinting bayonet in place. Without a second thought, I ran over and pulled up the gangplank. Scabby Five saw what I was doing and dashed up, but found nothing but empty air. 'Kongpi,' he growled, 'where did you get the guts to steal Deng Shaoxiang's memorial stone? Why the fuck don't you go to Tiananmen Square and steal the Monument to the People's Heroes?'

No time to reply. I picked up our axe and attacked the mooring hawser. Running away is always the best strategy; we had to get the boat away from the pier. 'Dad,' I shouted towards the canopy, 'we have to get out on the river!' Then I grabbed our punting pole, which we hadn't used in years – with no tugboat, that was our only means of getting going. We moved four or five metres away from the pier under the helpless stares of the four men, who began arguing about how to get on our boat. Scabby Five, first again, took off his shoes and rolled up his trouser legs, planning to wade over to us. 'Damn, this water's cold!' he groused. 'And where did those little whirlpools come from?'

'Don't talk like an idiot,' Wang Xiaogai said. 'How can there be whirlpools so close to shore? You ought to be brave enough to walk in water that shallow.'

But Scabby Five was having none of it. 'It's cold and it's deep,' he said, 'and the air pump is sucking my legs down. You're the leader of this group, the one who's supposed to be so brave, why don't you come down here?'

Xiaogai, not about to take the bait and having no luck with Scabby Five, turned his attention to Baldy Chen. 'That's a rifle you've got, not a fishing pole, so shoot.'

If I hadn't been afraid before, I was now. I crouched down and waited. Nothing happened. Then I heard Baldy say, 'Shoot what? You need bullets for that, and they wouldn't give me any.'

'Kongpi! What a stupid arsehole! Go on, try to run away,' Xiaogai shouted to me. 'The river won't help you. The Golden Sparrow doesn't belong to you, and how far do you think you'll get with a punting pole? You could punt all day and still be in Milltown's waters. Even punting for a whole month and getting off the Golden Sparrow won't do you any good. One phone call to alert the emergency defence forces, and you'll fall into our hands. But go ahead, try, maybe you'll make it to the Pacific Ocean! But not to the Atlantic. Or maybe you'll reach the shores of the American imperialists. Well, so what? We'll fire a missile and wipe you off the face of the earth!'

Police Chief Xiao remained calm the whole time. He knew what to do. Rolling up a magazine to serve as a makeshift megaphone, he stood on the riverbank and shouted, 'Barge number seven, Father and Son Ku, be warned. Seizing a revolutionary historical relic is a crime. If you don't want to be guilty of a crime, come back to shore. Turn back and the shore is at hand.'

We weren't about to turn back, because the shore was theirs, not ours. The battle for the memorial had begun. I felt a great sense of urgency. For all my eleven years on the water we'd plied the river behind a tug boat, and punting was something I'd never done. But I tried my best, pushing with all my might until I was bent over the fantail, and then walking towards the prow. That's how other people did it. But the barge refused to cooperate. When I walked, it stayed stubbornly where it was, lying perpendicular to the shore and trying my patience. 'Go over to the starboard side!' Father yelled. 'Get over there!' I dragged the pole over to the starboard side, but unfortunately that didn't work either. Father, who didn't know a thing about punting, was giving me useless commands. Then the boat began to move – floating back towards the shore! 'Now go back to the port side!' he shouted. So there I was, running helter-skelter from port to starboard, to the uproarious delight of the men on shore.

'Quit wasting time and energy, Kongpi, the picket ships are on their way, and when they get here it'll be like a racehorse chasing a turtle. Then where do you think that rust bucket will take you?'

I continued my fight with the barge. There was no time to worry about Father and the memorial stone. I could not have told you what was going on under the canopy, because by then I could hear the motor of the picket boat far down the river, which elicited whoops of joy from the shore. But they died out as quickly as they came. 'The canopy!' they shouted. 'Ku Wenxuan!' They started running parallel to our barge, saying something as they ran. I turned to look, and saw that confusion was setting in on the shore, as the first group was joined by several policemen; longshoremen, attracted by the commotion, had also come running. They were craning their necks to one side to see what was happening under the canopy.

The police chief stepped on to an oil drum and once again raised his magazine megaphone; but this time a note of anxiety had crept into his shouts. 'Comrade Ku Wenxuan, calm down, please calm down. Don't do anything you'll regret later.' Then he turned to me. 'Kongpi, are you a fucking idiot? Stop poling and go and stop your dad!'

I threw down my pole and ran over to the canopy, just in time to see Father, his arms wrapped around the memorial stone, about to fall into the river. I couldn't believe my eyes, I didn't think he'd have had the strength, and I'd never imagined that the battle over the memorial would end like this. My father, Ku Wenxuan, had tied himself to the stone and inched his way to the edge of the deck with it on top of him. The stone was crushing him. I couldn't see his head or his body, only his feet. A sandal was on his right foot; his left foot was bare. I ran up and grabbed one of his feet. 'Dongliang,' he said, 'I'm going down, I'm going down.'

Was this another miracle? In the final seconds of my father's life he was bound to the memorial stone, the two together a true giant. I couldn't hold him. A giant was falling into the river. I couldn't hold him. Now my eyes beheld nothing. The surface of the Golden Sparrow River exploded, sending a pillar of water into the air, accompanied by frantic screams from the shore, and my father was no more; neither were the memorial stone or the giant. I couldn't keep Father with me; all I held was a single sandal.

Fish

I SEARCHED FOR Father in the Golden Sparrow River for several days.

The riverbed was a vast world unto itself. Its scattered rocks longed for mountains in the upper reaches of the river; broken pottery longed for old masters' kitchens; discarded brass and corroding iron longed for the farm tools and machinery of an earlier time; broken skulls and frayed hawsers longed for boats on the surface; a dazed fish longed for another fish that had swum away; a dark section of water longed for its sunlit compatriot; I alone scoured the riverbed, longing to find my father.

On land, tortoises that, according to popular legend, travelled far with memorial tablets on their backs were enshrined in temples. But the chances were there was only one human who had carried a memorial stone into the river, and that was no legend, for that person was my father, Ku Wenxuan. No temple wanted to enshrine him, so he rested at the bottom of the Golden Sparrow River.

I located the stone on the third day and caught a brief glimpse of the body that lay beneath it. Unable to hold my breath long enough to swim deeper to get a closer look, I surfaced, then went back down, but the figure was gone. I reached out, and touched a large crack that was icy cold and felt as if there were life inside.

Something nibbled the back of my hand – a fish had swum out from the crack, and though I couldn't tell what kind it was, I could see how gaily it swam as it shot past my eyes. I tried going after it, but lost it almost at once. How could I, a human being, ever catch a fish in the water? So I just watched it go, believing that it was my father, swimming happily past me.

My father and I had got by for eleven years by relying on one another, but in the end he had left me. He obeyed the river when it told him to come down. The strange thing is, after he went down, the river stopped speaking to me. I spent three days in the river and on the boat, but it never spoke to me again, not once. Did the river see my father as a fish? He had disappeared into the water, but the river did not send me its condolences, nor did it offer me congratulations. I didn't know why that was. On the third day, I sat dripping wet on the sunlit bow; the hot sun sizzled the water on the deck, quickly reducing little puddles to a few drops. *Kongpi*, I said to those drops before they too evaporated. *Kongpi*, I said to the sun's rays on the deck. *Kongpi, kongpi*. Unlike the drops of water, the sun's rays stubbornly refused to disappear. Instead, they fervently shone down on my face and my body, and the entire barge, covering me with their warmth. As I slowly turned my gaze to the shore, I was struck by the thought that my grief was just like those puddles of water; it too was dried by the sun. Father had been gone only three days, and my thoughts were already on the shore. I didn't know why that was either.

I went first to the shipping office on the western edge of the piers to catch up on the barges' movements. I read that the Sunnyside Fleet had left the town of Wufu and would reach us in three days. Again, three days. I stood transfixed in front of the noticeboard, wondering how I'd get through the next three days.

'Kongpi!' Someone was calling me. 'Hey, Kongpi, come with me.' Baldy Chen walked out of the shipping office with a glass of water, took me by the arm and led me to the security-group office.

'What's going on?' I asked. 'Was I disturbing the peace by looking for my father in the river?'

'Take it easy,' he said. 'No one's going to bother you so long as you live by the rules. Somebody asked me to give you something.'

'Who?'

He wouldn't say. We walked inside, where he noisily opened a cabinet with a key. I thought my mother, Qiao Limin, might have come this way, so I stood in the doorway waiting for whatever she'd brought. It took a few minutes, but then Baldy came up with a bundle, which I took from him and weighed in my hand. There was something strange about that bundle. 'What are you afraid of?' Baldy said. 'It's not a bomb. You'll know who gave it to you when you open it.'

I untied the blue cloth and there was a tin red lantern, Huixian's red lantern.

'Huixian decided to swap with you,' Baldy said, studying my reaction. 'Her red lantern for your diary, her treasured item for yours. Fair?' My reaction puzzled him. 'You'd better not feel cheated. Your diary is just a worthless jumble of words, but what you're holding is Li Tiemei's red lantern. You get the better deal, Kongpi.'

Reminded by that lantern of so much that had happened, I felt my nose begin to ache and was nearly in tears. Not wanting to show weakness in front of Baldy Chen, I ran off with my lantern, confused and flustered, as if I were in possession of a priceless object or a keepsake that had been thought lost. It brought me consolation and it brought me pain. As I was running to my boat, a chewing-gum wrapper fell from under the lantern's shade. I stopped and picked it up. The image of a girl's head with a perm and a broad smile was printed on the red and white wrapper. Was that meant to symbolize the joy of chewing gum? How could something like that bring anyone joy? How strange. I didn't know how that could be.

It was a bright, sunny afternoon, that third day, as I strolled along the deck polishing Huixian's tin red lantern until it shone. The plastic shade gave off a red glow in the sunlight. Now I was content. As I was hanging the lantern in the cabin, I heard a strange sound from the shore. I stuck my head out and saw, to my surprise, that the gangplank was gone. How, in the few moments I'd been in the cabin, had it disappeared? Then a roar burst from the shore. 'We'll settle up later!' There was the idiot, Bianjin, standing on the bank in a blue and white hospital gown, a patch over one eye, a cold avenging glare emanating from the other. His forehead was badly scarred, but it was his nose that caught my eye: it looked white from a distance, but then I saw that the gauze had formed the character 年, for 'abundance', on his nose.

He'd been discharged from hospital to come and settle up with me. He was extremely nimble, with one foot on my gangplank and a portable noticeboard in his hands. He was looking for a spot to set it up.

I couldn't read what was on the board at first, but then he gave up looking for the right spot and simply held it up for me. It wasn't what I'd expected – shipping news – but something he'd had someone write for him, using the barbershop notice as a model. But what it said was a hundred times worse:

STARTING TODAY, KU DONGLIANG OF THE SUNNYSIDE FLEET
IS BANNED FROM COMING ASHORE.

Born in 1963 in Suzhou and now living in Beijing with his family, **Su Tong** is one of China's most iconic bestselling authors, shooting to international fame in 1993 when Zhang Yimou's film of his novella collection *Raise the Red Lantern* was nominated for an Oscar. His first short-story collection, *Madwoman on the Bridge*, was published by Black Swan in 2008. *The Boat to Redemption* is his latest novel to become an instant phenomenon in China.

Translator **Howard Goldblatt** is Research Professor at the University of Notre Dame. He is the recipient of two translation fellowships from the National Endowment for the Arts and has been awarded the Translation of the Year Prize from the American Literary Translators Association and the Man Asian Literary Prize. In 2009 he received a Guggenheim Fellowship for translation.